Ferryl Shayde

Book III:

A Very Different Game

By
Vance Huxley

Contents

Dedication
To my Noeline and to the Joy of my life

Acknowledgements

Thank you to my editor Sharon Umbaugh,
for turning my words into a book worth reading.

My thanks to Rachel at Entrada
for all her hard work and encouragement.

Aftermath

Centuries ago, when the church declared there were no witches and magic did not exist, most people never realised the true significance. The public declaration signalled the signing of a secret Accord, an agreement betwixt the church and the magical, an uneasy peace between them. The magically aware witches, warlocks, sorcerers and sorceresses agreed to stay out of the public eye. They moved out of any areas protected by a church and stopped targeting true believers. The church agreed the magicians would control the areas where there weren't enough believers to support a place of worship.

Both agreed to protect the humans in their areas from the magical creatures that still roamed the earth. Most of the largest, most dangerous entities had already been eradicated and any further attacks on humans were quickly hushed up, usually by the church. Most people lived on in blissful ignorance, unaware of the small, ugly, sometimes venomous creatures that still wandered, invisible, through their homes and food. Luckily, although many take a little magic from humans, the smaller creatures prey mainly on each other, small animals, plants, or insects.

Many years passed without any public mention of magic. Unfortunately, as belief in magic faded, so did the revenue for those who provided protection, either witches or priests. Large areas of the country, usually the poorer housing estates or small villages, are now overrun by invisible magical creatures such as hoplins, pictsies, and fae. All of them are ugly, most are fanged and many are slimy or have stings. None look like the versions in fairy stories. Despite none of the smaller ones taking much magic, the sheer numbers are having an effect on the health of the unprotected humans, especially the young or sick.

The Accord is still in effect but it no longer protects all the population. The remaining sorcerers are concentrated in towns and cities where they have lucrative contracts. Their main income comes from filling the logos on goods such as expensive cars and fridges with magic, so they work better and are protected from the likes of gremlins. The few magic-aware owners of gambling businesses, and those relying on delicate machinery or computers, pay heavily to have their premises hexed to keep the creatures out. The expensive fees give them a decisive business advantage over unprotected rivals. Some wealthy families have passed down the knowledge that magic exists, and pay high prices to divert the sorcerers from such contracts long enough to protect a home. There are no witches in the towns, because sorcerers won't let them work in the lucrative areas. Outside the towns, many villages no longer have enough believers in magic paying for curses and charms to support a witch or warlock.

The church hunts down any large, dangerous magical creature that comes near their places of worship, to protect the tithe-paying faithful who support the priest. The prayers of the faithful feed magic to the church cross, which repels all small magical creatures in the surrounding area. In places without enough tithes to support a priest, or enough prayers to power the cross, churches are closed and the protection it provided lapses. Over the years, more magically aware churchmen have been taken away to fight in God wars, against other religions. Today, most frontline priests are unaware magic even exists.

An increasing number of people live in areas where neither church nor sorcerers will spot the signs of magical awareness. The result is that potential magic users grow up never knowing, aware only of occasional movements in the shadows. Worse, if the person doesn't become aware of magic until they are in their mid-twenties, their brain can't adapt. Suddenly seeing all the magical creatures that surround everyone, without any way of driving them away, is enough for the unfortunates to question their sanity. The changes in their body and mind as the brain tries to control their new talent, without any idea of what it is, usually drives the person insane. In the village of Brinsford, tucked up against the Pennines in central England, a small group of teenagers are doing their best to change that.

* * *

Sixteen-year-old Abel Bernard Conroy, an accidental trainee sorcerer in a world mostly unaware of magic, has a big problem. The tall, skinny woman laid on a camp bed in the deserted church had been a possessed host, rescued during a frantic fight with a nest of blood leeches. The leech inside her had kept the woman completely under control, but conscious through forty years of killing and bloodsucking, which had broken her mind. During that time many of her vital organs had shrunk because the blood leech only drank fresh blood, using the magic in it to maintain the host's body. Now the only thing keeping the woman alive is another blood leech, a smaller one that has chosen to be magically enslaved rather than die.

Leeches usually prey on humans, living inside a host and controlling them. The creatures use magic to keep their host functional, even if organs are pierced, to give the leech more room to grow or access to blood. This blood leech is bound, magically enslaved, and is not allowed to cause more damage or drink fresh blood. Abel and his friends supply the leech with magic which it uses to keep itself and the host, the woman, alive even though her body is beyond medical help. Actually healing her needs a different, much more powerful magical creature.

Abel turned to his mentor, Ferryl Shayde, an ancient sorceress who currently possesses a red-haired schoolgirl, Claris. Ferryl had done so to save Claris's life, to heal her after a leech had been tricked into leaving her body. Now Claris could survive on her own and the woman on the bed needed a resident healer much, much more. "How soon can you release Claris and move into this one, Ferryl? The leech is barely keeping her going."

"Two or three weeks at least. I have to eradicate the worst of Claris's memories of being possessed by the leeches, and any knowledge of magic gained while I have been healing her. This is worse than my last host, Jenny, because I only had to alter her memories from when she had the accident. Even then, most of them could be retained once I removed any knowledge of how to work advanced magic." Ferryl/Claris didn't look particularly amused. "Life was never this complicated. I used to agree to heal someone in return for twenty years of possession, as I did with Jenny. Two hundred years ago that meant half their relatives were dead, and moving three villages away gave the host a whole new life anyway. Their memories didn't have to be precise or complete. Changing hosts every few months is very hard work." A smile brightened her face. "But a fair exchange for my life and freedom."

Abel glanced at his arm, at the tattoo of a furry catwoman that had been Ferryl Shayde's home for nine months. She'd moved in there when Abel freed her from a pit, because after being imprisoned for two hundred years Ferryl Shayde had faded to little more than a puff of wind. In return for her release and protection, she had promised to guard and train Abel for ninety years. Now a shimmer flowed out of the tattoo and hovered, smoky lines connecting her to the others present so she could 'speak' to their minds. "My life as well." Zephyr, or the Flying Fist of Doom as she'd been nicknamed, had been created so that nobody realised Ferryl had moved on to possess a human. The sprite pretended to be the sorceress to those who were aware of her existence. "What happens to the leech when you possess the woman? Why hasn't she got a name?"

"The leech says she's insane so it can't find an identity, or anything but pain and terror. After forty years of that she's better off with her mind asleep." Abel turned to his two best friends, also trainee sorcerers and fellow conspirators. "We'll have to try and keep her a secret for three weeks. Let's hope we have better luck this time. At least we all know how to cast a veil now so the neighbours won't see us coming and going." Last time they'd hidden a leech victim, Claris, their parents had found out but believed her condition had been a result of drug addiction.

Sixteen-year-old Kelis, tall and almost as thin as the emaciated victim, bent over the woman with a small lead bar in her hand. "Mum would go crackers. I'm still grounded because of the state I came home in at Halloween. I'd hoped mum might calm down and change her mind when the news showed there really were drunken yobs in Stourton, but no such luck." She held a small lead bar that had been filled with magic. One flat surface had a glyph, the symbols that helped a magic user to harness their power and intent, inscribed into it. This glyph controlled the transfer of magic from one object or creature to another. Kelis carefully aligned the glyph with a similar one drawn on the back of the comatose woman's neck. "Leech? Wake her up please, enough for you to draw the magic. Try to keep her dreaming."

The woman stirred, her limbs twitching as the leech inside her formed words using her lips. "I am doing what the Firstseed told me, but it is hard because her mind is gone. I learned to be less painful while living in the toad or it would have died." Ferryl/Claris flinched at the title Firstseed, which meant the senior leech in a nest, but Kelis smirked as the leech continued. "I cannot heal her, not properly, so I am trying to numb her pain. My given memories never taught me how to avoid hurting a host, and learning is slow."

"Well, at least you are trying. The seed you killed was eating her alive." Removing the lead bar, Kelis tested it. "That should be enough magic to keep you going. You can have another bar full later."

The woman stilled for long moments then began to twitch again. "My thanks for the magic. Please feed the host now, so she can sleep again."

"I'll do it." Rob, the other one of Abel's best friends and a fellow trainee, knelt and helped the woman into a sitting position.

As he did, Abel answered Kelis's earlier comment. "Being grounded until Christmas is sort of fair, I guess, since we organised the diversion that started the riot. We're not even properly grounded, just restricted to the village. I reckon it's the damage to our clothes that's upset our parents, the tears and burns. If mum thought I'd actually been part of the riot I'd never see daylight for a year."

Meanwhile Rob held a plastic beaker to the woman's lips. Despite leeches only drinking fresh blood, experimentation had shown they actually lived on the magic in it. They could utilise other forms of food, but never bothered since that was more difficult for them. "There you are, love. Liquidised raw rabbit because your passenger needs a little fresh blood. I've got some chicken soup with added vitamins to take the taste away afterwards." He looked up at the others, slightly embarrassed. "I know she can't understand, or even taste properly, but I can't treat her like a meat puppet."

"None of us can." Abel turned away as his phone played 'People are Strange.' "It's Vicar Creepio Mysterio."

Kelis, the person responsible for the peripatetic archbishop's unofficial nickname, grimaced because his phone calls were rarely friendly. "He said he'd leave us be for a while. After all, none of the news stories suggested magic so we didn't really break the Accord." She suddenly looked alarmed. "It's only been three days. Has he found out we opened Castle House?"

Castle House, a big old creepy building on the outskirts of the village, had been protected by layers of powerful and dangerous magic for over a hundred years. The peripatetic archbishop had threatened a massive response from the church if Abel and his friends opened it and released whatever lay trapped inside. Since nobody had a clue where the key might be, and even Ferryl daren't risk the protective magic, Abel and his friends had more or less ignored the building.

Then a Firstseed, a blood leech matriarch, had offered to sell them the key. Even then, they hesitated because the sale was a trap, but the Firstseed forced Abel's hand by attacking and threatening schoolchildren. Halloween had provided cover for a desperate battle that broke the leech nest, killed most of the leeches, rescued the woman now laid in the church, and left Abel with the key. As the Taverners escaped, with their friends using magic and goblins to spread confusion, the market town of Stourton suffered the most spectacular Halloween in its history.

Despite the warnings from Ferryl and the threats from Creepio, gaining possession of a key to Castle House had been just too much of a temptation. Unfortunately, opening the door hadn't helped very much, because only Abel could go inside. Some distant blood link to the sorcerer who used to live there meant the house recognised his right to enter, but only the entrance. Abel found a small chest on a table, containing a sovereign and brief instructions to take the coin to an address in Stourton, the nearest town. Further exploration had to wait because Abel couldn't do that while he was grounded.

"Creepio doesn't know or he'd have arrived without warning, along with God's SAS. The house isn't really open, just the front hall and only Abel can get in there." Ferryl/Claris turned from Abel to the seventeen-year-old schoolgirl who had just arrived. "Just as well or Jenny would have been in there trying to adopt the frog-dragon."

Jenny, Abel's ex-allegedly-girlfriend and Ferryl's ex-host, tried to look offended. "I wouldn't! Well maybe, because he's cute in a large frilly animated stone monster sort of way." She giggled, not that unusual after she'd filled up with tree magic. Jenny had told Abel she'd stay clear of him and Brinsford after Ferryl left her, because it would feel weird after the possession. The lure of magic had been stronger and she had continued to visit, and helped the trio as they rescued Claris. Now Jenny was the only other living human to know the true secret of Ferryl Shayde, that she possessed humans to give herself a physical form. "I can't see dad letting me keep a frog-dragon anyway, even in the shed."

"Hush or the vicar will hear." Abel answered his phone but then only listened, for quite a while. He eventually said "only if we are all here" before hitting mute. "He wants to talk to our patient, or to the leech inside her. He's trying to get the blood leech out of the priest he rescued." The possessed priest had been left alive but trapped when Abel and his friends smashed the nest.

The woman on the bed stirred, enough for the blood leech inside her to speak. "The leech in the churchman is Thirteenseed, the one created straight after me so it will have a firm hold in his brain. It will be bigger than you allowed me to grow, so pulling it free will kill the churchman." Her eyes opened in sudden fear. "He is a churchman, the one who spoke to me? He will kill me!"

"No he won't. He promised." Ferryl/Claris shook her head because that still surprised her.

"You are a strong Firstseed." The leech ignored the look from Ferryl/ Claris and the snigger from Kelis. "You will protect me? Please?" Its manners had improved dramatically after being magically bound to serve Ferryl.

"I have to." As Ferryl/Claris snarled her answer, Jenny tried to smother a snigger as well, because the sorceress really wasn't comfortable with protecting leeches. She absolutely hated being referred to as Firstseed, the title for a blood leech matriarch.

Abel had turned away, speaking quietly into the phone, but now he turned back and put it in his pocket. "I've told him we've all got to be here or no deal. He's agreed on tomorrow night, after tea because it's a school day. Come on Rob, we'll leave so mummy can take her baby to the loo."

"I am not that leech's mother!" Ferryl/Claris turned on her heel and called out. "Two goblins please." Two tubby green creatures with thin arms and legs came in. "Carry her to the toilet please. Gently." With a glare at Abel she rummaged in a bag for a clean nightdress. He got out smartish, as did Rob, both managing to stifle their laughter until they'd left the overgrown churchyard. Ferryl's voice floated after them. "Why don't you make yourselves useful? You could take some lead bars to Castle House and fill them up."

Both headed for Castle House gardens, protected by a magical barrier that excluded magical creatures and repelled most animals and all humans. The gardens and the wood behind contained a large number of trees without dryads, a huge reservoir of tree-magic for the five people who could pass the barrier. Once there the pair filled a stack of hundred-gram lead bars with tree-magic. Tomorrow they'd pass them around at school so the Taverners, local teenagers who'd become aware of magic, could use the extra supply to practice casting glyphs.

Controlling even the simplest glyphs took a lot of magic and hours of practice, but each human only absorbed a small amount from the air each day. Every living being absorbed magic but leaked most of it out again. Plants were an exception, they kept absorbing until completely saturated so the larger they were, the more magic they held. Grass and even bushes and saplings didn't hold much, but adult trees were the greatest natural reservoirs of magic in the world. Unfortunately, either dryads, the church or sorcerers claimed all adult trees, so even official sorcerers' apprentices had to manage on what they were grudgingly given or absorbed from the air.

Unlike sorcerers, the church or dryads, Ferryl, Abel and his three friends didn't mind sharing. This way their friends and fellow trainees were getting more practice in a month than any traditional sorcerer's apprentice managed in a year. While the youths transferred magic, Zephyr gambolled above them, creating tiny clouds of dancing leaves as she practiced her wind glyphs. A welcome change, because Zephyr had been subdued ever since Abel set her free to trap the leeches. Zephyr hadn't liked being cut off from her refuge, and since reconnecting she'd stayed close to Abel and firmly tethered to the tattoo.

As usual the fresh, clean tree magic left Abel and Rob in a wonderful mood, and even cheered up Ferryl/Claris when she and Kelis joined them. After filling up, Ferryl/Claris went to check the magic barrier in case anything had been trying to break through. Jenny had already left on her moped. She had to get home before the light faded or her dad would start phoning.

As they packed away the filled bars, Kelis told Abel and Rob what the three girls had been talking over while dealing with the patient. Creepio might come to the old village church while they were at school and take the host and leech away. The best solution they'd come up with was a sort of tripwire, and a bar across the inside of the door. Kelis preened. "Resting on hooks, then someone with good control of air glyphs will be able to send one through a crack in the door to lift the bar upwards. That will release the door for us, but anybody non-magical will think it's locked."

Rob's glum look didn't think much of the idea. "Creepio will just smack the door hard enough with a big glyph to break the bar."

"But Ferryl will set a trap. Not a lethal one like those in Castle House, just the sort that sends up a big, noisy firework, a fire and air glyph. Creepio won't want Mrs. Turner coming to look." The woman in question lived near the church and liked to know everything that happened in Brinsford. She'd come running for something like a giant firework, so Creepio would have to keep the leech and any magic concealed.

"We'd better warn Creepio it's booby-trapped, but not how. Tell him it's to stop the unwary getting inside and finding the leech. He won't be happy." Abel sighed, looking at the last lead bar. "Now I'd better throw some glyphs so I use up some magic. Then I can fill up from a tree afterwards to cheer up again." The rest joined him. Everyone but Ferryl needed the practice, and the tree magic really did feel fresh, clean, and invigorating.

*   *   *

The following morning started with a surprise. When Rob joined Kelis, Abel and Ferryl/Claris as they walked down the lane to catch the school bus, he brought his little sister Melanie. Not so little at fourteen, but her dad usually took her to school. "Apparently if I'm old enough to dress up like an idiot and play that stupid game with your friends, I'm old enough to catch the school bus." Despite the words, Melanie looked cheerful. "Which means I get there earlier and can natter to my friends in the canteen, and on the way to and from school." She nudged Rob. "And you can't avoid me when I want to ask questions about the game." Melanie had become an enthusiastic player of Bonny's Tavern, the board game devised by Abel, Rob and Kelis and adopted by many of their friends.

Unfortunately, when the trio discovered magic, they'd thought it funny to add a meditation exercise that really could levitate a leaf. The glyph should have been impossible to activate without more instructions but some of the beta players testing the game hadn't stuck to the rules. They'd drawn the glyph on their palms instead of imagining it, which made activation much easier. To make matters worse, some had drawn the Bonny's Tavern shield on their skin as pretend protection, having no idea it formed a real magical ward. The combination had led to over thirty test players, mostly schoolchildren, activating their magic and fluttering the leaf.

Some beta players didn't bother with the 'meditation' and some didn't draw the Tavern ward, but all the serious betas did. At least they'd stopped drawing the glyph on their hands, as the game rules now stated that would destroy the whole purpose of the meditation. Even so, Melanie had now begun playing with her friends using Skype so Ferryl/Claris thought there was at least an even chance she'd find her magic. None of them fancied trying to keep Melanie's magical training to a slow, safe schedule once that happened. Right now, Kelis looked alarmed about a more immediate problem. "You're not sitting with us on the bus!"

"No chance. You'll be rabbiting on about all that serious A-level stuff." Melanie stuck her nose in the air, then broke into a smile. "I can tell my friends the latest gossip instead. Mrs. Turner has seen ghosts in the churchyard, green ones."

The others laughed at how silly that was, but exchanged wary glances. They'd have to warn the resident goblins to be more careful. They'd also have to be more careful themselves instead of chatting about magic on the way to the bus. As a few raindrops pattered down all four looked at each other in dismay. With Melanie there, none of them dare create a magical rain shield.

*   *   *

True to her word Melanie sat with friends on the bus both ways, but she definitely stopped the four of them discussing Creepio's visit as they walked home. Instead Zephyr used her invisible one-way spooky-phone connection from Abel to suggest they meet a half-hour before Creepio arrived. Spooky-phone wouldn't be as useful if Melanie discovered magic, because then she'd see Zephyr and her connections as well as the myriad ugly little magical creatures that infested the world. So far, like most children and almost all adults, Melanie couldn't see anything magical.

After tea, Abel told his mum he would be meeting his friends at the abandoned church, to look the place over now the bishop had written about applying for a lease. At least that gave him an excuse to be there, though Mrs. Turner would no doubt notice the vicar. That would lead to some cross-questioning, so the four of them would have to pretend it was a coincidence. Hopefully none of the parents would investigate, because the leech victim couldn't turn invisible.

At the church Abel, Kelis, Rob, and Ferryl/Claris found Jenny waiting by her moped. Her happy smile and the shiny stone she waved at them probably meant Jenny had topped up her magical diamond. Diamonds, even magical ones created from pebbles with a glyph in the middle, made really good magical batteries. Gold and lead came a close second, with lead being the obvious economic choice because only Ferryl could make magical diamonds.

"Have you already filled it?" Kelis smiled and shook her head in mock despair when Jenny giggled, because that meant yes. "In that case you can test the door lock when it's fitted." Kelis, Ferryl and Jenny pulled a bit of boarding from one of the windows while Rob and Abel bashed in big nails and bent them to hold the wood in place. All five of them tried it out and even Jenny had enough control of wind glyphs to get in. At least that kept the five of them occupied rather than worrying about the vicar's agenda.

*   *   *

Though the teenagers still had no real idea what Creepio wanted ten minutes into the cross-questioning. The vicar kept pushing for details of leech seeds, which seemed strange because the leech in the rescued priest had grown past that stage. He wanted to know how fast they grew, how soon did they invade the brain, and when was it impossible to remove one? The leech, through the woman host, began to look really apprehensive. "Enough for now." Creepio whirled to glare at Abel, but he'd had a leech Firstseed and sorcerers do that and Kelis's glare worried him a lot more than any of them. "How about you tell us why you are asking, then we can get you some answers."

"Church business."

"You've come to a leech you tell me has no soul, a host you claim is no longer human, and five magic users who don't subscribe to your religion so we're heathens. That means it's well outside church business." Abel swept his arm round to include everyone else. "We will help you save anyone regardless of their religion, so why not tell us? Is it Thirteenseed, the priest?"

Creepio held his glare for a moment; he really didn't like anyone arguing with him. With an obvious effort he relaxed. "My report, or the report you all gave me, has caused considerable upheaval. Finding out how much pain these leeches caused their hosts is bad enough. An extensive investigation is trying to find out how many leech nests have abandoned the old ways of healing and releasing ex-hosts after their forty years. Any such nests will be eradicated, and the rest will be culled to teach them a lesson. In addition, many in the church are alarmed by a group of schoolchildren destroying such a large, unsuspected nest. Finding evidence of sorcerer-leech collusion and a priest being taken as a host has angered and worried them. The reaction to you rescuing an infected person, actually cleansing them of the leech, makes the rest pale to insignificance."

The vicar straightened and did his best to produce one of his enigmatic smiles, but didn't quite make it. "As usual, I am expected to deal with the mess. Dogma insists that the leech-ridden are lost, soulless, as they are no longer human. A leech cannot be removed." He pointed at Claris, unaware of Ferryl inside her. "There stands proof that a leech can be taken out alive and the human revived. A debate still rages over the person retaining their soul." His face relaxed a little more. "I believe that no soul is lost beyond redemption."

"You believe your churchman still has a soul, and you want him saved." Abel could go with that, regardless of the soul part. He didn't agree with the rest because if souls existed then Ferryl Shayde, Zephyr and probably dryads and goblins should have one.

"Yes, but that might not be possible. The answers so far tell me the leech has been in there too long." He hesitated for a long time. "When we arrived at the leech lair, after you escaped, we searched the lower floors before the fire spread to them. We found the female host with broken legs and kept the leech inside her, the Fourthseed, alive to answer some questions. The Church Militant also rescued three young women from a cellar beneath the building. All three have leech seeds inside them." His shoulders drooped and a painful memory showed briefly in his face. "We killed one leech seed but the girl died in agony. Our magical attack was as swift and clean as is humanly possible. Normally the best we could do for the other women would be to give them a quick, painless death, but you took a seed out of this woman. Now I would like to do the same for the two remaining women. I accept that the Thirteenseed leech in Father Curtis is too well developed, so we can't get his out without killing him. That's one reason the Fourthseed is still alive, we want it to order the younger leech out of Father Curtis but it mocks us." He stood up straight again and pointed at the woman on the bed. "I need details. How did you get a seed out of her without her dying?"

Abel ignored being ordered about again because Creepio didn't seem to know any other way. "We only know two ways to remove a leech. A developed leech might be persuaded or tricked into leaving the host and then the host might be healed. That doesn't work for a seed because it can't leave the host and can't be reasoned with. A seed is all hunger at that stage so you've got to kill it inside without it releasing toxins." He hesitated over the next bit but Creepio didn't wait.

"Which seems impossible. We killed it in a heartbeat then had to watch a young woman die screaming!" He pointed at the comatose woman again. "But she allegedly had a seed in her when she was rescued. Explain that, and the part about toxins."

"I didn't finish. The only way to remove a seed without killing the host is for an older leech from the same nest to kill it. We only know that, and about the toxins, because our leech told us. You know leeches recognise the presence of nest members?" Creepio nodded, intent. "The seed will let a nest member inside to share the host, then the leech can kill the seed and absorb any toxins before they spread." Abel pointed to the woman on the bed, in unconscious imitation of Creepio. "Better yet, the leech then stabilises the victim."

Creepio stared from the woman to Abel and back again, horrified. "The report can't have been totally clear on who actually killed the seed, or someone misunderstood the wording. Unfortunately, putting in a larger leech makes the situation even worse." His expression turned curious. "Though you claim to have bound this one, despite telling me you didn't believe in slavery." He curled his lip in the beginning of a sneer. "I wondered how long it would be before magic without faith corrupted you all."

"I asked, and the leech had a clear choice between death or life as a bound servant. As I understand it, the church allows that with either humans or creatures. Claris bound it, and as this leech's last victim she had fewer qualms." Abel wasn't going to tell Creepio that Ferryl actually bound the leech, and had no qualms at all. "Once the woman has recovered enough, the leech will leave and go into a rabbit. It will have a long, peaceful life if it causes no pain."

"Why not kill it?" Creepio jumped, startled by the laughter from four teenagers.

Ferryl/Claris didn't laugh, she scowled. "We gained entry to the lair because I carried this leech in a jar. The nest members detected it and assumed it still controlled me. When she realised the truth, the Firstseed attacked this leech as a traitor but I stopped her killing it. According to these lunatics I'm now responsible for making sure the leech lives a better life."

Creepio inspected all five faces, not sure if he should laugh. "Seriously? I thought the person saved from death owed a life?" He looked down at the woman. "Or the entity saved in this case."

"Nope. If you save a life, any life, it's your choice so your responsibility. You have to make sure the life was worth saving." Kelis didn't laugh or even smirk. Even Rob, Jenny and Abel weren't sure if she'd originally meant it or had just been winding Ferryl up, but now Kelis was adamant.

Creepio looked around them all again. "That's an intriguing thought." A smile flickered and was gone. "I really must drop that into the debate. The worst part is that is a truly Christian attitude, and you are definitely heathens." He turned back to the woman on the camp bed, his voice sombre. "But none of that helps me. How many bound leeches do you know of?"

"One?"

"Exactly, and it is keeping this woman alive. We can't bind the captured adult leeches, Fourthseed and Thirteenseed, because they'd rather die than agree." Creepio looked down at the woman for a long time, then heaved a big sigh. "In theory I should demand you save the two seeded girls, who have suffered nothing like the damage done to this host, but that would kill your patient." He stood debating for a while longer. "Thank you. I will explain to those trying to extract the leeches and seeds. The information about toxins might help."

"We might be able to save them in a couple of weeks?" Abel knew that in a fortnight or so Ferryl could leave Claris to possess this woman and save her. "By then this woman might be able to manage, then this leech could leave her and kill the seeds."

The nameless woman roused. "That will be too late. The seeds were set before the nest shattered. You must have been feeding the seeds blood to keep the hosts alive, so in another week or two the leeches will have grown enough to invade their brains." Her eyes closed again.

Despite trying to come up with a solution, there wasn't one, or not one that could be discussed before a very thoughtful Creepio left. If the church found out Claris was possessed by the entity he knew as Braeth Huntian, Creepio would call in God's SAS and probably armoured divisions to kill her. Instead Kelis told him about barring the door and setting an alarm to stop locals blundering in.

From his sour look the teenagers were sure Creepio knew exactly why they'd taken the trouble, though before leaving he helped them keep the church isolated. He renewed and activated the old church hexes on the lychgate, using his cross to fill them with magic. The activation produced a milder church version of the Castle House barrier, so anyone who hadn't been confirmed would feel uneasy and probably decide against going through the gate. The hex wouldn't stop anyone really persistent, nor would it affect anyone inside the graveyard, but the help was appreciated.

Even when Creepio had gone and the five teenagers discussed how soon Ferryl could move hosts, they couldn't find a solution. If Ferryl left her now, Claris's memories of drinking fresh blood from helpless victims and the pain as the leech grew through her organs could drive her crazy, and possibly to suicide. In theory Zephyr could learn to take a host just as Ferryl did, though Ferryl couldn't be sure how long the Sprite would need to learn how. Since Zephyr absolutely hated the mere idea of it, Abel wasn't going to insist. Over the next couple of days all of them returned to the problem again and again but there wasn't a solution. Ferryl pushed on with wiping out the worst of Claris's experiences as a blood leech host.

*　　*　　*

Just after lunch on Saturday the five teenagers were once again draining magic from trees to fill lead bars, a regular job with thirty-eight other trainees now depending on the extra supply. As usual Jenny had ridden over on her moped to help, and to top up her diamond. Zephyr seemed a little more relaxed today. She'd flown free briefly, but stayed close and soon came back to her tattoo and reconnected. Now she'd flown off out of sight because watching the others fill lead bars bored her, though she kept her tether firmly attached. Rob suddenly stopped in the middle of cutting a glyph on a tree. "Will a full intensive care unit keep Jane Doe alive?" They'd taken to calling the woman Jane Doe because the leech still couldn't find out her name.

"Maybe, or maybe only for a little while. According to the leech her organs are shrunk as well as damaged so she'd die without magical assistance." Kelis sighed and picked up another lead bar. "I already thought of that."

"But what if the two with seeds were right there, waiting? Could medics keep Jane Doe alive long enough to get our leech into each girl and kill the seed, then back into Jane to save her?" Rob sat frowning, looking at a lead bar and not seeing the growing smiles around him.

Abel's face fell again. "The NHS won't let a leech crawl around intensive care." Though now Abel wondered if the National Health Service had a magical division.

"Phone Creepio. If it works he owes us big-time." Kelis tossed her lead bar down in disgust. "No he won't because we'll do it anyway to save the girls, which is a pity."

"Never mind that. First we find out if it can be done." Rob lifted his bar as if to throw it at an inoffensive tree but changed his mind. "Flobberclomps. We're stumped anyway because we can't leave Brinsford and we daren't let Jane Doe go without us. Creepio is just waiting for a chance to kill our leech."

"Will you stop making up swear words! I've already imagined a bleddering, a sort of mermaid made of a Bedouin and bladderwrack seaweed. Now I daren't say it in case I create one. Flobberclomps will be really disgusting." Kelis scowled at a grinning Rob. "Just say curses, or blimey or heck. None of those will create anything dangerous like a hell or something bloody."

"Hush, children. Don't let the Creepio hear you squabbling." Abel called Creepio's number and as usual got the bland assurance someone would be in touch. All five returned to filling lead bars with magic, though the distraction didn't work. Abel, for one, had begun to wonder if they'd been crossed off Creepio's list when the phone finally rang.

As soon as Abel made his suggestion Creepio didn't waste any time at all. A few very short sentences later he rang off. "Well?"

"Give me a chance, Jenny. He'll be here with the two women and a complete intensive care unit within an hour. They'll blood-type Jane Doe in the ambulance, though it'll look like a delivery van on the outside." Abel stared at the phone, definitely worried. "I really hope it works after that."

"Flobwhatevers, we'd better break the news to the leech! What if it says no?" Kelis picked up the remaining empty bars, keeping them separate from the full ones.

"Then mummy will order it to obey." Rob chuckled when Ferryl/Claris growled at him.

* * *

Back at the church Ferryl/Claris really did have to order the leech to obey. It was utterly terrified of the church, with good reason, and didn't expect to escape if it went into a church vehicle. Oddly enough it had no hesitation over killing the seeds, because according to the creature they belonged to an inferior, defeated nest. Abel, for one, wondered if some of that attitude had to do with its Firstseed, mother in effect, trying to kill it. Zephyr worried more about the vicar getting close to her, because he seemed very interested in exactly what she was. After Ferryl reassured her even church magic couldn't get into the tattoo, she vowed to stay safely tucked away.

The five of them also worried about how to hide Creepio's ambulance, but there wasn't any need to veil the large furniture removal lorry that turned up. The vicar and two men dressed in overalls carried one of the infected women into the church. A veil covered her and the stretcher, while the vehicle stopped anyone getting a clear look at who went through the lychgate into the churchyard. The two supposed workmen switched the eighteen-year-old leech victim for Jane Doe.

Once Jane Doe had been carried out of the church, disguised as a pew, Creepio asked everyone to wait a moment before following. He kept his voice low, so the infected woman couldn't hear him. "I am worried that the seed inside her will sense if the other one dies, and release those toxins you spoke of." He gave Kelis a very stern look. "This glyph will block leech-recognition, stopping it from detecting other leeches. Don't try to repeat the glyph from memory, because you won't see it clearly enough and a mistake could be dangerous."

Kelis stuck her nose in the air. "I'm not stupid. Though if you drew it instead of just casting?"

A withering look was all the answer Kelis would be getting, as Creepio turned to the altar and sketched lines in the air. The smirk afterwards might have been because he'd cast the glyph very quickly, making sure Kelis couldn't follow his movements. Despite that, Abel had a lot of trouble keeping a straight face when Ferryl/Claris lagged behind in the church. He bit back a snigger as Zephyr asked to fly free and drifted off to join her without letting Creepio see her. The lure of a new glyph had overcome Zephyr's worries about losing her identity if she wasn't linked to Abel. The pair would be inspecting the altar, reading the flow of magic in an attempt to unlock Creepio's secret.

Creepio didn't even look back at Ferryl/Claris, confident there would be no trace. Even though the vicar knew that a few magical creatures could see magic, he had no idea an intelligent being could sometimes use the flows to decipher the original glyph. Now two such creatures were inspecting his work, one he believed was a captive Wind Spirit, Zephyr, and an apparent schoolgirl who shouldn't be able to see magic at all. As the stretcher came through the lychgate, Creepio worked a partial seeming to disguise opening the door in the side of the van. "Is the creature still willing?"

"No, it's scared you'll kill it although the leech will still save the two girls for you." Kelis didn't hide her sneer.

"For God, not me."

"Are they both confirmed? That might be a problem if their God mark, the cross on their foreheads, stops it entering." Everyone stopped in their tracks as Rob spoke, and Abel at least prepared for real trouble. He thought Creepio would force the leech to try anyway.

Creepio waved them on up into the van. "One is confirmed, the one I put in the church. I can nullify her mark to allow the leech into her, then bless her again if she lives, but I must see it come out of the other one first." He pointed at Jane Doe. "I will not let that thing claim another of God's children."

"Don't the two girls have names?" Kelis turned to look back at the church. "Or are they like Jane Doe, too badly hurt to remember?"

"They are possessed by blood leeches, and magical creatures do not have names." Creepio hesitated, glancing at Abel's arm where Zephyr, a named magical creature, usually lived. "Only those with souls have names, and are worthy of God's mercy. When the blood leech infected the women, it destroyed their souls and claimed two of God's children." Even though the vicar spoke with absolute certainty, Abel knew from their last conversation the vicar thought the souls were salvageable. The nods of agreement from three of the medics might have been why he'd stuck to church dogma this time.

Ferryl/Claris caught them up in time to hear him. "The leech in Jane Doe didn't claim any of God's anything, because I wasn't even baptised." She opened her mouth to continue but stopped just inside the back of the lorry.

Abel bumped into her, opened his mouth to say something but then the view shut him up. Now he'd moved through the seeming Abel could see that the apparently empty van had been stuffed with medical gear. The five medics weren't taking chances, they probably had enough equipment to put all three patients on full life support. Zephyr slipped back into her tattoo without Creepio seeing her and reconnected to her tether. "We have the flows, but it will take time to decipher the actual glyph." Abel wasn't even sure why they'd bothered, it wasn't something they'd be likely to need.

The young woman already in a bed looked pale and thin, but not anorexic like Claris had been. That had to be a good sign, because seeds were voracious so the hosts looked starved by the time the creature became aware enough to keep its host healthy. Jane Doe roused and the leech inside her spoke. "It is still a seed, without real purpose except to grow, though it feels relieved now I am here. Taking them away from the older nest members has frightened both seeds. Separating them has made that worse."

"Do they know you?" Abel wanted to ask if they'd know this leech had left the nest but didn't want the seed to find out.

"They recognise that I come from the same Firstseed. Please put this host to sleep or she will fight and scream when I release her." The leech spoke quietly, and very politely, but Abel could hear the strain through Jane Doe's voice.

The medic looked from Jane Doe to Creepio to Abel. "How does this work? Can we connect up the life support with the creature still in there? It would be best if we have everything working before it stops whatever it does." Even as she spoke another medic took a blood sample through a door into the front section.

The leech answered, through Jane Doe. "Tell me when it is safe to release her, then send her to sleep. Firstseed has told me to obey doctors." The medic didn't hesitate, she started to connect Jane Doe to the equipment and even asked the leech questions about which organs were most damaged. As the list grew the medic looked up at Creepio, confused, and asked how she'd been hurt so badly if this creature was under control. Jenny and Kelis helped Creepio explain there'd been a bigger leech in there for forty years, then a seed.

Meanwhile Rob had thought of another problem. "What about infection? I've got this for the leech." He brandished a plastic waste bin they'd washed out with disinfectant. "But shouldn't we be in white overalls or something?"

Another medic, tending the seeded woman, pointed to a large, very complicated glyph on the wall. "Ideally we would have everyone scrubbed and do this in a hospital, but we'll have to rely on that for anything you've brought in. Leeches themselves don't pass infection. It must be a survival mechanism to stop them poisoning their food." She looked the teenagers over and smiled. "If you are carrying a flu virus or you've got a mouth sore, it's history. Free medical care, compliments of the church."

Creepio cut in. "Don't try to copy that glyph, because you'll never remember it exactly. Get one bit wrong and it will kill all the good bacteria in your body as well. It also uses a lot of magic, enough to drain a human in about five minutes which is why we rarely use it. This vehicle carries a ton of metal charged with church magic, just to power that glyph." One glance at the tangled mass of curves and lines and Abel knew he'd never memorize the glyph. He didn't even fancy his chances of copying it accurately if he'd had pen and paper.

"I can try to memorise it? I will also memorise the magic flows so I know if I have it right." Zephyr had strict instructions to keep inside the tattoo, and not to send out spooky-phone. Ferryl wasn't sure how much information the church might get if she did so in a church vehicle. "I have nothing else to do."

"Good idea Zephyr, and it will keep you occupied so you don't see something interesting and forget to stay hidden. Ferryl will want to know how that glyph works." Abel had seen Ferryl/Claris's eyes sharpen so she was definitely interested, though he doubted even she could memorise the whole thing accurately. Out loud he answered Creepio. "No chance, I've already got enough trouble remembering my school work." Abel and the others waited as the medics finished preparing Jane Doe behind a screen.

Eventually a medic announced they could keep Jane Doe stable, though he didn't want to guess how long. The other one shook her head at the proffered waste bin and offered Rob a large stainless steel bowl from a cupboard. "I would prefer you to do this part. I've never seen a live one, just dying remnants as they dissolve."

"It's gross." Rob put the bowl near Jane Doe's mouth. "Whenever you are ready, leech."

As Ferryl/Claris lifted her hand to cast the sleep glyph, the leech came up with another request. "Please wake the other one once I am inside, so I can explain what is damaged. I may not be able to make the host talk if it is in a drugged sleep." That caused a short delay, because nobody had thought they'd be asking a patient the extent of internal injuries. As Rob proffered the bowl again all the medical staff drew in a little, obviously very interested. That included Creepio, so Abel quietly reminded him this leech mustn't be harmed. He still wasn't sure Creepio would let the leech survive if Jane Doe seemed to be all right on life support.

*   *   *

Rob tried to stifle his amusement at the medics' reaction when the leech's tendrils appeared, pulling on her teeth and lips, dragging it up her throat to slither out of Jane Doe's mouth. They were all torn between fascination and disgust, with most of them looking as if they wanted to kill the glistening, pulsing blood-bag on sight. The leech's physical body, slick with blood and with seemingly random feeding tubes and clawed tendrils sticking out all over, looked utterly gross. Since the medics must be magically aware they could also see the larger magical body, covered in throbbing veins and long, thin, ghostly wisps. The wisps were what the leech embedded in a victim's brain to control them, and Abel knew that a truly magical creature like Zephyr could see their full extent. The medics recoiled as the wisps sensed potential hosts and stretched towards them, though the connections recoiled when they came near Rob's ward.

The wisps withdrew into the leech's body once it landed in the bowl. It used the clawed tendrils to turn so the purplish brand of the binding glyph showed, but now a Tavern ward had been etched alongside it. Kelis looked curious but Ferryl/Claris smirked. "It does not trust the church. I know you can break through the ward, but that amount of magic might damage delicate equipment and kill your other patients." Creepio had a face like thunder but didn't answer as Rob took the bowl over to the seeded woman and the leech climbed into her mouth. Despite her medication she choked briefly as it slid inside, but soon settled again and the medics reduced her drugs to wake her up. By that time the two medics with Jane Doe had stopped watching. Their equipment began to beep, lights flashed, and they threw themselves into keeping Jane Doe alive.

The monitors attached to the seeded woman stayed quiet, but as she began to wake she shuddered a little. Even as Ferryl raised her hand, ready to cast a sleep glyph, the young woman quietened so the leech had taken control. A few lights changed colour while others lit up, and although no alarms beeped the medics looked worried. "How long does it take?" Abel put a finger to his lips and the medic shut up. Nobody, even the leech, could be sure how much the seed understood. If it could already understand speech it might learn it was about to die.

Though Creepio seemed to have forgotten that. "Wake her up now, properly. If she screams, the seed is still alive." He turned to Kelis. "In which case your leech has joined it and I will take her outside and kill them both."

His eyes opened wide as Kelis put a finger on his lips. "Shut up. Wait." Creepio must have realised why, because he didn't make any more comments. Instead Kelis, Abel, Rob, Ferryl/Claris, Jenny, Creepio and the medics waited for the young woman to rouse. Eventually she began to move again, her limbs twitching while her head shook back and forth. Creepio stirred but Kelis raised her finger again.

After a few more minutes that felt like hours, the young host calmed down and her eyes opened. "More magic please, Firstseed. Next time do not speak of killing. The seed began to release poisons and tore a hole in her heart. The toxins reached her stomach, kidneys and liver before I could absorb them. Now I am trying to heal her heart and other serious injuries where the seed grew into her organs. I have sealed the hole in her heart but the repair is still very weak."

Kelis wagged her finger at Creepio. "That's you and your big mouth. You were that keen to kill a leech you nearly killed three women." Behind her Jenny carefully drew the connection glyph on the young woman's skin and applied a lead bar full of magic.

"Three?" At least that part diverted Creepio from Kelis ticking him off. The way the medical staff were glancing at the pair, they were expecting fireworks.

"If our leech is killed then Jane Doe dies, and the two seeded women will eventually die because you can't save them." Kelis turned from berating Creepio because the two medics with Jane Doe were working frantically. "Is she all right?"

"We can't maintain her!" A syringe went in. "There's too much damage in there. How long do we have to keep her going?" The medic distracted the vicar and any angry retort died as he took in the frantic activity around Jane Doe.

"Leech, just heal that host enough to make sure she lives. She can finish healing naturally. Hurry!" Ferryl flexed her fingers but she couldn't heal from outside, and daren't switch hosts in front of Creepio.

Jenny swapped to another lead bar, testing the ones she'd taken off.

"They're both nearly empty. It's using a lot of magic in there."

"Have you brought enough?" Creepio actually put a hand to his cross, presumably to offer a leech some church magic, but Jenny showed him the bars in her school backpack.

A fourth bar went onto the glyph while the medics with Jane Doe looked more and more worried. Eventually the younger woman opened her eyes again. "Enough. Her name is Amanda. Her liver, kidneys, upper stomach and lungs were affected by the toxins but are working and her internal bleeding is stopped. Make her sleep." She turned her head to the side and tendrils appeared so Rob quickly put the bowl in place. He didn't quite run the three steps to Jane Doe but came close, and the leech quickly climbed inside.

"Do we stop?" The medic working on Jane didn't sound as if she thought that would be a good idea.

After looking at the blank expressions on the rest Abel answered. "We don't know so keep going. We'd better wake her up again, so the leech can let you know."

"That's not a good idea, usually." The medic watching a bank of monitors shrugged. "But what do I know? I've just seen one miracle. At least we'll know what to concentrate on." The way he hovered over the monitoring equipment probably meant he wasn't too sure. Moments later Ferryl/Claris annulled her previous sleep glyph and the leech began to explain the worst problems. Jenny moved over to Jane Doe, applying lead bars to feed the leech with more magic.

Meanwhile Creepio had gone to Amanda, the young woman who'd just had her seed removed, inspecting her while speaking to the medic. "How is she?" His eyes drifted to the door leading to the front section. "Will we need the surgeons?"

"Stable for now, though we'll want a full scan later. As far as I can tell she's just sleeping. The other one we freed had started dying by now. Her heartbeat is erratic but strong, which under the circumstances I'd call a win. The life support can keep her stable unless the leech repairs fail." The medic checked the equipment again. "We could probably let her wake up, but I'd rather get her to the convent for a scan first. We can get a better idea of exactly what we'll have to deal with, especially if that leech will answer questions before it leaves." He looked from Abel to Ferryl/Claris. "What will she," he glanced defiantly at Creepio. "What will Amanda remember?" This medic believed that the rescued woman still had her soul.

"Everything. Sorry. In my experience, most of the period with a seed is confused, painful and terrifying, so she'll wake up either crying or screaming. The really bad things happen once the seed is aware and takes full control." Ferryl/Claris laid a hand on the young patient's shoulder. "Amanda might not have the worst sort of memories but she'll still have nightmares. What will happen to her?"

Creepio hesitated, then looked around the room and spoke the young woman's name loud and clear. "Amanda will recover in a hospital, in a convent, with magically adept doctors to help her healing. She will stay there until she recovers, when she will probably turn to God and become a nun. That is the usual result, probably a combination of the environment and gratitude." Creepio stopped, suddenly looking unsure and definitely confused. "When the church rescues people from magical harm, the experience usually awakens them to magic. The lack of magical creatures in a convent is reassuring."

"But you've just remembered who actually saved Amanda." Abel shot a warning look at Kelis, who looked just about ready to blow, and offered a compromise. "Once she is able to leave the hospital, tell Amanda exactly what happened then allow her to speak to one of us. If she still prefers the convent, that's fair enough, but if not, we'll find her a home." He kept going right over Creepio's attempts to interrupt. "Not to recruit as a sorceress. We've got adults who have handled seeing creatures all their lives without church help. They can reassure Amanda and teach her which are good and which are bad." Behind Creepio, Abel could see Jenny fighting back a giggle, because there were no good magical creatures according to the church. She turned back to providing Jane Doe with bars of magic.

The vicar hesitated for a long time, struggling with his own belief that he'd be saving a soul. "You can't expect me to turn over both women!"

"Don't turn over either of them, just give them a free choice. The other one is confirmed and will probably take the nun option. She already believes in your God and is warded anyway, by the cross on her forehead." The last part puzzled Abel. "I know those are at least as strong as carrying a wooden Tavern hex, so how did the Firstseed get past it to seed her?"

"Her protection should have repelled the compulsion, or at least reduced the effect enough to let her get away, but as you know it won't stop determined creatures. We are more interested in finding out how it got past Father Curtis's protection. That should have been as effective as your magical wards in repelling any attempt to seed him." He glanced towards Jane Doe before continuing. "I agree, if your leech kills the other seed then both girls will be told the truth and given the option of meeting you or your friends. I also accept your leech is under control, or it would never have given up a healthier host. How soon before we can save the other one?"

Jane Doe opened her eyes. "This host needs help first. Please keep the machines working. More magic please." Jenny quickly swapped the lead bars.

*   *   *

Five bars-worth of magic later, the leech didn't actually need the life support to keep Jane Doe alive but she stayed hooked up ready for the next attempt. The leech insisted the host needed rest before it left again to avoid too much strain so Abel collected the empty lead bars. He intended taking them to Castle House gardens, but Creepio took him into the churchyard. Abel stood back while the peripatetic archbishop had what looked like a vicious argument with a dryad, then beckoned Abel forward.

"The dryad has agreed. The churchyard trees will supply you with magic if the church is attacked, or if someone is seriously injured. The dryads remain sworn to the church so they will not power a barrier for you." Creepio gestured to the huge Yew tree. "Fill your lead bars. Let it know when you are done so it can heal the glyph."

"We always heal the trees, it seems fair." Abel turned to the Elm, knowing that despite what Creepio said the Elm didn't agree. It had been ordered to help, presumably with Creepio's usual threats and no other options. "I thank you for your magic, dryad and tree." Abel ignored the startled glance from Creepio and quickly cut the glyph to top up the little magic stores. Maybe the dryad's feelings came through, because the Yew magic didn't cheer Abel up the same as magic from other trees.

As he came back out the lychgate, Abel heard someone calling out. Mrs Turner, the local busybody, had come to find out what was happening. To Abel's great relief, one of the alleged removal men went to meet her. When he mentioned it, Creepio assured Abel the workmen would tell any passersby that the church were clearing the building. Some of the men were carrying empty stretchers covered with a seeming of church pews out to the van to reinforce the deception.

*   *   *

An hour later, the other seeded woman came out of the church on a stretcher, hidden under a seeming of a church pew. Abel realised one of the alleged workmen had to be an accomplished sorcerer, a bishop at least if he could cast that glyph. He knew that Ferryl would be frustrated, because she couldn't inspect the magic and so far she hadn't remembered how to cast a seeming on an object. He bit back a smile when Creepio asked everyone to step back so they couldn't see what he did next. The vicar covered the girl's forehead with a cloth and drew what must be a glyph beneath it, another one Ferryl didn't know. The glyph overcame the patient's church protection, because the leech climbed into her mouth without hesitation.

Creepio kept his mouth shut and coincidentally the seed didn't release any toxins. As a result the victim needed less healing, which allowed the leech to get back to Jane Doe before she deteriorated as much. This time nobody hesitated before calling the rescued girl by name, Cecilia. Despite both his patients sleeping peacefully, Creepio kept his mobile hospital parked outside the church until the leech confirmed that Jane Doe was also stable. The medics, and a couple of doctors who appeared from the front of the vehicle, spent the time questioning the leech about the extent of the damage inside both young women.

The conclusions were encouraging. Despite the damage inflicted when the seed grew inside her, care and rest should leave Cecilia physically healthy. In Amanda's case, however, the toxins had left her with liver and kidney damage. Despite that, if she took care, Amanda should live a relatively normal life. If she actively practiced magic, casting glyphs, that usually enhanced the body's healing abilities so she might eventually make a full recovery. Unfortunately the leech couldn't repair mental damage. The girls would be left with their memories and the mental scars left by blood leech possession.

Once the church workers carried Jane Doe back into the church, Creepio wanted to talk to all five teenagers. "I can never work out who is actually in charge here, so I'll tell you all. The church is grateful for the help. Someone will let the local bishop know, and about the ungodly being resident in the church and graveyard." As he spoke, his eyes drifted across several gargoyles. "In this case only a few, and they have been on the side of the angels. How have you driven the others, the smaller creatures such as hoplins, thornies and globhoblins, out of the village? I don't see hexes on the houses or lamp posts, which is the usual way to clear a village. Except for the church way, but you haven't enough magic to set up anything as powerful as a church cross or I would feel it blanketing the area." He looked around again, trying to work it out. "Such an object would drive out goblins as well. There are even a few fae and faeries flying about."

"We use wooden stakes with hexes. They are driven into the ground all around the village, and we walk round now and then and top up the magic." Abel pointed to a gargoyle, actually a goblin under a seeming as the vicar must have realised. "The goblins and batlins catch anything that gets through, in return for the food from the rubbish bins and help if something larger comes into Brinsford. The fae and small creatures get past the posts when the residents drive home with some trapped in their car."

"Brinsford is the best protected, because we have the goblins. Our friends are all trying to use the same method round their villages, but they have to hunt down anything that gets through." Rob scowled at Creepio because the next part annoyed all the Taverners. "Those in town, in the estates, can't put stakes in other people's gardens so they are trying to put hexes on all the street signs and lamp posts. It's better than leaving them overrun like the church does."

Creepio didn't try to defend the church, ignoring that part entirely. "True barriers would work better if you had a large source of magic, though you've come up with a clever way to get a similar effect." The vicar's gaze fastened on Abel and hardened. "Assaulting the door to Castle House wasn't clever. That was downright foolish." As he looked from one teenager to another, Creepio laughed at their expressions. "There are scorch marks on the stone doorstep. What did you try?"

"We opened the door without any problem at all. What we didn't understand was that only one person can enter." Abel held up a hand and waggled his fingers. "The house likes me, but attacked the second person in. The key detected a distant blood relationship to the missing sorcerer, which must be how I got into the gardens in the first place." He watched understanding spread over Creepio's face, then calculation. "But I only got into the entrance. I have an invitation to get further into the house, but want friends along with me and more information. It should be possible because I can get friends into the garden."

For a moment, Creepio looked as if he would ask Abel to take him into the gardens. Not a good idea, because according to Ferryl, whatever lay at the heart of the house hated the church. "What sort of attack? Bound shades, guardians, traps?"

"All of them, but any sort would cause you a great deal of trouble. Your reinforcements won't be able to throw glyphs from outside, even with the door open. Worse, the house closes the door to trap intruders inside one small room." Abel shook his head. "So don't get ideas or you'll end up locked inside there with no backup. That's if you even get that far. The door relocks when I leave and needs my blood link to open."

"Very well. I must accept that." The wry smile conceded he didn't want to. "I can't even get into the gardens without using enough force to wake up whatever sleeps in there." A smug and thoroughly unpleasant smile spread over Creepio's face. "On a brighter note the mystery leech-ridden sorcerer has disappeared, and coincidentally so has one of Pendragon's apprentices. Apprentices can't escape their sorcerer's leash, so the miscreant must be conveniently dead. As a result, the church and Magical Council actually agreed for once. Pendragon has been creating protective hexes for leeches, so he is no longer allowed to place or power such hexes on any property in Stourton. That is a significant financial loss, and also humiliating." Creepio raised a hand to stop Abel speaking, and had definitely guessed the question. "A number of people in Stourton will be looking for someone to recharge the hexes protecting their homes and businesses. You can take over the business if you wish, because Pendragon is not allowed to stop you. Losing part of his monopoly, being forced to allow another sorcerer to operate in Stourton, is a part of

Pendragon's punishment."

"How will we know where to go?" Rob scowled as Creepio smiled. "That's bleddering mean, because I'll bet other sorcerers will know."

"But other sorcerers won't know the monopoly has been broken, not yet. As a thank you for your help today, young Abel will receive a list of customers that includes Pendragon's charges. There aren't many locations, but a moderate loss to Pendragon is a substantial income to others. Or it will be if you don't jump in quickly." With that he turned and walked away, leaving Kelis complaining, as usual, that she still had a million questions.

Though there wasn't much of a discussion straight after the van drove away because Mrs Turner, several other villagers, and then Kelis's mum wanted to know what the church had taken. Despite them wanting to discuss the mobile hospital, and the potential for a legitimate income, all five teenagers ended up answering Mrs Turner's questions. By the time they'd persuaded the villagers that a charitable refuge wouldn't mean Brinsford being invaded by drug dealers and violent husbands, the afternoon had flown by. Abel, for one, had to head home, sharpish. A text from his mum had threatened to feed his tea to their cat, Mrs Tabitha, unless he came home to eat it right now. Jenny had already left on her moped before her dad sent out a search party.

Endgame

True to Creepio's word, a list of names and addresses arrived midweek in a letter addressed to Abel. The prices alongside confirmed these were Pendragon's contracts. Abel passed the list to the Taverners who lived in town, and the older ones made appointments to visit the potential customers at the weekend. Several Taverners asked what the money would be used for, sparking a round of quiet, hurried discussions at school. Eventually the majority agreed the income from filling hexes should go towards fixing Frederick's large but run-down house. The fifty-three-year-old already had three Taverners as tenants, and had volunteered the place as a home for Stourton Refuge. Exactly what sort of refuge hadn't been settled, though it would be either a place for battered wives or a retreat for people with mental problems caused by magic.

Eric thought of one big snag, exactly who should the customers pay? He didn't want to put his own name on the receipts or the taxman would be chasing him. Jenny eventually came up with a workable solution, asking the customers to make charitable donations to Stourton Tavern Refuge. That way the drivers ferrying the glyph fillers round town could even claim back their expenses. Looking at the list of charges there'd eventually be enough money to fix Frederick's house up properly, using professionals.

While the rest of the Tavern worked on getting a steady income, Ferryl continued with repairing Claris's memories. She lifted her possession several times each night to wake up Claris's mind for short periods, so she could gradually integrate doctored memories of the missing weeks. Sometimes Kelis helped her to keep the eighteen-year-old calm while Ferryl worked on leech memories. Unlike when she had been preparing to leave Jenny, Ferryl couldn't keep Claris aware for very long in one session, because the schoolgirl's mind always turned to memories of her leech possession. Although that always led to her breaking down, Ferryl needed her reactions to decide which memories should be wiped out completely. Despite the distress, Ferryl reported progress. Even after the seeds were killed Ferryl still pushed on as quickly as possible, because Jane Doe needed more help than the leech could provide.

Ferryl had another reason to hurry. Kelis's parents might not be divorced yet, but the bank wanted the house Kelis and her mum lived in. If they became homeless so did their lodger, Claris, and her mother would want her back in Stourton. Ferryl wouldn't allow that. She insisted on being close to Abel to guard him, as she'd promised, though she couldn't say that publicly. The imminent eviction came up at a business meeting between Mr Forester, Jenny's dad, and the three mothers. He suggested getting the divorce lawyer to contact the bank. Throwing an abused woman and her child onto the streets before she had her divorce settlement wouldn't look good in the local news.

On the plus side, Mr Forester and Abel's, Kelis's and Rob's mums were all really pleased that there might be some charitable donations. Income from the game itself would be even better. All four were directors in the company now trying to develop and sell Bonny's Tavern, the game invented by Rob, Abel and Kelis. They agreed that even without giving the company direct income, a genuine charity supported by Bonny's Tavern players and linked into the gameplay could provide invaluable media coverage. Mr Forester pushed that aspect the hardest; the teenagers just wanted to help a few people who needed a safe place or were having magical problems.

Jenny had a very practical interest in the game succeeding. Not only had her dad bought her a small stake by financing the development, but actually producing and marketing Bonny's Tavern gave her invaluable Business Studies experience. At this rate she'd sail through her A-Level.

The three designers, with Ferryl/Claris and Jenny, worked hard on incorporating charity into the gameplay. They settled on a system where genuine proven charity work in 'Low Earth,' aka the real world, could be translated into extra health points during gameplay. Some Taverners, especially the younger ones led by fourteen-year-old Rachel, loved that idea. They were already on a real mission to clean up the school. Small groups were backing up anyone threatened by bullies, or picked on because of their colour or, in one case, her religion. The magically aware Taverners, hidden among the non-magical players, used invisible wind glyphs to confuse the aggressors or help the victims fight back.

The youngsters also found a bloke trying to give out drug samples near the gates. He had a really bad half-hour that he'd hopefully put down to a bad batch of whatever he used. If he came anywhere near Stourton Comprehensive again the dealer would get another session of falling down and ghostly hands pulling him about, and lose more stock down a drain.

* * *

On Saturday morning the four in Brinsford needed a diversion because they were still confined to the village. While others were busy in Stourton, negotiating contracts for magical protection, Abel decided to test his access to Castle House. After a quick text he waited until Jenny came over so she could back up Rob, Kelis and Ferryl/Claris in case of trouble. This time Abel walked right in and up to the double doors at the back of the entrance hall without any trouble. He tried the doors, which stayed locked, nodded to the frog-dragon when it opened its electric blue eyes, then turned and walked back out. Abel even stopped on the way back so that Zephyr, safely tucked away inside her tattoo, could inspect the magic flows inside the door.

Rob's magically inscribed rounders bat had definitely caused an overload when it stopped the door closing on the first attempt. A burned patch around a stone glyph set in gold marked a magical dead spot. Once outside, Zephyr explained to Ferryl, and the pair tried to decide if the emergency door closing glyph had been disabled.

Despite neither Castle House nor frog-dragon reacting to Abel going inside again, the letter and coin were useless until Abel's, Kelis's and Rob's groundings ended. Just Abel's grounding really, because only he could open the chest so the message "If ye lay claim, bring the box and coin" had to be for him. Jenny had gone into town to look so they knew the address below the message referred to a solicitor's office. After some debate Jenny suggested putting the chest with the letter and coin back inside Castle House. As she pointed out, that had to be the safest possible place to keep it, even better than burying it in the gardens.

Before Abel moved the coin beyond their reach, all five tried to pick up the magically aware gold sovereign. None of them could even remove it from the tiny wood and gold chest Abel had taken from Castle House. Every time anyone but Abel put a hand near the chest or coin, Zephyr and Ferryl warned of magic building up. Abel went back inside Castle House to place the chest on the table at the back, but the dead vine and frog-dragon didn't react beyond the eye-opening. Zephyr tentatively tried to come out of her tattoo, but barely and she stopped immediately. The air still felt as if it would burn her.

The five of them reverted to glyph practice and filling lead bars with tree magic, which still made Jenny giggle a bit. Her glyphs had improved rapidly because Jenny rode her moped over to Brinsford to fill up her diamond every night she didn't have Acro practice. Not only did that let her practice glyphs more often than most, but she also tried to fit in some tuition from the experts. Although she'd become competent with wind, Jenny preferred fire glyphs, and could already throw reverse fire to cause instant frost on her target dead branch. Despite coming to magic later than some other Taverners, she would soon be as adept as anyone but Abel, Kelis, Rob and of course, Ferryl Shayde.

The five went home for lunch, then came back to Castle House gardens to practice and wonder how the interviews for magical work were going. At last Kelis's phone rang, soon followed by Rob's and Abel's and then Jenny's. Ferryl/Claris didn't get any calls, despite allegedly being Abel's girlfriend, because none of the Taverners trusted her. Prior to her falling prey to the leech, the young woman had been a very unpleasant ally to the school bully.

As the calls continued, the group in Brinsford relaxed because most of the interviews had gone well. Either Creepio or the Magical Council had been thorough. Every person on the list had received a letter notifying them that Pendragon Enterprises had cancelled the contract for magically protecting the property. The letters didn't explain that Pendragon was being punished by the Magical Council, backed by the church, so several clients wanted to check the cancellation was genuine. Another client accepted the letter as being genuine, but wanted to speak to the sorcerer or sorceress in charge.

Much of the initial suspicion seemed to be about dealing with teenagers, rather than the adult apprentices Pendragon had sent. Most of them were satisfied when the Taverners produced tiny, controlled magical flames, well beyond the skill level needed to fill a hex.

The reactions to making payments as charitable contributions answered the Taverners' curiosity about how HM Internal Revenue dealt with magic. Magical protection for business premises had its own tax designation, but needed proof that only sorcerers could provide. Magical protection for private property couldn't be set against tax, but charity donations could, which explained why some of the new clients were so happy. The tax savings might be why the initial doubts over teenagers taking on the work were quickly abandoned.

Abel's calls were interrupted by an entirely unexpected one—from Creepio. "Since you are usually the spokesperson, can you make a decision about using your leech?"

"All five of us are here, including the leech's mistress. Do you have another seeded host?" Abel wondered if Creepio had found another one elsewhere. If it wasn't from the local nest this leech might not be able to help.

"No. We have a crisis." The phone fell silent but Abel waited, because that didn't need an answer. After a long pause Creepio continued, sounding less certain than usual. "The older leech, Fourthseed, has realised why we took the seeds away. If we try to remove Father Curtis it has instructed Thirteenseed, the leech inside him, to kill the host in the most painful manner possible. Now Thirteenseed has started hurting its host, hoping we will release them rather than kill a priest. We were resigned to killing the leeches so that Father Curtis could at least die free of infection. Meanwhile several of our trainees were reading the reports from Brinsford, as a part of their education about blood leeches. One young priest came up with a question we couldn't answer. You tricked an adult leech out of a young man, Henry, and killed it. We had overlooked that, probably because of your fuller description of the later removal." Another long silence followed. "Can you do that again?"

"I doubt it. The leeches will be expecting a trick, and will know you or God's SAS are nearby. Hang on, let me put you on hands-free so the rest can hear." Abel explained to his friends and they moved closer to listen and join in. Unfortunately everyone agreed Abel had been dead right; the leeches wouldn't go for something as simple as the trap that caught Henry. That had been cast in desperation, in the heat of a fight, by a very inexperienced trainee sorcerer. The only reason it worked was because Abel had made a purely magical trap, not realising anything non-magical could still pass through it.

"What if the leeches think someone has taken their hosts away from the church?" Jenny's eyes sparkled. "Someone who really, really hates leeches, more than the church does. Someone who might want to bind them and make them suffer a long, long time so they'll take any chance to get away. Especially if their new prison has a flaw." She looked around the other four with a little smile. "If it's a choice between taking their only chance or facing someone like the Hunter on the Wind?" That was the leech name for the entity now called Ferryl Shayde, the entity Creepio called Braeth Huntian. The leeches passed down partial memories of her, memories that terrified them.

"But you'd have to convince them the real hunter, a very old and dangerous hunter, had caught them. That will not be easy." Creepio stopped talking for a moment as the five teenagers started laughing. He didn't see the joke, but then he'd never met the real Ferryl Shayde. "Braeth Huntian is no laughing matter!"

"But those leeches already believe Braeth Huntian attacked their nest. They were shrieking about it when you caught them, so unless you told them it was only Abel's tethered Spirit?" Kelis smiled at Ferryl/Claris, because Creepio would never know Braeth Huntian really had been there.

"No. The leeches are so sure we began to wonder, until Abel finally showed me his shy passenger." There wasn't any humour in that, despite Creepio's name for Zephyr.

"So if something magical is nearby, hard to see and flitting about?" Kelis warmed to her theme. "We even have a bound leech to prove what the hunter is after. It will lie if we order it to. We can convince them."

Now Creepio sounded as if he'd seriously consider it. "It still won't be easy. How can we explain Braeth Huntian gaining control of leeches captured by the church? We would kill the creature if we ever found it, especially if it had captured a churchman." That sobered the teenagers, especially Ferryl. On the bright side Creepio had never connected the names, maybe because Ferryl Shayde was a cat-sorceress in the Bonny's Tavern game. The five of them, with Creepio and whoever else he had listening at that end, began to really plan.

At least Creepio wasn't expecting the impossible. If everything else failed he'd settle for Father Curtis dying leech-free and hopefully not in agony. The archbishop had no interest in Fourthseed surviving, unless it had been firmly bound and the church held the leash. Abel noted that for all Creepio's sneering about enslavement, the church definitely bound useful magical creatures. Despite Abel's misgivings, the other teenagers considered that would be poetic justice, because the church would use Fourthseed to detect and kill other leeches.

Carrying off the leeches would be difficult even with church collusion, but Creepio solved the main problem when he offered transport and equipment. Bonny's Tavern would supply the kidnappers and drivers, because the possessed Father Curtis might sense the church magic in members of God's SAS. Creepio agreed to bringing the mobile hospital, but refused to give them the glyph to nullify a church ward. That meant the plan couldn't rely on either the bound leech or Ferryl getting inside Father Curtis to save him, though Abel couldn't mention the second option.

Once Creepio rang off, all five began to make phone calls to find out which drivers and older Taverners were up for a late-night adventure. There was no time to waste, not if Fourthseed had started making threats about killing the churchman. Everyone who could get away from home tonight immediately volunteered, once they learned the mission would be to kill leeches. Unfortunately most Taverners were schoolchildren so only the oldest of those could be out that late, but there were also six people who didn't live at home and eight Taverners had driving licenses. Once that part had been settled, Abel and his friends went through the back gate into Dead Wood to talk to the only dryad allowed in there. They needed as much help as possible to both trick and trap their prey.

Dryad Sycamore discussed their plan and checked their preparations. Once it understood there would be no sorcerers fighting, no fire being thrown about, the dryad even offered to actively help them. After discussing ways and means, Rob looked relieved because despite being the best at it he wasn't really confident in his earth magic. The bound leech in Jane Doe seemed keen to help with killing the last members of its old nest. Learning it would be facing a much older leech didn't seem to worry it, as long as its mistress would be there.

Jenny went home just before dusk, leaving the rest to finish filling in the trenches. She took a new glyph, carefully cut into wood. Once activated it would ensure that her family slept soundly once they went to bed. They'd never hear the vehicle when a Taverner collected her.

The conspirators finished their preparations, went home for tea, and generally tried to act normal until bedtime. They daren't check by phone to see how the leech-nappers were getting on in case that distracted or alerted someone. At least a few more calls from Taverners in town, confirming contracts for magic protection, helped to divert them. The Taverners were down to the last few, all private houses on a gated estate.

*   *   *

Once in his bedroom, Abel waited for the silent vibrations to tell him he had incoming messages about tonight. The ones from the leech-nappers started soon after nine p.m., but he didn't answer those. The text messages reported success, so far. With God's SAS planning the kidnap-come-jailbreak and acting as the victims, Abel didn't really expect an upset yet. His only worry was that a kidnapper would say the wrong thing, a casual remark that let the leeches know the church had agreed to them being snatched. If Fourthseed or Thirteenseed realised the Tavern had captured them it wouldn't matter, because they'd soon know anyway.

The first call that concerned him personally came at 10:30 to tell Abel that Kelis's mum had gone to bed. Almost an hour after Kelis's call, Abel's mum came upstairs. When he couldn't hear her moving about any more Zephyr slipped out through the crack around Abel's bedroom door and reported she was reading in bed. Abel mentally apologised for how stiff his mum would be when she woke up, and activated the sleep glyph. Once Zephyr confirmed it had worked Abel texted Rob to let him know, then put on his jacket and sat by his window.

Since Rob was the last one, he put a little magic into his glyph to make his family sleepy, but even so his big sister Samantha stayed up until almost midnight. "Rob is coming." Zephyr had flown out into the street to keep watch. Abel cast a veil and joined him, quickly texting Kelis. Kelis and Ferryl/Claris, also veiled, were waiting when he reached the church. Abel's phone vibrated with a message saying Jenny had been picked up.

"Where are you going, sneaky but intriguing apprentices? You have Huntian with you, and are veiled, so is there danger?" Like all those aware of magic, the dryads on the village green could see through a standard veil although a shimmer betrayed its presence. The veils were to stop the non-magical humans seeing things that might send them crazy.

"No, Chestnut. The answer is free, a special offer just for tonight." A joke because the humans never charged Dryad Chestnut for answers, though it was notorious for demanding honey if they asked questions. "We are going to trap blood-bags, with the help of a dryad. One who trusts us a little more than you will." Abel pointed to the big Yew in the front corner of the churchyard. "Though you trust us more than they do. I left a jar of honey as a thank you for the magic, but even so, the Yew dryad didn't speak. Though the jar was empty when I came back."

"That one is very old, and is still angry about humans building a place of worship near its tree. If it ever talks to you, it knows more about Sorcerer's Keep than any of us." Dryad Chestnut creaked a few branches in humour. "Though you will need many, many jars of honey."

"But not tonight. I really must go, Chestnut." Abel waved goodbye and hurried to catch up with the others. He would have loved to ask more about trees that were here before the church, but not tonight. When he caught up, four goblins under a veil were already carrying Jane Doe out of the church, supervised by Ferryl/Claris. "Did Claris agree?"

"Yes, twice. I woke her a few minutes ago to ask again. She'll live with a few more nightmares if that's what it takes to save another leech victim. I've wiped out a big section of Claris's memories about the leech growing in her but she won't tell anyone about the gap. That way the doctors won't get involved and try therapy." Ferryl/Claris sighed and glanced at Kelis, who nodded.

"I was there both times and heard Claris agree. She seemed happier the second time, after losing all those memories. She wants to stay at my house for a while before going home, so she can come to terms with it all." Kelis gave a wry smile. "Regardless of what a cow she used to be, I've got to agree to that." None of them mentioned the real fear, that once free, Claris would go running off to the church or the cops screaming about possession.

All four headed towards Castle House, extending the veil to cover the goblins and Jane Doe on the stretcher, but only Ferryl/Claris went into the gardens. Rob took the goblins and the stretcher round the edge to the rear of Dead Wood. He would send the goblins home and watch over

Jane Doe until the rest arrived. Ferryl/Claris would take advantage of the privacy and virtually unlimited tree magic in the gardens to tear out her wits, magical knowledge embedded in bone, and heal the wounds. Abel and Kelis carried on past Castle House and out of Brinsford.

*   *   *

Neither Kelis nor Abel felt like talking, Abel, for one, was much too nervous and worried about all the ways this could go wrong. In the absolute worst scenario, Creepio might realise Braeth Huntian lurked inside Claris and start a pitched battle to kill her. He stood mulling over ways to delay the vicar so Ferryl could get away without getting anyone killed, until the first vehicle lights came up the road. Both stepped onto the verge, because with their veils activated anyone non-magical might run over them. Instead the large black SUV with tinted windows pulled up next to Abel and the window purred down. "I want to keep these wheels!" Shannon patted the leather seats. "Do we have to give it back? Oops, sorry, that's sinful but so are these seats. The other two are about five minutes behind me, driving vans, each with a leech aboard. I claimed the decent transport to pick up your ex and her moped."

Jenny waved from the passenger seat. "Hi Abel, Kelis. Nice to get a word in. We've brought extra muscle." Two hands thrust forward between the seats to wave. "Is everything set?"

"All ready." Abel tried to look stern. "When they get here, try to keep quiet please, Shannon. We want silent, threatening, mysterious figures stood all around while the legendary leech-killer Braeth Huntian terrifies them. Comments about nicking the church transport would sort of spoil the effect. Have you left your cross at home?"

"Yes, don't worry. Sorry, I can't help being a bit excited. I'm only an innocent church-going schoolgirl, not an agent of darkness. Or I wasn't one until tonight. I should have brought my Saint Georgeous cloak to hide under so the minions of evil don't realise I'm an angel in disguise." With an obvious effort Shannon stopped, her face sobering as she peered up the road towards Castle House. "I'll stop babbling now. Though to be honest, if it wasn't for the archbishop being in on this I'd be a bit worried. Thank God we won't be dealing with the real Braeth Huntian, whatever that is." She glanced at her watch. "I can only stop for another hour because my parents think I'm at a dance, and three of the others have to be home by one.”

“But that’s all we need. Once everything is in place your job is to swan about in luxury, playing taxi for the muscle. Just grab a real taxi back home before the coach becomes a pumpkin. And don’t mention Creepio again.” Abel grinned and wagged a finger at her. “You can’t be a lost cause if you won’t give the archbishop his game name.” At least that made Shannon smile again. “Park on the grass and we’ll cast a veil around the car in case the wrong person comes along.”

Kelis plonked a lead bar on the car roof to supply magic, because the veil for a solid object that wasn’t held or worn by living creatures needed an independent supply. “I’ll get that set up. Good practice for later.”

*   *   *

Five minutes later two anonymous white transit vans parked on the grass verge behind the veiled car. Eric, Warren’s nineteen-year-old big brother, leant out of the driver’s side window. “Two leeches as instructed. The tranq guns caught the church guards completely by surprise. Where does Braeth Huntian want them?” He’d got his lines dead right. Shawn gave them a thumbs-up from the second van, so his part had also gone well.

“We’ve got to carry them across the fields, but Shannon brought extra muscle. Did you get the stretchers?” Kelis felt sure they had, because Creepio had promised to put them in the vans along with the tranquilliser guns and harmless darts.

“Yup, and we brought extra people as well so we can take turns carrying.” Shortly afterwards both vans had lead bars on the roofs to feed their veils. The two struggling but securely trussed leech hosts were carried across the fields to Dead Wood, also safely hidden under veils. The leech-nappers had even taped the casts on the young woman’s broken legs together, because leeches could over-ride pain in their host.

The struggling had started once Eric mentioned Braeth Huntian, a promising start because the plan relied on both leeches being terrified. Rob and Ferryl/Claris were waiting with Jane Doe, Ferryl/Claris showing no signs of the wounds inflicted as the bone shards came out. Rob tapped his pocket significantly, where Ferryl/Claris couldn’t see, so all memory of the wits had been wiped out. Ferryl would want as little as possible left to erase as she left.

*　　*　　*

Jenny and Rob directed the stretcher bearers as they laid the captives out well apart, ten metres clear of the magical barrier protecting the trees. Both leech hosts were taken off the stretchers and untied except for their legs, but their gags were left in for now. Abel and Kelis drew the magical traps in the earth around them and led the lines of magic to the tree nearest to each one, either side of a small clearing. Both cut a draining glyph deep into the bark, clearly visible from where the leeches lay, and Abel connected his to activate the trap around Thirteenseed. As far as Abel could see, Father Curtis, the leech's host, didn't look badly damaged.

"Thanks everyone. Braeth Huntian is coming now, and will want to deal with this personally. It will be safer if you have left." Abel's arm swept across to include Kelis, Jenny, Rob and Ferryl/Claris, though Zephyr still stayed hidden. She had her part to play, and very soon. "We are sworn to Huntian so we are safe. Come back at dawn to help us bury the bodies if necessary. You will be rewarded then." He held his breath but the snatch squad all turned and left without anyone giggling or making a smart remark, taking the stretchers with them. Nobody would be back at dawn; the Taverners were all heading for their beds.

As soon as they were out of sight Rob, Jenny and Abel stood between the two leeches so they couldn't see each other. If Father Curtis survived, he mustn't know the alleged Braeth Huntian wasn't Zephyr. Ferryl/Claris strode up to the young woman, the Fourthseed, and seized her head in both hands. She whispered, "Braeth Huntian is already here," and let her true nature come to the surface before stepping back. As she did, Zephyr soared up in plain sight of Father Curtis, and his leech. Kelis had plenty of time to activate the trap and stop the Fourthseed leech escaping as its host tried to scrabble away from Ferryl/Claris with casts on both legs. Ferryl/Claris sneered at it once the trap sprang to life. "You can both take off your gags and free your legs."

As soon as it had its mouth clear, Fourthseed shouted to let the other one know this really was Braeth Huntian but it couldn't get past the church ward. Kelis laughed at it, while Zephyr swooped in lower and both leech hosts cowered. "Huntian doesn't want to possess a churchman, but fancies having one as a servant. A servant with a bound leech inside so he can stand some pain. If you oppose Huntian, your host will make a good home for our leech, even with broken legs."

As she spoke Jane Doe sat up, with an obvious effort. "That is a fine young body and cannot be damaged too badly inside. Much better than this one. Braeth Huntian has promised me a new host once I have told her all the secrets your Firstseed left behind."

"Traitor!" Compulsion lashed out at Jane Doe with absolutely no effect.

"Firstseed tried to kill me. Braeth Huntian stopped her, then killed her and accepted me into her nest. A nest that destroyed yours. I have already killed three seeds for my new Firstseed. You two are the last of the nest, and tonight you will be bound or die." Jane Doe smiled, which with her gaunt features looked ghastly in the moonlight. "If Thirteenseed is foolish and refuses the binding I will get the churchman as a host. He looks strong and healthy, and is hardly damaged at all."

"Why? Why does Huntian want to bind us? Huntian kills leeches. All the memories say so." The young woman, the host, whipped her head back and forth, looking at the four teenagers around her in total confusion. Even so she avoided looking directly at the fifth, the one possessed by Braeth Huntian, or the wraith hovering above them.

But that teenager answered. "You have just spoken to a bound leech, because we have found a use for them. Just killing leeches is not enough now. You will be bound, to be used as hounds to help us find more leeches. Huntian has been away for too long, and leeches have grown bold." Ferryl/Claris produced a classic evil cackle that rang out over the fields. "It is time to spread some fear again." She leant closer. "Bound servant or bound shade? Make a choice." Zephyr swooped in again and the leech host tried to scramble away, but couldn't with her legs in casts.

"I will wreck this body. I will make it unfit even for a shade." The host looked back and forth again. "You can't bind Thirteenseed, not with a church mark."

"But we can kill the body, slowly, if you refuse. We can cut both of you out of the corpses and take you into this wood." Kelis wore her Windcatcher cloak, which she opened to reveal Una's sword. Producing her very best sneer, she pointed to Dead Wood. "Take a good look.

Nothing magical goes in there except Braeth Huntian and her sworn apprentices." Zephyr swooped down on cue. "But before the wood kills you, we will cut the hosts open and drag you out. You will agree to be bound or die screaming in terror, and then we will bind your shade. A leech shade without a host isn't much use but Huntian can amuse herself torturing you when something annoys her."

Abel wondered if Kelis might really mean that but despite his misgivings added his part. "Even if you compel something, it can't get to those trees to break the glyphs because of the barrier around Dead Wood. Trying to cross the barrier will send them crazy, then kill them. You've got until an hour before dawn to sit here and think about your choices. Watch all the magical creatures that try to get in there and think of being in there yourself, helpless. Use compulsion to try and force a few and watch them die." He didn't try for a sneer because he'd never match Kelis's, so Abel gave an evil or possibly crazy grin. "Life, even as a bound hunting hound, might seem more precious after some thought." The next bit had total conviction, because Abel really didn't like leeches and this was an old one. He'd no idea just how many people it had killed or tortured, or sent insane. "I really hope you say no. I might even ask if I can bind your shade personally because I hate your kind."

Compulsion battered at each of them, desperation because the leech had to have tried that on the other Taverners. All five laughed, Ferryl loudest of all. "You two, wait in Sorcerer's Keep. Take the bound leech." Kelis and Rob picked up the stretcher with Jane Doe and headed into the nearby clearing. Ferryl/Claris's imperious gesture included Abel and Jenny. "We will find something to amuse ourselves. Waiting until the leeches decide will be boring, and a hunter's moon shouldn't be wasted. If we kill enough local wildlife it might make up for letting a leech live." Ferry/Claris strode between the two magic traps, out into the field, before turning back towards the wood. "Fourthseed! Thirteenseed!" The hosts turned towards her. "You have until we come back to think about your options. One way or another, alive or dead, you will obey before dawn." She beckoned to Abel and Jenny as Zephyr headed across the field. "Come, Abel, you and your woman can flush the game." She held out her hand, waiting for Abel to come and take it before stalking off across the field after Zephyr.

*   *   *

Despite the spooky-phone and skin connections, nobody commented until they reached the far side of the field. "What do you think?" Ferryl/Claris held out a hand and Jenny took it so Ferryl could talk silently. She repeated her question.

"About being Abel's woman again? You might have asked." Jenny smiled at Abel but then sobered. "It went well I think. I hope. You kept saying 'we' and left it sort of unclear exactly who Braeth Huntian was, so Father Curtis might think you are Huntian's senior apprentice or something."

"Both were frightened of Zephyr and if Father Curtis is as confused as Claris, he'll never be certain who was what. Hopefully they are too concerned with escaping to have a long involved conversation about who each of them thinks is the real Braeth Huntian. At least both of them looked away from the wood for long enough, providing that glyph on Jane Doe works." Abel didn't seem too sure about that. "Fourthseed seems very sure of itself, and that it can stop you taking Father Curtis."

Ferryl/Claris let go of their hands. "Maybe talking silently is a bit paranoid. They can't hear us now." She looked back towards the wood again. "That glyph is the one Creepio cast on the altar so our leech will be masked. Don't mention it to Creepio, or he might be more careful when he casts other glyphs near us. I wish we could hear, then we'd be sure."

"I can sneak in, a quiet Zephyr rustling through the grass?"

"No need to risk it, Zephyr," Abel spoke aloud. "The Firstseed tried to kill our leech just by ordering it to die. Can Fourthseed do that to Thirteen?"

"Possibly. It is now the oldest, so might take the role of Firstseed. If it wasn't for the binding and ward, Fourthseed could probably either command or compel the leech in Jane Doe." Ferryl/Claris sighed, looking back again as they walked into the next field and a hedgerow hid the Dead Wood. "I hope that leech is smart enough to see the flaw in our trap, and can't see the rest of it. I also hope it knows how to draw the glyph the other leech used to get into Dead Wood when it came after you. I should be nearer, just in case of trouble."

"It's all a bit iffy, but the leech in the badger must have had the same glyph as Henry to get into Dead Wood, so Fourthseed should know it. In any case, this is the only chance Father Curtis has so it's worth a shot. How about we actually hunt a few skurrits instead of hanging about worrying, or maybe find some of those things that attacked the school? Just to keep us occupied. Will there be any out here?" Jenny looked around at the hedgerows and occasional magical creatures browsing on the magic in grass and leaves. "I don't want to kill the grazing ones, just nasties like those creepy snakes with spikes." She squinted in the gloom. "That's if I can see them."

That distracted Ferryl, briefly, because she reverted to tutor mode. "I doubt you'll meet most of those creatures again, but you ought to know what they are and how to avoid them. Lone varglin, the spikey wolves, might be hunting along the hedgerows but they prefer packs and woods. The turtle types, amanatik, are from South America so there won't be many in England and they'll be by a seashore, waiting for the Goddess Amana to return. Satan-steeds, the white lizards, prefer old bogs where sacrifices were once buried alive, while the beinsnork, bone snakes, only appear in graveyards. Ganshbaal, the little black scorpion rats, lurk by pathways in thickets or other places difficult to travel through. It's some sort of connection to Ganesh the elephant god, their creator. Wealth toads and catspaw beetles are rarely seen in the wild, and are not usually belligerent. There may be some ruttlyte, the grey ratlins with purple and blue veining, lurking in the hedgerows. Legends claim they were a failed attempt to bind a complete goblin meld. Most of the other little creatures in that attack are even weaker, secretive and daren't come near magic users like us." Ferry/Claris stopped, shrugging at the two intent faces. "I doubt you'll ever get three of those types together again."

Jenny pointed back the way they'd come. "At the time, the St. John's man wondered how anyone managed to get all those different creatures together to invade the school. Now we know. A combination of sorcerer commands and bindings, and compulsion from eight or nine leeches, must have been enough. Even so, Firstseed must have spent weeks preparing that attack."

"True, which makes it a really good thing the sorcerers and most of the leeches are dead." Abel smiled and obliged as Jenny raised a hand for the celebratory high-five. "Any other time I'd want to know more about all of those creatures and how come they've ended up in England, but right now I can't stop worrying about Kelis and Rob. I suppose we'll just have to settle for hunting skurrits and maybe the occasional thornie and hoplin. I'm not really in the mood but it might distract me."

"There's always fae. They're nasty and take concentration." A tiny, hot glyph arrowed out from Jenny's hand but missed a passing fae. "They also need better eyesight than mine."

Abel raised his hand to cast a glyph, about to point out he could see better than Jenny in the dark, but Ferryl/Claris interrupted him. "That might be a way to keep us amused. Zephyr has been practicing as she promised."

"Practicing what?" Jenny glanced towards the spooky-line from Abel's shoulder because she couldn't see Zephyr's shimmer in the moonlight.

"Adapting eyes. She passed her final test, giving Stan's dog better vision and enabling him to see the magical creatures more clearly." Ferryl/Claris laughed as Jenny spun to look at her, then Abel, her eyes wide with excitement.

"I get night vision?"

"Only if you keep quiet about it." Abel wagged his finger at her but Jenny pointedly ignored it. "No letting it slip like you did about getting extra magic from a tree, or every Taverner will want the same. Zephyr will spend weeks doing nothing else, then someone will show off to a sibling or parent and there'll be a trip to the optician."

"That'll be fun, when they end up on national TV with a dozen top opticians trying to work out if they're some sort of biological freak." Ferryl/Claris added her wagging finger to Abel's. "Creepio will not be amused, and Stourton will be knee-deep in reporters."

"Opticians? It isn't just a magical coating?" Now Jenny looked a little apprehensive. "You'll physically alter the inside of my eyes? I know you said Zephyr had to learn to get inside my eyes, and that's why I couldn't have mine done as soon as Ferryl left me, but you didn't mention surgery!"

"More a case of re-growing some parts in a slightly different way, but it's the only way if you want permanently enhanced eyes. You'll see better in poor light, not in pitch darkness, and if you concentrate the faint lines of magic in leaves and grass are visible. The glow from the magic in smaller, thin-skinned creatures is quite pretty, and makes them really easy to hit at night." Ferryl/Claris tried to be stern but the huge grin spreading over Jenny's face didn't make it easy. "Zephyr will do what I did to Rob's, Kelis's and Abel's eyes. She will alter the cones in the back of your eyes, making them more sensitive but also more adaptable so you aren't dazzled by ordinary light. Zephyr will also adjust the lenses, your cornea, so that with a little concentration you will see further, clearer. That will include a thin magical coating to see magic better. Active hexes will appear bright red instead of a faint glow."

"How long will it take?" Jenny looked towards Dead Wood. "I don't want to be fumbling about because the job's only half done when the trap is sprung."

"When Ferryl fixed mine it only took a couple of minutes so there's plenty of time. The leech will still be waiting to make sure we aren't sneaking back." Abel looked up at Zephyr. "Are you ready? Zephyr, the gentle breeze for this, not the Ffod."

"Very gentle. You know I practiced and practiced on mice and rabbits, before fixing Bugsy. I will adjust one eye at a time so Ferryl Shayde can check." Zephyr drifted slowly closer to Jenny. "Part of me will go inside her eye, a little way, so I must keep coming back to my tattoo. Just to remind me who I am." Zephyr still worried about losing her identity when she merged her magic into any living being, even though it was only a little way.

Abel pointed to the grassy verge around the field. "Sit down Jenny, and close your eyes until it's done. Remember you have to trust Zephyr completely or she'll not get past your ward. You'll have to keep trusting her for a long while because Zephyr wants to do this slowly and very carefully."

"I'm good with the slow and careful bit." Jenny found a place without nettles or thistles and sat, before looking nervously at a very close Zephyr. "What do I do?"

"Relax." Ferryl laughed as she said it because Jenny wouldn't be able to, and Jenny's nervous giggle confirmed it.

"What about Claris? Will she remember the eye thing, that we can all see better? You said you'd left the minimum to erase as you left, but won't this bit take time?" Jenny looked a little embarrassed. "Sorry Claris, if you remember that eventually, but I'm worried you'll say the wrong thing."

"Just before I leave Claris, I will erase everything from when we untied the leeches. She'll be a little confused by the passing of time, but there'll be plenty going on to distract her." Ferryl/Claris smirked. "I've mazzled some memories so she doesn't notice the gaps after the leech left."

"Did you do that to me?" Jenny almost stood up again, definitely alarmed.

"And spoil all the memories of the hand-holding and Abel trying to work out kissing levels? No chance." All the humour dropped from Ferryl/Claris's voice. "I trusted you, but I'm in Claris's mind now and I can't totally trust her." Ferryl/Claris hesitated, then pushed on. "Claris might not even realise she was truly possessed. A mild mazzling has been spread over the whole period I've been in here, so I might seem to be nothing more than a voice in her head like Zephyr."

"Why did you do that? Knowing how much you did to save her should be enough to keep her quiet about how." Jenny looked uncomfortable, still wondering just how real her own memories were. "You could have explained like you did with me."

"You knew about me within days, to work out the kissing, then had time to think as I woke you up without the memory of leeches clouding your mind. There hasn't been time for Claris to understand and come to terms with what happened." A little smile touched Ferryl/Claris's lips. "She might not appreciate Abel's hand-holding like you did."

Which was Abel's cue to change the subject, before the others started teasing. "On that note of doom and gloom, can we get on with Jenny's eyes? Watching her afterwards will cheer us up." He laughed, remembering how excited Kelis and Rob had been when they could suddenly see in the dark. Jenny didn't laugh, closing her eyes and bracing herself as Zephyr drifted in towards her left eye.

*   *   *

Twenty-five minutes later Jenny wiped her eyes with a tissue soaked in drinking water from her bottle. "You never mentioned the stinging. Not as bad as chopping onions, but not much fun either." She kept her eyes closed for long moments, bracing herself, then opened them. "There's not much.... Oh, wow. It sort of comes in slowly, a bit like after walking out of the sun into the shade." Jenny turned her head back and forth and stood up. "Not as good as daylight, but definitely much better and I can see what you mean about fae and faeries glowing." Her hand came up, a small fire glyph arrowed out and a large fae burst into flame, dissolving into oblivion as it tumbled to the ground. "Oh yes, that's better." Another glyph shot into the shadows at the base of the hedgerow, sucking a thornie out into the field. "Much better." A fire glyph nailed it.

"Fae bop!" With that Zephyr hurtled off along the hedgerow, soaring into the sky seconds later gripping a fae. Though even as they laughed, none of them could stop worrying about what might be happening back at Dead Wood. Adapting Jenny's eyes had helped, but not for long enough.

*   *   *

On the outskirts of Dead Wood nothing happened for a long time, at least half an hour. Eventually a wave of compulsion swept over the small creatures in the field nearby, magical or flesh and blood. They all attempted to enter the wood, pushing forward until one by one the magical types, even the armoured hoplins, stilled and bubbled away into nothing. Fourthseed concentrated on the larger magical creatures it had snared, grazers from those similar to rabbits, if rabbits had four prehensile ears, up to a long-legged caterpillar-type a little larger than a sheep. The caterpillar lasted longest, its proboscis curling and thrashing in pain as the leech's mind drove it forward across the magical barrier. Halfway through it shuddered, and with a low rattle it collapsed and began to bubble away.

Several rats and mice, two rabbits and a dozen birds roused from their sleep survived crossing the barrier then fled in panic. Compulsion needed structured thought, but the magical deterrent latched onto that until sheer terror disrupted the leech's hold. When the Fourthseed ran out of victims it carefully inspected Dead Wood, an inch at a time, and then the field.

"Thirteenth, your host is magically aware. Look for another trap, or a veil. Take your time and inspect everything in sight. I do not trust the Hunter on the Wind. It is well named and might have flown back unseen." Fourthseed tried to stand on legs that were encased in plaster casts but failed. "This host is not healed enough to move far."

The other host, Father Curtis, stood and looked around slowly and carefully. "The only signs of magic are the traps and the feeds. I have decided. I do not wish to be a bound servant, but a bound shade kept for torture would be worse. Huntian might torment us for a thousand years before it tires of the sport. Was that truly Braeth Huntian?"

"I am sure. I saw it's true-self so there is no doubt. Keep looking for any other magic nearby. If the fools really have left, Huntian has made a mistake. A sorcerer's mistake." Fourthseed looked around again. "If we can get free of these traps you can carry me to the nearest house. We will compel whoever lives there to drive us away."

"Huntian will follow."

"We can take different hosts and disappear. If we phone the church, Huntian will be running from them long enough to give us a start. It will need a different disguise, and new followers." Fourthseed tried to get up again, and failed. "Keep searching. There is a way to break free, if we are truly alone." Though the leech still wasn't sure enough to say how, not yet.

Over an hour after Huntian had left, Thirteenseed confirmed it still couldn't see any sign of magical activity outside of the traps. Waves of compulsion lashed out for the third time but there were no victims, magical or otherwise, lurking nearby. "It is time to find out if we have a chance." Fourthseed picked up a handful of earth and threw it at the trap wall. The earth flew through, unobstructed, as Thirteenseed stared in confusion and Fourthseed sneered. "Typical of a magic user. Huntian set a purely magical trap, forgetting we might use pure physical force."

"But we are magical so it still holds us." Thirteenseed threw earth and watched it fly through the barrier.

"We are magical but what Huntian forgot is that our hosts aren't. Mine can't walk, and is too damaged and wasted inside to live without me long enough to crawl to the tree. Yours has only been a host for a few months. If you seal up any holes when you withdraw from the host's organs it can survive long enough to free us. Remember that you can still command your host even after you leave it, despite his ward, if you do not allow the compulsion to lapse. Don't falter, not for a moment, or the church ward will reject you." Fourthseed looked around, especially at the wood. The trees were spread out here, with a clearing between the two powering the traps so the leech could see a large area of rough grass and nettles.

"Will he be able to enter the wood?" Thirteenseed inspected the Dead Wood. "It killed or frightened everything you sent."

"Send him here to look at this glyph, the one I draw in the earth, then he must draw it on his skin. Thirdseed and Ninthseed used it to overcome the fear while partly protected inside a host. It should maintain your link through the barrier into the wood, so you can overcome your host's fear. Compel him to scuff the glyph on the tree, spoil it so the magic feed to your trap is broken. He can use a stone, or his teeth if he has to. Then break my trap, and get the host to swallow you again. Hurry. I do not trust Braeth Huntian to wait until an hour before dawn." Far out beyond the edge of the nearest field a small spark rose and burst. "We must leave while it is still hunting."

Father Curtis sat quietly while his leech withdrew tendrils from his organs and brain, and patched his internal damage. After a few minutes he went down onto his hands and knees and began to heave. He coughed, heaved again and choked as his throat bulged. The leech dropped free, and the churchman rose to his feet to totter through the magical barrier. He spoke, though it wasn't by his choice. "It works!"

"Yes! Quickly now." Fourthseed crawled to the edge of its trap to watch the man draw the glyph on his arm, using dirt and spit, then stagger towards the Sycamore tree. Five steps short of the trunk, inside the barrier around the wood and well clear of the magical trap, the man stopped.

"No!" He raised a hand in defence.

Two large, pale eyes had opened in the bark. "Hello, blood-bag." Branches creaked and both leeches and the man looked up, exactly as the dryad wanted. Roots swarmed out of the ground, twisting and writhing as they wove a net around the priest's feet and shins, starting up his thighs while he was still distracted. In one moment of shock the leech lost its link, and when it tried to reconnect the church wards rejected it.

"Push him forward. Make him ignore the pain and tear free to break the glyph." Fourthseed looked across at the other leech, sensing guilt and remorse. "You lost him!"

As the compulsion died Father Curtis tried pull away, to get away from the magically inspired fear already burrowing into his confused brain. He might have peeled away the roots and done so, but Dead Wood pressed in and robbed him of coherent thought. A voice brought Fourthseed's head back around to the wood. Impossible though it should be, two people watched from the middle of the clearing. Three, because Jane Doe could be seen through the nettles.

"No you don't, vicar." Rob's hands flexed, the glyphs flew, and earth rose to bind the roots together. Despite his frantic struggles the combination quickly held the churchman immobile, even trapping his hands as they pulled at the roots. He still moved slightly, because the cast didn't tighten onto his skin.

"How? I can see you but not feel you, but how?" Fourthseed couldn't tear its eyes from Jane Doe, a leech who'd stayed completely undetected mere metres away.

"Magic, the real thing, not that crappy blood magic you use." The other person in the clearing sat slumped in exhaustion. Kelis raised her head, sheer hatred all over her face as she raised her phone and pressed send. "Don't need magic to call Huntian, blood-bag. Braeth Huntian or the archbishop, time to make a choice." She slumped again. "I hope you've got it, Rob. I'm done."

"No problem." Rob pulled a lead bar full of magic from his pocket before casting another glyph with his free hand. More earth rose from the ground to coat Father Curtis's arms as he tried once again to pull his hands free. More roots snaked out of the ground, burrowing through the earth covering to bind it together, then reach up his thighs to his waist. Despite the magical protection offered by his church ward, the sheath held the priest immobile. His head thrashed back and forth and he began to moan in fear.

"Enough. Just keep the earth hard around the roots, apprentice, so he doesn't overbalance and break our hold." The dryad had come out of its tree, and now turned towards Fourthseed. "You consider yourself old and wise, but you are young and foolish compared to Braeth Huntian. Even her apprentices are beyond you." Branches creaked, definitely dryad humour this time. "You should have joined her when you had the chance." It raised a limb, the twigs on the end pointing across the field.

Fourthseed twisted to see. Three figures raced towards it, with a flying hunter leading the way. Out of sight, beyond the wood towards the road, engines roared into life. Fourthseed's host turned towards the sack-like creature with waving tendrils laid in the other trap. "You failed! I will not let you join Braeth Huntian. Die!" The leech struggled frantically as the compulsion hit it, trying to crawl away but the trap held it fast. Its tendrils lashed out wildly, blood spattering the earth around it as it thrashed and writhed before it began to bubble into oblivion. Thirteenseed gave a last shudder before collapsing, its tendrils falling limp and the rest quickly dissolved back into raw magic. Once it had gone, the dryad healed the glyph cut in its tree and the magic trap collapsed.

"You let them cut your own tree?" The leech looked as confused about that as anything else because dryads jealously guarded their trees from anything and anyone.

This time the branches creaked and thrashed enough to bring down twigs, almost hysterical laughter. "But it was my idea, my way to thank the master of Dead Wood for this fine tree, and a chance to squash another arrogant blood-bag. He has even promised me honey, and this sorcerer keeps his word." The dryad glanced towards the sound of approaching engines and stepped back inside its tree.

*   *   *

Ferryl/Claris and Jenny staggered to a halt, panting, but Abel carried on to Kelis. "You okay?" He collapsed to sit next to her.

"Maybe better than you." Kelis stretched cautiously, her face twisting in pain. "Ouch. I've never worked so hard and all I did was sit here. I began to wonder if the rotten thing would take the bait, because I'd never have lasted until an hour before dawn."

"Crikey, weren't three trees enough?" Abel glanced at the nearest tree, linked underground to another two with a third underground link to where Kelis sat. The magical links had been buried deep enough that even the dryad and Zephyr couldn't see a hint of them.

"Probably plenty, but it's the continual casting, sucking the magic up one arm then pushing it down and out the other palm. My arms are dropping off. I've no idea how much that super-speed veil uses but don't even think about it without at least one tree to supply the magic." She stretched again, very carefully. "I'm pleased it'll be Sunday so I can sleep late and laze around all day. Come on, help me up. I want to sneer at that thing and it isn't as satisfying from down here." Abel hesitated. "Don't be an idiot. An arm round me won't activate our connection, even if there still is one." Abel knew some sort of connection survived, he could feel it as he helped her up but was relieved because Kelis didn't know.

By the time Abel had helped Kelis across to Fourthseed, her sneer had to take second place. Two Land Rovers bounced up and Creepio jumped out of the first one. "Is he alive? Is the leech gone?" He stopped to stare at Father Curtis, frantically trying to pull away from the woodland while tears poured down his face. Creepio's stare might have had something to do with the earthen cast holding the priest bent over with his hands clutching at his knees. "Can you release him?"

"Yes. The leech is dead but we needed you here before setting him free. He's inside the barrier so he'll be terrified and try to run away." Rob looked a little embarrassed. "If he'd got out of the wood, the leech might have been able to get to him again. I didn't want to wrestle a priest to stop him." His hands worked, the glyphs flew and the earth began to crumble. As it did, roots wriggled free and slithered back into the ground.

"A dryad is helping?" Two pale brown eyes opened briefly when Creepio looked towards the tree.

"Yes, another nasty evil magical creature helping you to save a soul. You might want to rewrite that dogma of yours." Kelis smirked happily as Creepio ignored her comments.

Instead the vicar gestured two men forward as Father Curtis tripped and rolled away from the wood. The priest scrambled further away, moaning in fear with an arm up to hide his face. "Father Curtis will need a sedative. Check his vitals and get him to the ambulance as quickly as possible." The men placed the Father inside their vehicle and began to check him over.

"Fourthseed said he could survive for a while without the leech. Thirteenseed sealed up the major organs so he'd last long enough to free them." Kelis finally got her chance to sneer at the Fourthseed. "This miserable specimen killed the other leech as a failure when we trapped your man, but doesn't look any more successful from where I am."

"I'll kill the host if you touch me. She'll die in agony." Though the leech glanced at Ferryl/Claris as it spoke, fully aware Braeth Huntian didn't really care. "I will trade Braeth Huntian for my freedom? It is a bigger prize."

The vicar burst out laughing as Zephyr swooped low, now tethered to Abel. "You still think that is the real Braeth Huntian? You really are stupid." He quickly sobered, fixing the leech with a cold stare. "I don't care what happens to you, as long as you are bound or die." Creepio turned away, speaking to the teenagers. "Do you need us for anything else?" As he spoke one vehicle roared off across the field with Father Curtis aboard.

"Possibly, in a few minutes, but you can't watch." Abel turned to Kelis, and Zephyr connected them by spooky-phone. "I want life support for either the host or Jane Doe if necessary. Do you have paper and a pen?"

"Always." Kelis produced a little pad and a marker pen. "My instant glyph-copying set." She laughed at the suspicious look from Creepio.

Abel scribbled on the pad. 'We might need life support for the woman if we can kill the leech fast enough. You'll have to wait out of sight while we do something ungodly.' He offered the paper. "Can you do this?"

Creepio read it. "These men are paramedics, and the ambulance is nearby." The two men in the remaining vehicle nodded. With that the vicar climbed in the Land Rover and the churchmen set off after the other vehicle.

Zephyr reached out to connect Abel to the rest through spooky-phone. "Fourthseed will not give up so we go to the alternative. I'll give Rob a hand to bring Jane Doe, then Ferryl will kill the leech and we'll try to save the girl, the host."

"I'll get a tree ready for Claris." Kelis walked past Jane Doe and into the wood, across the clearing where the three of them had waited. Ferryl had been right, the leech hadn't even suspected the advanced veil that blocked even magical sight. Very few knew of it, and fewer still used it because of the amount of magic needed. "My thanks, tree." Kelis sealed the underground links to the tree before cutting an ordinary draining glyph into the bark. She put away her knife and came back to the rest, her hand outstretched. "Let me have the marker back please, Abel, so I can draw the glyph on Claris's palm."

Rob and Abel put the stretcher down near the magic trap, while Ferryl/Claris stood looking down at the Fourthseed and host. "Have you made up your mind?" As she spoke Jenny healed the glyph feeding magic to the leech trap and it disappeared.

Even as the host opened its mouth, a sneer starting, Abel and Zephyr struck. Abel jammed a compressed air glyph inside its mouth to keep it open and the Sprite flew straight in. Barely a second later Zephyr shouted "got it" down the connection.

"She's got the brain." Abel meant that Zephyr had severed the magical tendrils the leech used to control the host. She absolutely wouldn't even try to control a brain. Ferryl/Claris had been poised so she quickly dropped a cloud of small glyphs, glittering in the moonlight, straight into the open mouth. She turned away as the cloud disappeared inside, hunting the Fourthseed, and knelt beside Jane Doe. The bound leech was already crawling out of Jane Doe's mouth, into the bowl Rob held ready. He hurried over to kneel beside Fourthseed's host, ready to tip their leech into the open mouth once Fourthseed died.

The old leech fought hard, both against the cloud of magic and sharp ice particles tearing into it and to regain control of the host's brain. Zephyr fought to keep the magic tendrils from regaining a purchase and shredding the victim's mind. Unfortunately that meant she had to slip just a little way inside, partly blending with the host. "Help me Abel. I am losing me!"

"Hang on Zephyr. Don't lose you, don't lose the link. Hold tight."

"But it tugs on me, the mind pulls. I know I could but I want to stay me." The sprite definitely started to panic, though she stayed in the struggling host. "I don't know who I am!"

Abel started to worry, but daren't show it. "You are the mighty Flying Fist of Doom, the wondrous Ffod fighting for the Tavern!"

"But I am slipping inside, it is too easy. It is hard to stay me, to be your hunter. Some of me wants to give in." Zephyr sounded horrified over the link, more so as it started to fluctuate.

"No! You must come back! Back to your home. You are Zephyr, the wind with a name." Abel pushed magic down the link without being asked, something he'd never tried, and it firmed up. "Don't worry, I won't let the link fail. I'd rather lose her than you." Abel felt ashamed but it was true. If he had to choose between his magical friend and a nameless woman he'd do it.

"Truth. You will not let me lose myself. I am safe if I hold tight. I am Zephyr, your watcher in the night." The link strengthened as did Zephyr's 'voice' and Abel remembered, she could read the truth on a link. "Ffod is strong with Abel magic. The leech cannot get past me." Abel fed more magic down the link, until Zephyr no longer needed it. "The Fourthseed is fading. Please put in our leech so I can come home."

"Rob, tip it in." Rob tilted the bowl. The leech scrambled down the host's throat and disappeared while the host trembled, spluttering and coughing blood. Zephyr stayed inside, holding on until the woman's brain was safe, then flew out of the open mouth and into her tattoo. She gave the impression of crouching in there, trembling.

"Bad, very bad. Don't like it. Very bad. Home again, the Ffod is home. Not in her head, in my home. Belong here. Puff of wind home."

While Abel reassured Zephyr, Rob noticed Claris knelt over Jane Doe, still hesitating. "Do it Claris." Ferryl must have withdrawn her control, completely ready to transfer hosts, wiping out the last couple of hours. Unfortunately Claris, now completely aware and in control of herself, was also totally confused by the memory loss. She had baulked at making mouth contact with the gaunt figure on the stretcher. Jane Doe opened her mouth and began to thrash about and scream.

Jenny pinned Jane Doe's arms and glared at Claris. "Come on bitch. This is how we saved you." Claris jerked in shock then leant forward to press her mouth to Jane Doe's. She froze, then shuddered for long moments as Ferryl flowed out of her. Even as Claris fell away and crumpled to the ground, Jenny pressed her magic diamond into Jane Doe's hand. "Here you are, Ferryl. Plenty of magic." She placed Kelis's much larger magic diamond into Jane's other hand. "There's more in that. We've got to deal with Claris."

Abel reached down to help Jenny get Claris to her feet, because he knew exactly how she felt. Ferryl had drained Claris of her physical strength as well as all her magic, just as she had when leaving Abel and Jenny. Jenny got a shoulder under Claris's arm, and Rob took the other one. Kelis finished her call to Creepio and took Claris's hand. She drew a glyph on it, then slid a glyphed pebble into Claris's pocket to protect her from Dead Wood. "Creepio is on the way, Rob. Try to keep Claris well away so she doesn't say the wrong thing. I'll feed magic to our leech." She moved over to the young woman with broken legs, now beginning to thrash about a little. Kelis drew a glyph on a trembling and twitching hand, holding it still while she pressed a lead bar full of magic into place.

Jane Doe had quietened now but the other ex-host thrashed and struggled even more, making mewling, bubbling noises that were almost words. Jane Doe opened her eyes, turned to look, and released a small glyph. "Sleep." The young woman quietened though her chest still heaved erratically and her limbs twitched. "It isn't deep sleep, so leech can still talk. Food please." Abel opened the first flask of oxtail soup. They'd known that Ferryl would need food as soon as possible, to turn into new flesh inside Jane Doe. By the time he held the cup to Jane Doe's mouth a Land Rover screeched to a halt and two paramedics rushed up.

"Here. Deal with this one." Kelis beckoned them to where the ex-host lay, fighting for breath and occasionally blowing out a fine mist of blood.

Her eyelids fluttered open and blood spurted from her mouth. "Very bad. Too much bleeding." The medics pounced, one quickly finding a vein while the other rigged up a drip. "Lots, she needs lots. It was big and fought hard." Blood bubbled as the host spoke, making her hard to understand but driving home how serious it was.

The medic pulled a second bag out of his kit. "We've done this before." An oxygen mask went over the woman's mouth and another needle went in. "Come on love, don't let go. Fight it." The medics worked frantically for long minutes until one looked up at Creepio and shook his head.

"Get the leech out. Let me save her." Creepio, his face set, brandished his cross. "Her soul at least." The two paramedics kept working on the young woman, so Abel and Kelis hesitated.

A paramedic glanced up at Kelis. "He's right. She's fading fast. If it gets out now, we will keep her going long enough to die leech-free. That will give the archbishop a chance to save her soul." He put a hand on the mask, ready to move it aside as Kelis extended the bowl.

"Come out leech, and thanks for trying." Kelis took the bowl away as soon as the leech tumbled free and the mask went back on. The amount of blood trickling into the mask underlined the urgency. Creepio, or rather the peripatetic archbishop right now, knelt beside the dying woman with his cross in his hand and began to speak quietly. Abel turned back to Jane Doe as Kelis came over to join them. "What do I do with this?" She held out the bowl with the leech inside.

"Let the Firstseed find it a new host once she's up to it." Though that would have to wait until the vicar left. Abel waved a paramedic away. "This one will survive, thanks." The man turned back to work on the dying girl. Inside the wood Jenny and Rob had managed to get Claris to the tree and persuade her to draw magic. Now she sat beside Rob, hanging onto him and crying her eyes out. Jenny looked over towards Abel and shrugged, tree magic must have a different effect on Claris. For some endless time the tableau held. Claris sobbing, Jane Doe leaning on Abel while she drank soup, the paramedics working on the girl and Creepio's voice reciting what Abel assumed had to be Latin.

Behind Abel the young woman's laboured breathing stopped, though the archbishop carried speaking on for a little while. The paramedics kept murmuring, and working frantically, but Fourthseed's host didn't breathe again. A few minutes later the vicar spoke just behind Abel. "We will never know who she was or if she ever belonged to a church. Even so, I would like to bury her in hallowed ground."

Abel turned to have a dig about hosts being soulless but stopped. He wasn't facing Creepio or the archbishop, just a man, his face gaunt with grief and a tear in his eye. "Thanks. We'll be okay here if you want to take her now." Despite what Creepio had said, he'd obviously hoped to save the host. Abel saw the vicar look over towards Claris, still sobbing loudly. "Memories, probably. She had the same experience but made it."

"I will be in touch." For once that didn't sound like a threat.

"Her name was Beth." Zephyr sounded cautious, and ashamed. "I went into her mind a little. I tried not to!"

"I know you didn't mean to, but finding her name was a good thing."

Abel looked up at Creepio. "She's called Beth. Our leech caught her name when it first went in there."

"Thank you." Creepio hesitated, looking towards the leech in the bowl for long moments. "Please thank your leech." He turned away quickly, probably to avoid any comments about evil creatures being helpful, and went to help the paramedics. The paramedics already had a stretcher beside the body and were packing up their gear. It didn't take them long, but by the time the noise of the vehicle had died away Ferryl had drunk one flask of soup and started on the second.

Claris still sobbed, quieter now, with her arms round Rob and her head on his shoulder. From that, and the way Ferryl kept drinking soup, Abel figured they'd be here for a while. "Ferryl?"

She stopped drinking. "This woman is very badly damaged inside. The leech did well to keep her going."

"I wanted to ask about our leech. What host does it get?"

"Something harmless. Considering how hard it tried, something big enough to hold it. No need for the cleaver." Ferryl turned back to the soup.

Abel met Kelis's eyes and they both shrugged. "Fox?"

"That's not harmless." Kelis thought a moment, eyeing the glistening, tendril-covered, bag-like creature in the bowl. "A hare might be big enough? The leech can't run away because it's bound, so it can live in the fields nearby. We'll have to let Stan know or he'll shoot it."

"We can paint its ears red, or put a luminous stripe on its back?" Kelis nodded agreement with a little smile. "I'll send Zephyr to look."

A shimmer rose cautiously from Abel's shoulder, no bold moves now. "I will search for a large hare. My tether will bring me home." Abel had a feeling the last bit had been Zephyr reassuring herself. She drifted off across the field, working back and forth to search any likely hiding places.

*　　*　　*

While Zephyr searched, the rest of them topped up lead bars, then themselves, with tree-magic. Jenny used fire glyphs to burn away any trace of blood, the leeches or the hosts, then took both Ferryl's diamonds so she could top them up. According to her she could do with the lift from the trees, though for once Jenny didn't giggle afterwards. Claris quietened to an occasional sob but tears still trickled down her face and she wouldn't talk yet. Rob kept his arm round her, patting her back now and then though he didn't seem comfortable with his new role. Kelis sat quietly, looking at the place where the young woman had died and occasionally rubbing her arms because they were still sore.

"I have one. It is a big adult. I am bringing it home." Abel warned the rest, who all looked towards where Zephyr's tether disappeared over a hedgerow. The spooky-line wavered back and forth, which seemed odd until she came into sight. A large hare raced over the field towards them, trying again and again to break away to the side. Every time it did Zephyr zoomed up to cut it off and threw a tiny glyph to herd it back onto the right track. "Yee-hah! Run, bunny, run!"

"Ferryl? How do we catch that without injuring it?" Abel supported Ferryl as she turned so she could see.

"Everyone stay very still. I'll stop it as near as possible." Ferryl raised a hand, waiting until the hare skidded to a stop, staring at the humans. "Sleep." As the glyph shot across the field and the animal crumpled, Kelis jumped to her feet to collect it. She laid it next to the bowl containing the leech and everyone pointedly looked elsewhere.

Zephyr flew into her tattoo and chasing the hare had done wonders for her. "Did you see me! Ffod needs a hat and a lasso. Yee-hah!"

A few minutes later Ferryl woke the hare again and it staggered to its feet, looking around but not frightened. It hopped, cautiously, and sniffed at the grass, then the air. After moving away a little, very tentatively, it looked back at the humans. Ferryl waved 'go away' and the hare set off across the field, gradually speeding up as it disappeared from sight. The leech had very specific instructions. Since it wasn't allowed to grow it wouldn't need blood, just a daily dose of magic from Ferryl, and it should use compulsion as persuasion rather than commands. The hare might never realise it had a passenger.

Just after three a.m. the weary group headed back into Brinsford. Despite not actually doing anything physical, running so much magic through her arms had left Kelis incapable of helping with the stretcher. Once Jenny had helped to carry Ferryl Shayde to the road, she banished the glyph hiding her moped and set off home. She didn't put on the lights until she reached the main road so nobody in Brinsford would see her leaving, not a problem with Jenny's new eyesight.

Rob and Abel carried Ferryl to the church while Kelis kept everyone under a veil, then escorted the girls home. At Kelis's door Claris finally let go of Rob, apologising for her reaction. The sight of the leech had kicked in a lot of very bad memories. Kelis offered her a tiny glyph drawn on a page of her notebook, and told her to wait outside until the sleep glyph in the house had been broken or she'd collapse. Then, according to Ferryl, if Claris held the paper while Kelis activated the glyph it should give the ex-host a solid night's sleep. Rob and Abel headed for home after letting Dryad Chestnut know the blood-bags were dead.

Once he got home and into bed, Abel broke the wooden sleep glyph. If his mum had gone to sleep in an uncomfortable position she could now wake up and get comfy. He didn't think about tonight for long, quickly drifting off to sleep with Zephyr curled up in her tattoo. She'd already told him there'd be no flying about tonight.

To The Woods!

After their late night, Abel and Kelis slept late, but Rob had a little sister and wasn't as lucky. On the way through the village to meet up after lunch, several villagers told one or the other teenager about the noise in the night. Creepio's Land Rovers and possibly some of the other vehicles had been heard. Mrs Turner blamed teenage delinquents with stolen cars, but others thought a couple of off-roaders might have been racing. A look in the fields near the village had shown enough tracks to support the off-roaders idea.

Abel, Rob, Kelis and Claris met at the church, because Ferryl wouldn't be up to walking to meet them anywhere else. Just Ferryl Shayde now, because this host had no other name. Claris seemed very quiet, and once again put her arms round Rob when she met him. Right now she needed some human contact, someone normal to remind her what normal felt like. Claris seemed very confused, which might be Ferryl's mazzlement, but definitely remembered she'd been possessed by a leech and saved by the four teenagers.

Once Claris went back to her room, Ferryl Shayde had bad news. The bound leech wouldn't have realised, but this woman hadn't been six feet tall when the leech Firstseed took her. Her joints had been deliberately stretched, enough so that even standing must have been painful. That wouldn't have bothered the Firstseed, but now Ferryl wanted to bring her bones back into proper alignment before building muscle. In the interim she would continue repairing the worst-damaged organs.

The biggest problem from Ferryl's point of view would be staying in Brinsford while Abel went to school. She had sworn to defend and train Abel for ninety years, and now for the second time she would be physically incapable of doing so. Eventually Ferryl accepted there were plenty of Taverners at school to keep everyone safe, but only because she couldn't do anything about it. Zephyr promised to guard Abel, changing her tattoo to a cat-cowgirl with a big pistol, riding a hare.

It wouldn't just be school that felt strange without their resident sorceress. Abel, Kelis and Rob, and lately Jenny, had become used to practicing their glyphs in Castle House gardens or Dead Wood. Nobody could interrupt them, and there were plenty of trees to replenish their magic. Tattoo Ferryl, Ferryl/Jenny, and then Ferryl/Claris had been there to help them progress faster. Right now, with darkness falling early, none of them dare practice even minor glyphs in the churchyard where Ferryl could check them. Mrs Turner still claimed the churchyard had ghosts so mysterious lights would just make her worse.

Though there were still some bright moments. Stan, the allegedly retired poacher, thought being asked to come out into the fields to meet a hare must be Abel winding him up. Eventually he agreed but without Bugsy, his old Jack Russell, or any hares coming near would have had a hard time. Ferryl had already used her bond to send the leech to the field, so Abel sent Zephyr out to look. He saw her spooky-phone connect, completely invisible to Stan. Kelis had begged to be the one to do the next part. She cupped her hands and shouted, "Here bunny, bunny. Come home bunny."

Within a couple of minutes, a large hare cautiously approached the humans. After getting over his initial shock, Stan agreed he'd notice the odd markings long before shooting. Ferryl had turned those into a lesson, insisting her trainees change the colour of the hairs rather than dye the white stripe down its back and round each ear. Once Kelis told it to go and play, the hare left. The leech would take it round to the church after dark, where Ferryl would supply a daily dose of magic and a safe place to sleep.

Between spending time in the church with Ferryl and being restricted to indoors by the darkness and weather, magic practice suffered over the next few weeks. All the Taverners at school complained about the early nights and finding some privacy, though most of them still managed to use up an extra two lead bars-worth of magic each week. On the plus side, everyone had plenty of time to get their school homework done. Mrs. Svengy in particular saw an increase in extra studying, though she didn't realise it came from her magically-aware biology students. Learning that sorcerers could self-heal if they had precise biological knowledge had come as a shock to the trainees, but also an incentive.

Through it all Claris stayed withdrawn, though she rallied enough at school so nobody realised it. Claris and Rob gave the gossip mill some ammunition for a few days, but it soon became clear they weren't an item and interest waned. Once Rob explained that her ward would stop any leeches getting to her, Claris decided she didn't want to learn magic. The whole idea scared her, she didn't even like seeing the others practice so she never even asked to come into the Castle House gardens. Abel saw her staring at his tattoo several times, fascinated, but definitely worried, and hoped she wouldn't say the wrong thing to anyone.

While Claris dealt with her problem, the older Taverners had to deal with the new contracts in Stourton. Along with the few Taverners not in school, they worked out a rota to fill hexes for their new customers. At least the charity could now reimburse the hex fillers for their petrol or bus fares. Once everything settled down, the older members would take some younger Taverners to help, and to train them. For now, Abel and his friends supplied extra bars full of magic.

It wasn't long before the clients wanting confirmation from Pendragon signed up, because the sorcerer verified the letter. Abel even received a letter from Pendragon reminding him they had an agreement not to poach any other type of work. The one client who wanted to see the new contractor agreed to the Taverners maintaining her hexes until the sorceress returned from a trip abroad. Abel wanted Ferryl Shayde present at that meeting in case the client wanted a demonstration of competence.

Jenny had her own extra work, though at least part of it meshed with her Business Studies homework. Mentored by her father, she continued with setting up the launch of Bonny's Tavern. As she'd feared, it wouldn't be ready for the market by Christmas and Abel, Kelis, and Rob still refused to sell a beta version. Mr. Forester had also made progress with creating a charity, but had been hesitating over what type would be best. Eric sent a list of the fees for the magical work in Stourton, which the customers were happy to pay as charitable donations. Once he saw the size of the donations waiting for registration and a bank account, Jenny's dad told his lawyer to get the job done as quicklyas possible. The Taverners kept out of the details, except to make certain none of them would be personally liable but they'd have some control over how the donations were used.

Laurence, Kelis's aristocratic ex, came to see Kelis, not as her ex-boyfriend though he hoped for a favour. He confessed to almost kidnapping a couple of goblins when he collected them in Stourton for the diversion at Halloween. Now he'd come to ask, officially, if he could take a few to his home. Having seen the seventeen-bedroom slightly run-down stately home Laurence lived in, Abel and the rest knew he could provide a home for several stonelins and batlins. The house and gardens already had gargoyles and statues of various sizes, so a few more magically inhabited ones would fit right in.

This time the goblin meld didn't debate long. Late one evening Laurence parked his family's 4X4 outside the church while he attended a meeting to play Bonny's Tavern in Kelis's house. When he went home, six stonelins and eight batlins went with him. The latter would hunt any stinging fae as well as gnats and other annoying insects. The stonelins would raid the rubbish bins but also eat rats, mice, and a variety of small magical creatures.

Before he left, Laurence asked if the local members of the Tavern would like to hold a meeting at New Year's, at his house. Despite starting work he'd continued playing the game, both with Taverners in town and his cousins in Germany, and had kept up his magic practice. He'd broached the subject of a fancy-dress party to his parents, and they were pleased he'd increased his social circle despite leaving school.

Laurence didn't want all the people who played the game, just those who could cast glyphs. He hoped to get rid of the huge fursomnium, the Dream Stealer, that Ferryl had discovered sleeping in his attic. Despite Ferryl's assurance that it would probably sleep for years yet, and that Dreamcatchers now protected the bedrooms, the young aristocrat felt uneasy. If it woke when Laurence had gone abroad on business nobody else in his family would know and it might prey on them or staff. A Dream Stealer that size could drive an unwarded human insane if it followed a dream back to its source. The stronger magical Taverners gleefully accepted their invite to a New Year fancy dress party at a real mansion, one with a real resident monster.

Claris remained quiet and withdrawn, not attending Tavern meetings and spending much of her time in her bedroom at Kelis's house. She still sat with Abel, Kelis and Rob at break times in school but said very little. Eventually she asked, tentatively, if she could move out of the village. She'd laid for too long in the village church with a leech eating away inside her, so Brinsford gave her the creeps. Claris had also spent a whole summer as Abel's girlfriend, whereas before that she'd despised him as one of the Geeks. She remembered that summer, and enjoying herself despite the weird voice in her head, so it felt strange being in Abel's company.

Abel, for one, worried she might be thinking of confessing all, including Ferryl's possession, but Claris didn't want to go home. She still wasn't ready to face her mother's inquisition about the alleged drug addiction. Instead, Claris wanted to move into Frederick's house in Stourton where she could still get magical support if necessary. Within days her mum came to help Claris move into her new digs, pleased the supposed withdrawal regime had worked and her daughter was recovering. Claris's mum even insisted on paying for decorating the room and her rent, a real boost for Frederick's finances. That gave him five paying tenants, because Effy had also rented a room. The twenty-seven-year-old found being with Frederick, someone even older than her who was also just learning to handle glyphs, was reassuring.

Kelis's mum cheered up a bit because she wouldn't be looking for a room to rent, not just yet. Her lawyer spoke to the bank and, as Mr. Forester had suggested, they wouldn't ask her to vacate the house until the divorce had been settled. That still might mean Kelis moving into Stourton, because her mum couldn't afford a house in Brinsford even if one came on the market. Jenny suggested they moved into Frederick's house, but Kelis thought that with so many magic users coming and going her mum would realise magic was real. At her age, that could give her a breakdown.

While the rest of the world carried on, Ferryl Shayde concentrated on getting mobile again. With massive amounts of magic and an almost continual supply of soup and then solid food, she finally pulled her new host's bones and ligaments back into shape. The first time she managed to stand unaided came as a shock to everyone, because the host had shrunk ten centimetres to just over a hundred and seventy. Ferryl thought she might end up a little shorter as her joints finally settled. After that first attempt Ferryl's new body walked for longer periods every day.

While shrinking, Ferryl Shayde had also filled out a little, and her features had softened from the haughty leech queen look. The original tall, thin woman had looked pale, but the new shorter version had fuller lips and a tanned skin. According to Ferryl she now looked Egyptian or

Bedouin, some Middle Eastern mix, which should stop Creepio making any connection between her and the ex-host. The long straight hair had originally been dyed, but the gleaming, wavy black tresses now framing her face were completely natural.

Her four apprentices knew Ferryl must be pushing her recovery so she could accompany Abel and the coin to Stourton, but now she explained her long-term plan. After forty years as a leech host this body had no history, and the mind inside it was totally insane. Ferryl couldn't find any memories of childhood, friends, or a name, nothing but pain and terror, so she'd already put it into a deep sleep. If Abel agreed Ferryl would build the woman a new life.

Ferryl would create a new name and identity, complete her schooling, learn to drive a car, and act just like anyone else for the next ninety years. During that time period, she would assemble enough detailed memories to give the woman a history up to the age of twenty, then wipe out all the pain and terror. Once Ferryl Shayde moved on, leaving the woman with a twenty-year-old body, her host could live out a normal lifespan without ever knowing about the leech possession. In the interim Ferryl would be the same age as Abel, Kelis and Rob so it wouldn't look odd if they stayed friends.

None of her trainees could understand it, because Ferryl had complained about the detailed work involved in fixing just a few months of Jenny's and Claris's memories. Now she'd volunteered to construct twenty years, minute by minute. Ferryl became embarrassed and quite defensive before finally confessing. She'd seen how Abel and his friends reacted to possession, so she wanted to take this opportunity to abandon her usual method of switching hosts every twenty years. More than that, she felt certain Abel wouldn't agree to her using this woman for ninety years without giving something in return.

Kelis, Rob, Abel, and Jenny talked it around and around, but that seemed like a good solution for both the woman and Ferryl Shayde. The church would never expect Braeth Huntian to live as a human, a schoolgirl, rather than flitting from victim to victim. The biggest problem would be to explain the original ex-host disappearing and the new, shorter, younger girl appearing. Jenny thought the first part might not be too hard, because few people even knew the woman existed. After three days of discussion Abel finally agreed. If Ferryl could arrange a new identity and admission to the school as a sixteen-year-old pupil, she should.

Privately Abel thought that the modern world wouldn't allow a person to appear out of nowhere. Magic might be able to create false documents and change appearances, but it wouldn't create a new National Insurance number or Birth Certificate in the computers at the General Register Office. Right now, he worried a lot more about the impending visit to Stourton with the letter and coin from Castle House. Rob, Kelis and Jenny stood guard twice more as he went in through the front door of Castle House, but the defences remained quiet.

* * *

School broke up with a surprising number of people coming to ask if Bonny's Tavern could have another meeting, a Christmas dance. Not a magical one, these were the pupils who were playing the game as entertainment. Unfortunately, over a hundred people had turned up to the outdoor meeting in the summer, so a winter meeting would mean hiring a hall. Despite being disappointed, the queries soon turned to when the weather might be good enough to meet outdoors. Some groups were working on having their own miniature Tavern parties at the Christmas dances in Stourton, especially if they could find one where they could wear costumes.

On the way back in the bus, the three teenagers talked about that rather than what was really bothering them. Tonight, their grounding ended, so Abel could go to the mystery address in Stourton. The rest could come too, but Castle House only allowed Abel to touch the key, go in through the front door, or pick up the small chest he found on a table beside the next door. The letter had to be for him. Despite hours spent discussing the message, "If ye lay claim, bring the box and coin," the guesses still varied from claiming the magical coin up to the whole house. Abel kept claiming that the Castle House and gardens had been Rob's suggestion, but the rest thought that wasn't even remotely likely. How could a sixteen-year-old boy claim a huge house and all that land?

Kelis had already asked her mum for the loan of the BMW, and Shannon had agreed to come over in two days to drive it. Abel daren't make it sound urgent, because nobody else knew about the key or opening

Castle House. All the Taverners would want to come and see, then the villagers would notice, and in the end the house would kill someone. Jenny had started driving lessons, so hopefully she would soon be able to act as chauffeur instead of relying on others. The weather took some of the edge off their excitement, as they had to walk in the rain because of Melanie.

The weather became a big part of the discussion later when the three of them met Ferryl in the church. It wasn't a long meeting, because Mrs. Turner would spot any lights. At least the three of them could use heat glyphs, while Ferryl swore the cold didn't affect her or the body she wore. Without the enhancements Ferryl had added to their eyesight, Kelis, Rob, and Abel wouldn't have been able to see the clothes show. Ferryl tried on the clothes donated by Jenny and Claris, because the ones originally supplied by Kelis were now too long and much too tight for her new body.

The sorceress settled on a shirt and jumper to go with the best fitting of the jeans and shoes, but suddenly realised she didn't have a jacket or coat. This body had only been outside the church once since arriving in a leather catsuit, and had been wearing a nightdress and wrapped in a sleeping bag then and ever since. A quick phone call to Jenny arranged for a fleece, then the three humans headed gratefully for Kelis's house and the warmth in Bonny's Tavern, the old library. As soon as Ferryl could arrange a new identity she would be able to attend meetings as well, and maybe become a lodger just as Claris had. When he mentioned that, Abel had to suffer the usual digs from Kelis about collecting girlfriends.

*   *   *

Nobody made any jokes at all when Shannon arrived just after lunch to drive the BMW, because they were all on edge. Ferryl had already gone into Stourton, on the bus, which would give her time to inspect the address. By the time the rest arrived, she should have found signs of any magical traps or protections. There wouldn't be anything too blatant, because the office building stood in the old town centre. Despite the number of shops closing down since the big shopping centre opened, enough businesses remained to make it a very public location.

Today Shannon picked Jenny up on the way into town so she didn't have to ride her moped in the driving rain. Jenny had her school backpack with her, whispering to Kelis that it held a waterproof hoodie for Ferryl. When Shannon pulled up in Stourton she didn't recognise the young woman with an umbrella who waved and came to greet them. The umbrella didn't exist, just a seeming, but it gave Ferryl an excuse to divert the rain around herself. After a quick hello, Ferryl introduced herself as Fay before an intrigued Shannon drove off to find a parking spot.

Everyone else crowded into the doorway of a boarded-up shop, where Ferryl dismissed the umbrella seeming and put on the waterproof hoodie from Jenny's bag. "That's the office, directly across the road. The place is warded but only against the likes of fae, hoplins, and none of the wards, bar strong magical beings. Some of them are dormant so if they are awakened that might change." Ferryl glanced across the road. "I think these solicitors deal with magical customers, advanced magical beings as well as human glyph-users." She pointed, then dropped her arm with a tut of exasperation. "There are magical flows on the wall above the door, invisible to anyone but the likes of Zephyr, me, or dryads. The language is vaguely familiar, so it may be stored on one of my lost wits."

Abel had another explanation. "It might be a warning?"

"No, there is an arrow to the door. The door has no glyphs that would bar me from entering."

Abel passed on Zephyr's message to the rest. "Maybe Zephyr should connect us up before we go inside."

"No, that might be considered rude or threatening. Anything or anyone in there who can read those signs will see her." Ferryl looked really nervous, as bad as any of the humans. "I wish I could read it. I need my wits!" She stared in surprise as the others laughed.

"It's been ages since you said that." Kelis looked past Ferryl and braced herself. "Here comes Shannon. Remember, you just arrived in town but you are an old pen pal of mine."

"From Germany, which explains my name." Ferryl smirked at the puzzled looks.

"What, Fay? Is that German?" Rob looked as baffled as the other two.

"No, but my surname is, because I have been thinking about it. My Shayde is spelled with a y, and the German one usually has a c between the s and the h, but it's near enough." Her smirk grew as she saw comprehension spread across the other three faces.

Rob finally managed to splutter out an answer. "Fay Shayde? Seriously? The Taverners will connect the dots straight away."

"But then Kelis will admit that Abel got the name for the sorceress from mine. Zephyr will tell those who know about her that there is a real Ferryl, and that she took the name because her true one can't be revealed." Ferryl laughed at their expressions. "Those who have heard us mention Braeth Huntian will wonder, but Zephyr will tell them her true-name is much older than that." Which Abel knew was true. He also knew her true-name, Pungh Hmmshtfun, which even his closest friends didn't.

"Here's your first chance to try that out. Shannon is coming." Jenny pointed down the road.

"Let's save the surname part until after we've been in there." Abel hunched his shoulders and stepped out of cover. "I don't fancy hanging about in this rain while we work through the full explanation." As soon as Shannon arrived, the group headed across the road, through the double doors and into a spacious reception area.

*   *   *

"Wards on all the doors, magic in the desk and the plant is aware." As Zephyr warned Abel, Ferryl glanced at him so he nodded that he knew.

Shannon leant over to whisper to Kelis, eying up the plush surroundings. "What exactly are we doing here? This is not the sort of place that gives free advice."

For a moment Kelis debated telling Shannon about the box and coin, but none of them actually knew what would happen next. "Ferryl says we have to come here to make the magic contracts legal, the ones we took from Pendragon."

"Which I'd better do now." Abel headed for the receptionist, opening his pack and extracting the letter without showing the small chest. "Hello. I've no idea how this works. Does this letter mean anything to you?"

As he placed the sheet of paper on the counter the eyes in a small statuette of a mermaid glowed yellow, just briefly. "Yes sir, I know who you should see. One moment while I find you a guide." The receptionist didn't read the letter or go to find anyone, waiting until a door opened and a smartly dressed middle-aged woman came in. He pointed at the letter, then Abel.

She looked at the group, her eyes lingering for a moment on Ferryl and Abel, then produced a professional smile of welcome. "Welcome to Woods and Green. If you would bring the letter with you?" She held open the door, then led the six of them down a short corridor and through an intricately carved door. Abel paused in the doorway for Zephyr to have a good look round, but the woman continued to a desk before turning and smiling again. "This room is not a trap. I am sure one of you can read the glyphs? They are either defensive or to ensure privacy. Could I see the letter, please?"

"The glyphs do not look threatening." Zephyr seemed certain.

Ferryl went to take Abel's hand then stopped, probably wanting to tell him the same thing but she wasn't his pretend girlfriend this time. Instead she returned his small nod. Abel walked in, holding out the letter. "As you said, nothing threatening."

"That wouldn't be good for business. I am Terese Green, and have no objection to being called Terese." Terese took the letter as the group introduced themselves by their own first names, reading the short message before looking up. "You have a box and coin?" When Abel took out the chest she narrowed her eyes. "Please put that on my desk, near the Salamander."

Abel placed it near a brassy-looking frilly lizard with webbed feet. The ornament's eyes blazed bright red. "Please don't touch the box."

"Highly unlikely. It is a long time since I saw that strong a reaction." Terese didn't look at all relaxed now, watching the box very warily. "I will pass you on to a senior partner, but only one person can make the claim." She looked very pointedly at Abel. "Presumably you."

"Two would be better." Ferryl moved up alongside Abel. "I should be present. I have a business matter that should be discussed at the same time." Kelis, Rob and Jenny moved up as well, but Shannon hesitated, obviously confused.

Terese considered that for a while, not convinced, but an old-fashioned phone rang. She answered, then put the phone down before answering Ferryl. "Two people, Abel and yourself. You are to keep your hands in plain sight, and must not summon any glyphs. Any attempt to do so will be met with lethal force."

"If nobody attacks Abel, there will be no need." Ferryl turned to Abel. "If that's all right with you, Abel?"

"Happy to have you along, Fay." Abel picked the box up, retrieved his letter, and put them both in his pack. "Will the rest wait here?"

"I will send for refreshments, in case you are here for a while. If you will go though there? The glyph above the door is defensive. It will only react to an active offensive hex or glyph." With that, Terese started asking the others to take a seat. Abel glanced at Ferryl but she just shrugged, so he opened the indicated door. The large room beyond looked empty when they walked in, apart from a small table in the centre and a large, gnarled bonsai tree on a rock over a pool that took up nearly a third of the space. Sunlight from a skylight sparkled on the small waterfall, which with a little birdsong created a soothing background noise. Neither calmed Abel, especially when he remembered it was raining and overcast outside, not sunny.

"There are more of those glyphs in the walls, and in the doors." Like those in Terese's office, the doors were carved with riotous writhing branches and leaves.

Ferryl took Abel's hand but let go after warning him. "There are more of those glyphs in the walls, and in the doors."

Abel chuckled, he had to, then looked around startled at a quiet, amused voice. "An unusual reaction. Please ask your passenger to remain inside its haven, young man." An unfelt breeze rustled the leaves on the tree. "You are in absolutely no danger while you hold the coin. The same might not be true for your companion." The tree trunk blurred slightly, then a small dryad stood in front of it. "I had hoped that the news of your return was just a rumour. Why do you accompany this human, Spiritus qui Furabatur?"

Abel looked at the dryad, then Ferryl, completely baffled, but Ferryl answered. "That is a very old name. I have agreed to help and protect this human for ninety years, using the name Ferryl Shayde. As part of that agreement I have abandoned my old ways. You and yours are safe if you do not threaten him. There is no dispute betwixt myself and the Wild

Wood, I swear it on all my names."

The dryad and tree both drooped a little, just for a moment. "The wind has held no word of the Wild Wood for much too long. We fear the church might be to blame." The little not-breeze fluttered the leaves on the bonsai again. "Though we thought you were gone, so there is hope."

"The church hunted both of us. For now, they've lost track of me. I hope they will not learn of this identity?" Abel heard the faint threat under Ferryl's words, not blatant, but clear enough.

"The storm may blow down a tree, or a tree provide shelter from the storm, but the wind and the forest are not enemies." That raised a list of questions for Abel, but Ferryl seemed to be reassured. "Welcome, Ferryl Shayde. Strange days, the strangest since the Accord or possibly the coming of the Normans." The dryad noticed Abel staring. "This tree grew here, on this rock, before the Romans came to these shores. When we say we are an old established firm, it means I dealt with contracts between druids and their demi-gods. You may refer to me as Woods. It is my little joke and the reason for the carvings on the doors." The dryad stopped for a moment. "I must be nervous, I'm gossiping. You have a box, a letter, a coin and a key. From that I must assume Celtchar is dead."

"Celtchar?" Abel looked at Ferryl, baffled again.

"The sorcerer. I refuse to use their pathetic play names. The real Celtchar was an ancient Celtic druid." Abel didn't need more explanation. Ferryl only used that tone when speaking of one person, the one who put her in the pit.

He took out the chest and presented the letter. "Where do you want these?"

The dryad gestured with a clump of twigs. "On the table will be near enough. Do you lay claim to Celtchar's legacy?"

Abel looked at the box and hesitated, but that was why he'd come. When he glanced at Ferryl she nodded. "Yes." He looked round but monsters didn't burst out of the walls and no pits opened under his feet. "Is that it?"

"Not quite. Pick up the coin in your bare hand, without using magic, and hold it in plain sight." Abel did. "Repeat after me. I claim it."

"I claim it."

"By blood and power, it is mine."

"By blood and power, it is mine."

"I command you, obey."

"I command you, obey."

The dryad shuddered, the tree branches shook, and the coin glowed. Abel felt a tingle, then he only held an ordinary gold sovereign. "Please take great care of that. You hold my life. I would rather not tell you, but then you might spend it on wine or lose it on a wager."

"You mean the command bit? Bloody…er, Blobberwhats, no! I don't do that!" Abel stared at the coin, horrified, then held it out. "Here, take it."

"It would kill me, and anyone else except another male of your bloodline. Watch out for sons, siblings, fathers and grandfathers." The dryad cast a small glyph towards the door and raised its voice. "Two comfortable chairs please, Terese, and refreshments. As usual, my clients have not been properly informed. I will need the Celtchar files." The dryad moved down the rock until its roots were in the water. "I may as well make myself comfortable. When I send the next glyph, please state your beverage of choice, clearly. Alcohol might be a bad idea. You will need clear wits."

With that in mind Abel asked for coffee though Ferryl wanted cola. She considered cola to be one of the greatest inventions in two hundred years. Shortly afterwards a young man brought in the chairs, then the drinks, and a few minutes later a large black box which he opened to reveal bundles of papers and some scrolls. The coffee came in a large pot, with a jug of cream and a bowl of sugar. Abel wondered just how long this might take.

The dryad started with the coin. A hundred and sixty years ago Celtchar had come to this office. Nobody had thought his appointment would cause any trouble, because Woods and Green already dealt with his legal affairs. This time Celtchar wore a suit of ancient armour. Every defensive glyph that came near him activated, and none of them even scratched the metal. He had walked straight to this room, breaking the doors without any apparent effort, and watched as the defences flared and died.

The sorcerer made Woods an offer, an alternative to being a bound servant, though it had a similar effect. The coin held a sliver of heartwood from the tree, and another from Woods, both linked magically to their origins. Celtchar had demanded that Woods and Green held his property safe from any attempt to usurp his claim, and managed it if he was busy elsewhere, without charge. Abel had just proved his right to the property, the coin, and the link to Woods's life. Only a magically aware male with a blood link to Celtchar could have survived saying those words while holding the coin.

While Abel tried to absorb that, Woods moved on. The laws of England would not allow Abel to legally inherit property until he was eighteen. Abel couldn't see how he could inherit it at all, legally, but Woods waved that away. All over the world there were a second set of laws, hidden provisions for sorcerers and magic, because they were there before any government or ruler. Sorcerers could take a new identity, disappear for centuries, or leave wills with provisions that couldn't be acted on for lifetimes, but their properties remained safe. The few attempts to overturn that had been brief, bloody, and fatal for those proposing the change.

The new identity part definitely caught Abel's attention. He knew someone wanting a change of identity, but had a nasty feeling it would be expensive. The plush furnishings didn't come from low fees. He listened to the list of property in some sort of shock. It probably didn't make him filthy rich, but there were parcels of land in several locations around the UK and Ireland. The two in Scandinavia were called forests, which had to mean enormous. Abel reassessed the filthy rich bit when Woods explained they all included accommodation, but sometimes only a hut or a cave.

That meant some were better than huts. "Could I live in any of them?"

"Yes, in all of them though none are modern. They have not been used for over a hundred years."

"Ruins then." Abel cancelled plans to get his mum to move or give Kelis a new home.

"No. Magically sealed, so they have remained exactly as Celtchar left them. Some are hidden from normal sight, some are in places that deter the curious. They will open for you once you unlock Castle House." Woods pointed twigs at the file box full of papers. "Their locations are in there."

"Back up a bit please. I already unlocked Castle House." Abel put his hand in his pocket and produced the key. He'd brought it just in case the solicitor needed proof.

"No, you gained access to the box and the sovereign. Now you have claimed the sovereign it will allow you to attempt the other doors. You can make multiple attempts and the house will simply ignore them unless you use the right method." Woods paused, watching Abel's face. "You have no idea? This is worse than expected. I always suspected that Celtchar tried to make it impossible for anyone to inherit. Too many related males died mysteriously. He had to make a will of course, that's the law, magical law." Branches rustled, sounding very like a sigh. "There are an unknown number of doors, each of which will test your prowess as a sorcerer. Each one will open part of the house. The last one will give you access to an item that unlocks everything, either marking you or attaching itself. In the interim you can visit your land, the actual acreage, and even access the trees there."

"Trees?" Abel perked up again. A few available trees elsewhere would be useful for other Taverners, or for him if he travelled.

"Yes. There are substantial woodlands on every plot. They supply the barriers or preserve the houses but you can access their magic. There are a few dryads in each location, given trees in return for acting as watchdogs. Many strong sorcerers make similar arrangements, scattered plots of protected woodland, so they are always relatively near a large source of additional magic. If I can continue?" He extended twigs towards the papers so Abel nodded.

Next came a list of parks in towns and cities. Like much of the woodland they were open to the public, but any attempt to drain magic from a tree would bring massive retaliation. When Abel asked, many sorcerers claimed parks in towns so they could collect extra magic without a trip to some remote estate. The public access stopped anyone non-magical from noticing large clumps of woodland that nobody could visit, but the traps stopped anyone magical taking advantage. Once again, the coin would allow Abel to draw magic, but nobody else.

"Don't sorcerers believe in sharing?"

"No." Even as Woods answered, Ferryl laughed.

"I told you, Pendragon told you, and Creepio told you. The sorcerer code is hands off, it's all mine. Even apprentices don't get to share, just dribs and drabs as a reward or for special jobs." She sighed heavily, looking at Woods. "Abel shares the trees in Castle House gardens with forty of his friends. None are bound or even tethered. He even refuses to bind houseflies."

Woods didn't answer, just looked pointedly at Abel's shoulder, then the small chest containing the coin. Abel looked at the chest as well and made a decision. "You dealt with the sorcerer's affairs before he created the coin. Do you deal with magical legal matters for others, such as magical beings?"

"We will represent any magical entity who will pay. Except leeches." Abel could actually hear the humour as well as the creaking branches. "Considering what I am, you should be asking if I accept human clients."

With a smile Abel pointed at the big box of papers. "Can I afford to hire you to look after this lot until I can? Probably after that as well."

Woods shifted its eyes to Ferryl. She shook her head in mock despair. "I should have known. Answer him, Woods."

"I told you, I am not allowed to charge you. If I could there is more than enough income from harvesting timber here and in Scandinavia. The estate also sells permits for wild stalking and many large tracts of farmland are rented to nearby farmers. You have access to the rental income from now on but not the accumulated balance, not until you reach eighteen. Fifty years after Celtchar went missing I also took the liberty of renting out houses in large towns and major cities." The dryad paused, glancing at Ferryl then back at Abel. Its eyes came back to the small gold-bound box.

"So how do I break this coin?" As he spoke Ferryl took hold of Abel's arm, then her hand dropped away.

"I almost said that wasn't wise, but that won't stop you. He means it,

Dryad Woods, this one really doesn't like binding living creatures. There is no trick or trap." Ferryl shook her head, then chuckled. "I wish I could tell Creepio, just to see his face. Sorry, the archbishop. I've actually talked to one and lived." She chuckled again as the tree branches rustled briefly and the dryad stared at her.

Dryad Woods recovered, looking pointedly at Abel's shoulder. "While I would like to hear about the archbishop at some time, I must doubt your first claim." His eyes locked with Abel's. "You have bound a feral spirit, a strong one."

"She is not bound, nor feral. Will your defences target Zephyr if she flies free?

"Not if it…. She? Not if she flies free, unbound, and does not attack."

"Zephyr, please fly free. You can come back if you wish." Though Abel would miss her if she didn't. "You can always come back if you need to, even without connecting the tether, but you know that."

"I do. Zephyr will fly, but not far. This is not a place for a free Ffod. Back soon."

Abel felt the tether part, then the emptiness in his tattoo as she flowed out. Zephyr flew slowly round Ferryl, then hovered halfway towards the dryad. Abel pointed at her. "No tether, no binding."

Woods still sounded wary. "In that case, if you really mean to free me, breaking the bond is simple. Hold the coin and let a drop of your blood fall on it. Repeat 'I release thee' three times, then say 'You are free.'" The dryad looked at the box again. "The coin will still give you access to everything else, but not to me or my tree." Its eyes stayed on the box as Abel opened it, then followed the coin as it came out.

"Ferryl? Get my knife out please and nick my finger." Instead Ferryl took hold of Abel's hand and touched his finger end with one fingernail. A bead of blood appeared. "Perfect." Abel smeared it on the coin, where it promptly disappeared. "I hate blood magic." He held the coin out. "I release thee. I release thee. I release thee. You are free."

Nothing happened for a few moments, then both the tree and dryad shook briefly. The dryad sagged a little, then straightened. "True intent. I could not tell you that part, that you had to mean it. I thank you." The tree branches creaked a little. "As your solicitor I should tell you that was a mistake. You should have negotiated the contract first."

"Then you would have tried to break it. There is another contract to negotiate as well. Ferryl Shayde needs to be a schoolgirl arriving from Germany, living locally, and wishing to enroll in Stourton comprehensive." Abel put out his hand to squeeze Ferryl's as she made a small, protesting noise. "If there's enough money in the bank."

"There is, though it will have a definite impact on your income this year. You will still have enough money, since if you are staying at school you shouldn't spend too much without an obvious income. That is unusual for a sorcerer, and so is what you intend. My clients are usually several hundred years older than you, or who Spiritus… Ferryl Shayde wishes to be." The following discussion took another cup of coffee, cheese and onion sandwiches for Abel and beef ones for Ferryl, and a visit to a sumptuous rest room. Despite all Abel's misgivings, his and Ferryl's youth seemed to be what would cause most trouble. By then Zephyr had flowed back into the tattoo and offered her magical hand to reconnect her tether.

By the time Dryad Woods had worked through all the possibilities, Abel felt overwhelmed. He took away a short summary of the options for Ferryl, a list of the locations of the woodlands, a proposal for supplying a legitimate income, and a thousand pounds in twenties.

*   *   *

None of those waiting made any comment on how long it had taken until they came outside, when they all stopped dead. Shannon and Rob looked at their watches. "Never! Three hours?" Rob looked around and then up, where the sun behind the clouds looked much too low.

"My watch says it's past four. It can't have been later than one when we went in." Shannon turned to Abel. "Three hours to drink a cup of coffee and eat a couple of biscuits? And what's with the magic box? How can that be a contract?"

"Magical waiting room, it had to be. Either they slowed time or put us out for a while." Kelis rounded on Abel. "How long did it seem to you?"

"At least three hours." Shannon still looked suspicious so Abel tried to explain the amount of time. "Magical contracts have to be held in a magically guarded box like the one I brought in, a sort of safe. Nobody else can touch it so they can't get at the papers. That took a long while because the solicitor and Ferryl Shayde had to adapt the protection so it didn't hurt them or me, and put glyphs on the papers so they couldn't be altered." He touched his arm when he said Ferryl Shayde, to remind everyone but Shannon that the other Taverners still thought the sorceress lived in his tattoo.

Kelis narrowed her eyes at him before turning to Ferryl. "Were you bored, Fay?"

"No, it was fascinating because I am new to all this as well. Though I was also able to employ the solicitor in a non-magical way, to help me settle in England." Abel heard just a trace of vas instead of was, and realised Ferryl had spoken like that when meeting Shannon the first time. She now had a very faint accent, presumably German. "I have only played Bonny's Tavern and practiced glyphs at home. This is the first time I've seen any other sort of magic at work." She looked up the street, at the charity shops that had taken over any empty premises. "Is there still time for me to visit a few shops? I'd like more clothes so I can stay longer."

After Shannon called home to reassure her mum she hadn't pranged the car, and the rest told their parents they'd met friends and been delayed, the group of teenagers went shopping. Ferryl had some money left from selling the gold statuette so they visited several clothing shops, especially the charity outlets. She wasn't interested in current fashions, and seemed perfectly happy buying second-hand clothes. Ferryl looked particularly pleased when she found a pair of mid-calf leather boots that fitted her properly, and wore them immediately.

During the shopping Ferryl 'let slip' her surname, and that she had come to Stourton on holiday. Kelis had sent her a beta version of Bonny's Tavern, and she wanted to visit the place where it had been created. Now, if things worked out, she might be staying in England, in Stourton. The solicitor would be looking into it. Kelis promptly phoned her mum, then invited Fay home to stay the night. After Abel treated them all to a huge, fancy frothy coffee he confessed to stealing Fay's name for the game character. Zephyr confessed she used Ferryl Shayde because she didn't want enemies to recognise her old one. A very thoughtful Shannon, somewhat reassured when Zephyr swore she'd never been called Braeth

Huntian, drove them back to Brinsford. Jenny looked annoyed that she had to be dropped off at home, because she wanted to know what had really happened.

*   *   *

Kelis waited until Shannon drove out of sight, but only just. "Right Abel, give." She looked up at the rain and then at the dark, cold church. "No, not yet. After tea. Better still, you can come home with me now, Fay or Ferryl, and explain. Remember, we met you in town, where you were staying in the hostel. I told mum I didn't think that was good enough for a Taverner from abroad, which is why she agreed to you stopping over." Kelis poked Rob and Abel in the ribs, laughing at their expressions. "I'm blaming you two for that. Mum will think it's Abel's fault because she knows what he's like when he meets a new girl. He just can't wait to drag them back to Brinsford."

"Don't you dare!" Abel considered jabbing Kelis back but settled for wagging a finger. "Not a girlfriend, not this time."

"I never mentioned girlfriend. That takes you a couple of days at least." Kelis turned towards home. "Come on Ferryl. Sorry, I mean Fay. We'll leave these two to stand in the rain and argue with each other. They'll have got it over with by the time Bonny's Tavern meets. I'll bet Jenny rides over for this one, rain or not." Ferryl grinned, shrugged, and followed Kelis as instructed.

"Not a girlfriend, not this time. Else I'll never get a real one." Abel glared at Rob's grin but didn't dent it one tiny bit.

"You don't want one. Well you do, but can't have her."

"I don't want anyone just now. Kelis has moved on."

Rob laughed out loud. "I could have meant Jenny, Claris, Fay or half a dozen different Taverners but you immediately thought of Kelis, which just makes my point. Never mind, you'll have a bigger choice under the mistletoe this New Year." Despite being true, that didn't cheer Abel up very much.

*   *   *

The long Bonny's Tavern meeting that evening included Jenny as expected. She had an advanced lesson in water glyphs as soon as she walked in, as the rest cast tiny glyphs to dry her clothes. Once she'd been promised proper lessons the five of them, six with Zephyr, went through the high points of Abel's interview.

Looking through the options for Ferryl, they ranged from her appearing with a full identity as a twenty-one-year-old with an inheritance to a long-lost penniless orphaned relative of Abel's. One stood out, but with a few differences because Abel's mum might be too curious about a long-lost relative. Not only that, but Abel occasionally holding a relative's hand to get answers would look really odd. Hopefully Woods and Green could act as trustees for an orphan, Fay Elle Shayde, with no link to Abel's family. Abel would pay for creating details of her identity, dead parents and a small inheritance through the magical law system. The inheritance would pay for her rent and living expenses, when Mz. Shayde found lodgings. Although the idea hadn't been mentioned to Woods, Ferryl hoped that would be with Kelis's mum.

Some options already included Woods and Green contacting Stourton Comprehensive, asking if a foreign student could pick up the school year in January. Her preferred subjects would coincide with Abel's, and her school records from Germany would show a suitable level of academic achievement. Dryad Woods really liked that idea, simply because it would be something different from a sorceress becoming a different adult to hide her age. Altering or creating all those records would be difficult, so it would be interesting.

Abel described the inheritance, a rough outline of what he could claim because of his blood link to Celtchar. As he finished the list Kelis sat back, shaking her head in confusion. "You keep saying when you are older or when you open doors, so are you filthy rich or not?"

"Yes and no. We can visit lots of trees and slurp up enough magic to reduce Jenny to a heap of happy giggles, but can't get into the properties." Jenny produced a small giggle but stopped, more interested in the next part. "We can get a small but steady income for the company marketing the game if we make a slight alteration to the game setup and the illustrations. The changes will make Jenny curse unless we fill her with tree magic first." That brought a waved fist, not a giggle, because Jenny had thought she'd done with changing the background scenario. When Abel showed them the extra, and how much they'd be paid, she agreed the artwork and rulebook would need reprinting but it would be worth it. Abel held up the gold sovereign. "Meanwhile this lets me try to open a series of locked doors. It'll be well over a year before I'm eighteen and can officially inherit, and even then explaining could be a bit awkward. Though it could take that long just to get the final big key because Castle House sounds like a puzzle box."

"We should ask Creepio to come and look." Rob wasn't put off by the reaction from the rest. "Seriously. We can ask him one question. Is something evil lurking behind that door? Ferryl insists there's something very nasty in there, but Creepio should be able to tell us how deep the whatever is inside." He pointed at the coin. "We know Abel will be safe trying the doors, but is he safe from what's behind them?"

"Theoretically, because of the coin, but he may not be strong enough to control it. In either case it could lash out at anyone else nearby." Ferryl stood up and paced back and forth, just as she used to in Abel's tattoo. "I am sure the entity I helped to trap and hopefully control is not behind that door. Even so, and even though I really don't like the church, Rob has a point. Though I'd like to sleep on it? In a proper bed? In the warm?" Her face broke into a smile. "Just because I can deal with sleeping on a camp bed in the cold doesn't mean I like it."

Jenny looked curious at that. "What have you told Kelis's mum? How long are you staying here?"

Kelis smirked as everyone looked at her. "I've asked if Fay can stay a few days while her accommodation in Stourton is sorted out, and Fay offered to pay. I've hinted Fay has a problem, something sad in her past, and mum is a sucker for a sob story. Ferryl might have to sleep in the church a few more times but by New Year I reckon she'll be a lodger." Her face fell as she remembered. "For as long as we've got the house."

The four of them set into making a list of the most important questions Abel hadn't asked. He couldn't ask them over a phone, so they'd have to wait. One thing could be settled over the phone. Abel called the following morning and when he gave his name the receptionist put him straight through to Terese Green. When he told her Fay Elle Shayde would like her affairs in Germany put in order so she could attend Stourton Comprehensive, option four, Mz Green chuckled and promised it would be a priority. Abel's extra stipulation, that she wouldn't be related to anyone local, apparently simplified the job.

*   *   *

Abel had a number of other mundane things to do before visiting Dryad Woods or Terese Green again. First among them involved his clothing. All the exercise, building up his strength to cast glyphs, had filled him out a little even if he stayed wiry rather than muscly. Abel knew his mum couldn't afford to buy new clothes so he nipped out of school at lunchtimes and went shopping. A second-hand school blazer looked the same, it was just a size larger, and providing he bought the same brands from charity shops, things like jeans weren't obvious.

While he did that Abel worked on his big problem. He could get a few quid out of Dryad Woods, so he wanted to give some money to his mum. Not a lot of money because even if Woods insisted his blood link to Celtchar made Abel the magical heir to the sorcerer, he couldn't suddenly announce it. Even without reaching the centre of Castle House, or turning eighteen, he had access to thousands of acres of land and the income from it. Abel himself still had difficulty accepting that all he needed was that trace of Celtchar's bloodline-his mum certainly wouldn't believe it.

Just proving the blood relationship would be impossible without magic, and Abel daren't bring magic into the equation. Abel's mum, one of the few adults who saw magical creatures, walked a fine line. She'd had years of therapy in her youth, to banish the hallucinations, but now knew they were real. That, and the Tavern ward for meditation that also frightened creatures away, were a big hint that things weren't as she'd always been told.

Stan the poacher, the second of the three adults Abel knew of who could see some magical creatures, had a similar problem. He admitted to not asking questions or thinking about it too hard. He said he could feel the loony bin sneaking up on him if he did. Frederick, the other adult, had actually had a major breakdown and only recovered when a dryad befriended him. Ferryl Shayde assured Abel that breakdowns were common if an adult, someone over twenty-five, discovered how to activate their magic. Now Abel, sure his mum did the same as Stan, didn't push too hard. She slept better, her hip didn't hurt as much and most creatures avoided her, so her life had improved. She even put out saucers of warm milk and sugar for the brownies and pixies that helped to keep the house clean.

Abel declaring himself a trainee sorcerer would destroy whatever scenario his mum had come up with to keep her sanity. He went round and round it, alone or with his friends, but couldn't come up with an answer. Abel wasn't old enough to have a convenient win on the lottery, or to bet on horses or cards. For the first time in his life Abel could buy his mum a really nice Christmas present, except he couldn't.

*   *   *

To take his mind off it, and stop him sending his friends crackers, they all decided to have a proper look at the next door in Castle House. Not to open it, but Woods had said there were puzzles to solve. They should try and find out if that included the first door, or they'd look pretty stupid when Creepio turned up.

Abel opened the front door with the key and walked into the entrance hall without any problem. The room didn't react, except as usual the frog-dragon opened its electric blue eyes. Abel inspected the double doors that should let him into the house proper. Apart from a curved, carved handle on each one there wasn't any sort of keyhole or snek. He'd promised not to actually touch the doors, so Abel could only think of one way to see if anything had altered. He took a deep breath and pulled the coin from his pocket.

Abel nearly jumped out of his skin, not just because of the shout of alarm behind him but because the frog-dragon moved! It turned its head a little, enough for a long thin tongue to press on the wall. A panel about half a metre square turned transparent and a small rectangular opening appeared at the bottom. Abel held up a hand to stop the others shouting questions and inspected the view behind the transparent panel. It looked like a maze with five levels. A cube behind the panel had been divided up into different sections by more transparent panels, some with holes in them. At the top far corner, as far as possible from the opening, was a horizontal slot. Abel wasn't jumping to conclusions but it looked about the right size for the sovereign.

Moving very slowly Abel used his phone to take half a dozen pictures at different angles, zooming to get a good shot of the little slot, then shut it down and put it away. He took a step back and the panel became a featureless patch of wall. "I can still see the outline, though it isn't easy because magic swirls all around and across it." Zephyr made a very tentative move to leave his tattoo as Abel turned and headed for the exit. "I think I could come out now. The air does not seem to burn."

"Wait until we reach the door, Zephyr, so we can take a dive outside if necessary." One step from the outside door Abel stopped and raised his voice. "Someone tell me if anything behind me moves. Zephyr thinks she can come out now." Despite Jenny's objections, the rest agreed he could manage one step before anything could trap him inside.

Zephyr trickled out of her tattoo, into the open. "The magic tickles. It is inspecting me but is not hurting." She moved out a little further, then more. "Too much. The air is starting to warm so that must be a warning. I will come back now." The sprite eased back into the tattoo and Abel walked outside. As he passed the threshold the front door closed, gently but firmly, but this time he had to physically lock it. Zephyr connected to everyone to explain, while they collected round Abel to look at his phone.

"It's a multi-storey maze made of glass. Passages and little rooms, some dead ends, and those look like holes in some walls and in the top of some passages and rooms." Jenny cocked her head one way then the other. "Dad used to play these with me on the computer, when I was a lot younger. The idea was to move a little ball through a 3D maze that became more and more difficult. There'll be a lot of dead ends but one path that winds its way right through from the bottom to the top. Then pop the coin in the slot and the door unlocks."

"A path for what? Whatever it is has to carry that sovereign. How big are those passages?" Rob took a closer look. "The panel looked to be about half a metre square, and there's five horizontal sections."

"Floors. Five floors in the crazy maze hotel. Are you supposed to train a mouse to carry the coin?" Kelis took a turn looking at the phone. "No, because the defences would fry it before it got near. Maybe the house would allow you to use a pictsie or brownie if you bound it?" She held her hands up at Abel's expression. "Okay, okay, no binding. Sheesh, I didn't mean killing it! Though even if you bound something like that, and the house allowed it to try, it might not get up from one floor to the next. There doesn't seem to be much grip and those holes would be a bit tight."

"Look below the slot at the back, students. You have not inspected the whole inside for clues." Ferryl moved the pictures back to the zoomed shot of the little slot at the rear and tapped the screen. "Do the simple part first."

"Yes sensei." Abel's phone went round everyone again and all of them agreed. The glyph for wind had been etched very, very faintly just below the slot at the back. If Abel hadn't zoomed in to get that picture, even Ferryl might have missed it. The first conclusion floored Abel. "I haven't got enough control of wind to blow a gold sovereign around the corridors and up through the holes. If I drop it I'll never get enough purchase with wind to lift it off a smooth surface."

"But I could." Ferryl sounded thoughtful rather than smug. "This is designed for someone with superb mastery of the glyph, a very experienced sorceress. Dryad Woods may be right. Celtchar might be trying to make sure nobody ever inherits. He killed any relatives he knew of, so whoever finally tried would be young and inexperienced. It could take you years to reach the required level, years during which you would be relatively unprotected and might be killed."

"Will the hallway allow one of us in it now that Abel's got the coin? It let Zephyr out to fly." Jenny glanced at the door and back to the phone. "Ferryl could try, then if she fails Kelis could go because she's the best of us with wind.For now." After getting to a certain stage with fire, Jenny had decided that wind seemed to be easier after all. With Kelis concentrating on water, Jenny now wanted to be the mistress of wind though she'd already started on water as well.

Abel took the coin out of his pocket. "One step inside the entrance, then I'm stopping while you follow. I'll be watching the plant and dragon, and if the front door tries to close it should just help to shove both of us clear." Five minutes later a despondent group stood outside watching the door lock itself, again. "Plan B or 6 or whatever. It won't let anyone else in so I've got to practice wind glyphs until my arms drop off."

"I am wind with a name, a thinking wind glyph, and I am allowed inside. Will the coin let me touch?" Zephyr flew out of Abel's tattoo. "The room let me move as far as your arm would reach. That is far enough to reach the back of the box." Abel took out the sovereign and Zephyr slowly flew nearer. "The magic is reaching for me, but is not gathering as it did before. Though I did not try to touch before."

"Wait, let me try again so we know if that's a change in the coin or how it treats you, Zephyr." Ferryl slowly put her hand out but stopped well short of the coin. "No, the magic is already gathering and it doesn't look at all friendly. From the amount, the coin must be supplied with magic through a link, probably from inside the house."

Zephyr flew close to the coin again, waiting until the magic reached out to touch her. "It tickles, the same as the room did." None of the humans could see any change.

"Move closer, Zephyr. I am watching the flows as well and it still looks friendly. There isn't as much magic gathering." Ferryl watched intently until Zephyr touched the metal. "The only reason I can think of is the tether. The house treats Zephyr and Abel as one. I suggest Zephyr tries to pick up the coin." Ferryl tried to keep the excitement from her voice but all of them were thoroughly wound up now.

The shimmering ball of wind slowly lifted the gold coin clear of Abel's palm. "Oh yeah. Up yours, Catch-a-car!" Kelis punched the air. "Team Tavern wins."

"Not yet." Though even as he tried to calm everyone down Rob wore a big grin. "We still need Creepio."

"Why? Zephyr can solve the puzzle, then Abel peeks through the door. If the big bad is there he slams it smartish." Kelis smirked at Abel. "After all, he's got the get out of jail coin."

"Unless the outside door closes when the inside one opens and he hasn't got time to close it again. Oops, as you wouldn't have time to say." Ferryl tried to scowl but the smile kept winning. "Though if Creepio's creature can't sense anything nasty waiting for Abel we can get into the house itself before Christmas." She stopped smiling, looking very thoughtful. "Abel had to find a missing magical key for the first door, then take a trip to Woods and Green and pass the claiming test, then solve a puzzle to open the next door. We've no idea how many more doors there are, and the rest are likely to be harder. I doubt we'll get this lucky again."

"I'd settle for finding a way to bring everyone inside the house so we have somewhere warmer and drier to meet. We can clean the place up a bit, or if the furniture has rotted we can bring in some chairs and a table." Abel held out his hand and Zephyr dropped the coin for him to pocket it again. "If the next door is harder to open, I want us all to be able to inspect it." He pulled out his phone. "We'd better get Fay's story straight before she meets Creepio." A phone call to Woods and Green confirmed that any inquiries would be met with legal confidentiality. Anyone magical asking about her would learn that her father had been a warlock and Fay had some ability, so her inheritance came under the magical laws.

The phone call to Creepio resulted in dire warnings about proceeding without him. A patient Abel pointed out he'd phoned so he wasn't being secretive, and would appreciate something less than Armageddon. That calmed Creepio down but he wanted three days, to arrange for a creature that would recognise danger but remain under control unless attacked.

Knock, Knock

With three days to spare before Creepio came to check out the door in Castle House, the friends had time for another trip to town. Rob bought Melanie's Christmas present, a big floppy witch's hat for her Cackle the Crone outfit, but asked Kelis to hide it. He didn't have anything like enough cash to buy what his big sister wanted, high top leather boots like Robin D'Ritche. The whole gang had extra money because Abel split the thousand pounds with Kelis and Rob and, after some thought, Jenny and Fay. Jenny had never hesitated to back them in anything magical, and actually did more work towards selling the game than all the others put together.

Despite the jokes about getting preferential treatment because she'd once been Abel's girlfriend, the diamond and extra magic and tuition weren't because of that. Jenny had somehow become one of their gang, or whatever a collection of trainee magicians should be called—a "turmoil" according to Rob. To cement Jenny's new status, Ferryl drew an invisible glyph on her skin. Abel ceremonially took her pebble glyph away, and Jenny had free access to Castle House gardens. As with Dead Wood, she found it made the place welcoming rather than just not threatening.

Claris hadn't become part of their gang—quite the opposite. She spoke to Abel, Kelis, Jenny, Fay and Rob when they called in on Frederick, and occasionally at school, but otherwise kept to herself. According to Frederick, she seemed to be coming to terms with what had happened, helped by the soothing effect of stroking her ward. Despite being magically aware, Claris refused to practice glyphs. She seemed content to help the younger Taverners such as Justin and Warren with decorating Frederick's house or concentrate on schoolwork. Effy, nearly twenty-eight, spent a lot of time reassuring Claris and had forged a real friendship.

Ferryl, as Fay, began to build her new life. Kelis's mum welcomed the extra cash from her new lodger while the solicitors organised the orphan's affairs. Her final home might be a flat or lodgings, depending on the eventual state of her finances. While in town, Fay allegedly reclaimed her clothes from the hostel, using more of the remaining money from the gold statue to kit herself out properly. The five of them split the rest, just over six hundred pounds, between them. While in town Abel nipped in to see Woods and Green, leaving a message at the desk asking if he owned any property in Stourton. The following day a letter told him he didn't.

Abel now had over three hundred pounds, and still couldn't spoil his mum. Rob and Kelis had the same problem, as did Jenny though she had a little more pocket money to explain a better present. She still didn't have enough to suddenly splash out, or her dad would ask questions. Ferryl offered to make cheap jewellery into the real thing so it looked better, but someone would get it valued for insurance. Then the allegedly cheap gift would attract questions.

Meanwhile, in the three days before Creepio came, Rob constructed a computer version of the 3D transparent maze. He even created a cyber-coin that could be moved through the passages, rooms, and openings to work out the best path to the slot. Abel went back twice for more pictures at different angles to help place the openings exactly right. By the time Zephyr had to go into the puzzle box, Abel had a print with a red line showing the best route from the entrance to the destination.

While they stood outside Castle House, waiting for Creepio, Abel, Kelis, Jenny and Ferryl debated the benefits of Ferryl casting a seeming of Claris. Abel thought that would stop the vicar prying about the new person inside Castle House gardens, Fay. Better still, Creepio wouldn't be tempted to find Claris to question her. Ferryl finally persuaded them not to take the chance. Creepio would be bringing some means of detecting a dangerous entity lurking just inside Castle House. If it detected her seeming, the vicar wouldn't appreciate them trying to fool him.

When Rob finally arrived, he wanted to talk about his troubles at home. His little sister Melanie had run downstairs last night claiming that a troll had looked over the back fence. Rob and his dad had gone out to see what had upset her and found nothing. Despite the fact that the troll was not found Melanie insisted that she recognised it from the picture and description of trolls in the Bonny's Tavern gameplay. If a troll really had been there, she might have seen it even if Melanie wasn't magically aware, because the soil and rock bonded into their skins made them visible to everyone.

Melanie's dad declared she'd been playing Bonny's Tavern too much and started imagining the game's monsters, so he'd banned it for three days. Rob might not have worried too much and come to the same conclusion, except there'd already been one troll incursion into the Dead Wood. He'd also remembered Abel talking about trolls in the fight at the leech lair. Ferryl racked her brains but she couldn't remember if leeches could compel or inhabit trolls. She felt almost sure a troll couldn't be a leech host because they were mostly magic inside their tough hide, without any blood at all.

There must be an adult troll somewhere close to Brinsford, because although adolescents like those in the leech lair might roam, a juvenile like the one in Dead Wood wouldn't stray far. Even so, a troll should have no interest in Brinsford, where its identity would be too obvious and quickly killed by the church. Unless someone controlled or employed it because, being almost immune to magic, trolls could pass the hexed posts that protected the village. The others promised that tomorrow they'd join Rob in a search of the grounds around Brinsford to see if they could find any sign of a real visit.

By the time Rob had calmed down, the five of them had to walk up to Castle House to meet the vicar.

* * *

Creepio kept his visit low-key, as he'd promised. Only one car arrived, pulling up just before reaching Castle House gardens. A very serious archbishop came to see them on his own, leaving his driver sat on the car bonnet. "The driver carries something powerful." Ferryl squeezed Abel's hand as she passed the message. Zephyr, out in the open and connected to the rest, passed everything on.

Creepio eyed the five of them, standing in a line holding hands, and his eyes narrowed at the way the light rain neatly parted around them. He almost commented, then switched his attention to the door of Castle House. "There doesn't seem to be any more damage."

"No need. Not only can I walk in any time I wish, but I'm pretty sure I can open the next door. As agreed, I've told you first." Abel hesitated, but they'd come too far to back out now so he pushed on. "When I open the front door you will see the entrance hall. Please don't throw glyphs, because the doorway won't like it and they won't get through. What I'd like to know is if anything truly nasty lurks behind the second set of doors." He glanced left and right at his friends. "We can't detect anything we can't deal with."

Creepio inspected the front door, then the five of them. "I can answer you now, without using our creature. Yes, something powerful and evil lurks in Castle House. You know that, so what you really need to know is how far inside." The vicar hesitated, then sighed and continued. "If I tell you not to open any more doors, please don't. I've made tentative enquiries and even the Sorcerer's Council don't know exactly what Celtchar captured. They know it's strong enough to stop any of them finding out more, which should be enough to make you very careful." One hand gestured back towards his car and his tone lightened a little. "My driver has a tattoo that contains a bound shade, which he will partially summon. The creature should be able to sense the strength of whatever lies just behind the next door. With luck it can also sense where the really dangerous entity is waiting. I doubt the house will respond if our creature stays on the road."

"If something comes out please don't try to enter the gardens, or even throw glyphs at it, unless the creature or guardian breaks out. The garden and house would react badly. We have our own precautions." Abel wasn't happy about it, but Rob carried the bone glyph captured from a sorceress. If activated, it would kill and bind whatever it had been aimed at by latching onto and invading their own magic.

"You are that confident?" The vicar glanced at Ferryl, then Jenny. "We must talk about that later. But first, do you want us to leave while you open the door or do so before my driver releases the creature?"

"Opening the front door isn't a secret. I have a key." Abel let go of Jenny's hand to take it out of his pocket and hold it up. "There you are, a big old-fashioned key with lots of gold and jewels on it. Don't try to steal it because it will fight back. I'll hold it at the edge of the boundary and let you inspect it with your cross, from there and very carefully, just so you don't try."

The vicar did, looking very thoughtful once the pale tendrils of church magic retreated to his cross. "There is too much magic in there, and it rejects any attempt to investigate it. Is the key linked to the house?" Abel nodded, because that had been their best guess. Creepio turned to beckon the man by the car. When the driver reached them, the vicar passed on the warnings, all of them. He turned back to Abel. "Please don't be alarmed. It is under complete control." Creepio turned back to the driver. "Make sure you keep tight control. Do not let it attack even if it sees an enemy, not unless the target crosses the boundary."

"I can do that if it isn't fully materialised. It doesn't need to be very solid just to sense danger." The man put his hand inside his coat and the air near him shimmered and then smoked. The cloud grew rapidly, upwards and outwards, and thickened until something about six metres tall and three wide appeared within it. Glowing green eyes opened but only suggestions of huge limbs, possibly a tail and definitely forked horns could be seen. Abel assumed the creature was under control, because the driver's voice sounded calm and relaxed. "Ready when you are."

Ferryl let go of his hand, Zephyr flew into her tattoo, and Abel went up the path and opened the front door. He walked in and up to the double doors at the back, then froze. Instead of just opening its eyes, the frog-dragon came awake! It half-slithered, half walked on its eight little legs past him and up to the opened door, then coiled up blocking it. When Abel turned he didn't have to see its eyes to know why, its whole attention had fastened on the smoky creature.

The creature reacted immediately, lunging towards the boundary and Castle House. Beside it the driver took two steps backwards, putting his other hand inside his coat. As it flapped open, Abel caught a glimpse of several big crosses hung on his chest. Creepio raised his hand, calling out to his struggling companion. "Hold it, John, hold it!" The vicar had his own cross out, hesitating between the frog-dragon and the huge thing trying to become solid in the road near him.

The frog-dragon began to uncoil, moving out of the door so Abel shouted, "No!" To his great relief it stopped. "Guard, not attack." The stone guardian settled back into coils but watched intently, with Zephyr hovering above it. She exuded the same sort of intent wariness. Outside Abel's friends split up, all building glyphs as they raised their hands towards the monster in the road. Its outline solidified, with massive limbs, clawed paws and a body covered in square, metallic-looking scales or armour taking shape in the smoke. A short, thick tail lashed.

Creepio didn't wait any longer, his glyph hit it and coated the front of the creature with ice that shimmered and changed from blue to green and back again. Behind the translucent barrier the creature recoiled, its fanged maw opening in a bellow. "Call it off. Get it back inside, John. Now!" The driver, John, switched his hand to another cross, so they were probably magic stores. He staggered and doubled over but Abel could already see the creature becoming less solid, smokier. Once that started, the monster quickly became shapeless and shrank until the last trickle disappeared inside the driver's coat. He straightened but staggered again, almost falling until Creepio took hold of his arm.

The driver, John, pointed at the doorway and the stone frog-dragon. "It recognises that creature even if I don't. They must be old enemies." He turned away, doubled over and once again struggled as a little smoke appeared. It cleared quickly.

"The feeling was mutual, and that thing didn't seem afraid of an ogre or either of us. Perhaps these young people were right and we have underestimated what lives here." Creepio raised his voice. "Can you call it off, Abel? Our servant will not be appearing again."

Abel wasn't sure just how much control he had. "Come back, frog-dragon. It's all over. No danger." The stone flowed as if made of real flesh and scales and the guardian's head turned. For long moments it hesitated, so maybe it disagreed about the danger. "Please. I invited those two men to watch, and they have removed the threat." Zephyr's spooky-phone connected and she assured the creature she'd keep watch. The frog-dragon seemed to accept that, uncoiling to move back to its usual position beside the inner doors. This time its head stayed turned to watch the doorway. "Thank you. I will be going outside to speak to those men. They will not enter the garden." The frog-dragon turned its head to look at Abel, then back at the outer door. It didn't need words. Abel clearly understood they had better not, for their sakes. As he walked back outside and the door closed behind him, Abel heaved a big sigh of relief.

Zephyr flew back into her tattoo. "I promised to keep watch. Can I warn our guard if the enemy comes into the garden?"

"Oh yes, because if that thing comes past the boundary we'll need everything we can get."

*   *   *

Abel joined his friends and nodded towards where Creepio and John, the driver, had their heads together discussing something. "What did Creepio say?"

"Something about underestimating what lived in Castle House. It's about time he got that message." Ferryl's smug tone disappeared as she looked towards Castle House. "Though I've never seen anything like that. Stone guardians are controlled by a set of instructions on a glyph inside, so they either defend or attack. They do not react as living creatures, assessing the situation and listening to other instructions."

"Living? Could it be a bound shade, but in stone?" Kelis concentrated, her forehead crinkling. "I can't remember my lessons. Can stone hold a bound shade or does it need something pliable, wood or plastic?"

"A bound shade can move stone, but the result is slow and clumsy. Stone guardians are more agile, but that creature is true living stone." Ferryl also seemed deep in thought. "There were legends of creatures that could do that, animate stone, or rather turn the living into stone but retain movement and some sort of intelligence."

"The gorgon?" Jenny's eyes sparkled. "Fraggon is the gorgon's pet? Rock on!" She giggled then stopped. "Rock on? Get it?" Her smile faltered and she looked a little bit embarrassed. "Sorry, I'm still getting over the heart attack. Imminent death has an odd effect on me."

Rob let go of his bat and flexed his hand, slowly. "And me. Would earth glyphs or my bat have any effect, Ferryl? With it being stone."

"No, because it isn't truly stone. I'm sure the glyph we used to destroy the first stone guardian would just bounce off that." She frowned towards Creepio and the hunched figure with him. "I wasn't sure what Creepio brought with him, because he was very careful not to name it. If he hadn't been so secretive I'd have been better prepared. Until he said ogre, I thought the driver might have bound a giant. The half-materialised figure wasn't clear, and giants use armour that is similar to ogre scales." Ferryl turned back towards Castle House, obviously worried. "I'm racking my brain but I don't recognise our creature at all."

"The fraggon?" Abel turned to Jenny. "Why fraggon?"

"Frog-dragon isn't a proper name and I didn't like drogg, dragon-frog. Can we keep the name? I'd try the innocent smile but you know me better." Jenny took a deep breath, though she still looked pale and shaken. "I'll stop babbling now, providing all the monsters will just stay where they are."

"We'd better ask him about that." Kelis nodded towards where Creepio had started across the road towards them.

*   *   *

For once Creepio really looked apologetic. "My apologies. We are still not entirely sure what happened. A stone guardian shouldn't trigger that response, unless there was a bound shade in there. An old enemy of the ogre might react like that, but that isn't any creature I've ever heard of." The vicar looked at the door to Castle House with a little frown on his face. "That thing in there isn't really stone, not the sort a guardian is made of, but neither is it a living magical creature. We are trying to find out what it is, but the ogre has difficulty communicating at the best of times."

"Stone, but not as you know it. Could Fraggon be one of the gorgon's pets?" Kelis watched Creepio's face very carefully as she asked, and caught the calculation after the shock.

"Fraggon?"

"We just named it. You didn't answer the question." Five very interested faces were watching the vicar now.

"The creature that gave rise to legends of the gorgon was probably a wandering skoffin, an Icelandic dragon. There are other legends such as the basilisk, but they all come back to the skoffin. Skoffin had wings and spines and are now extinct, as are all dragons. That type could turn prey to solid stone, despite some claiming it could only burn them to solid charcoal. There are a few entries in our church records that suggest a skoffin could keep a victim alive as living stone, but none are substantiated. None of the records I've seen even hint at anything as mobile as your pet." Creepio turned back to the other churchman. "John, can you ask your ogre if that was something created by a skoffin?"

John concentrated for a while before replying. "It's still not happy so I can't communicate very well, but I'm sure you are on the right track. The ogre's anger could be about the skoffin part, or what that was before becoming what it is." He straightened with a big sigh. "All closed down now. I couldn't get much of a read on the rest of the house once the stone creature started moving."

"The fraggon." The churchman stared at Creepio, who chuckled. "They've named it. You'll get used to this sort of thing if you meet these youngsters very often."

"Maybe not a good idea, not carrying an ogre." The man paused, collecting himself. "When the, er, fraggon moved, the ogre stopped sensing beyond the locked doors and concentrated exclusively on its perceived enemy. Either that, um, fraggon or the original creature were very dangerous."

"So, is it safe for me to open those double doors?" Abel shrugged when Creepio turned to frown at him. "That's why you came." The vicar turned back to John and nodded for him to answer.

"Before it all went to pot, the ogre detected something very, very dangerous, something that frightened it, very deep inside. Possibly deep as in underground but it didn't have time to fix a location. There is nothing as dangerous as the fraggon on the other side of the closed doors." John shook his head after he said 'fraggon.' "Will it obey you?"

"While you were busy he called it off." Creepio gestured towards Abel.

"I asked it to come away, and explained you wouldn't come into the garden." Abel smiled quietly. "It didn't answer, but I got the impression it wasn't worried about that."

"No, it wanted to come out here and fight an ogre, an archbishop, and what you would call a bishop-level sorcerer. I am relieved it didn't." Creepio leant back a little and looked up at the building. "If we ever have to force our way into Castle House, I can't be sure we will be able to avoid some damage in Brinsford. We will have to be prepared for more fraggons at least, and then the creature in the centre." The vicar's harsh features softened a little. "I will try to bring allies like the ogre. They are living missiles, aimed at the greatest threat they can detect so they won't deliberately target the village."

"Thanks. I'll try to persuade Fraggon it doesn't have to guard the road, just the house." Abel debated with himself, briefly. "I won't open the double doors until you leave, in case anything behind them has a similar reaction."

"We will drive to the main road and wait, in case you have trouble. I would like to talk to you all including you, young lady, at your convenience." He looked towards Ferryl and managed one of his little smiles. "I am known as Vicar, regardless of what these reprobates call me."

"I am Fay, and I'm hoping to move into the area." Ferryl managed a really good version of Jenny's innocent smile.

It didn't seem to fool the vicar. "I hope you can explain more when we meet, Fay. Judging by the glyphs you summoned, Abel has attracted someone already proficient in magic." He turned back to Abel. "I will wait an hour. If there are no explosions, no smoke and no rampaging monsters, we'll go home."

"Thanks for coming." Abel raised a hand in farewell.

"I'm pleased we did. If something wants to eat me, I like to know what it is." The vicar put an arm round his compatriot. "Come on John, let's get you home so you can rest. Tomorrow we can spend long hours going through dusty archives to find a drawing of a fraggon." The pair moved slowly to his car and left, with the vicar driving.

*   *   *

"Are you really going back in there right now?" Kelis's voice told Abel her opinion without her crossed arms.

"If it goes wrong we've got an ogre to help?" Rob shrugged when Kelis glared at him. "Just saying. If we do it later, Creepio won't be there if we need him."

"Hah. Abel will just set Fraggon on anything nasty. After all, it came to heel when he called." Jenny cracked her fingers. "Fraggon? Heel, boy. Girl?"

"Boy. When Abel called it back it had that sulky look all boys have when they're stopped from doing something stupid." Kelis had recovered her humour now she'd got a target. "What do you think, Ferryl?"

"Although it might come as a shock, I agree with Rob. He has to be right once a year." She raised an eyebrow at Rob's face. "Hey, I'm supposed to be a teenage girl so I have to practice." Her face and voice sobered. "Everyone ready?"

A shimmer shot skywards before looping and swooping back down. "Ffod is always ready!"

* * *

When Abel opened the front door, Fraggon had moved its head back to the normal position instead of looking straight at the opening. As usual it opened its electric blue eyes when Abel drew level, then licked the wall when he produced the sovereign. The panel turned transparent, revealing the maze. "Here we go, Zephyr. Do you want to fly free, in case you have to run?"

"No. I am part of you this way. Please hold the coin next to the opening so I can go straight in."

"Do you want to look at the print?"

"The cheat sheet? Yes please, though I am sure I can remember the path to the coin slot." Abel felt sure Zephyr could remember every line after the amount of time she had spent hovering just above it. He took out the paper and unfolded it, holding it open for Zephyr to inspect her route.

As she did, Abel glanced towards Fraggon, then jerked and stared hard. He couldn't be absolutely, totally sure, but that wide, curved frog-like mouth looked as if it had more curve. A smile? Abel racked his brains, had it always looked like that? Why would the guardian smile now? He glanced at the cheat sheet, then looked back at Fraggon. "Are you watching to make sure we don't cheat?" Fraggon didn't answer, or not in words. Instead, the stone creature turned its head to look straight out the entrance. That meant it couldn't see the panel!

Abel really, really wanted to tell Zephyr to hurry, but daren't. After a couple of minutes, or three hours to Abel, Zephyr sighed, a strange sensation in his mind. "Looking more will not help. I am ready. Keep a tight hold on my tether, Abel."

"Always, wind with a name." Abel took the coin out of his pocket and held it up.

"Down near the entrance, is the way in, so I can take it straight inside." Abel lowered his hand and the coin. Zephyr hesitated, then plucked the coin from his fingers and was inside in a split second. She stopped there for a moment. "It works!" Abel heard the excitement in her voice, but didn't want to tell her to calm down in case he distracted her. The coin, held fast in a shimmer, moved deeper, turning two corners in the narrow passageway then sideways through a partition. It looked really strange as the tether, a smoky line still connecting them, followed Zephyr as she turned back towards Abel, through another partition and then up to the next level.

Despite his good intentions, Abel couldn't help commenting. "Perfect." The route through the next level took longer, and the level above was even more convoluted. Zephyr moved slower and slower, finally hesitating under a hole up to the fourth level. Abel glanced at the cheat sheet. "That's the one."

"I keep wondering. I know what I remember, then wonder if I just think I do. Then I wonder what happens if I take the wrong turn. Will the box close and cut my tether? Will I be trapped in here forever?" Abel could hear the fear creeping into Zephyr's contact. "No more fluttering leaves in the trees, no more fae bop?"

"Woods said I can try this as many times as I like, so if I fail the coin must come back. You don't need a tether to find me, because you have already flown free. Hold tight to the coin and you will come back with it." Abel glanced down at the cheat sheet again. "Stop at each turn or hole and I'll tell you yes or no. After all, we've got the cheat sheet. Tavern rules, not Celtchar's."

"The Tavern rules. Ffod will not fail the Tavern. She throws a bonus twenty!" Zephyr had been fascinated by the set of seven RPG dice, especially as she could throw any number she wanted. Though despite her confident words, Zephyr stopped at each of the crucial turns and openings until Abel confirmed her choice. She moved faster now, and soon hovered in the final chamber with the coin held in front of the slot.

"Well done Zephyr."

"But what happens when I let the coin go? If the box closes then I cannot hold it. I have looked at the slot, and it will not allow a being such as me inside it." The coin jiggled a little as Zephyr became more agitated.

"I know you can stretch out long and thin. How much of you can come back outside and still leave enough to hold the coin?" Abel thought fast because he really didn't want Zephyr frightened, let alone actually hurt. "Will more magic help you to stay strong while you get thinner? I can send extra down the link."

"Then I can cast a strong wind glyph to hold the coin and come right outside! When I am safe, I can tell the glyph to tip the coin into the slot." Abel heard the sheer relief in Zephyr's voice. She'd been a lot more worried than she'd let on, but had still kept going.

"More magic ready and waiting." Abel concentrated and pushed a little magic, then felt the small additional drain as Zephyr cast her glyph.

"A puff of wind casts wind. The sorcerer never thought of that." Despite the humour in that, Zephyr extracted herself slowly, feeding her shimmer back through the puzzle while leaving enough to hold the coin until the last moment. Abel felt the pull on his magic as she strengthened the glyph, but the coin barely moved. A flicker of movement and the rest of Zephyr shot out of the box. "Now?"

"Now." Inside the box the coin tilted, slid into the slot, and the transparent panel turned back into wall. "Curses. Did we do something wrong?" Abel looked at Fraggon and found two electric blue eyes looking back. Its gaze dropped so Abel turned to see why. The coin lay on the little table, right where the chest used to be. Abel picked it up and put it in his pocket, turning to tell the rest what had happened. The door was closed! He'd no idea when that had happened, or why. Maybe the house didn't like anyone watching him work on the puzzle. Though if he'd failed it should open again. So maybe? He reached for the handles on the double doors.

"I will hide. I remember the first time, and burning air."

"Good idea Zephyr. Here goes." Abel pushed down, and with a soft click the handles moved and the doors opened a crack. He pushed them right open but the metre-thick wall meant all he could see was the opposite side of a corridor, with soft, pale yellow light coming from either way. A picture on the opposite wall showed volcanoes and ice, and in the middle of them a fraggon. Its eyes moved, resting on Abel, then looked upwards. Abel looked up. On the ceiling the plaster had been shaped like an octopus, or decimus, or some other "uss" because Abel lost count of the tentacles when it opened its eyes.

"That doesn't look welcoming." Zephyr sounded hesitant. "Though it might be. None of the flows are threatening even though magic coils through everything. Are we going in?"

The tone suggested Zephyr didn't fancy it, and neither did Abel. More to the point, he wanted to let his friends know how he'd got on. "Not yet Zephyr. Let's talk to the rest." Abel hesitated because he'd love to peek, but he'd have to take a full step inside to see into the corridor. Then if the doors shut or the octopus grabbed him the others would never know what they were facing when they tried a rescue. They would try, he felt sure of that, which was really good reason to reassure everyone. He closed the doors, turned, and walked back towards the exit. The door stayed shut. Abel took hold of the doorknob, and staggered as his knees buckled in relief when it turned. He hadn't realised just how worried he'd been.

The raucous cheer as the door opened sounded like the sweetest music he'd ever heard in his life. Zephyr must have been relieved as well. As soon as Abel stepped outside she shot into the air in a series of spiralling loops, connections zapping out to everyone. "We did it! Abel and the mighty Ffod have unlocked the doors. Tavern rules rule!"

*   *   *

Abel didn't fancy standing in the wind and rain to explain everything, or going back in straight away. Instead he called Creepio's number to leave a message that there wasn't a problem behind the door, then the whole group headed home for their tea. They'd meet in Kelis's house later for an impromptu meeting of Bonny's Tavern. As they passed the first house in Brinsford, Stan came out to wave them over. "Tell that vicar bloke that if he brings something like that again I'll shoot it." The old poacher looked pale but determined. "I couldn't see it proper so it was like the other weird stuff, and nothing bloody holy. Are you sure he's a vicar?"

"Very sure, Stan. That thing is supposed to fight the bad stuff, but it got confused." Abel worried about Stan shooting because he had a nasty feeling that not only would the shot bounce, but the ogre would treat him as a target. Worse, Creepio had veiled it so Stan's magical sight had sharpened to where he could see through one.

"It was trying to get into the garden to you kids. Just tell him."

"I will but ordinary shot might not affect it, or just make it angry, so be careful. How's Bugsy?" As expected, Abel asking about his dog diverted Stan.

"He's doing okay. I thought his eyes were going, but he seems as sharp as ever now. It must have been an infection or something." Stan grinned, relaxing a bit. "He wanted to go and bite that vicar bloke."

"Be good. You know he only bites properly if you let him." From Stan's smirk he might still let Bugsy get a holy mouthful, so Abel kept going. "Seriously. We need the vicar's goodwill if we want to lease the church."

"You should buy the village shop if you want to do something charitable. It only opens in the afternoons now, and the Slummers are selling up. They've had enough of real life." Stan waited, but nobody wanted to argue about him using Slummers instead of Summers. He'd had a feud with Mr. and Mrs. Summers, the shop owners, ever since they'd banned Bugsy from their establishment. "You could flog computer games in there instead of lentils and sunflower seeds." The health food also offended Stan, who preferred pies and puddings.

"I'll tell mum. She deals with the finances, but I don't reckon there's enough in the kitty for the stock, let alone the shop, even if they sell up cheap." Abel hadn't actually seen any sign of the shop closing, though it didn't do much business with nearly every family having at least one member working in Stourton every day. A village shop couldn't compete with supermarket prices, especially when vans would deliver orders for next to nothing. The group split up, with Jenny coming to Abel's house to eat with him because her dad knew she wouldn't be back until late.

At the Bonny's Tavern meeting after tea, Jenny thought buying the shop and the flat above it might be worth considering for Kelis and her mum if they wanted to stay in Brinsford. Kelis wasn't so sure. She doubted her mum would have enough for a deposit, and neither of them knew the first thing about running a shop. If Abel would have received his full legacy he might have bought it as a Tavern headquarters, but none of them thought he should tie up the income to pay a mortgage.

Before getting down to what Abel had found, Jenny presented the rewritten Bonny's Tavern paperwork. On the new box lid, a small shack near the Tavern sported a sign proclaiming that Woods and Green, solicitors, were in residence. "All magical contracts negotiated" had them all laughing. The regular payment for the advert would persuade Jenny's dad to alter the artwork, while the gameplay now included the adventurers signing a contract to split the proceeds according to their skills and strengths. According to Woods, those with any magical knowledge would recognise the glyph on the sign as belonging to a real magical solicitor and it might even bring them business. Until then Abel paid for the advert out of his legacy, to help get the business started.

Abel finally got to the part they'd all been waiting for, and with Zephyr occasionally interrupting, he explained what happened. Nobody could be sure why Fraggon turned away, though Rob wondered if it had got lonely so it didn't mind bending the rules. A hundred years staring at the inside of a door didn't sound like much fun. None of them had known what happened after that, because the door closed. Kelis admitted they'd spent the time discussing ways to break in, just in case the door didn't open again.

Despite going around and around what Abel had seen, there wasn't an alternative. Ferryl, and then Kelis would try to follow Abel inside the entrance, just in case something had altered. If not, he'd have to go through the double doors on his own. This time there'd be a time limit. Abel had to come out in thirty minutes, or his friends would be testing doors and windows with serious intent.

Kelis remembered Creepio's remarks to Ferryl, or Fay as he knew her, about being magically proficient. Ferryl admitted she'd activated two very potent glyphs just in case the ogre kept coming. One had been similar to Creepio's ice, adapted specifically hurt an ogre, the other was a mixture of shattering and fire for a mist or frost giant. She really needed her wits, to provide better memory of other creatures and ways to deal with them. The fraggon might be in her missing wits under its real name, though at least it hadn't been offended by Jenny's choice.

The five of them rehashed Fay's story so they'd all got it straight the next time Creepio met them. Her knowledge of advanced glyphs would explain her using a magical solicitor, while the Accord and magical privacy laws would stop Creepio from prying too much. Where to meet Creepio might be a problem, because the deserted church wasn't really very hospitable if the meeting dragged on for too long. Unfortunately, if he came to one of their houses the mothers would want to join the discussion. They were the directors and should be involved if the bishop really might let Stourton Refuge lease the church.

An attempt to play Bonny's Tavern ended up in a fiasco as Zephyr kept throwing bonuses for herself, and probably Abel though nobody could catch her. She was in a terrific mood, probably reaction after being in that box. Ferryl might have been able to spot the cheating, but she kept throwing exactly what she needed as well. As Kelis became more and more frustrated, Jenny, Abel and Rob collapsed in laughter, which probably did all of them more good than a serious game would have. Even Kelis saw the funny side in the end and started using wind glyphs to control her own dice throws. When Jenny went home, the rest made arrangements to meet at Rob's in the morning, to look for trolls.

*   *   *

An inspection of the grounds behind Rob's house didn't reveal any signs of a troll, possibly because Rob and his Dad had trampled everything flat while searching. Melanie sulked, both because she couldn't play Bonny's Tavern and because nobody believed she'd seen a real troll. If so it had been another baby, because Melanie would have mentioned the size if it had been as big as a truck and there'd have been definite gouges in the earth. Between Melanie's mood and tramping around in the rain, none of them wanted to hang about at Rob's, so the four of them headed for Kelis's house and Bonny's Tavern. This time Rob and Abel brought drinks to help out, because Kelis had heard her mum on the phone talking to the solicitor. She wasn't broke, but the days of a fridge full of free drinks were definitely over.

A phone call from Creepio, suggesting they all met in an empty chapel in Stourton, might be his way of avoiding the weather. Since he didn't want to see them until after Christmas, that set the timetable for Abel's foray into Castle House. He wanted it over with before Christmas anyway, preferably this afternoon so he could relax a bit. Una had offered to drive them all into Stourton on Christmas Eve, to finish their shopping, so he only had two days anyway.

At least the rain stopped after lunch, so the group in Castle House garden only needed small wind and heat glyphs to stay comfortable. Somehow today seemed more solemn. First Ferryl, then Jenny, then Rob and even Kelis gave Abel a quick hug, which made him even more nervous. This time when Abel showed the coin to Fraggon it didn't move. He looked back over his shoulder and put his hands on the door handles, and the outer door closed. Celtchar had definitely been shy.

When the double doors swung open, the picture of a fraggon looked upwards and the octopus opened its eyes. Abel waited, but nothing else happened. He put a foot over the threshold, then the other, then finally leant forward to look up the corridors and sighed. Four metres away in each direction wooden doors with carved fraggons on the panels blocked his view, though neither had a keyhole. Halfway to one door a small table held a stone or plaster toad. Its eyes opened. Abel could take a hint.

He wasn't sure what the hint was when he walked up to it and the toad opened its mouth a little. It wasn't a slot, though the coin would fit. "Any ideas, Zephyr?"

"I am testing the air. It feels tingly, but not dangerous, so I will come out if you need me. The toad is a seeming over something else. There is a concentration of magic, and a very strong link to the wooden plaque on the wall behind it."

Abel inspected the plaque, a smooth square of polished wood with a carved border, then a plain strip and a carved outer edge. There were two glyphs carved into the outer plain strip. "Zephyr, what about those two glyphs? They look odd, just two of them at one end of the top like that."

"They seem dormant, though each holds a little magic. Most things in this house do."

"I'm going to hold the coin to the toad's mouth. I'll keep firm hold. Warn me if nasty things start to build up."

"Always." Abel extended the coin, very slowly, until the edge went into the mouth. "Stop. Magic is flowing over the coin and extending over your fingers. It is not aggressive. Now it is withdrawing." Abel slowly removed the coin.

"A generous gift. Thy finger would suffice, master." The toad shimmered and became... a three-legged toad. A furry toad with three straight horns on its head, so Abel took a careful step back. The last time he saw one of those it attacked his school friends. "I am a wealth toad, also known as a luck toad. In this instance it means I will protect thy wealth, and will be bad luck should thine enemies invade."

"Good, I think. Some creatures looking like you attacked my friends at school for no reason so forgive me if I'm suspicious." Abel inspected the creature but it made no move towards him. "Have you been sat there a hundred years?"

"I would not know, master. Most of the house closes down if the master locks the door, unless a guest remains. Did the last master die?" The creature didn't seem the slightest bit bothered about skipping a century, or a dead master.

"We think so." One part of the toad's answer snagged Abel's attention. "How did he bring guests inside? The guards won't let my friends into the entrance, let alone past these doors." Abel looked back and upwards. "I'm guessing that won't like visitors either."

"The board behind me shows which entities are welcome. Their glyph glows if they are inside the house. Only two are still welcome, but neither has been able to enter since the master locked the door." The toad turned, so it wasn't a talking statue. "To remove their invitation, cut a line across the glyph."

"Who were they?"

"One was an apprentice, the other a young woman who had no magical knowledge. She lived here for some time before the master left, in the guest rooms because he never gave her permission to pass the next portal."

"Which is a door with a fancy magical lock, no doubt. Guest rooms?" Abel reined in his curiosity. "Though first, how do I get a friend onto that board up there?"

"Now you have taken possession of this section of the house, keep physical contact while escorting your friend through the doors to the plaque. If they place the back of a hand, paw, or other limb on the square in the centre, they will be marked and a glyph will be added to the border. Not the part of the limb used to cast glyphs as the mark may interfere, which can be very dangerous." The toad turned back and fixed Abel with a stare. "Tis best to keep the numbers low, new master, or they may try to pillage your wealth. Stopping them might damage your goods."

"These friends are welcome to pillage, if they find any wealth. Do I offer the coin or my finger every time I come in?" Abel looked up to see if a glyph had appeared for him. "Do I put my hand up there?"

"There is no need for either, because now the house knows you. You are the master."

"No, I'm Abel."

"I will address you as Abel if you wish, but unless another claims that coin you are the master. I can keep it safe if you wish, though it should be placed in the chest with the letter, on the table just outside this door." The toad looked towards the entrance. "So that if a mishap befalls you, the next in line can claim their inheritance."

"I'll put the chest back later, but first I'll get my friends." Abel looked at the two tempting doors and hesitated, but he'd already beaten this part to death with his friends. If he could get them inside then that became the top priority. As expected, when Abel retraced his steps he didn't have to close the double doors. They closed themselves when he went to open the outer door. This place would drive Creepio crackers because he'd never be able to peek.

*   *   *

Abel explained to everyone and as expected they all wanted to come inside right now, immediately. When Abel asked who wanted to come first, the three girls warned Rob that if he waited until last Abel might not want the competition. Worse, they might not let Abel leave because warmth and wealth could have an odd effect on young women. Jenny had them all laughing again by pointing out they didn't know the effect wealth and warmth would have on Rob.

Ferryl waited until last. As she pointed out, the house might still object to her. Three times Abel took a friend inside, and three times they pressed the back of a hand to the flat wood. Each time the panel lit up briefly, then a glyph appeared as if carved into the border and began to glow. Even though there were similarities, each one looked different to the others. To everyone's relief, whatever mark they received didn't show. The only fright Abel got came when Jenny reached out to pat Fraggon on the way past. According to her she'd been dying to do that since seeing him. Once again Abel couldn't be absolutely certain it smiled.

"Ready?" Abel held out his hand.

Ferryl looked at it and laughed. "A hand. Traditionally, sorcerers carry young women into their houses over their shoulders, often kicking and screaming."

"What about sorceresses? Kelis will want to know." Abel went along with it because Ferryl's smile looked too bright, too forced.

"Hah. Sorceresses simply crook a finger." Ferryl did so. "The sucker follows that anywhere, or maybe it's the glyph."

"So, do I carry you in, or learn the glyph?" Abel paused, then held her eyes. "Or will you tell me why you're so worried? The rest went in without any trouble, even if Jenny patted Fraggon."

"She wants to adopt it." Ferryl heaved a big sigh, glancing nervously towards the door. "I'm worried the house will let me in, then kill me. I am inside this body, remember, two in one."

"Zephyr has been in and out several times."

"But Zephyr is inside her tattoo, accepted as a part of you. I wish I could get back in there." Ferryl looked at the jacket covering Abel's bicep and tattoo, then reached for his hand.

"I can make room, if you wish?" Zephyr shimmered into view, then flew back inside.

Ferryl stopped midstride, her hand almost touching Abel. "Truly? Yes truly, or you would not offer. That is very kind, and generous." She patted Abel's jacket over the tattoo, very gently. "If the hunters ever close in and I need a safe haven, I will remember that."

"So now you know. The Ffod is keeping guard, I've got the coin, and I'm sure the fraggon is smiling. Let's go for it." Abel took her hand and set off for the door, quickly opening it before Ferryl could object again. "There, see, no prob.... Oops. Calm down, Fraggon." Abel cringed inside, because up to now nobody had actually called it that.

Fraggon didn't seem to care, or notice. It stared fixedly at Ferryl. "I'll leave. It knows I'm in here." Ferryl tried to back out but Abel hung on.

"No, it just needs to understand. Fraggon, I know there is something else inside the human. Someone else, a friend, Ferryl Shayde. I don't care what other names you have for her, I know them back to the very first."

That got Fraggon's attention. It shifted its eyes to Abel. "Yes, her true-name as well. She will not harm me." The eyes moved back to Ferryl and somehow, without any real movement, Fraggon told her she'd better not try.

"He speaks truth. I can touch you to tell you, so you can read the truth?" Fraggon extended its head about ten centimetres, not exactly welcoming, especially when it bared its teeth. Abel hadn't seen them before, and could probably live without seeing them again. The smaller teeth looked like small daggers, the largest might be baby swords and Fraggon had a very wide mouth. Abel and Ferryl approached cautiously, hand in hand, and she carefully placed a hand flat on Fraggon's head. "I am now known as Ferryl Shayde. See my true-self. I have promised to guide and guard Abel Bernard Conroy for ninety years."

"I watch over him as well." Zephyr popped into view as her spooky-phone connected to Fraggon as well as Ferryl. "Though if you want to help?" Abel and Ferryl froze, but Fraggon shut its mouth, hiding those teeth. After a moment it moved its head back to the usual position.

"That's a pass then. Come on." Abel hustled Ferryl through the double doors and down the corridor. This time he explained everything to the luck toad before Ferryl came close, but the luck toad only had one proviso: Ferryl had to let her true-self touch the wood as well as the back of her hand, so the house recognised both. After that Zephyr flew out to touch the panel so she could fly free in here if necessary. The board gave Ferryl two glyphs, overlapping, while Zephyr had a single, normal sized one.

"Now can we open the door? Please?" Jenny had her hand on the doorknob, ready.

Kelis shook her head. "Not until Abel gets rid of those two original glyphs. The woman has probably died, but a sorcerer's apprentice might still be alive. As far as I can make out from what Abel said, that glyph allows the apprentice to come in again now the house is open." When Abel checked, the toad agreed, so he scored through each glyph with his penknife. The glyphs faded straight away afterwards, leaving smooth wood.

"Now?"

"Yes, but be care…. Never mind, too late." Abel walked through with Kelis, behind Jenny, Rob, Ferryl, and Zephyr.

✳   ✳   ✳

The door opened onto a shorter stretch of corridor with a door halfway down one wall and another door at the end. The end door led to a large corner room with a view of the gardens at one side and Castle Lane out the front. Within seconds Jenny and Ferryl were off back along the passage, opening the door in the wall to check the room behind it. By the time Abel had glanced at a room with sinks and worktops, they'd moved back past the toad to check out the other side of the house. Abel caught up as the pair reached the top of the stairs, intent on checking out every room as fast as possible. "Whoa, hold up everyone. I wanted a proper look at that library. I barely saw the shelves before you shut the door again."

Jenny kept going, opening the first door she reached. "You could go and look at that, while I investigate this dressing room?"

"Good idea, just like every horror movie. The idiots split up and die horribly." Despite her light tone, Kelis jerked them back to reality. A quick discussion agreed that the safest way was for Jenny and Ferryl to stay with the rest until they'd checked every room. Once they were sure there were no nasty surprises waiting anywhere, the group could split up.

Half an hour later everyone returned to the first room, a sort of sitting room at least eight metres square. Rob flopped into a well-padded easy chair, but shot to his feet as a footstool carved and stuffed to look like a tortoise waddled towards him. While the rest laughed at him, Ferryl dropped to her knees next to the animated furniture, inspecting it. "A bound shade, a small one."

"You said walking furniture was difficult," Kelis nervously inspected the rest of the furniture. "When Abel teased me about animating my bedroom door by accident."

"None of you seem to get it." Ferryl spread her arms and turned to include the room, gardens and house. "You have seen how my old name frightens leeches and worries Creepio, yet Celtchar kept me like a caged rat to use in his experiments. The man who owned this house, and created these things, would have brushed away Creepio and the ogre as minor nuisances. He was hundreds of years old, all of them spent learning to manipulate glyphs and magic. He probably made the walking footstool to amuse himself on a wet afternoon." Ferryl stopped, sighed and flopped into a chair, raising her feet for a footstool to position itself. "But he's dead. Now you've got the benefit of Celtchar's defences while you try to learn enough to survive in the wider world."

"Well that certainly ruined my mood." Jenny sat down, more cautiously, then pulled her legs up as another footstool waddled over. "I'd rather it didn't do that."

"I can kill the shade, or move it to another job? Whatever it is probably volunteered as an alternative to absolute death. The only reason I'm not in furniture or in a plant in the entrance is I refused that option." Ferryl looked across at Abel and a smile started to grow. "You are the master of the house, or this part at least. Tell your furniture to behave."

At least that broke the mood, as did Abel ordering some of the footstools to stay where they were. Everyone tried the big armchair, but nobody liked how it moved to cradle them so Abel asked it to stop. As usual, Abel wasn't keen on anything being bound, but he didn't have many options because releasing a bound shade simply meant it had finished dying. Once the furniture behaved itself, the friends all came up with their favourite discovery. There were plenty because Abel now had access to the first two floors at the front of Castle House. That made eleven rooms in all, four downstairs and six upstairs plus the entrance hall.

The ground floor consisted of two large corner rooms and two smaller ones, one set out as a dining room and the other as a scullery with sinks, wide marble worktops and metal cupboards. Upstairs a huge master bedroom filled one corner, with a walk-in wardrobe or dressing room next door and a bathroom connected to that. The other rooms were two smaller bedrooms with a bathroom between them. Running water and a toilet, even late Victorian versions, came as a great relief after all the history lessons about the lack of hygiene in the past.

Kelis chose the large room at the opposite corner of the ground floor as her favourite, because of the books lining the walls. Some would have been new a hundred years ago, but others were tomes about magic and glyphs that looked much, much older. Abel could see her spending long hours tucked up nice and warm in there during the winter, reading about glyphs. Definitely warm, because despite a lack of fires or radiators they'd all taken off their coats.

Rob liked the scullery, it fascinated him once he found out it was a full kitchen. That had taken a little while, but eventually he'd realised the worktops and cupboards all contained glyphs. Reverse fire kept some parts cold, so those metal cupboards had to be magical fridges or maybe the coldest one was a freezer. Other glyphs would heat portions of a flat metal plate, or individual shelves in a metal cupboard to make an oven. The amount of magic put into those glyphs must decide the heat and enough intent would time the cooking. The pipes leading to some of the taps had heat glyphs stamped into them, but getting the water exactly the right temperature would take very precise control. Rob wanted to experiment, and had already made plans for an extra cold box for soft drinks.

The dressing room, also a walk-in wardrobe, really fascinated Jenny. While training as a sorceress Jenny kept switching between game characters, but she'd currently settled on Bonny the Barmaid. She'd even bought some cheap jewellery and lace to decorate a skirt and blouse. Now Jenny's imagination had caught fire because the dressing room held clothes for women as well as the sorcerer, very expensive-looking clothes. She'd found a complete outfit, dress, shoes, gloves, wig, hat, brolly, and jewellery, carefully arranged on a dummy. Unfortunately, there wasn't a Tavern character who dressed as a posh late Victorian, though Abel felt there might be one in the near future, possibly one with a pet fraggon.

The clothes also caught Ferryl's interest because she'd been in the hole before those fashions developed, but the aquarium interested her more. It covered half of one wall in the library, almost two metres tall, four metres wide and extending maybe three metres back into the wall, full of exotic fish she didn't recognise. Despite sometimes living near rivers or the sea, Ferryl had kept out of the water. She didn't know what magical creatures lived there, or how vulnerable she might be. Now she had a whole tank full to look at, without even getting wet. Though it wasn't just the creatures catching Ferryl's interest. There were glyphs maintaining the water temperature and presumably keeping it clean, controlled by at least one bound shade. Ferryl wanted to investigate, to copy and understand the glyphs, but worried about killing the fish and other aquatic life.

Something more practical had caught Abel's attention. There were vases, pictures, ornaments and furniture in every room, not a lot of them but they all had to be at least a hundred and eighteen years old. That meant they were antiques, so going by their pristine condition Abel felt sure everything must be valuable. Providing Woods would let him take things away, and convert them into cash, Abel could help mum out. Even if he had to keep the money secret, surely it could be fed into financing the game which would mean more money for all their families. The dryad had told Abel that Castle House belonged to him now, and only the inheritance laws stopped him moving in so that should apply to the contents. Unfortunately, "the dryad said it was okay" might not work in an antiques shop.

On the way out, Abel picked up a small, cheap-looking vase, just to check if he could take it away. When questioned, the luck toad repeated that Abel was the master and could do anything he wished. The small chest, sovereign or key would still kill anyone else who touched them, but the visitors could handle everything else if they didn't cause damage. If a guest tried to remove any item they hadn't brought in with them the house defences would stop them, unless Abel was present and authorised it. Stopping thieves might damage the décor and could destroy the item, but luck toad seemed very certain the offenders wouldn't escape.

After Jenny went outside and came back in so the rest could watch her glyph dim, the luck toad also confirmed that the others could come inside the house when Abel wasn't here. He could stop that by deliberately locking the door. After the warning about the key, coin and chest, Abel left them inside the house. He placed them on the table and Ferryl put a coloured bubble over the lot to remind Kelis, Rob, and Jenny. That should stop anyone getting accidentally killed.

There'd be plenty of time to explore the eleven rooms, because there wasn't a short cut or puzzle to open the next locked section. The double doors sat at the end of a seven-metre-long, three-metre-wide corridor at the top of the stairs to the first floor, with a tall slim slot in a glowing panel on the wall next to them. Abel needed another key, and there wasn't any clue where it might be. Nothing would be getting past the locked section until the door opened, not even an inquisitive puff of wind, judging by the gathering magic when Zephyr came near. At the same time, Ferryl reported magic gathering in two stuffed heads, a lioness and a black bear, one on each side of the door. Seemings stopped her from seeing what the heads really were, and she couldn't tell if the rest of the animals' bodies were hidden inside the wall.

The five of them went back to Kelis's house, to the original Bonny's Tavern, where they could get a drink while they talked. They'd got inside Castle House, and out again. Now what could they do with the place?

Loot or Legacy

Ferryl had another bit of news once everyone had a drink. "The charred stone near the door, the one in the dead patch, is one of my wits. I looked very carefully on the way out, and I can't see why the sorcerer used it. The only reason I can come up with is as a tripwire, one that would recognise me if I ever entered the house." She smirked happily and lifted her cola as if toasting someone. "Despite how he treated me, Celtchar must still have thought I might break free one day."

"Can you get to it? More importantly, can you read it? Or repair it, because the surface is definitely damaged." Kelis hitched forward a little. "You said you put all Jenny's and Claris's schoolwork on a bone wit. How hard is that?"

"You can answer one question at a time, just so the rest of us can keep up." Rob pretended to duck as Kelis turned towards him. "Help, Jenny, call up Fraggon."

"Soon. I patted him again on the way out. I'm sure he likes me." Jenny turned to Ferryl, her voice losing any hint of levity. "You've stolen all my schoolwork? How? I can still remember what I've learned, I think? Or have I lost some?" Now she definitely looked worried.

"Your memories are intact. I copied all the knowledge you and Claris had learned at school, to help me with the modern world. That made one of my wits larger, which hurt more than usual when it came out. I'll create a new one and transfer that knowledge, and future schoolwork. The knowledge is etched into the bone using intent, a section at a time, and any mistakes can be erased by healing. The etching is slow. It takes hours of concentration to enter the magically charged marks, I suppose you would call it code, to hold the basics of something like a new language. Fluency would take another long session, more hours of concentration even if the information only takes up a very small space." Four heads leant forward, all wearing rapt expressions because Ferryl had them totally hooked. "How do you think the sorcerer remembered all the glyphs from the captured wits he forced me to put into my bones? He always cut them out once I'd read them and he'd recorded them, and probably destroyed the original." Everyone flinched at just the thought, especially as they'd heard Ferryl scream when only two bone wits came out.

"So, I cannot have a wit." Zephyr sounded downhearted.

"No, but as you grow you can remember more. Storing knowledge in wits needs a solid body." Ferryl sounded sympathetic, but adamant. "It took me many, many centuries to learn that, centuries during which I had to relearn again and again. Take care, Zephyr, severe damage will leave you smaller and might destroy some of your memories."

"I'd have to know how to heal my body before I could mess about with my bones." Kelis looked glum, her interest waning. "I fancied learning German, but there just isn't enough spare time. One of Laurence's cousins, the ones I saw at that last dance, keeps emailing and he's asking if I'll come and visit. I can't go, but I'd like to learn to at least talk to him properly when he visits England."

Despite the chance to tease Kelis, Abel stuck with wits because he had his own use for one. "I wouldn't mind putting maths on a wit. It isn't cheating if it's in my bone instead of my brain, is it?" He looked around the rest, startled by the smiles and laughter.

"Only you would ask about cheating. Actually, in Henry's case, brain and bone are the same so it can't be. I'd like to put all the things I'm learning about human biology on permanent storage. I'm sure I lose a page-worth for every two new pages I read." Jenny tried for a bright smile but failed. "Chicken and egg, and all that. I need human biology to create a wit, but can't learn human biology quickly without a wit."

"No, you don't. As I said, if you heal the bone the knowledge will be gone." Ferryl thought hard, obviously working something out. "I've been talking about me, and I need healing when I move my wits from one body to another. Humans never need to take wits out, so they don't have to heal the damage or force a wit into a new body. That means you don't need to keep them small and concentrated, to start with at least. All you need is the control to etch and magically mark the bone inside your body without disturbing the flesh. Wits are magically locked etching, the same as creating glyphs inside a tree, or a stone guardian, or a magic diamond or gold." Her eyes fastened on Jenny. "The other three can already reach inside earth compressed into a very small rock, to place a locking glyph at the centre. Further practice will get them deeper, and some bones are very near the surface."

Despite just getting inside Castle House, everyone concentrated on creating wits. The sheer scope of what they could learn made it more important than exploring. With a wit, any of them could remember enough to pass their exams, or every page of those glyph books in the library.

A reply to Abel's email to Woods and Green asking "Remove vase and sell?" brought them back to discussing Castle House. The reply simply said "All yours. As you wish. Please consult first." Two more emails confirmed an appointment the day after tomorrow, on Christmas Eve when they'd all be in Stourton anyway.

Jenny left soon afterwards, before her dad started worrying. He still didn't like her riding her moped in bad weather, especially in the evening. The rest thrashed it about, but then Rob and Abel went home to eat. The humans wouldn't be thinking about treasure tonight, they all had school work to finish. They'd all made that mistake in the past, leaving holiday homework until later and then remembering too late.

*　*　*

The following day the four school students worked on homework, then on how to raise some money from Castle House. Jenny worked from home because she didn't fancy a rain-lashed fourteen-mile round trip on her moped. She had already started on fixing that particular problem, even if she complained the rain made it harder to learn to drive a car. Meanwhile internet enquiries about selling the valuables came up with the same thing time after time. Sudden finds of anything old and valuable needed a verified source or proof of ownership, and selling on websites such as eBay was restricted to over-eighteens. Their investigation turned to other ways people had come into possession of valuable items.

Meanwhile Ferryl had plenty of work to keep her occupied. The morning post delivered a thick parcel full of papers, her new identity and history. After glancing through them she took several and went to see Mrs. Ventner, Kelis's mother. Half an hour later her mum called Kelis out of Bonny's Tavern, leaving Rob and Abel to wonder what was happening. The big smiles when Ferryl and Kelis came back reassured them. "Kelis's mum has accepted me as a lodger, in Claris's old room, for as long as she has the house. Woods and Green supplied paperwork confirming that I have a small legacy." Ferryl bowed to Abel. "From my deceased parents. The letter asked me to decide where I wish to rent accommodation, because I can't buy my own home until I am eighteen. I will have a small lump sum to purchase school uniform, a laptop, that sort of thing, then a regular income to cover rent and board."

To Abel's surprise she came over and kissed him on the cheek. "Thank you, Abel. I have never been a real person, just me alone." She held up some of the papers. "These need a signature, my signature, not my host's. In all my years, I have never had a signature of my own."

The rest gathered round her, really interested now. Somehow, they'd never really processed how Ferryl only experienced life through her succession of hosts, or that she'd never had a real body. Everything they took for granted, Ferryl experienced second-hand. She still would experience life indirectly, but for ninety years she could react as if the body she was inhabiting was hers, because the host would never know. The celebration only involved soft drinks, but then everyone wanted to do something to mark the occasion. After eating the hot bacon sandwiches Ferryl's new landlady provided for lunch, Rob came up with the perfect answer. Ferryl wanted the burned wit from the door inside Castle House, and now Abel had been accepted as the master of the house she should be able to get it.

*   *   *

A long, careful three hours later, Ferryl came out of Castle House with a blackened nub of bone. The luck toad had agreed that Abel could alter the house protection, but advised against changing the intricate web of magic and glyphs. After that warning, Ferryl and Zephyr inspected the wit and the surrounding area very closely, but removing it shouldn't make any difference. The difficulty would be in repairing the underlying webs and whirls of magic in and around the wall itself. Neither Zephyr nor Ferryl could work out what most of them were for which meant it might be a bad idea to change anything.

Abel carefully explained all that to Fraggon while hoping the dead vine listened, didn't care, or would follow Fraggon's lead. The living stone creature uncoiled and came across the room to where it could watch Ferryl directing Abel, Zephyr advising, and Abel extracting the wit complete with the gold surrounding it. Once Abel removed it completely, both Zephyr and Ferryl directed him in repairing the magic flows across the wall until they met across the blank spot. Finishing the task successfully came as a big relief, nearly as much of one as Fraggon slithering back to coil by the inner door. This time Abel took a picture with his phone. He felt sure it had smiled again.

Despite everyone else thinking she should put the wit into her bones straight away, Ferryl demurred. She'd wait until tonight, when she had chance to deal with whatever the wit held and make sense of any damaged portions. If they were too badly damaged, portions of memories might be distracting or confusing so Ferryl wanted time to erase them.

Instead, she wanted to go through the loot taken from Castle House. Ferryl had told the other four which items had been created with a glyph at their heart, or were charged with magic. According to Ferryl, none of those would be as valuable as the naturally created art so Kelis, Abel, and Rob had all chosen non-magical items. Having genuine valuables rather than those formed with magic had become a status symbol with sorceresses, even two hundred years ago.

Now everyone carefully wrapped the jewellery, half a dozen odd coins in a case, three small vases and a few statuettes and ornaments in gold and precious stones. Kelis had brought two books that caught her eye, Faustus and Queen Mab, both printed in 1821. An internet search showed the same editions on sale for two thousand pounds each.

*   *   *

When Una arrived the following day to play taxi driver, she looked Fay over very carefully. "Shannon has told us about you, which is why I volunteered to drive you all today. Are you living here now?"

"I will be lodging with Kelis and coming to Stourton Comprehensive after Christmas." Fay held out a hand. "I am Fay Shayde, from Germany. Pleased to meet you, Una. Kelis and her friends told me about you, and your sword."

The attempted diversion didn't work, for once. Una stayed much too interested in the new mystery girl from Germany with a familiar name to be sidetracked into talking about her sword or boots. The polite interrogation helped in a way because it allowed Ferryl, Abel, Kelis, and

Rob, then Jenny when they picked her up, to practice the story. At least Ferryl had a good excuse for going to the solicitor, a sheaf of papers she brandished when the subject came up. Una had heard of Shannon's visit to Woods and Green and had no intention of sitting in there for hours. She drove off to visit Frederick's house to catch up with gossip.

Just as well, because this time the group weren't split up. After checking that everyone knew exactly who Woods and Green were, Terese Green dealt with them. "Does your name mean you are a partner?" Kelis looked a little embarrassed. "Sorry, but Abel told us Woods is incredibly ancient and you aren't."

"You shouldn't ask a lady her age." Terese's little smile took any sting out of the words. "Or try to work out her age from her appearance, especially if she needs a history book to calculate the answer. I am the junior partner, and consider myself very lucky to be. My predecessor only lasted four hundred years, but times were more turbulent back then." She watched with a little smile as the four humans decided against asking when that might have been, though they all really wanted to know.

Ferryl took pity on them, putting the papers on the desk. "I would definitely prefer an abacus to work out my age. I would feel more comfortable if you had a Greek one, left to right. The right to left versions confused me."

"I only ever used one type so I never had that problem, though Woods might have come across others." Terese picked up the papers and glanced through them. "Your signature is precise considering how extravagant it is."

"My first signatures, ever. I enjoyed signing papers." Ferryl leant forward a little. "Are they in order? I have already arranged to lodge with Mrs. Ventner in Brinsford."

"I will need one other signature. Mr Conroy?" The solicitor pushed a paper forward. "This authorises us to free the funds to create Mz. Shayde's legacy. While not extravagant, it will affect your income for the next three years and eventually add up to a substantial sum."

"But I can do this without anyone else knowing?" Terese nodded so Abel signed, smiling quietly at the little tut from Kelis. He probably wouldn't have understood the wording if he'd read it. Either Abel trusted the solicitor, or he was stuffed. "We have been looking at ways to free up a lump sum in cash." Abel pulled his pack onto his knee and started to remove the items. Rob and Kelis followed suit. "These were in the house, so according to you and the toad we can sell them. Unfortunately, we can't just produce them out of thin air."

"Ah, right. I thought of something. Boot sales and markets. I found a bit on the internet where people bought things for a few quid and made thousands, even without a receipt." Jenny looked a bit embarrassed. "I couldn't tell you with Una there, and by the time we could talk freely I'd forgotten. We'd still have to wait while things were valued."

"Then we can give the money to our parents if we want. That's if Abel still wants to go for splitting the loot. It's all yours you know, not ours." Kelis's quiet smile at Abel turned into a smirk as she turned to Rob. "Though as ex-girlfriends, me and Jenny have a better chance of any loot than Rob."

"I keep telling you we are all in this together, the five Taverners. Otherwise I'll get all snooty and big-headed." Abel almost reached out to take Kelis's hand, then remembered he shouldn't. That stupid link might connect again. Instead he turned back to Terese Green. "Once I'm eighteen we'll talk about making that legal. Jenny, for one, needs her own clump of trees so she can giggle in private."

"If you still feel the same way, we will advise you. Woods mentioned you have a refreshingly different outlook. May I offer my personal thanks. That coin was a knife in his heart." Terese straightened, becoming more business-like. "I cannot advise on the best way to present these openly, except to offer receipts for them. Those will show you bought them recently, legitimately, at a value similar to their current one. The main problem with that is you can't explain how you paid for them."

"But if we bought some for pennies along with some really worthless rubbish?" Kelis unwrapped the two books. "If I bought these from a market stall, then discovered they were two hundred years old, we'd pocket about four grand."

"Then I could discover these vases at a jumble sale, Rob could buy a couple of those ornaments or the coins from a boot sale, and Jenny can discover that jewellery among some tat." Abel held up a vase. "That should work?"

"My apologies. I didn't ask how much you wanted. The vase you are holding would make national news, as would several of these items. A similar vase brought over three hundred thousand pounds in a recent auction. Those coins would bring a lot of attention, because they are probably the only complete set in the world that aren't badly worn or damaged." Terese smiled at the shock on the faces in front of her, even Ferryl's. "In common with many senior sorcerers, Celtchar collected exceptional treasures, items that weren't made magically. Others like the coins are valuable because sorcerers keep items for hundreds of years. The books are rare now but not then, so he probably bought them for their content rather than value. The jewellery is relatively low-valued, a few thousand pounds for each piece."

"That came from a dummy wearing the full outfit, hat, dress, boots, all of it." Jenny eyed the necklace in Terese's hands and sighed. "I'd love to find an excuse to wear it, all of it."

"That ensemble was Celtchar's, and explains why this jewellery isn't more valuable. He would travel around dressed like a moderately affluent merchant's widow, with a bound servant girl." Now the solicitor looked as if she'd sucked something really nasty. "Since he didn't use a seeming he could get close to the wives and daughters of the rich and famous or politically powerful without magical hexes detecting him. Once they were alone, he could use magic to gain influence or blackmail material. Such women would never have been left alone with a strange man."

"A cross-dressing sorcerer? Yeuk. Though I still like the dress." Jenny concentrated on the necklace. "So, Abel could sell those without causing a big fuss?"

"Just don't repeat it too often or it becomes a business and you'll be taxed. If you stray over your allowances, there will be Capital Gains Tax. We have an accountancy section to minimise your liability of course, though if the items are sold through the magical community the liability will be much less." She smiled quietly at the looks from the teenagers. "Yes, there is the magical equivalent of HM tax collectors, but they are nothing like as greedy." After some more discussion on the best items to sell, and warnings about overdoing it, the meeting broke up. Before they left, Terese repeated her offer to supply receipts for more expensive items at some time in the future.

As the rest left the office Abel turned back, waving them on to keep going. Terese promised to look into the extra matters for him, without ever mentioning it to the rest. As she pointed out, she was his solicitor, not theirs.

The rest of the visit to Stourton turned out to be a lot of fun. The five of them wandered through the Christmas market and the attached boot sale, buying silly bits of this and that. Jenny collected some truly tacky rings, brooches and necklaces from four different stalls, ideal for her Bonny the Barmaid costume. Rob couldn't find suitable ornaments or coins, but he discovered a big plastic sword with plastic gems on the hilt. It would be perfect for his barbarian costume. He also bought a box of battered lead soldiers, for the lead rather than the figures. Abel splashed out on a real leather jerkin, a cheap second-hand sleeveless one that the bloke on the stall swore would be perfect for a building site. From the look it had already been on a couple, just the thing for a hardworking sprite hunter. He picked out a couple of cheap vases and two framed prints, from a stall full of assorted rubbish the man reckoned came from his grandma's house. Ferryl collected a selection of crystals, because they would be easier to turn into magical diamonds than pebbles. Kelis kept searching for wands or small staffs, but couldn't find the right look. She settled on three reels of thin steel wire, for Ferryl to use with her crystals, and two old books from a stall full of them. She also bought a pair of black driving gloves, the ones that left the palms uncovered, so she could still cast glyphs while keeping her hands warm.

When Una finally picked them up she had news. Claris wanted to come to the New Year's bash at Laurence's, to apologise to everyone and thank them. She would be going home to her mum in the New Year, before school started again, so she wouldn't catch everyone together again. Claris had asked Laurence when he came by, but he wanted Abel or Kelis to okay it. That wasn't a problem for either of them. Claris had been warded against magic, so it didn't matter if she saw the Tavern hunting the fursomnium.

Una dropped Jenny off at home, clutching her purchases. She kissed Rob and Abel on the cheek, for Christmas, and more or less skipped up her path. Rob, Kelis and Abel had agreed that if she could come up with a viable game character to wear late Victorian dress, Jenny could use the one in Castle House. The three of them weren't sure it would fit her, but were certain Jenny would get around it somehow.

*   *   *

Christmas morning Abel smiled quietly as his mum oohed and aahed over the pair of earrings with small gold leaves dangling from a central diamond. Later all four teenagers exchanged glances as Rob's mum and Kelis's showed off their necklace and brooch. None of them suspected the gifts were anything but paste or maybe crystal. They could compare because all three families spent most of Christmas at Kelis's house.

Mrs. Ventner didn't throw a party this year, because she didn't have the money. Instead the other two families took food around and helped to cook it and set out the table, so they all ate together anyway. Abel's mum supplied the cake, of course. The Tavern game, and the three mums being directors, had drawn the three families even tighter together over the last year. This time Melanie insisted on coming into Bonny's Tavern to play the game with them, so Ferryl couldn't cheat and Zephyr couldn't play. At least that gave the others a chance. Despite her still not being a playable character, Melanie insisted that today she could be Cackle the Crone. After all she had the hat, and a toy fox as her familiar.

The only slight hiccup came as Abel's and Rob's family left. A hare with white stripes sat in the middle of the lawn watching them. With a sudden pang of guilt, Abel realised that with Ferryl living in Kelis's house she must have forgotten to give the leech its daily magic. The sudden shocked look from Ferryl confirmed it, though she recovered. "Ooh, a pet hare. Who does it belong to?" Nobody knew so Ferryl, as Fay, insisted on petting it. The hare let her close, of course, so she could provide a good dose of magic while stroking its ears. By then Melanie had gone to stroke the hare, then Rob's older sister Samantha, until even the parents joined in. It added a really different, genuinely magical end to Christmas.

*   *   *

Over the next couple of days Abel found himself tempted again and again. He wanted to see his mum's face when she found out her earrings would buy her a replacement for her ailing car. Not new, but a good, reliable second-hand one. Abel would have loved to take her to a showroom and offer her anything she liked, but that could take a year or two. Kelis, Rob and Jenny were all tempted going by their occasional comments, but the big reveal had to wait until they'd been to town. That took some of the fun out of it, because they'd be meeting Creepio.

In the interim, the teenagers had a new skill to practice. They'd already practiced the theory to turn earth into almost-rock, but reaching deep inside their own skin would be a new application. Ferryl had wanted everyone to put a glyph under the skin for drawing extra magic from storage belts, so they didn't run out during a fight. They'd all perfected drawing the magic by putting a thumb on the belts, which didn't involve possible pain and scarring so the urgency had gone out of the skin glyphs. Now the trees in Dead Wood, and chunks of dead branch carried inside to avoid the weather, suffered magical assault. Again, and again the etching appeared on the surface, or the surface twisted and splintered, but gradually the visible damage grew less. At least the trainees could work on the test pieces in Castle House. Kelis's mum might have worried about them dragging branches into her house.

Practice had to stop for the meeting Creepio had arranged. Jenny's dad must have been pleased with her work on Bonny's Tavern, because he offered to run them all into town. He solved the usual problem of getting a driver to Brinsford, and at least this time having him along wouldn't cause any problems. This meeting, with a vicar, would allegedly address any problems the church had with Bonny's Tavern being linked to a leased church.

Abel phoned Creepio to tell him about Mr Forester, so the vicar could insist on talking to the actual designers of the game. After all these alleged meetings about it, Abel hoped the church finally let them have the place, especially now he could finance the lease through the allegedly charitable donations.

For once Jenny stayed relatively quiet and subdued on the way into town. So did the rest, there wasn't too much they wanted to discuss in front of an adult. Sure enough Mr. Forester insisted on having a quick word with the man wearing a vicar's dog collar before coming back to the car. "I'm still not totally sure why he doesn't want me present. He claims it's because he wants to talk openly about the moral background, and a parent might inhibit you. Don't sign anything and I'll sit here and wait.

Jenny, hit send if anything odd happens."

"He's a vicar, dad!"

"Who has had some very odd press sometimes. I'm not really worried, it's just a bit of dad paranoia." Everyone got out of the car sharpish before they got a lecture as well.

"It's good to see a protective parent." Creepio gestured to the door, but kept his eyes on Ferryl. "After you, ladies, gentlemen." He smiled, just briefly, as both Abel and Ferryl stopped to inspect the chapel.

"Faint signs of church magic, almost faded." Zephyr sounded eager, ready to do something, anything. Abel attempting to reach into wood bored her, because she could do it easily by partially blending into it. Ferryl looked at Abel and nodded so he went in. Definitely an abandoned chapel, there were cobwebs and an air of neglect but the seating seemed intact.

"The bishop can't go any further with the lease until he sees the result of this discussion." No small talk this time, Creepio leapt straight in as soon as everyone had found a seat. "There are two schools of thought in the church." He paused, a smile flickering briefly. "There are two thousand opinions, but in your case, they come down to two." He fixed Abel with a look. "The first believes that you are extremely dangerous and should be killed immediately, then the full weight of the Church Militant should descend on Castle House. Your friends would become collateral."

If he'd wanted them speechless, Creepio had succeeded. Kelis recovered first. "Which church? What do the other churches say?"

"In this case every church, or all the important ones in England. We may squabble in public over exactly how to spread our message but the Church Militant, the magical arm, is united. Not truly one, but we never fight among ourselves and will combine against threats to the one God." His eyes came back to Abel. "You have gone into Castle House and emerged unscathed. The argument is over eradicating you before you gain complete control of whatever is inside."

As he finished speaking Zephyr shot out of the tattoo, hurtling up and through some miniscule crack she found in the roof. Her connections zapped out to everyone but Creepio. "The fearless Ffod stands guard over the Tavern. I will tell you if an enemy approaches."

Creepio looked up to where the spooky-connections disappeared. "A watchdog? A good precaution after what I said." He turned to Ferryl. "Are you going to take precautions, Fay?"

Ferryl looked him straight in the eye. "I will take whatever action I need to if danger approaches."

"You don't think I am dangerous?" The vicar moved a finger towards his cross but without touching.

"You won't attack Abel on your own, not with us all here." Ferryl pointed to Abel, Kelis, and Rob. "Fire, Water, Earth, and I have a particular affinity for Air. That is a truly difficult combination to tackle. Jenny likes to switch about, and all the rest are adaptable if necessary. They all carry extra magic."

"And you are an unknown sorceress, who produced two very powerful and complicated glyphs from memory. I could dismiss the others, perhaps with some difficulty, except for you being here. Why is a real sorceress joining this happy band? Everyone else is an amateur, dangerous but not yet skilled. You looked like another amateur teenager when we first met, until you thought the ogre was attacking." Suspicion crept into his voice, and he kept glancing at the others to see how they reacted. "Have you made friends with Abel to gain access to Castle House?"

Creepio looked shocked when everyone laughed at him. "Fay has free access to the house whether I'm there or not, as do the other three. I trust them all, for various reasons." Abel narrowed his eyes, his face sober again. "I don't trust you."

"I know you don't. Creepio Mysterio, church investigator and possibly assassin. Sneaky, dangerous, magically powerful." His own eyes narrowed. "May betray you for a higher cause. That part of the character description is entirely true. Luckily I do not pay attention to those who find your game characters funny." Creepio's eyes swept across the group, resting on Ferryl again. "Personally, I find it useful for everyone to know who they are dealing with. What character do you play, Fay?"

"You already know or should. I am called Fay Shayde, so Ferryl Shayde the cat-sorceress. Or didn't you know where Abel came up with the name?" Ferryl watched surprise and then calculation appear on the vicar's face. "Abel Bernard Conroy helped me out of a great deal of trouble. I would take it very personally should anyone seek to harm him. That does include the church." She leant forward, meeting Creepio's look with her own.

Abel almost held his breath. He didn't think Creepio would appreciate a threat to the church. Several breaths passed without all hell breaking loose until Creepio slowly relaxed. "That is what I had to find out, your relationship to this young man and if he knew what you are. I am not afraid of you, Fay Shayde, as you well know, but I respect that kind of debt. You should know that I am not one of those who wish to attack your friend." He broke the eye-lock, shifting to look at a relieved Abel. "Though if the church had decided on that course, I would have helped. It is my calling. I had to speak to you for two reasons. Three really. Where is the host, the one who had the leech? Did you put it back in her?"

"No. She is safe and her body is healing. Her mind is destroyed so she sleeps while someone much better than me tries to put her life together." Every word gospel truth, so Abel didn't blush or falter. "The leech is hopping about in a hare with white stripes so the local poacher doesn't shoot it."

The burst of laughter from the vicar might have been more shocking than the threats of doom and gloom. "I might offer a prayer of thanks for that, just for the sheer effect it will have when the discussions get a little tense." His humour didn't last, or not completely, though the tone stayed lighter. "Another of the reasons for concern is your army. If any sorcerer gathered over thirty apprentices and trained them as you are doing, it would herald a magical war. Your neighbours would act to stop you. As it is, not a single one is tethered so they do not count as apprentices. They are simply a large group of young, partly trained warlocks or sorcerers with no allegiance to anyone."

"It might be a bad idea for anyone to think that means they can hurt any of us, or try to tether anyone without permission." Kelis smirked, getting back on balance. "We had to tell Pendragon that when he talked about recruiting. Nobody wanted to join him voluntarily."

"Who do you think has raised all the alarm about your possible army? Nobody paid any attention to him until you wiped out a nest of leeches, and word leaked out you defeated trolls and sorcerers." The vicar shook his head in disbelief. "I wondered myself, even after finding out the sorcerers were only senior apprentices. That attack looked very much like a power play by an arrogant new sorcerer or sorceress. Then you rescued a dying host from the middle of that mess, and killed those two seeds for me. Why didn't you ask for the village church as payment when you freed Father Curtis?"

"We'd have liked to, but we don't charge to save lives." Jenny smiled sweetly at him, her patent innocent one. "How are they all doing?"

Creepio even responded with a brief smile. "Both the young women are very well. Father Curtis lives, and may recover in time. Your reminder about the young ladies isn't necessary, because Amanda and Cecelia have already been told how they survived. They both want to meet their saviours. I suggest your refuge in Stourton, the big house." The old Creepio smile came back, along with his usual mocking tone. "That place really did throw the pitchforks and bonfires brigade off-course, as did using the income from the contracts to support the charity. Teeth were gnashed and beards pulled."

"Why do you find it funny when church leaders are upset?" Rob asked, but they'd all wondered now and then.

"For the same reason I am the peripatetic archbishop for the Church Militant in our fair country. I do not blindly follow dogma, I follow my heart and my faith. Sometimes the two clash." His humour died again. "Then I support my faith, always." Silence fell, with the vicar obviously thinking how to proceed and the others wondering what the last bit might mean.

"What about the third reason, or the first? The other one." Rob shrugged at the looks from the others. "Is there another? I lost count."

Creepio stirred, abandoning whatever he'd been thinking about. "That solves my problem, how to bring up the subject without being too abrupt. I must ask some very straightforward questions, ones I really hope you will answer." A wry smile might be admitting he couldn't force answers from them, or at having to ask carefully rather than demand. "Some people use ignorance to create a greater threat from a small one. I must know what type of glyphs you have learned, and have some indication of your skill. You, Kelis," he said, looking at her, "hid in plain sight of a priest aware of magic. I know how, I think, but need confirmation."

"A very super-fast anti-clockwise veil glyph to conceal us from even magical sight, while casting a clockwise one to extend it to conceal Rob and Jane Doe as well. We set it up behind nettles, so the leeches couldn't see an apparently bare bit of ground when the grass disappeared." Creepio opened his mouth but Kelis kept going. "I used a magic link from three trees, buried deep enough so even a dryad couldn't see it. I kept the veil going over an hour which hurts, believe me." Everyone heard her pride in the last part.

"I've never held one that long, but I believe you and that is exactly the sort of thing I need to know. Normally only an experienced sorcerer would even know the glyph, and only a very strong one would use it. I doubt more than half a dozen apprentices in the country have been taught how to hide from their masters. Rob?" His eyes moved across. "How did you hold an adult man captive with just earth?"

"The dryad helped. We did it between us. I could raise the earth and harden it but not enough to hold Father Curtis, so the dryad threaded roots together to create a reinforcing mesh. We made a slightly loose prison that never squeezed him so his ward wasn't threatened, but he couldn't get out. He panicked, which helped because it gave us the chance to capture his hands as well." Rob paused, glancing at the others before continuing. "You knew I could cast earth glyphs."

"Not those, to construct a solid earthen shell, though you have now explained that it wasn't completely solid. Your previous demonstration destroyed a small patch of road in Stourton, turned it to dust, which is easier as you pointed out at the time. Now I'm trying to assess how knowledgeable you are, and how adept, but not for the church. The church has decided to leave you all alone for now, largely based on your charitable actions and for saving leech victims." He didn't smile, but Creepio's face definitely lost its stern edges for a moment. "Especially Father Curtis. He is still in great distress but his faith is strong, so we believe he will recover in time. You will never know how much that means to some very influential people. I know you didn't do it for that, but take the credit and bank it."

"I thought the church had been considering killing us all? We can't have got much credit." Her tone matched Kelis's sour expression, because she'd really hoped someone in the church would be grateful.

"Unfortunately, some of what Father Curtis said caused real concern because he remembers his leech truly believing they faced Braeth Huntian. Only some fast, serious talking stopped a few rash individuals from heading to Brinsford loaded for something much worse than fraggons. It soon became clear he'd mixed up Claris being seeded with your claims of possession by Braeth Huntian and the appearance of Abel's passenger. I have already reported that Abel's shy friend is just a strong tethered spirit." A hint of a smile appeared again. "All of that is immaterial now. I need to assess your strength to get the Magical Council to back off."

"Why? You are the church, they are the heathen."

The smile widened as they all stared at the vicar. "True, Abel, but we have an Accord. We try not to fight each other, or have private wars rampage through our people. The Magical Council is all about power, and limiting the amount other sorcerers have. New sorcerers, those who qualified since the rule was made, are limited to eight senior apprentices. A sorcerer, or," he said, looking at Ferryl, "sorceress with as many apprentices as you seem to have could demand a seat on the Council and probably get it. My advice is don't be tempted; it's a cesspit. Knowing that, will you tell me the truth?" His trademark slightly supercilious smile appeared at last. "I think the truth will be enough to scare them glyphless. It will certainly back them off."

"We'll try. If we don't like where you are going?" Abel shrugged and the vicar nodded his acceptance.

Creepio wasn't kidding about wanting to know the full extent of their glyphs, though Fay didn't take part. According to the vicar, the Council would have to be satisfied with his assessment of her as an accomplished sorceress. For the rest of them, while he didn't want anything flashy, the vicar asked for small controlled demonstrations of some skills. Once he had what he wanted, the vicar moved on to the Taverners who weren't present. He didn't ask for names, though Abel, for one, felt sure he knew most, if not all of them. Instead Creepio seemed more interested in the breadth of glyphs taught, and the criteria for progressing. The idea of studying human biology before qualifying to learn how to heal themselves fascinated him, though he wouldn't mention the idea to the Council. He agreed with withholding the part about extended life, so that those who never progressed that far didn't feel deprived and bitter.

Eventually Creepio sat back and smiled, a big happy smile. "Definitely glyphless even if I won't give them the details, or even tell them who is capable of what. I certainly won't tell them you are giving away magic bars like penny toffees. I will just let the Council worry how these young people are progressing so fast because that should keep them wary. There are apprentices out there who would tear out their hair if they found out, which they won't. Their masters won't allow the knowledge to spread. Some men and women have given forty years of their lives and only just learned the first steps to self-healing, and have no background in human biology to help them. Others have never gone beyond air and maybe fire, because they are used as human batteries to fill up hexes to earn money for their masters. Your not-apprentices would tear through them like a fireball through a cornfield." Creepio paused, laughing quietly. "I'm getting a bit carried away, maybe."

"We wouldn't do that, attack others." Abel looked at his friends, who seemed just as startled. "We just want to be left alone."

"After I report, you will definitely be left alone. The Council will use your refusal to tether anyone as an official apprentice as a fig leaf, an excuse not to challenge you over exceeding the permitted limits. Right now, your not-apprentices might not actually rip the usual apprentices apart, but in a year they will. In the meantime, the Magical Council will equate skill and control when casting some glyphs with much greater skill in the lesser ones. That's the usual process, and why only senior apprentices would want to take on any of you four. Thirty of you? Forty?" He laughed again, obviously very happy with that idea. "Definitely glyphless."

"Why are you so happy? Aren't powerful people more dangerous if they feel threatened? Surely the Magical Council will be worried we are going to lead an uprising or rebellion, or just disobey them?" Jenny looked back and forth between the others. "That's what happens in books or films, the chiefs or rulers lash out at any threat."

"Not this time, and not just because we aren't strong enough to actually threaten the Council. They are a collection of the most powerful magic users and any one of them could probably wipe us all out, but a sorceress has hundreds of years of life to lose so she is cautious." Ferryl watched Creepio but she spoke to the other four. "One mistake and she is dead, or a bound servant, or a bound shade. Then all her years of learning, all her power and wealth, belong to someone else. Some of the most powerful sorceresses withdraw to strongholds, surrounding themselves with slaves, bound creatures and humans incapable of harming them." Creepio nodded gently as she continued. "Now it has been put like this, I think I understand. A concentration of reasonably adept magic users like ours, uncontrolled, will stop any lesser sorcerer starting a war in case some or all of us align with the other side."

Creepio bowed towards her while remaining seated. "Exactly. Peace, sorceress, blessed peace. While not individually powerful, thirty of you could easily tip most disputes one way or the other. If you are attacked, you may find others offering help just to gain your support elsewhere. I suggest asking Woods and Green to take some minor part in the legal affairs of your game and charity. Their clients are sometimes killed, but if the first strike fails, Woods in particular is well known for negotiating lethal combinations of allies so their clients usually win. They also tend to do well in the legal wrangling over reparations if neither side is wiped out. All for a hefty price of course."

"So, this Council is using us as a sort of balance? That doesn't seem a particularly clever idea, letting a bunch of uncontrolled amateurs get more and more powerful." Abel looked from Creepio to Ferryl and shook his head. "They should stamp us out now, use their minions or whatever so they aren't harmed."

"Possibly true, if they could all agree, but some of them will not risk killing the master of Castle House. You are their first chance to get at whatever Celtchar left in there for over a hundred years. Rumour insists at least two Council members tried to get into Castle House and disappeared without trace. Now you have succeeded, but if you die before reaching the centre they may never find another blood relative." He stood up and stretched. "I will apologise to your father, Jenny, for not including him in this discussion. I have explained that I had to assess the overall moral stance of you five, personally, and your game. He will be pleased to find that neither your personal beliefs nor the game are at odds with the aims of mother church herself. That is the truth as it happens, loosely speaking."

"We get the church? To lease I mean." Kelis came to her feet, a big smile starting.

"You get to meet the bishop to persuade him face to face, or rather Abel does. Your local bishop voted to watch and wait, so I am hopeful. He knows Father Curtis, personally. To show my own appreciation for your efforts with Father Curtis, I should mention that the sorcerer who once controlled Elmwood Park is long dead. His protection has lapsed, but Pendragon never bothered to take over because the only adult tree left has a dryad. You could claim the park for your Tavern? The other trees will soon be old enough for dryads, which means big enough to supply you and yours with magic." The happy smile had a large slice of malicious. "Pendragon is unlikely to make a fuss about anything just now." With that Creepio turned and walked out!

*   *   *

"As usual, I had another million questions." For once Kelis didn't seem too upset.

The five of them turned to each other, smiling at Kelis's usual complaint after any meeting with Creepio. "But we get a good report from Creepio, he'll back off the Magic Council, and the bishop dealing with the lease likes us!" As Jenny finished, the Taverners came together in a completely spontaneous group hug. Even so Abel took care not to hug Kelis, or she avoided him, but right now that didn't bug him as much as usual. When they parted Ferryl kept hold of Abel's hand. "I enjoyed being able to admit what I am. Perhaps we can slowly let the rest of the Tavern know? Not that I am the one who lived in your arm, just the sorceress part. Then if there is trouble, I won't need to hold back." Abel squeezed her hand for yes, because Zephyr had them all connected now and Ferryl obviously wanted to keep this private.

"I win the sweepstake, I think." Jenny pointed at the joined hands. "The reassuring hand holder strikes again."

For once Abel just laughed, because the idea of an ancient magical being as a girlfriend was ridiculous. "I thought I'd try it with a girl who isn't enchanted or being rescued."

"C'mon Rob, try it." Jenny took his hand.

"Maybe it's an older woman thing. He's been headed that way with you and Claris." Kelis caught hold of Rob's other hand as they came out through the door and Jenny took Abel's so the five ended up hand

147

in hand. Creepio, about to get into his car, looked at them and then up at Zephyr and shook his head. This was how they usually faced him at Castle House. Laughing at his expression, the group split up and headed for the Mercedes.

At least Mr. Forester didn't want details. He always claimed the actual game confused him, because his brain had already fossilised. Instead he seemed really happy about the church approving, and had done what Rob once suggested in jest. The vicar had apparently laughed when asked about advertising Bonny's Tavern on church noticeboards. Mr Forester treated them all to frothy coffees, then turned them loose for an hour in town. According to her dad, joining Jenny in a walk around town would be an invitation to bankruptcy.

The walk didn't take long, just enough time to get a couple of pieces of jewellery priced. The shop assistants should remember the gang of excited kids who'd struck lucky buying from a market stall. On the way back to the car Jenny confirmed that her mum loved the ring she'd been given for Christmas, but she didn't wear it much. Probably worried she might damage the paste diamonds or wear off the gold plating, but that would soon change.

*   *   *

Abel felt sure everyone else felt as tempted as him once they were home but they'd all agreed to break the news as casual comments, the following morning over breakfast. He cheated a little bit, getting up early. Once he'd made a bowl of porridge, it was porridge weather right now, Abel braced himself. Casual, he reminded himself, once again. "When we went to town, Jenny took a ring into a jewellers to get it priced."

"For insurance? If we could afford insurance I'd have a job finding something worth putting on it." Abel's mum looked around the kitchen. "Maybe the TV and digibox?"

"Maybe your earrings? Maybe not, because we aren't sure where we bought everything. Jenny wanted costume jewellery for her character and we bought job lots from several stalls so there'd be spares for others." Abel glanced at his mum, but she wasn't getting the message. "We all gave our mums jewellery for Christmas, because when we collected it all together some pieces looked really nice, better than the rest."

His mum reached up and tapped the leaves on her earring to set them swinging. "Very nice, which is why I'm wearing them. As nice as anything else I've got."

"The thing is, Jenny priced up one of the other nice rings yesterday. It's real. Proper gold and diamonds, but old stuff." He almost held his breath as his mum froze for a moment, then reached up towards her ear.

She very carefully took off the earring and put it on the table, then put her hand next to it. "That rock might be real? It's bigger than the one on my engagement ring, and your dad splashed out on that. Spent his bonus." She reached up to take off the other one, laid it with the first and sighed. "If they're real I'll sell them and put the money into Bonny's Tavern."

"No!" Abel put out a hand as his mum jumped. "Sorry. No, don't. Sell them if you like, but I gave them to you so you keep the money. Promise?" He managed to force a laugh. "After all they might not be real. Most of the rest is obviously plastic and glass."

"There's only one way to find out, providing the car will start." She picked the earrings up and put them back in. "I may as well show them off in case they've got to go."

"You can keep them anyway? The others might." Abel clammed up but too late.

"Terri's and Jess's presents as well?"

"They all might be real, or none of them." Abel knew full well every piece held real diamonds and gold, because Ferryl had looked into them. "You can take Kelis's mum in the BMW, and Rob's mum if she wants to know." He smiled happily. "You might finally meet Jenny's mum, in the same shop."

"Jenny as well? What about Kelis's new lodger? Fay Shayde? Did she get jewellery for Christmas? Is she another secret girlfriend?" Abel wasn't sure if the smile might be winding him up, or seriously trying to find out.

"No, but that's where the name for our sorceress came from. Kelis's internet friend who got to know all of us and then became a beta." He shrugged casually. "That's why she came to England when her mum and dad died. From what she's let slip, her family were reclusive and a bit odd, even if I'd never say that to her, so she didn't really have friends."

"I got all that from Jess. Even so, that's a big move for a young girl." Abel recognised that tone, Mum on the scent, except there wasn't anything to find out. "Come on, eat up. I'll call Jess and Terri, and Jake so I can talk to his wife. What's her name?"

"Pass? Jenny's mum? I met her twice. She probably told me but I can't remember." Abel swallowed more porridge, then stopped eating. "You don't need me."

"Yes, we do, all of you, and the rest of that jewellery. Whose is it?"

"Ours? The Tavern's? We bought all sorts of junk for costumes because it only cost a few quid." Abel looked at his dish. "We won't all fit in the car, not even in the BMW."

"So, some of us go in Terri's or get Jake to bring his family over in that great big Mercedes and collect any spares. Now eat up." As his mum started calling, Abel gave up and ate.

*　　*　　*

Jenny had still been working up to telling her mum, Stephanie. Rob's mum, Terri, had thought he was winding her up. Kelis's mum had placed her brooch next to the engagement ring she intended selling anyway, compared the rocks, and told Kelis that either her husband totally stiffed her over the ring or the brooch was real. Since the engagement ring had been to impress his new model girlfriend and had been shown to all her friends, the chances were that it was real.

Abel ended up in the Mercedes with Jenny and Ferryl, because according to his mum, "We should keep him with his mystery women." If he hadn't already known the truth, Abel would have been worried by now because his mum already thought her earrings must be the real thing. The disappointment if they weren't would have been a real downer. The rest of the trip went to plan. The shop assistants recognised the five teenagers, and the ring Jenny had shown them, and were happy to confirm both to the parents.

Abel had wondered about the next part, but sorting through the big heap of cheap glitter didn't take the adults long. A few pieces needed a closer look before going into the reject heap but soon all the real gems and gold were laid out on the counter. Mr. Forester wanted to know who actually bought what, but all five swore they had no idea. At least the rejects kept Melanie and Jenny's sister Diane occupied as they sorted through the heap for some brooches that might be witch's curses.

Once she realised there wouldn't be any real stuff heading towards big sisters, Samantha settled for helping the two younger girls sort through the rest. After Rob waved a casual hand when she asked about a necklace, the trio set into the bag of tat in earnest. Meanwhile the negotiations started over the cost of a real appraisal of each valuable item. When sell or keeping the items came up, Abel pounced. He suggested the mums might want to sell their Christmas presents, maybe to buy a better car or TV, if the gems were good enough.

For now, the valuables went into the little velvet lined boxes Mr. Forester bought, though four of the items stayed firmly attached to four mothers. Each family would decide what to do about the gifts, while the teenagers and their parents would discuss what to do with the rest. There wasn't a fortune, but if Abel, Jenny, Rob, Kelis, and Fay invested the proceeds it would mean Jenny's dad would no longer be the only real investor in Bonny's Tavern. Abel expected close questioning about Fay getting a share. To celebrate the windfall, Mr. Forester suggested lunch for everyone, including Fay. He meant a proper restaurant, so as Abel pointed out it was a good job he'd learned to eat peas without a spoon. He tried to keep his mouth full to avoid the questioning.

When they got home Abel soon knew what his mum had decided. She really did like the earrings but couldn't afford to keep them, not if they would replace her car. It failed to start about one day in three, so she ended up relying on the minimal bus service to get to her part-time job. She'd ended up missing out on extra work over the holidays. Abel diverted her by talking about the rest of the stuff. He'd already decided to try and find out where mum sold the earrings, and to get Woods and Green to buy them. One day, in a year or two when he'd got legitimate money of his own, he could accidentally find them in a shop.

Eventually his mum came round to the other subject Abel had dreaded, Fay. Abel stuck to his guns. Fay had bought some of the heap of rubbish, maybe the good stuff, so she got a share. He felt sure the others were getting similar earache.

Monster Hunt

Despite some definite heart-searching and genuine regret, all the mums, but Jenny's would sell their Christmas presents. Stephanie Forester considered selling to donate the money to the charity side of Bonny's Tavern, but Jenny persuaded her not to. The rest would go to really good causes, in a way. A car for Abel's mum, a new three-piece suit for Rob's mum, and cash in the bank for when Kelis' mum had to move. Jess would have extra, because after some negotiation Rob's mum wanted to buy the furniture from Kelis's snug and use the rest of her windfall for a TV.

The children kept out of it, because they had their own plans to make. Jenny had come up with a way to wear the dress she'd found in Castle House, as a steampunk character. That would take serious adaptation, so Jenny searched through the rest of the dressing room. Either the sorcerer did a lot of cross-dressing, or he kept his girlfriends' clothes when they left. A quick check on the internet showed that some were over three hundred years out of date, but those would need work for Jenny to wear them. Eventually Jenny found an off the shoulder gown that looked like a French one on the internet, from the mid-eighteen hundreds, one without a really wide skirt or a bustle on the back.

A pale blue almost transparent skirt covered in embroidered flowers had been pulled up at the sides to show off the deep blue of the floor length dress. The lace around the top that left her neck and shoulders bare was probably a bit racy back then, but well within dad approval zones now. With the petticoats pushing the skirt out it looked nothing like any game character costume, but Jenny didn't care. She could even wear her own modern, comfortable shoes under it, safely out of sight.

Abel asked Kelis if she wanted to raid the clothing, but she pointed out with a big smirk she already owned an outfit that had the desired effect. He couldn't argue with that, though he thought a couple of the lighter coloured cloaks in Castle House might suit her Sorceress Windcatcher ensemble.

Abel couldn't find anything in his size to start with, except hats and cloaks, until he looked at the casual clothing. He found a pair of old-fashioned leather jeans, buckskin breeches, and a shirt. A couple of hours spent carefully drawing the allegedly magical symbols from the Bonny's Tavern game onto his leather vest, and he had Wind Chaser's costume. All the boots he found were a bit big, but he could wear two or three pairs of socks for one night. Abel had two Angry Birds balloons filled with helium as pretend sprites because the real one could fly around in the open at this party.

Rob had worked on his Roughly Hewn, especially on the torn shirt which now sported several wooden badges showing similar symbols to those on Abel's jerkin. The big plastic sword, slung across his back in a rough sheath made from sacking, definitely looked better than his old papier-mâché club. After inspecting the buckskin breeches, Rob went for a pair as well, though they fit him better. Pathetic pleading to Samantha persuaded her to help him fix loops so he could wear a belt instead of braces.

Ferryl just laughed when asked about costumes and pointed out she'd be herself. To avoid confusion with Petra, her fur and face would match Abel's tattoo and she'd create a skirt so Petra could wear shorts. Her tail would have been a problem because if people touched a seeming their hand would go through, but Kelis had the answer. Next-day delivery brought an electric tail, bought on the internet. A phone call to Petra also meant the real Ferryl Shayde would have a real leather skirt instead of a seeming over a fabric one.

*   *   *

The first surprise on New Year's Eve was the chauffeur. Abel had suggested a taxi, but Laurence offered to come and drive the BMW. Not alone, he turned up with another young man, one of the cousins he introduced as Emst. That made him the cousin, the one Kelis seemed keen on talking to in German. While they waited outside for the two girls, Abel kept half an eye on him to see the effect of the full Glyphmistress look. Emst would have only seen a toned-down version at one dance, just before Kelis and Laurence broke up. Then Abel forgot the cousin, because Kelis caught him out as well.

Abel had assumed Firstseed's clothes were thrown away. They were bloody, muddy, might be too tight even for Kelis, and she'd never wear that leather anyway. Kelis wouldn't even want the red cloak, because she still didn't like Ferryl talking about red being the right colour for a

153

bloody-handed sorceress. That didn't stop Ferryl from trying, but Kelis seemed determined to be a gentler sort of magic user.

The crimson cloak now swathing Kelis meant Abel had been completely wrong, and definitely tended towards the bloody-handed look. He still wasn't properly prepared for Kelis opening the cloak to give them a twirl. She'd kept the lot, the long boots and the form-fitting leather catsuit, and added her black driving gloves. Abel tried to shut his mouth, or breath, because with her sorceress hairstyle and makeup, that really did take his breath away.

"Sniggleflitting heck." Rob's voice squeaked a bit, probably shocked.

After fighting back a laugh and snatching a breath, Abel answered. "I second that, whatever it means. Gobsmacked?" He almost said 'snugglefitting,' but that would be too near the truth.

"No, that'll be the other two suckers. Especially the German sucker." Rob sniggered, definitely recovering. "Someone should shove his eyes back in."

Kelis smirked happily, satisfied by the reaction. She started forwards, waving to Laurence. "I thought I'd better wear something tougher if we'll be chasing monsters. Ah. Right." She looked at Emst, suddenly uncertain.

Laurence recovered enough to lift a hand and say hi. "Don't worry, Emst knows we are putting on a show. He's hoping he doesn't doze off and miss it." Abel understood the glance at his shoulder. Laurence wanted a glyph to make sure his cousin slept through the hunt.

A familiar voice with a touch of German accent interrupted. "Surely not." Abel knew exactly what to expect, but hadn't properly processed the full effect. He'd got used to the miniature Ferryl Shayde wandering about on his arm, and now Zephyr could control the tattoo to do so again. A completely accurate version the same height as him came as a shock, because she even had the big green eyes. He'd mentioned the ones on the tattoo were unrealistic but Kelis and Ferryl found clips on the internet where women were putting on anime eyes. The whiskers stuck out as well, rather than Petra's drawn-on versions while Ferryl's darker skin made the whole effect more realistic somehow. "Will you be sleeping, Emst?" Abel cursed under his breath, because Emst perked up when he heard the hint of accent. He answered in German!

Probably German, Abel privately conceded, because he didn't know. He certainly didn't expect a stream of the same coming back, or a more halting but still definitely foreign contribution from Kelis. Kelis came past him on her way to the car, where Laurence had opened the front door. "I made a wit." Now he watched her in a different type of shock. Abel had managed to get to his shin bone, but it hurt when he tried to scribe on it. Kelis always did get obsessed with a new glyph and usually mastered them first, but she'd outdone herself this time.

Abel wondered for a minute how everyone would fit in the BMW, but Emst headed for Laurence's car. He definitely glanced hopefully at Ferryl, but she nudged Rob. "Go on Rob. You can learn German." In a lower voice she continued, "Too close for too long and he might realise these eyes aren't makeup."

Rob opened his mouth, to volunteer Abel from his glance, then smirked and shook his head. "Watch out Abel. You know the effect fur had on me." He turned towards the smaller car. "Hard luck Emst. Abel wants to hold hands with his new pet."

*   *   *

Ferryl really did hold Abel's hand during the trip, so she could make jokes about Laurence. Most of them were about how it was lucky Kelis wrapped the cloak around her as she sat down, or he'd have run off the road. The others had to do with Laurence's tights, because he'd finally found striped ones for his costume. Abel kept quiet, because he'd started worrying about Ferryl's outfit. If she danced with anyone and they put an arm round her they'd realise the fur was a seeming. Nobody in the Tavern could cast a seeming on skin yet, only on cloth over the skin.

Abel stopped worrying when Laurence drew up outside the big country house. Maybe it was because they'd had time and some had become more competitive over costumes, maybe because these were all the people who could throw glyphs, not just flutter a leaf, or maybe they'd all made a special effort because they'd be in a real stately home. For whatever reason, the Taverners had produced a dazzling array of costumes.

The first one Abel noticed made him smile. A wide-brimmed black hat, a black cloak and a plain black collarless jacket, and trousers could be anyone. The big white cross on a chain, the white dog-collar and the way he kept creeping up behind people made this one Creepio Mysterio. Despite what he'd said, Abel didn't think the vicar would find it amusing. The rest of the costumes were just as good.

There were no bits of rope for tails, roughly drawn symbols on old pin-on badges, or a fancy jacket, hat or boots with otherwise ordinary clothes. Some costumes were relatively simple. The two rugby players had come as Champ the Bouncer and a frost giant, with their physique providing most of the costume. Someone had a cloak and a wolf's head, probably from Halloween costumes, but the furry forearms and shins looked real. "A seeming over bandages." Abel realised that he still held Ferryl's hand and she'd seen him looking at the wolf-sorcerer.

"It's a good job I improved my costume." Everyone here knew about Zephyr and spooky-phone so Abel may as well use it. "How much of this is seemings?"

"Not that much. Several people are using magic to create fur, or unusually coloured skin or hair, and one is making his shoes look like boots. Many of them are using makeup for the main effect, then adding just a little extra. Very ingenious, and that uses less magic than a full seeming." Ferryl waved to Rob and Emst as they came over, followed by Petra with a huge smile on her face.

"No fair! If you weren't the real deal, the original Fay Shayde, I'd be really ticked off about now. You've even found the same fur pattern as the tattoo." Petra sighed dramatically. "Upstaged. Though looking around this lot, I'm going to have to invest in the electric tail to keep up." She looked closer. "Ooh, I want to know where the eyes and whiskers came from."

A mental giggle from Ferryl meant she wasn't too worried. "It's a good job I actually looked them up on the internet, or Kelis did. I'd better pretend I haven't met all these people before." She introduced herself properly and explained where the makeup came from, promising to send Petra the web address. Her hand held on as Abel started to move away. "Keep hold, then if I make a mistake I'll swear that Ferryl Shayde told me their names."

"Not hand holding. Zephyr can do that."

"Except she'll be talking to lots of people at once. This way Ferryl allegedly tells me privately through skin contact." Her laugh echoed in Abel's head. "A girl should have a date for New Year, and I'm new to England. Tomorrow I'll walk away and leave you broken-hearted. Unless you were hoping to catch someone special under the mistletoe?"

"No, and that includes sorceresses with a warped sense of humour who hide in furry seemings." Abel noticed Kelis's pointed look at their hands and asked Zephyr to explain to her, Rob and Jenny. Zephyr told him Jenny wasn't here, not quite, because her Dad's Mercedes was still coming up the driveway.

Mr Forester got out to open the door for his daughter, but forgot for a moment. Instead he stood there staring around at about thirty young people in extravagant costumes, creatures and people he'd only seen as drawings in a game. He shook his head, opened the door, and said something as he swept an arm to invite Jenny out. Some sort of joke by the laugh on her face as Jenny stood up. Abel wasn't sure if Mr Forester had deliberately come a little later so his daughter got her entrance, but it worked.

A ripple of quiet swept across the Taverners as they turned to see what had caught other people's attention. Jenny wasn't dressed as any game character, which made her stand out. The Victorian dress suited Jenny perfectly, her hair had been put up the same as the internet picture, and either Jenny had a secret jewellery box or her mum had donated dangly earrings and a necklace. "Have you invented a new character, Jenny?" Laurence strode forward, his hand out to her dad. "Don't worry Mr Forester, we'll summon a fairy coach to get her home."

"There's a taxi booked for twelve-fifteen, so no need. Don't worry, I've had the lecture about fathers hovering at dances." Mr Forester waved a greeting to Laurence's parents, stood at the top of the steps to their house. "Though it looks like you are stuck with yours. I'm going home to read the paperwork for that game, and try to work out who all these people are supposed to be." He shook his head with a rueful smile. "I'll be looking under the bed before sleeping and probably have nightmares." With that he got into the car and drove off.

"Whew. I'm sure he'd have disguised himself and stayed if he could work out how to." Jenny put down her school bag, gave a twirl and giggled.

"Well?"

"Out of costume, definitely. Unless there's a new one?" Laurence turned to Kelis, which meant Jenny got a good look at the leather and cape and then Ferryl. The conversation descended into accusations of keeping secrets, and plotting to introduce more characters just to keep the rest on their toes. There'd definitely be a sorceress in leather and a crimson cloak, a real baddie. The big floppy hat with a huge plume that Laurence produced from the boot of his car came in for its own share of admiration and ridicule. Despite worrying about looking outlandish, Abel now found he didn't feel the slightest bit conspicuous.

*   *   *

The first hour, up to 9:30 PM, went like any other party. The buffet took a hammering while people who rarely met outside school, or not even there, exchanged news. Most of it, the conversations away from the two cousins and Laurence's parents, involved how they'd progressed with glyphs and who had recently discovered magic. Eventually all the twenty-nine Taverners had met Ferryl Shayde, and none called her Fay after the first introduction. Abel knew that, including himself and his four friends, there were now fifty-five locals who could flutter a leaf, with another seven further afield. Frederick and Effy were getting better with glyphs but had begged off tonight, both worried about fighting a large, dangerous monster. Eight of the less able users wouldn't be safe here tonight and another nine were too young. At least the rate of discovery had slowed down.

A slight undercurrent of excitement built as Zephyr passed messages and the Taverners moved into position. Kelis went to sit on one of the chairs along the wall, inviting the two cousins to sit with her so she could practice her German. Other Taverners spread out through the house. When Zephyr reported that there were Taverners near to every member of staff, Abel asked Zephyr to contact Laurence and Jenny. "All ready. Bring them in."

Laurence, with Jenny on his arm, brought his parents into the ballroom where two easy chairs had been arranged at one end. "We need judges for the fancy dress. I'm barred, because you'll be biased about me, and Jenny isn't in game costume, but the rest are really keen." As Laurence explained, most of the Taverners began to form pairs. Kelis kept the cousins in place by making a big show of choosing one as a partner.

"Everyone ready." Abel started to pour magic into the steel glyph Ferryl had made. As the magic built up everyone in the house who didn't have a ward felt sleepy, then fell asleep. The Taverners quickly made them comfortable and hung Dreamcatchers around each sleeper's neck. Ferryl had spent hours creating a metal sleep glyph so it had a wider, stronger effect. She'd also turned the reels of steel wire into gold and created magical gems from the crystals she'd bought before Christmas. The other four had spent a similar number of hours bending and joining wire into glyphs, then fixing and filling the gems to make cheap decorations into genuine magical dream protection.

"Give me a minute." Jenny headed for the door. "This isn't a monster-bashing dress." Several other Taverners, the ones in the more fragile costumes, headed for the door as well. When Jenny came back everyone knew what had been in the bag, jeans, sweatshirt and trainers. Others came back in wearing similar clothes, while some like Laurence just put jeans or a jacket over part of their costume. Kelis took off her cloak, because it wasn't very practical for chasing about in. She seemed oblivious to the reaction from several of the lads when they got a proper look at her in the form-fitting leather.

"Will you be able to keep that up and throw magic? Won't you run out?"

Ferryl smirked, which Abel thought was a hell of a look with the whiskers. "I've got some of the new diamonds set into my bone and filled with magic. Since the wits were going to hurt going in, I decided to make it worthwhile. If the seeming slips a bit the skirt is real and I'm wearing a crop top under here." She turned away from Abel. "Okay, where's this monster we're supposed to kill?"

"How good are you at glyphs Ferryl, er, Fay?" Warren looked worried, as did some of the others. This would be a serious fight according to Ferryl Shayde, the one in Abel's arm.

"My dad was a warlock, but I never told Kelis until I got here and found out how much she and the others already knew." Fay raised her hand and a tiny fire glyph enclosed in wind danced across the room.

"Don't waste magic. We may need it." Kelis looked around the room where several people had raised hands to join in. "Has everyone banished any seemings? You can't afford the wastage right now." The wolf-sorcerer looked guilty and his fur turned to bandages. Eric had already taken off the head so he could see better.

Abel turned as the last two Taverners came in, pulling on jackets. "Ferryl will be trying to keep everyone organised, but if she can't you'll all have to remember the important part. We have to drive the fursomnium out of the house, into the open where we can be sure of killing it. Once we surround it, don't let even a fragment get away to find another victim." He beckoned to Laurence. "We've got a treat for you. Let me have your rapier for a minute."

"I'm not allowed to...." Laurence looked at his sleeping parents and his face hardened. "There are several swords on the dining room wall. Genuine ones with steel blades. Who wants one?" As half a dozen people rushed off to collect the weapons he handed the rapier to Abel, hilt first. "I didn't think they'd hurt magical creatures."

"But you knew my wooden bat did, you just need the same addition." Rob held up the bag he'd just brought from the BMW. "Extra Tavern hexes, already charged. I need volunteers to lay them out to guide the fursomnium out of the house. If it looks like breaking past them, hit it with everything." He glanced at Laurence. "Try to avoid fire in the house, or be very controlled."

"I'll take the blame for a few little scorch marks if necessary." Laurence looked upwards towards the attic. "I get the creeps just thinking about that thing lurking up there, even if it is asleep."

"Look at this lot!" Una came in with a sword in each hand. "Can I have one of these instead of my fake one?"

"For magical bashing, your fake one works just as well." Abel put his palm on the blade of Laurence's rapier, then snatched it away leaving a small Tavern hex burned into the steel. "Give that a moment or two and I'll fill it with magic."

"I'll do that bit." Kelis blew on the blade. "I'd use air but I'm saving magic." As Abel put his palm over the next blade, she spilled magic into the hex.

"Will you have enough magic?" Petra held out a curved sabre. "We don't want you running dry later."

"I brought enough." Abel wore four of the belts made of small gold blocks linked with gold wire, each one holding at least eight lead bars' worth of magic. He'd wondered why Ferryl gave him her magic belts, even when she claimed they would be hard to hide under her costume. The remark about diamonds in bone explained, she'd got a better way.

Ferryl reached for Petra's sabre. "I've got extra lead bars just for this." Not really, but she'd probably got more spare magic than anyone else. "So has Kelis." Kelis had her hand inside the leather suit where she'd unzipped it at the neck, and would be holding her supersized magic diamond.

"Come here Eric." Jenny waved him over and gently slapped him at the side of the head. "How much magic did the seeming for the fur use up?"

"Not that much." Despite being two years older, Eric looked like a kid getting scolded by mum. "Quite a bit, but I wanted it to look right and I brought the extra lead bars I use for the contracts."

"Then it's a good job I brought extra magic as well. Give me the one you've used." Jenny had two gold belts and her diamond, so she'd got plenty to spare. A few moments later she handed the lead bar back with a grin. "Now behave." She raised her voice. "Anyone else use up magic on a seeming?" Several others congregated round her and Kelis.

"What about you, Rob? Can you give me some magic?" Rob rolled his eyes but topped up magic bars as three of his fan club gathered round.

Meanwhile Abel and Ferryl quickly worked through eight swords and sabres. Abel stopped at the last weapon. "Crikey, who's going to use that?"

The frost giant pushed forwards, picked up the long-handled axe and hefted it. "I can do it. Just don't get in the way when I swing." He swung it, but very gently. "This will be a lot better than punching, though I'd better not use it indoors."

"In that case you'll be waiting when we drive it outside. We'll want you and a few others to make a line and try to slow it until we get out of the house." Abel burned the little hex into the blade and shook his hand. "I'll have a blister if I'm not careful."

"Just one more. Can I have a bigger hex please?" Una fluttered her eyelashes, but her laugh spoiled the effect. "After all, you won't be taking mine off me again."

Abel shook his head but did as she asked, though this time Kelis used a tiny reverse heat glyph so she didn't have to wait before filling the hex with magic. "There you go, extra zap in there as well. Robin D'Ritche would pay for the best."

"Pay? Hah, steal the best." Una peered at the sword, squinting a bit. "It's got a tiny red glow like the hexes we fill up on the houses."

"I told you, extra zap." Kelis glanced at Abel. They sometimes forgot the rest of the Taverners hadn't been given the Ferryl eye-boost. Even the small active hexes glowed to the four who had, and that reminded Abel of something else.

"Zephyr, ask Rob, Kelis, Ferryl and Jenny to help me if the creature gets somewhere really dark. The others won't be able to see as well as we do." The spooky-phone zapped out and all four nodded. A general movement started towards the ballroom door, with the swords being taken by those with the least skill in casting glyphs. The three armed teenagers going outside took two strong glyph-casters to back them up.

*   *   *

Getting everyone into place, and setting the hexes to herd the fursomnium down a given path, took time. Again and again Zephyr shot out her connections to move someone a little, to tighten the trap. While they did, Abel wanted a quick word with Ferryl. "What happens if the fursomnium gets a firm grip on someone?"

"Their ward should fend it off, stop it getting a clean connection. Even so it could damage them. We must keep at arm's length." She looked around at all the Taverners getting into position. "We'll have to be quick, cut off any connection before it gets a real grip on their mind." Her hand caught hold of Abel's. "If I had my wits we'd have shields!"

Zephyr cut most of her connections so the others didn't hear Abel. "What about that slippery type protection glyph you used when we chased the Aryadne's hound? You said that made it harder for a glyph to catch hold." Abel had been thinking about it, and the next bit made sense to him. "Will it stop a magical creature getting a grip?"

"Of course! Stupid, stupid, stupid me! I am used to casting big, powerful glyphs, not the type a witch would use." Ferryl looked around at the Taverners again. "Is there time for them to learn?"

"I learned it when I'd barely started, while walking across a field at night. All these are a lot better than I was then, and you taught me in minutes." Abel tapped his tattoo. "We don't even have to tell them individually."

"Brilliant." The hug surprised Abel, because Ferryl wasn't the spontaneous type. Maybe it was the excitement of the hunt. "Ask Zephyr to connect please. This glyph will help to protect her as well." Heads began to turn as Zephyr connected. From the relieved smiles as the Taverners carefully drew the glyph with their fingers and activated it, Abel didn't think he was the only one who'd been worried.

In a surprisingly short time everyone reported they were ready. The strongest glyph casters climbed to the attic to launch the attack, the five with the most magic tucked away and the most practice. The real reason only five people led the assault was that most of the bulbs in the attic had failed. The end of the corridor lay in darkness, so nobody else would see the fursomnium properly, though the rest didn't know that.

"Is it stirring yet?" Kelis peered into the gloom. "You said all the extra hexes downstairs might disturb it."

"It's stirring, but the next ones will wake it. Be ready." Ferryl turned to Abel, reaching out a hand to hold his. "It's time." Jenny put her hand on top of Abel's and Ferryl's, with Kelis and Rob quickly adding theirs. Zephyr wrapped around them all.

Kelis raised the joined hands. "For luck. One for all. The Taverners are go." She let go and glyphs began to build in both hands. "Whenever you like, Abel."

"Dream bop!"

"Now, before I need an emergency toilet break." For once Rob's humour didn't lighten the mood.

Abel and Ferryl crept forward, past the closed doors of the old servants' quarters up in the attic. The fursomnium sprawled in there, spreading through the walls across several rooms and under the floor of the corridor. Abel paused, looking at the third door. "Aren't we past yet?"

"No, it's bigger than I thought so hurry up. I can feel it above us and on both sides, and it is waking." Two doors later, nearly at the end of the corridor, Ferryl stopped. "Quickly now, or it will surround us." She turned left and Abel turned right, each opening the last two doors their side and throwing a hex inside the small, dusty rooms. "Three, two, one, go!" Both of them cast reverse wind glyphs down the corridor, dragging open doors. Halfway down the corridor Kelis and Jenny did the same as Rob finished throwing hexes into the empty rooms at that end. Zephyr hovered, spooky-phone connecting through the floor to warn the Taverners below. The fursomnium, dream stealer, infiltrated rooms by extending webs through the walls so the Taverners below slapped hexes onto the walls it had claimed.

Something scratched the inside of Abel's brain, or so it felt. "The wards aren't working!" Rob scratched at his head, then Jenny did the same. Kelis looked irritated, both hands filled with glyphs.

"Yes they are! That is pain and anger. The hexes downstairs are hurting the fursomnium as they attack its webs. Be ready." Ferryl needn't have bothered with the last bit. As Zephyr told the Taverners below to ignore the itchy feeling, and those in the attic stopped scratching and concentrated on glyphs, the creature boiled out of eleven little rooms. Zephyr snatched a connection back as a limb reached for it. Ferryl had warned that this creature could use them to get inside a person's head.

"Fly free Zephyr."

"The Ffod flies into battle!" Abel felt the tether part, because the fursomnium might even get into his connection. He had been rotating his cupped palms, facing each other but well apart as if smoothing a big snowball. Now he hurled the result, an ice ball, into the heaving mass filling the corridor. Even as he did so, Abel reflected that trying to suck out his brains didn't stop the fursomnium from being pretty. A faintly luminous, transparent pale blue cloud billowed and flowed, full of tiny sparks of light. The effect would be downright peaceful if it wasn't for those long tentacle-like limbs. Each one ended with a large web like a spider's, the edges waving and reaching for him.

"That's all wrong." Kelis sounded really upset. "Monsters shouldn't be pretty. Die, lovely nasty thing." Abel could see her right through the fursomnium. Kelis's long ice spear flew towards him, or rather the pretty monster, propelled by Jenny's wind glyph. It drove deeper and deeper into the amorphous mass as Abel's ice ball did the same from his side.

Abel released the ice glyph, and the much larger fire glyph inside the ball exploded deep in the fursomnium's guts. The sparks kept expanding until they finally ran out of magic, he'd wanted the first shot to count. Ferryl had been building something that glowed a deep red. Now a web bigger than anything the monster had extended flew down the corridor, unravelling as it went. The reaching limbs fell in bubbling droplets as the mesh diced them in passing. Ferryl's web clung to the main body for a moment, then the edges moved forward and drew in. As the edges came together, it tore a huge hole in the blue mass then shrank to a dull ball before flying back to Ferryl's hand. Abel saw the glow start to build again, but paid more attention to his own glyphs.

He threw a big, quick-and-nasty fire glyph into the hole torn by Ferryl. Even as the fire glyph burned and died, Zephyr shot into the open wound, spinning in place to produce her patent firework display but not as a signal. The stream of fire glyphs ripped and tore away inside the hole, but it slowly closed as the fursomnium shrank away. Zephyr flew back out before being sealed in, straight into her tattoo. "Magic please." Her magic met Abel's and they connected. He used one hand to draw magic for her, and himself, from a belt before she broke the link again. Meanwhile his free hand threw reverse fire at a fresh crop of limbs, freezing them until they broke off, fell, and bubbled to nothing.

*   *   *

At the other end of the corridor, Kelis's ice spear finally stopped deep inside the mass, then exploded into shards. Each shard drove into the gloop around it, then exploded into steam. The steam froze and spun, each shard now a sharp ice blade shredding anything nearby. Kelis had taken care over her first shot as well. Jenny stayed with simple and brutal. Windhammers smashed the limbs to bubbling goo, with Rob using his bat to clobber any that got through.

Rob's first shot had a double whammy. He threw a handful of what looked like pebbles boosted with wind, up at the top of the fursomnium. As they hit the mass, each one glowed and burned in, then warped. They became spiked balls, spinning madly as gravity pulled them through the creature from top to bottom. Rob reverted to plain glyphs, smashing at the limbs or freezing them off. He couldn't use earth here without tearing lumps from Laurence's house. Once she saw how well ice worked, Jenny switched to freezing the webbed limbs.

"This is much bigger than expected. It must have spread into the attic as well as all those rooms and the walls." Ferryl's glowing web disintegrated after chewing off another lump so she switched to freezing off the nearest limbs. "Hit it hard, drive it downstairs because we don't have enough magic to destroy it here."

For long moments the creature fought, reaching out again and again as everyone including Zephyr now concentrating on destroying limbs as fast as possible. Abel, Rob and Jenny used reverse heat, or Windhammers if a limb came too close. Kelis wrapped the base of each limb in frozen water, which contracted to nip it off. Ferryl cast out tiny ice particles as if she were throwing grain for chickens, but each sparkling shard tore into anything it touched. Despite her being careful, they occasionally scored the walls and ceiling of the passage.

The creature no longer completely filled the corridor, so Rob began to throw carved hexes through any gaps. The rest did the same when they could, and room after room received one of the potent little creature repellents. Ferryl threw a few right into the glowing, billowing mass. "Keeping going. The hexes won't kill it, but they'll irritate and drive it away. Not long now, it's had enough!"

The heaving mound in front of them began to sink, swirling and draining away through the cracks between floorboards. Abel waited until Zephyr came back for more magic. "Warn the others it's coming, Zephyr. Tell them to concentrate on freezing or cutting off the limbs."

Zephyr shot down through the cracks between floorboards, reappearing soon afterwards to fly back into her tattoo. "Could only reach the ones right below because it's already filling the rooms in between. They are shouting to the rest." Abel could hear raised voices below. Zephyr flew out again to shower the web on the end of a limb with reverse heat until it frosted and disintegrated. This time when she came home Zephyr connected for more magic.

"Spread the hexes out. Quickly!" Ferryl darted forward to spread out the ones already thrown and to fill in gaps as the last of the creature oozed out of sight. There'd be no retreating back to its lair.

"Are we done?" Kelis hesitated, torn between wanting to chase the fursomnium and worrying about it doubling back.

"Go right down to the ground floor so it can't break sideways to reach the sleepers. It won't stop in the next two floors. Too vulnerable." Ferryl dropped to one knee as the others headed for the stairs. "But I'll make sure." A cloud of those vicious ice shards spilled down through the cracks in the floor. "Just in case some is lurking." She followed Abel down the corridor.

*   *   *

From the shouting and the thump of air glyphs, the fursomnium tried to break out into the other bedrooms. Only a half-hearted effort, because by the time Ferryl and Abel stumbled out of the door at the bottom of the servants' stairs it had begun to ooze out of the dining room ceiling. Once again it tried to break out sideways, towards the sleeping staff in the rear of the house, potential victims whose dreams would strengthen it.

For the first time Abel saw the hexed weapons at work. True to what he'd told her, Una's sword cut straight through the heaving luminous cloud of stars. Not a clean cut, the magic in the blade left bubbling tears that grew into wide, ragged gashes. Better yet the blade glowed a deep red as it did, which probably accounted for Una's "pow!" every time she swung. Abel took a moment to build another ice and fire ball to hurl deep inside, but nearly lost the glyph when he realised who wielded one sabre.

Claris wore a crone's outfit, so she must had been hidden behind a plastic witch's mask. Abel had forgotten about her asking Laurence for an invitation. Now her face contorted in rage as she swung the glowing blade again and again, double-handed. Abel got a grip, finished his glyphs, and hurled the ball deep inside the monster. Fire exploded, gouging a hole out of the centre. "Careful of the drapes." Laurence came past, his rapier flicking out to lop off a limb. He really could use the thing, and the hex meant it cut through like an axe. Two more flicks and the last two limbs reaching towards the sleepers in the ballroom, including Laurence's parents, dropped and bubbled. "Not ready to inherit yet." Laurence moved off towards where the creature still tried to get into the kitchens.

A raging storm of red-hot sparks tore into it and the fursomnium retreated. Rob, Kelis and four others including Petra appeared from the kitchen area, releasing another cloud of very small, hot glyphs. Some Taverners only managed one or two, but the combined assault really hurt the monster and it recoiled. "Watch out, it dropped Tez. A web thing grabbed him though we lopped it straight off." The teenager waved a sword. "He's sat up again but he's out of it." The Taverners stopped going for the main body unless all the nearby limbs had been destroyed.

At last the fursomnium stretched limbs out through the open front doors, and the rest of the cloud began to follow. More and more Taverners appeared in doorways to hurl glyphs into the sides and rear of the creature, or slash with magical weapons. "I'm done." Warren reached out to Una. "Come on, give me that. I'm out of magic. Ugly please?" She hesitated, pouted and handed her sword over before building a cloud of ice shards.

"You owe me." Una drove her missiles into the target. "Pow doesn't feel the same with ice."

Warren swung and the blade glowed red. "Pow! Try yelling 'Cold as Ice' or 'Ice, Ice, Baby' like the songs." He swung and shouted again but then had to run to keep up as the monster decided on full flight.

Behind him Una hurled more frozen shards, shouting "Ice, Ice, Baby" then shaking her head in disgust. As the last of the fursomnium flowed down and off the wide stone steps, over twenty Taverners poured out of the main doors and the French windows from the dining room. Some were definitely slowing now, and their glyphs weren't doing much damage. One after another the youngsters were running low on magic while a voice warned them someone else had been tagged and was out of the fight. Justin staggered down the steps, a hand to his head. He'd been caught as well, touched briefly, which had dropped him in his tracks. The momentary contact had drained a lot of magic and left Justin with a banging headache, but he'd topped up from his lead bar.

Abel still had plenty of magic because of his gold belts, but also because his hours of practice had made his glyphs more efficient. He looked around those who were faltering. "Warren?" The sixteen-year old looked over. "Catch. Lead bar plus." Abel fumbled for a moment before releasing one of his belts, a half-empty one. With a quick swing he threw it over. "Works like a lead bar. Find the bit with the glyph. Fill up and pass it on."

Warren turned the belt, saw the row of little gold bars joined by gold wire, and put his hand on the glyph. He jerked his head up and a big smile spread across his face. "Thanks, I'll pass Una's sword along." Abel had already started running across the lawns. Somehow the fursomnium didn't look as big out here, or maybe they'd trimmed a lot off it. At a quick estimate he thought if it pulled itself into a ball it might be the size of an elephant, but only an Indian one. At the moment the creature flowed over the grass like a giant animated cloud-duvet, still incredibly beautiful with all those sparks floating about inside it.

Twice the fursomnium changed direction, but the five figures spread across its path ran to block it. The creature couldn't swerve too much because it only moved just above walking pace and the Taverners were right on its heels. Some were already running up both flanks and more glyphs flew from behind, burning or freezing lumps off, goading the monster onwards. The front thickened and produced dozens of limbs, then it surged towards the five people in the way. They didn't flinch. Abel saw the axe and two swords go up, ready.

The webs on the limbs were only a couple of metres away from the first target, shy nervous Sarah who'd worried about approaching Frederick in the park. Now she put her wrists together and thrust out her hands, cupped as if to catch. A flamethrower erupted from between her cupped palms! Sarah swivelled at the hips, playing the stream of fire glyphs along the front of the fursomnium like a fiery water hose and it recoiled. Limbs quickly retracted or shrivelled and burned, and for a moment none reached for anyone.

The other Taverner without a weapon, Eric, spread his hands apart, palms almost facing down. A line of glyphs scattered across the clear space between the five defenders and the monster. With an audible scratching, rustling sound the lawn surged up, growing higher and thicker than grass ever should. The fursomnium lunged, its limbs pushing through but jerking back as stumps as the swords and axes did their part. With a crackling noise, frost spread along the luxuriant growth, thickening to ice as the creature pushed against until it recoiled. Another storm of glyphs tore into the amorphous mass from behind and now each side as well. "Don't let it get round the end!" Other voices took up the call and some of those still running up burned or blasted the bulge each side, forcing the fursomnium back behind the barrier.

Rob staggered past Abel, panting, and dropped to his knees about halfway along the beast. He put both hands flat on the grass and hunched his shoulders, while Ferryl dashed down the other flank and copied him. "Now!" This time earth surged up, a wall from Rob to Ferryl two metres high. For long moments the creature draped over the wall, but then began to thin and flow down each side until the new barrier cut it clean in half. "Harden!" The soft crumbly brown barrier smoothed out, looking almost glassy.

Abel stopped building yet another fire glyph. "Anyone who can, make it rain on the back half. Weapons, keep the front half trapped. Those with just air glyphs, make the rain fall harder." He drained magic from a belt and copied Sarah's pose, but aiming into the air and with his hands opened up further. A sprinkler this time, not a hose. Clouds formed above the rear half of the fursomnium as glyphs sucked moisture out of the air, forming raindrops. The front half of the monster kept pushing limbs over the ice wall, but they came back as stumps. Swords glowed red as others stopped it getting out from between the earth and the frozen grass.

A small concentrated rainstorm began, turning to a savage downpour as wind glyphs drove it down. Abel let his glyphs go, a continual stream of reverse fire that turned each drop into a tiny ice missile. With more wind glyphs driving them downwards harder and harder, everyone could see the ice chewing away the top of the fursomnium, lower and lower until it began to fray. Larger and larger holes appeared, and then it broke apart! Smaller bits tried to escape, but the rain and wind stopped as everyone switched to hunting them down.

"I'm out."

"No magic."

"I'm done." At least half of the Taverners were out now, though the rest of the monster stayed firmly trapped.

"Extras, anyone?" Kelis held up a belt. "Fill up for one last push." Jenny raised a belt, and Abel calculated what he'd used. He could manage with what was left in one belt. He held up the other partly used belt and his emergency lead bar. No matter how hard he tried to use them in order, Abel ended up partly draining each one. While the best glyph users sucked up magic, Zephyr came back from hunting down any remnants. She flowed into her tattoo to fill up.

"Sarah has collapsed. The ice wall will fail soon."

Abel raised his voice. "Listen up everyone. Don't waste magic. Take it in turns to use really tight hot or cold glyphs and eat it away. Those with weapons can stop any attempt at a breakout." He waved to Ferryl. "Fay, will you go round and help Sarah keep the ice strong, please?" He didn't want the rest to know she'd collapsed, though looking around Sarah wasn't the only one. Even as Ferryl disappeared around the end of the frozen grass, he could see the top begin to crumple. Eric was getting low as well, despite bringing extra lead bars. Frost reappeared on the melting parts, then ice, so Ferryl's diamonds were holding up.

"I know what Kelis meant when she made that veil." Rob rubbed his forearms. "That hurt."

"Yeah, but can you imagine Creepio's reaction." Abel sniggered and pointed to the grass and ice wall. "To both of them."

"Creepio is swinging Una's sword. He's run out of magic." Rob headed for the last of the fursomnium. "Some of the swords look less bright so they're running down as well. Let's put this thing out of its misery." Rob more or less summed it up. The creature was trapped and now the Tavern executed it, a piece at a time. Several times the fursomnium lunged to try and get free, and even managed to get a web onto one of the weapon wielders but the advance always shredded away or fell back. The girl it webbed collapsed, holding her head, but once the limb had been sliced off she sat back up.

As the fursomnium shrank, the Taverners began to relax, but the creature must have reached some critical point. It burst into a cloud of smaller pieces, each containing one bright spark, surging outwards like a huge, slow-motion firework. Just for a moment the Taverners were stunned, pausing their attack, then the first few pieces struck and three people crumpled. "Hit it! Hard! Get every bit!" Laurence sounded desperate, probably because even one piece might eventually grow big enough to threaten his family again. The Taverners responded, a blizzard of small glyphs tearing into the rapidly spreading fragments to destroy them one by one. The youngsters spread out in every direction, running down every scrap they could see. At least that pale, luminous blue and the spark in the middle made it easier to find fragments in the dark.

If the fursomnium could have truly flown, some would have got away, but it seemed incapable of getting more than about three metres off the ground. Zephyr zipped back and forth, dodging stray glyphs and picking off any mini-monsters blown up higher than the rest. As Abel staggered across the lawns, panting as he caught the last couple of bits escaping this way, he could feel the strange itch in his head fading. When he turned round only six people were still chasing blue sparks, and one by one they hit their targets and staggered to a halt.

An echoing silence heralded the final destruction of the fursomnium. Complete silence, as everyone put a hand to their heads because the scratching inside finally stopped. Heads turned, smiles broke out, and the cheering started. Not for long, the exhausted Taverners scattered across the huge lawns didn't have the breath to keep it up for long. As silence fell again they began to trudge back towards the house.

*   *   *

Laurence hadn't joined in with the cheering. He stood with a hand on his hip, swishing his rapier with the other, a worried look on his face. "The gardener will be upset." He pointed his rapier at Rob's earth wall. "The gardener will have a shrieking fit, father will do the stiff-upper-lip disappointed-in-me thing, and mother will probably need a week shopping in Harrods to recover." He glanced at Abel with a half-smile. "Not really but we can cancel any future parties. We haven't enough magic to fix this, have we?"

"I've still got some, but probably not enough to fix the lawn, let alone any damage inside." Kelis looked around at the Taverners, her hand inside the leather to hold her diamond. "I'll be using what magic I've got on anyone who collapsed. I think most of it is magical exhaustion." She turned back to Laurence. "Did you manage to bribe any of those dryads in the woodland?"

"For magic? No. They'll answer questions for honey, or some of them will, but that's it." He scowled at the wood behind the house. "I'd need a truckload of honey, but it would be worth it. Was the monster supposed to be that big?"

Abel felt a hand slip into his. "No it wasn't. Half of it must have been above us in the roof spaces. It must have lived here for centuries, feeding from all the servants. I wouldn't be surprised if it killed residents in those bedrooms at some time."

"Can I come home now please? Ffod needs to be Zephyr again." Zephyr flowed into Abel's arm and extended her magic. "Shake hands please." Abel did, then asked her to pass on Ferryl's assessment.

Once he'd heard the explanation, Laurence looked back and up at his ancestral home. "It might have killed people, if it did so by sending them crazy. There's a history of mental instability in the family but it's not talked about much. Stiff upper lip, never admit there's a problem or lock it in the attic and all that, and mental problems weren't really understood back then." His face hardened as he gestured with his rapier towards the mess where the fursomnium died. "Though maybe it wasn't really instability, just the monster in the attic, and the last victim might not have been that long ago. A great-aunt died in one of the bedrooms just before I was born. It's supposed to be haunted. I wonder how many of my ancestors or their servants died in the upper floors?" He rounded on Abel, looking at the tattoo. "Why weren't they hexed like the lower rooms?"

"Not all sorceresses would recognise a fursomnium, and witches wouldn't. They are rare here, but more common around the Mediterranean. Keeping the bottom floors hexed would stop most other dangerous creatures, and be much cheaper." Abel passed that on as the Taverners trudged back towards the house.

He stopped by Claris, sat on the grass with her head down and her shoulders slumped. "I thought you weren't having anything to do with magic?" Two tear-filled eyes looked up at him, her eye makeup leaving tracks down her cheeks.

She turned to the others nearby. "I need a private moment with Abel, please?" Once Ferryl let go of Abel's hand and followed the rest, Claris gave a big, long sobbing sigh. "That was the plan, to hide with the sleeping staff, protected by your friends and those hexes. Then I thought about what I was doing. I considered getting Rob to lend me his bat, but you started magicking swords." Her eyes drifted to the sabre on the grass nearby then across the wreckage of the lawn, but she wasn't really seeing it. "I watched helpless while that leech did things to me, made me do things, and then while you scared it into treating me better. I was just a passenger again when you tore the bitch's precious lair and nest to shreds. I still didn't do anything when you rescued the two seeded girls, or when you freed the father. Well, one thing, I gave up the spell inside me to help Jane Doe, and I nearly screwed that up." Another big sigh shuddered out. "I dreamt my way through it all, and Ferryl healing my memories and body. Then once you got me free and healed, I ran away and hid from you all in Frederick's house. But I can't keep hiding."

"You aren't…." Abel stopped as Claris shook her head and kept going.

"I hid from you after being your girlfriend, then even in my head I hid from the memory of monsters and being helpless. I can't remember any of it, not clearly, and don't want to. You all came here to help Laurence but I wanted to do that again, hide until the danger was gone. I treated Laurence like shit but he forgave me, enough to treat me like a human being, but when he needed help I wanted to hide. Poor little helpless Claris, too frightened to even learn magic to defend herself." With another of those sighs Claris looked back at the shambles where the fursomnium had died, but this time her shoulders straightened a little. "Well not this time. I still don't want to learn magic, but now I know. I can beat the monsters." A sad, hesitant smile peeked out of her tearstained face. "Though I'd like a magic machine gun for the next time?"

"A magic baseball bat?" That would fix non-magical threats as well, but wouldn't get her locked up.

"You mean it?" Claris held out her hand and Abel helped her up. She bent to pick up the sabre. "In that case I won't try to smuggle this home." She leant on Abel and they followed the rest to the ballroom.

Some people were drinking or eating from the buffet, but most of them were sat or stood around completely wiped out. At least this room seemed almost untouched; other rooms looked like a tornado had passed through. Parts of the house had hexes scattered all over, or just a few chairs tipped over and a scuff on the wall.

"Damn. The rest doesn't really matter now." Laurence looked down at the remains of what must have been a large vase or urn. "Family heirloom, a real antique. That's my wages gone for the next thousand years or so."

"Maybe not." Ferryl knelt and looked at the heap of pieces for a few moments. She held a hand above them, palm downwards. "Just now, freshly broken, the pieces know they should be together, how they fit. They've been together a long time. Not proper knowing or thinking, but they'll just make sense if they fit a certain way." She shrugged and stretched out the other hand. "Father taught me this because I was a clumsy child. Words don't really explain it. So." Glyphs floated down towards the pieces, then a few drifted away and returned with shards. "Like that." Another cloud of glyphs drifted down, each one attaching to a fragment until a few floated aimlessly. Ferryl turned both hands until she cradled an invisible something and the pieces began to lift.

Nobody spoke a word, completely entranced as the shattered fragments and even bits of ceramic dust lifted and swirled around each other. They began to fit together, one or two to start with, then faster until with an audible click the last shard fitted into place. "Now to lock it." Ferryl wasn't speaking to them, she was far away in her mind or maybe the vase.

Abel, for one, jumped when Ferryl took a deep breath, a firm hold of the vase, and stood up. "There's a tiny glyph inside the base now. It'll be all right for a couple of months but feed it more magic when you've recovered and it'll last forever."

Laurence took the vase as if it was made of spun frost, very, very carefully, and placed it on a small table. He stepped back and let out a long breath of relief. "Thank you. Everyone go home and leave the sleepers. I'll wake them up in the morning and take the heat. It's the least I can do after that."

"Not until I've talked to your trees. I want to make them an offer they won't want to refuse." Ferryl's and Jenny's eyes opened in shock, but Kelis narrowed hers when they met Abel's and Rob nodded gently.

"You don't mean one they can't refuse, do you?" Kelis's wry smile swept across the rest. "Abel won't offer to burn them, though I'd love to know what the hamster in his head has come up with."

"So would I. How much will it cost?" Laurence shrugged as the others looked at him. "I'll find it somehow if you can fix this place before anyone wakes up."

"If we fix the Taverners, fill them with magic, they can fix the place. With luck it won't cost a bean, or even honey." Abel smiled confidently and headed out of the door. "I'll need you all to keep back so you can't hear."

"That's got to be a clue." Though Kelis didn't try to work it out, or not out loud.

*   *   *

Abel wasn't quite as confident as he looked, because a lot depended on who the wind whispered to. As he approached the wood, Abel looked back and smiled. The Taverners had all come out to watch, standing in a group well out of hearing. Much closer, only just about far enough away, four people stood in a line. The other four Taverneers, his friends, ready to step in if he needed them. Abel swallowed the little lump in his throat, blinked away the sudden stinging in his eyes, and turned to the nearest adult tree.

"I greet you, tree and dryad. I bring a proposition that may be to your benefit." Complete silence followed. Abel waited, then moved to the next adult tree and repeated it. At the third, branches creaked just a little. "I did not threaten. Any attack from you would be unprovoked, and fatal." He kept his tone level, with absolutely no threat in it.

"Not if the attack works."

"The four behind me would not be pleased. You already know that, unless the wind no longer whispers here." Abel looked up at the branches above him. "Think about what the wind whispers of the Dead Wood, or what the goblins gossip about."

Two deep brown eyes opened in the tree. "Goblin gossip is not reliable. Nor is the wind."

"But both together? Perhaps the wind whispered of Dryad Woods." Branches rustled on several nearby trees. "If there were time, I would ask Woods and Green to vouch for me. Unfortunately I am in a hurry, so I am willing to make a contract that Dryad Woods will consider foolish."

"No sorcerer makes contracts with dryads." A dryad came out of a tree further into the wood. "Just agreements they break when they feel like it."

"Yes they do. I have a signed contract with Dryad Woods to represent me. Better still I believe any agreements are binding, signed or not. Ask the wind, I don't break them. I have one with Dryad Sycamore to watch over Dead Wood in return for an adult tree. There will be other trees for its young when they ripen this summer. The dryads in a whole orchard protect my friend's house from magical creatures, and we protect them from sorcerers. I have an agreement with three young Willow dryads. I am protecting them until they are strong enough to protect themselves. In return they will supply some magic to help protect my village once their trees can spare it. There will be an empty tree there as well, for some lucky dryad seedling." The rustling continued for some time, but Abel waited patiently.

"Why is this urgent? I would rather hear from Dryad Woods." Abel didn't have a chance to answer, the dryad in front of him butted in.

"Everything is in a hurry except the trees." Its eyes moved to look past Abel. "Are they here to threaten?"

"No, they are asking you for help. You saw us fight the fursomnium?"

The leaves rustled a little, but not threateningly. "Yes, a very large one. I did not realise they grew to that size."

"I didn't realize what it was. Why isn't the sorceress talking to us?" This dryad appeared from one of the trees that hadn't answered Abel's first offer. "She is stronger than you, so she should be the mistress."

Abel glanced back for a moment. "We don't have a master or mistress, because none of us is tethered or bound. The sorceress stayed back there because she can't offer what I can. I am the master of Dead Wood and Castle House gardens, by blood and power." The wood stilled. "That was not a threat, just information. I have also claimed the house, but have not reached the centre yet."

A voice from deep in the wood finally spoke. "The wind whispered of the church sending their sorcerers, and a bound ogre."

Abel chuckled, trying hard not to sound nervous. "I thought it might, in which case it spoke of the ogre leaving again without entering the garden. The church will not interfere, in Dead Wood or any of the other woods I own. Sixteen woods and two forests, where only I can decide if a dryad seedling can live or not." This silence became so deep it almost felt like pressure. Somewhere an owl hooted, and something rustled in the grass nearby but nothing stirred in the wood. The silence stretched on and on, until few leaves rustled.

"What is the contract?" More leaves fluttered and rustled and branches thrashed and creaked, so not all the dryads wanted to negotiate. Abel waited until things settled down a bit.

"It can apply to one dryad, three dryads, all the dryads here, or none. None means that some of my friends drive me away, some hours pass, and I come back with what I need. That would cause trouble between a friend and his parents." Abel sighed, deliberately loudly. "Then the foolish dryads would have many long winters to think of lost opportunities. Worse, when my friend plants new trees here, he will not look to this wood for guardians." Abel would make absolutely certain Laurence didn't, even if it hadn't been mentioned yet.

"Magic, you want magic. How many trees do you expect to use, and for how many years must they supply magic?" This came from the nearest dryad as it stepped out of the tree. "How many seedlings will your friend make room for and how soon?"

That opened a whole new avenue to explore, but later. "Right now everyone out there needs magic, quickly. I will trade you a home for a seedling for each person who is helped, but you must allow them to top up themselves and their lead bars twice. One seedling for each diamond or gold belt you fill. If one dryad helps six people, six seedlings." Abel took a deep breath, because he knew this would be the bit the dryads might baulk at. "But not here. The seedlings will be taken to other woods. You can still make the deal to help my friend in return for a home for your young in the future."

The storm of thrashing and creaking went on and on, but Abel waited. Eventually it quietened enough for a dryad to be heard. "We will not give seedlings to a sorcerer! The only way to do so is as a shade, unless you can carry whole trees about."

"Not so. Humans can carry saplings, and even larger trees." For a moment Abel thought he'd got a convert but the dryad turned to him. "But I would not put my seedling in one and give it to a sorcerer."

"Not even if Woods and Green organised the transport and the transfer to an adult tree at the other end?" Abel had expected silence, but the thrashing started again. Eventually it hushed to a rustling, then a few last creaks.

"An adult tree?"

Abel smiled in relief because one had taken the bait. "One never inhabited by a dryad or used by a sorcerer for over a hundred years. No need to wait for their home to grow strong." He opened his arms to take in the whole wood. "There are enough for every one of you to send a seedling." Abel had stressed adult, because seedlings usually moved into saplings and hoped to survive until the tree matured.

Though that still hadn't convinced at least one dryad. "But we must give the magic now."

"Yes. The urgency is why I will pay such a high price. But that's it, no higher because if you say no I can go and get the magic tonight. There is only one dryad in the whole of Dead Wood, so I can drain every other tree if I wish." Abel held up a belt, now almost empty. "I will fill this and others, bring them back, and fix the damage. The wind will laugh at you. Hah, even goblins will. After all, you risk a very small amount of magic against a large gain." It was melodramatic but Abel took a good look at his watch. "Time is moving on. Human time, so it moves quickly. I'll give you five minutes." He turned on his heel and left.

Kelis still had a little smile when he reached her. "Well?"

"Five minutes. If not, the five of us and a heap of lead bars need transport to Dead Wood and we'll give pebble glyphs to the drivers so they can help." Abel looked past them to the rest of the Taverners. "The sleepers can be woken up much later and it'll take some fast talking, but we'll get there."

"If we get some magic quickly, we could fix enough to wake up the sleepers but make sure they stay dopey and go to bed without looking outside? Regardless of what it felt like, killing that thing didn't take long. It's only twenty past ten." Rob nudged Kelis. "You can put Emst to bed if you like. Tuck him up and kiss him goodnight?"

Kelis replied and Ferryl laughed. The other three looked baffled. "No fair. When did you learn to speak German?" Jenny smirked and nudged Kelis. "Exactly how long have you spent chatting him up on the internet and Skype?"

"I've just got more wits than Rob. Which isn't hard."

Rob just laughed at Kelis. "Maybe some of us have a better use for our wits than chasing Germans."

Before Kelis could ask what Rob meant, Ferryl pointed over Abel's shoulder. "I think you have an answer." He turned to see four dryads standing clear of their trees in plain view. Another two appeared from deeper in the wood. "That looks hopeful. Now do we find out the deal?"

"Only the four of you. None of the Taverners can know the exact deal, just the result. Come on, you may as well listen." Abel headed for the waiting dryads.

*   *   *

Almost an hour later the sleepers woke up, though Ferryl made sure any that had been laid on the floor were mazzled more than the others so they didn't remember that part. Some of the staff still felt tired and went to bed, but the ones on duty for the party just felt confused. The Taverners carefully arranged themselves before waking Laurence's parents and the German cousins, then swung straight into the judging. The cousins soon took up wrangling over who would make the best companion for Kelis. Everyone knew Emst would get the job, which kept his mind off the time. The Taverners arranged for three young women to compete over being the other cousin's partner, so he didn't look at a watch or clock either.

Since the first couple were posing for the judges as they opened their eyes, neither did Laurence's parents. Despite the mazzlement, Abel kept expecting someone to realise what had happened. Once the judging finished the sleepers were astounded at how time had passed, but decided it was because of how long each couple spent explaining their characters. The dance kicked off again after Friends in Fur, Eric and Petra as wolf-sorcerer and cat-sorceress, won. Remarkably most of the Taverners still had enough energy to dance. Two doses of tree magic seemed to be a good antidote to exhaustion.

Abel danced with Ferryl and several others, not his strong point so he didn't do much of it. He avoided the slow stuff entirely so he didn't trample anyone, because he'd never learned any steps. As midnight approached Laurence's parents made themselves scarce while Laurence turned on the TV for the countdown. A hand caught Abel's and pulled. "Come on, it's the last dance before midnight." He smiled, because Ferryl actually sounded excited and she must have done this hundreds of times.

"Mind your toes. Or your boots, since you haven't got paws like Petra." Ferryl wore her leather boots rather than chase monsters in bare feet.

"They'll survive. I'm pleased dancing is still in style."

Abel took her hand, put his arm round her and froze. "Oh. Sorry. I forgot." Because his hand had gone through the seeming, of course, and hit Ferryl's bare back.

"I don't mind a hand on my back. Neither do Una, Lovingly Sculptured, the frost giant or a half a dozen others with bare waists. Have you got a thing about skin contact?" At least Abel could see Ferryl's face because they were the same height, but with those huge eyes and her whiskers he couldn't tell if she was teasing or not.

"No. I just forgot. How come nobody else noticed?" When he thought about it, Ferryl had definitely slow-danced with others.

"Because I do this." The smooth skin of her back suddenly tickled his hand. Maybe not quite fur, but maybe that was because Abel knew it wasn't. "That's air, rippling a little. It feels furry, doesn't it?"

"Sort of. If I didn't know it wasn't, I'd be fooled." He braced himself. "Right, dancing. You do realise I don't know how?" Either Ferryl was very fast on her feet or Abel's dancing was good enough, because he didn't scuff her boots even once. Kelis swept past with Emst and winked at him, followed by Laurence and Jenny, but Abel stuck to slow and steady. The dance ended, Laurence turned up the TV and Abel counted down to midnight with the rest.

The tickle of whiskers came as a shock, as did her lips, then Ferryl pulled back. "New Year kiss. It's traditional. I kept it to the kiss you negotiated with Jenny." This time Abel could see the humour in those great big eyes.

"The whiskers were a shock. I thought they were a seeming."

"They are." She winked. "It's magic." Before Abel could ask how she did that, Shawn turned Ferryl away for a Christmas kiss.

A loud clap quietened everyone, and a voice called, "Attention everyone, please." Abel turned to see Claris, her makeup repaired and wearing a big smile. She raised her hands to make sure everyone knew who was talking. "I wasn't really keen on coming here tonight. It went better than expected, because I got to find out I can hurt those monsters. I still owe you all a huge apology, and hope you'll accept it." A ripple of clapping, not a lot, went round the room. "I know, hard to believe. Still, finding I've got some mojo left means I can keep a promise. When that leech was in me, Ferryl asked if I'd kiss someone to get it out." Abel started to get worried, and so did Rob, Kelis and Jenny. "She meant to let the magic inside to heal me, but I said if I had to I'd snog Abel's brains out as often as necessary." A ripple of laughter spread out, relieved laughter from four of them. "Mr Hand-Holder never collected, because he's a gent. Look up Abel."

As Abel did so a bunch of mistletoe held in a wind glyph slowed and stopped right above him. There were a few whistles and some applause. Abel opened his mouth to say no chance, but as he looked down Claris connected. The mouth part was a mistake because snogging brains out involved an open mouth, apparently. He certainly felt as if his brains had been scrambled as Claris stepped back and high-fived Jenny. "Okay girls, he's all trained up."

Jenny laughed and pushed forwards. She lowered her voice as she put her arms round him. "I owe you one as well, a proper kiss instead of those careful chaste versions." This one wasn't snogging his brains out but it definitely went beyond Jenny's previous kisses. "Thanks, Abel." Abel watched her go in a daze.

Kelis bent down and whispered, "This is all you're allowed, idiot," before kissing him on the cheek. "At least you got to kiss someone without using magic."

Abel lost his temper, just a bit, because the magic link to Kelis had been a genuine mistake. Worse, she'd pushed the boyfriend thing with the other two girls but kept tweaking him about it. "And I won't be binding anyone here even if I kiss them properly. They're all warded." He turned as someone pulled his shoulder, put his arms round her and kissed back, hard. For a moment he thought he'd made a mistake because her back felt furry, but it was Petra.

"Hey, he really is learning." As Petra pulled away Sarah smiled and held out her arms. Abel was either still mad, or maybe enjoying himself, he didn't care which anymore. He didn't kiss many girls, but none of them were possessed or magically linked. Or most weren't, the fur on the last one's back suddenly felt like skin and he realised her whiskers were tickling.

Ferryl laughed at him. "I'm your date tonight, so I get the last kiss and it was a lot better than the first. You seem to be in the mood now so come on, I want a proper smoochy last dance." Abel almost said no, but then he saw Kelis smooching with Emst.

"Why not? It's about time I learned how. Maybe I can get a dancing wit." After all, Ferryl said she just wanted to have a date for tonight. The least he could do was go along with it. Abel didn't even get uptight about the kiss at the end because Ferryl kept it to the Jenny original, or thereabouts. He'd lost track of that somewhere along the way.

The party broke up soon after, with Jenny's taxi arriving within minutes. Abel smiled as he saw Petra in her Ferryl Shayde costume leave with Creepio Mysterio. That sight really would give the actual vicar a heart attack. Claris checked he would fix up a baseball bat if she bought one, and left looking downright cheerful. Poor Emst looked really upset when Kelis went towards the BMW, then she laughed and got into the Corsa with him. He'd borrowed her cloak as a costume for the fancy dress, but Kelis insisted on taking it back when they all arrived home.

Abel walked home from Kelis's hoping this New Year would be just a bit less traumatic. He even had an answer when Rob teased him about Claris's kiss, because he'd seen the fan club bushwhacking Roughly Hewn under another bunch of floating mistletoe. Tonight Abel didn't even have questions from mum. She must still be at the New Year dance in Stourton.

*　*　*

Ferryl Shayde lay awake for a long time, her mind whirling. Something had happened tonight, something that frightened her, something that had never happened in all her thousands of years. Perhaps it had started sooner, when she had become embroiled in the lives of these children? They had somehow wrapped her, Pungh Hmmshtfun, into their dreams and schemes. Humans only ever spoke to her host, because Ferryl always hid herself to avoid the church. These children spoke to her, not the host, and they knew she wasn't human, that she was incredibly old and that she possessed bodies. Despite that they took her into their homes, and introduced her to their friends.

Perhaps it started because she had almost faded in the pit, had looked extinction in the eye and then been snatched back to the world. Maybe it had been the time spent riding in that tattoo, a vessel within a human and powered by that human's magic, but without any binding. Those three, then four frail, short-lived children had accepted her as one of them, not a monster to be controlled or destroyed. Even her ex-host Jenny, knowing what she was, laughed and joked with her. With her, using her name and not a host's.

Ferryl could have understood if they had bound her, or held the secret of her existence as a threat. Instead, all four had agreed she could stay herself for ninety years and had lied to church and sorcerers to keep her secret. Abel had signed away his new-found wealth, a large part of his income, to let her stay. He'd done it without hesitation, because he considered her a friend. She liked that too much, being accepted. Somehow it made her feel less like Pungh Hmmshtfun, perhaps like a Ferryl Shayde.

Tonight she had risked her existence to attack a creature that had been no threat to her. A small risk but Braeth Huntian would have wriggled away from the loose agreement with Abel and run, as she had so many times before. Instead she had led the attack, deliberately trapping herself in the attic with the creature to give Abel, Rob, Kelis and Jenny the best chance of survival. She had stood watching Abel walk towards the dryads and worried about him, then felt a fierce pride when they had all kept Laurence out of trouble.

Afterwards the entity Ferryl Shayde had cheered and danced with the Taverners, basking in a very odd sensation that as yet had no name. It felt similar to sensations she remembered in her hosts, their feelings, which she had mimed to conceal her existence but never understood. Was this friendship? What was friendship? Ferryl had never understood those helping and supporting others without any promise of return.

Perhaps Zephyr was to blame? Ferryl knew her own kind were rare, created by chance and dying without trace. With Abel she had deliberately brought a new life into the world, not a mindless slave but something that thought. Something free, with magic and will of her own, a hybrid that included some human traits, Abel's traits. Had the magical equivalent to a child awoken something inside herself?

A child only partly hers. Zephyr would never act as Pungh Hmmshtfun had, possessing human after human to supply her with a form that could hold knowledge and magic. That aversion came from Abel because despite his growing strength and skill, he had flaws. Abel gave up control of a powerful ally, Woods, without hesitation, and released Zephyr knowing she might never return. He squandered tree magic training two score potential rivals, with no tether or even an oath of fealty. Abel cared too much for the lives of others, for their freedom, to reap the rewards that his growing skill and powers had earned him so far. His plan to share the magic from his trees with strangers all over the country relied on the basic good nature of the recipients. Ferryl knew that magic brought out the worst in those who used it, fed their ambitions and greed. Sooner or later, a spared enemy or a faithless friend would stab Abel in the back.

In the darkness, Ferryl Shayde's lips peeled back in a soundless snarl. He would need someone or something at his back, one who would not hesitate to strike. If Abel Bernard Conroy really was her first friend, then regardless of what Pungh Hmmshtfun should do, Ferryl Shayde would not allow the world to take him from her. She lay in the dark, trying to work out where the threats might come from so she could be ready.

Though time and again she came back to possibly having a friend, or friends. Did that explain the feeling she had whenever she thought of Abel? Is this what caring felt like? How did she find out for certain?

Gathering Wits

The week between New Year and going back to school turned out to be busy for everyone close to the five Taverneers. Their parents were discussing either the Christmas presents and the extra windfall their children had found, or the letter that arrived from the bishop. The bishop wanted a proper explanation of how the charity would use a leased church, and the alterations they might want to make. The latter part came down to Jenny's dad. The goblins in the churchyard had to be very still gargoyles during the three days Mr Forester and two of his men measured up and checked the condition of the stonework, timbers and roof.

Abel found himself looking through internet pages of second-hand cars with his mum. She now had a rough idea of what the earrings would bring, and what she'd get as trade-in for her old car, and wanted the newest car she could manage. Abel kept steering her away from the larger ones, insisting the Tavern could supply their own transport. She wore the earrings most of the time, especially the two days she went to work, and now Abel wished he'd kept quiet and found another way to replace the car.

Kelis's mum had made definite plans to sell her engagement ring and the brooch as soon as she was divorced. The divorce still dragged on because some of the evidence was tied to the court cases for assault. Two cases because as Abel had thought at the time, the police were charging Mr Ventner with assaulting their officers. Kelis would eventually have to give evidence about her own and her mum's injuries, probably at the end of January because Mr Ventner's lawyer kept wriggling and putting off the final reckoning. There'd definitely be no money at all left from the house or the business after the bank and the lawyer were done. Mr Ventner would probably end up both bankrupt and in jail, so there'd be no maintenance money either.

In the meantime Kelis finished scribing her German language onto a wit, becoming more fluent even if Emst had now gone home. She'd taken a break after getting the basics because the scribing hurt, just as Ferryl warned. Abel could testify to that, because he'd managed to put all those complicated geometry equations onto a small wit in his shin. He could manage because that bone wasn't deep, but it certainly felt sore. Rob explained his comment about a better use for his wits, he already had one containing the entire periodic table and had started on a long list of facts he needed for his Science GCSE. Since he could read and manipulate earth better than the rest, getting below his skin and scribing on bone turned out to be relatively easy once Rob got the knack. Not that he would be recording anything he didn't think was essential, because of the pain.

All three agreed that actually turning the knowledge into a sort of cipher, not actual letters but a representation in thought, had been the hardest part. They'd only managed it after Ferryl passed the feeling, how her mind felt the sensation as the memory turned to a solid mark, to Zephyr. Zephyr passed the feeling on to Kelis, Rob, Jenny and Abel. Even then Kelis and Abel had chosen subjects where a mistake wouldn't matter too much. Jenny still couldn't manage reliable scribing under the surface of a length of branch, but ferocious practice would soon solve that.

Between that and homework, and keeping up general glyph practice, none of them even thought about how they'd open the next door in Castle House. They'd got plenty to do right now, even Ferryl. Her charred wit held several languages, though many were old ones and often didn't include the written version. She'd also found information on seemings, like the ones Creepio cast over the lorry door and the stretchers rather than the ones cast on bandages or skin. She'd found different ways to bind various types of entities, and some knowledge of the weaknesses of the more dangerous magical creatures, but much of that was incomplete. The charring meant Ferryl had to work through all the memories to make sure she'd got it right before re-scribing the missing portions. Her fluent German had come from the wit, an older version she'd had to update once she saw Kelis's books and heard her tapes.

Rob had an extra distraction, at home. Either something visible to ordinary sight kept looking over the back fence, or Melanie had started to get hints of creatures. According to Rachel, one of the few Taverners the same age, there'd been no sign of Melanie activating magic when they played Bonny's Tavern over Skype. The latest peeping whatevers had supposedly been toadstools, which Ferryl couldn't match up with any magical creature. They all hoped Rob's dad wasn't right about Melanie playing Bonny's Tavern too much and imagining monsters. At least

Melanie had promised Rob she'd only tell him if she saw any more, so her mum and dad didn't get uptight.

Abel had a ticking off rather than a distraction. Dryad Woods, through Terese Green, politely told him he'd carried out the whole negotiation with Laurence's dryads the wrong way. As Mz Green told him four different ways, having a legal representative usually meant including them in any agreements before finalising them. Abel apologised, feeling about ten years old again as he explained why, and asked Terese to organise the details. She promised that Woods and Green would be in touch with the dryads near Laurence's home to find out when each one could ripen seeds. A lorry carrying saplings in pots would transport several at a time. Terese Green suggested she should explain the rules to the seedlings, or in a few years' time they would start seeding all over their new home. Abel didn't argue.

The comments from Laurence's dryads led to the Taverneers having a long conversation with Chestnut, the dryad on the village green. After negotiating the price in honey, Chestnut explained that dryads would sometimes agree to guard woodland for a sorcerer or supply magic for a limited period. In return the dryad would be allowed to ripen a seedling and place it in a protected sapling. The seedling usually stayed within sight of the dryad, because sorcerers were notorious for either breaking agreements or binding young dryads if they caught them alone. The sorcerer didn't have to negotiate if the dryad was bound and would put them into different trees on a whim, which could be painful and very confusing. For the first time, Chestnut seemed genuinely interested in homes for seedlings in Dead Wood.

* * *

The visits to Chestnut used up the last of the honey. Since Chestnut had just had some, Abel felt it might be past time that Dryad Sycamore, the one watching over Dead Wood, had a treat. The simplest solution, now they all had a few quid, was to buy a pot from the village shop even if it would cost a bit more. Mr Summers was his usual grumpy self. He didn't want to talk about the huge For Sale sign beyond grumbling that if the locals had bought more honey, he wouldn't be leaving.

After buying the honey, the five of them set off for Castle House and Dryad Sycamore, but Stan diverted them. "Careful Abel, if you start shopping there the Slummers might stay." He looked the group over before turning back to Abel. "How's that lass, Claris? I haven't seen her lately."

"Still doing well, thanks Stan. She might be visiting, so I'll ask her to call in." Claris would be bringing her baseball bat sometime and Abel would insist she called in on the old poacher. Stan still worried about how Claris was coping with whatever had been inside her, and drinking blood to feed it.

The pensioner turned his attention to Ferryl. "Watch him love, he's a real lady-killer. I can't keep up with them." Stan winked at Jenny. "As this one and Kelis can both tell you." He looked back towards Ferryl with a cheeky grin. "Though you've been around here too long already. You're either hooked or immune."

"Hooked, Stan, definitely hooked." Ferryl turned to inspect the other four. "Though is it Abel or Rob, or maybe Kelis or Jenny?"

"Don't start that sort of shenanigans, young lady. My heart won't take it." Stan paused, then finally got to why he'd come out to intercept them. "Are you going into that house again?"

Abel didn't bother denying it. Stan lived almost next door, with just a bramble and shrub-filled empty plot between him and the wall around Castle House gardens. "We kept exploring the gardens and found a key in a box, so we tried it in the door. It must have been left there for deliveries or something because it only lets us in the front bit. Most of the house is still locked up but the front entrance is warmer than that cave, and we don't need a chicken." As expected Stan laughed, though he looked a bit curious because Ferryl laughed as well.

"You know about that? I thought you were from Germany?" Stan had definitely been asking around. "How come you know all about the weird stuff?" There wasn't any point hiding it, so Ferryl looked sad and explained about being an orphan and seeing creatures. As expected, Stan apologised for prying, though the old poacher would no doubt do so again if he felt like it. The five of them left laughing at the parting shot. Stan had offered to give Abel refuge and loan him the shotgun if his women ganged up on him.

* * *

After opening Castle House, and suffering more teasing about the shotgun, Abel headed for the library. He'd brought his own reading, a history text book, but found the room relaxing. Kelis and Jenny headed upstairs. They were cataloguing all the old clothing so Abel could decide if he wanted to sell some or give most of it to a museum. Rob went to study in the sitting room, because he couldn't concentrate on school work with other people in the room.

As Abel made himself comfortable and opened his book, Ferryl came in. "Do you mind? I want to look at the aquarium again." She had become fascinated with the actual mechanics, trying to work out how the magical maintenance worked.

"I don't mind if there's someone in here while I study, I'm not like Rob. Though I'm curious about what you expect to see. You spend hours just staring through the glass." That part puzzled Abel, because Ferryl didn't seem to do more than look or occasionally raise a hand towards it.

"I'm tracing the magic controlling every aspect, and I think it's one item working many glyphs. Magic is maintaining water circulation, the types of food for different species, keeping the tank clean, salinity, aeration and several other chores. I'd like to see the actual glyphs that can do that, and now I'm wondering if they are controlled by a wit." Ferryl sat cross-legged on the floor near the fish tank. "Maybe not mine, because the whole point about wits is I can't remember what is on most of them. If it isn't mine, it will hurt if I put it in but could give me valuable information. I have lost so much."

"Can I help?"

Ferryl looked almost embarrassed. "I could use Zephyr's help in deciphering the flows of magic, but she will disturb you when we talk."

"Zephyr, would you mind flying free for a little while, in here? So you can help Ferryl?"

"I can come back? I would like to understand the flows because the more I know, the better I can guard, but I do not want to leave you or my home."

"The tattoo is always open, Zephyr. Fly free, wind with a name."

"But a gentle Zephyr, no need for Ffod." The connection tingled and disappeared and the shimmer headed for Ferryl, definitely a bigger shimmer since fighting the fursomnium. Abel wondered if Zephyr had absorbed some of the smaller scraps trying to get away at the end. She settled around Ferryl's hand.

"Perfect, thank you. We can talk without words now." Ferryl turned to the aquarium and Abel to his book.

*   *   *

Abel read through the two chapters he wanted, then again, slower. This time he tried to work out how to turn the information into the thought patterns for a wit. Ferryl kept trying to explain better, but she found it difficult because the whole process seemed to be second nature to her. She claimed it was like teaching the colour-blind the difference between green and red. Abel glanced up at the thought, and kept looking.

Ferryl sat forward, intent, with the hand covered in Zephyr almost touching the glass. Her other hand moved in the air, palm towards the aquarium, following a strange bright blue swimming thing that seemed to have a starfish with long thin legs growing from every limb and its rear. There were also longer bits almost like tentacles. Abel had thought it must be magical but the internet called it Glaucus atlanticus, the blue sea slug.

The slug wasn't holding his attention now, Ferryl was. Concentrating on her magic, with the soft light of the aquarium playing on her face, she looked both exotic and beautiful. Abel felt sure the effect was deliberate, because although some of the students and Taverners had African, Indian or maybe Far Eastern ancestry, none looked quite like her. Her skin wasn't olive, more of a softer mid-brown, which with her full lips and those eyes definitely stood out. Abel had even looked on the internet under Egyptian eyes because he thought she'd created something unique, but Ferryl had told the truth. There were even a few faces that looked just like her, though he couldn't be certain because they all wore makeup and Ferryl didn't.

Ferryl turned towards him and Zephyr lifted from her hand, flying off round the room in a slow circuit to inspect the glowing globes that provided light. "Do you like me, Abel?"

Curses, she'd seen his reflection in the glass, gawking at her. Abel took a quick breath. "I'm sure anyone would tell you you're pretty, deliberately so I'm sure." He felt relieved to manage that without a blush. "Wait until you get to school and see how many lads want to help the new girl."

That brought a little smile. "I told you, this face is like other faces I lived among for many, many years, which is why I chose it. I didn't ask if my host looked pretty so does your answer mean you like me, Abel? Not just the face, me."

"How many years, Ferryl, and who is the real you?" Abel didn't want to answer the other question because it had to be a bit weird, fancying an ancient being. Abel seized on who Ferryl really was, because he'd often wondered. "Woods called you Spiritus qui Furbatur. It sounded Latin so I looked it up." Ferryl looked a little apprehensive, but Abel ploughed on. It was long past time to find out. "It means spirit thief, and you said Huntian means hunter, a hunter who scares leeches bloodless." He took a deep breath. "What does Braeth mean, and did someone scientific give you that Latin name or did the Romans?"

"I'm surprised you didn't ask before." If he didn't know her better, Abel would have thought Ferryl was poised on the edge of flight. "The Romans named me, as did the Greeks and the Mongols, the Danes and many others, all with different names. Me and a very few creatures similar to me, or like I used to be. Braeth means breath. Breath Hunter, Spirit Stealer, do you need to know more?" Ferryl looked towards the door and almost stood up.

"Yes, I do. Why used to be, how have you changed? I have to assume those weren't nice names." Abel wondered if he should be ready to run himself. He was in a room with an ancient sorceress who stole spirits and hunted breath. Even so, he didn't feel threatened. Zephyr slipped back into her tattoo and Abel shook hands without any real thought, intent on Ferryl.

"I told you it took me many years to learn how to use solid bodies, so I could save my memories." A wistful smile touched her face. "Or I told Zephyr, the first life I have ever created. That I will never regret. Before that I lived on magic stolen from animals including humans, and from magic creatures. Some died." Ferryl paused and braced herself before continuing. "The first animals I possessed died, either because I did it wrong or I couldn't get out again. I learned, stealing magic from each host before moving on, then learning to live longer within them until eventually I could control them. I started with small hunters, usually cats because their thoughts are not complicated, before working up to humans. Once I could do that, I learned more about the world, and copied the leech's method of making a bargain to get hosts. Though I always kept the agreement, if possible. I have always been hunted, so I dare not break my deals and leave a trail." She stopped, watching Abel carefully.

"The church hunted you, from what Creepio said. But they don't know who Ferryl Shayde is." Ferryl nodded. "How come?"

"The church has my previous name, Braeth Huntian, a name I earned in the years following the Norman Conquest. You felt me pass to another host, dragging out all your magic and leaving you breathless?" Abel nodded, unwilling to speak and interrupt the flow. "A few hosts confessed to the church, about how I took their breath and left them helpless. Most of my names come from that sensation. Though when challenged I have killed sorceresses, witches and occasionally churchmen, sucking the breath from the weaker ones to taunt my hunters. I have also killed many types of magical creatures in self-defence, or for their magic, or sometimes because I wanted to remove opposition such as blood leeches." She might be embarrassed or frightened, but Abel couldn't be sure which. "I really am an inhuman monster."

"Not necessarily." It came as a shock, having it all laid out, but put that way Abel couldn't see any other way to survive. "I can understand why you fought back, or hunted your rivals. Most of mankind did that, and some still do, so it doesn't make you a monster. You are non-human, like a goblin or dryad, but not inhuman." Abel tried to sort out why he wasn't running for help, or horrified. "I know the church wants you, and Hunter on the Wind is fairly self-explanatory, but you don't seem like some crazed mass murderer. You told Zephyr you stopped killing hosts when you worked out how."

"Once I could think of such things, it seemed the clever thing to do. I even began to collect a small amount of wealth, mostly gold coins to make life easier when I changed hosts, but the sorcerer took all that. Wealth is why I came here. I heard about this house and its treasures, and wondered how well it might be protected. I am a thief of goods though I would rather steal knowledge, glyphs. I moved a long way away from here, changed hosts, gave myself another name and came back. It didn't fool dryads, but they see more than most. Then I tried to break in here." The rueful smile accepted that had been a bad idea. "I took weeks sneaking through the Dead Wood, and made it over the wall. I even crept to where I could study the house. Maybe I became too eager, maybe I missed a trip or a hidden watcher. The sorcerer set a trap and I ended up in the pit. One of my first tasks was redesigning the barrier, to make sure nobody else could survive in here by using another's body as a partial shield."

The answer would probably be gross, but Abel had to ask. "That thing you showed me really was your body?"

"My host, the last one, or a hint of her form using dust and a breath of magic. I broke my bargain with her. She never did get her new life and Celtchar tore pieces out of her living body. I shut her mind right down, so despite the holes in her bones she died peacefully." Ferryl took a deep breath, obviously bracing herself for something. "I've been expecting this ever since you rescued me. I will leave. If you wish I will leave this host, or I will keep our bargain and make her some memories. They will not be the ones I intended." She stood up.

"Sit down please, Ferryl. Why must you leave? We know you possess people and all that, but you've also helped them. You saved Jenny's life, and Claris's." Abel opened his arms to include the room. "We'd have never got in here without you. You belong, a Taverneer."

"Still?" Ferryl sat, but perched uneasily right on the edge of a seat. "Time after time I keep thinking one of you will scream and run away or denounce me. When I first appeared, or when I flew around in Kelis's house, or when I terrified the leech, and so many other times." Her little laugh sounded uncertain. "The real me flew out around that room, and you all offered me a home. Nobody gives me a home except as a bargain to save their lives. Then when I showed my true-self to the leech, Kelis found me a bed in her house and you used your legacy to buy me a new life." Ferryl looked and sounded lost, uncertain, casting her eyes around the room without looking directly at Abel. "I don't know what to do, how to repay that. I already owe you ninety years for my rescue."

"Why not just keep on being Ferryl Shayde? Build memories and a new life for that poor woman as we planned? Be my friend? I don't have enough to lose one." Abel stopped and thought about that. "Though I seem to have more since you arrived."

Ferryl finally looked straight at Abel, stood up and walked over to sit on the settee next to him. She reached out and took his hands. "I've never had friends, not even one. My hosts do, but their friends don't know about me. Does anyone have friends for ninety years?"

"A hundred and ninety years? A thousand and ninety? Friend isn't a bargain with a time limit, unless you stop wanting to be a friend." Abel looked down at her hands. "I really should stop doing this, holding hands with your hosts."

"I'd rather not." He looked up at the humour in her voice and straight into her eyes.

"I thought you'd made those eyes bigger than they should be. They're stunning." Abel closed his eyes and mouth. Foot in big mouth, again.

"No, they are natural and normal where I came from. Though you finally answered the question about liking my host." Her hands squeezed a bit and Abel heard humour and maybe a little tease in her voice. "Now you also know me, the real me. So, Abel, do you like me?"

"Of course, but you're an ancient sorceress. It could be glyphs or anything." Or a girl sat too close and Abel's face started heating up.

"Why do you always do that with girls, try to avoid them or make a joke if they get near? I understand about Kelis and the link, but what about Jenny and Claris? As far as I can remember, a young man like you shouldn't have been so reluctant to kiss them."

Abel glanced at her face, and those eyes, and away again. "They weren't in charge. Of themselves."

"I was completely in charge of myself at the New Year dance, but you still worried about touching my back. You wouldn't kiss me, or anyone else, until Claris bushwhacked you." Now when Abel glanced he could see a little sparkle in her eyes and her voice had definitely started teasing him a bit. "After that you kissed some of the others, properly, and I thought you had got over it. Then you froze again when you realised I was kissing you the second time. Though I did get a proper last dance, which was really nice."

"Still possessed." Abel knew he'd mumbled that, but he daren't admit he'd enjoyed the kissing. Even the one at the end, after the last dance when he knew exactly who he'd kissed. Abel closed his eyes because even if Ferryl had aimed at ordinary, he thought she looked stunning. He couldn't look in her eyes and lie.

"No I'm not, or not really. I didn't truly realise until the dance." Ferryl stayed silent for a long time, and if she hadn't been very gently squeezing his fingers Abel would have thought she'd finished. He certainly had no idea what he should say. "I have never known true friendship, or cared for another being. I'm not sure I know how to. When the host meets another person she gives me a reaction to use, to respond with, one I can alter if I wish. Not an emotion. I've never tried to understand emotions, because there would always be a new set that clashed with the old."

This time Abel thought the silence needed some sort of answer. "You laughed with us, and joined in the Glyphmistress celebrations. You seem happy or nervous sometimes, even while you lived in the tattoo." He smiled just a little. "You are definitely proud of your command of wind glyphs."

"But that was how any host including Jenny or Claris would have felt, or so I thought." This time when she fell silent Abel opened his eyes to look at her but Ferryl seemed sunk in her thoughts. She raised her head and Abel quickly looked down at their hands. "When I lived in the tattoo, I thought maybe I used your reactions. Now I'm wondering, and if all the ones with Jenny and Claris were totally theirs. I've been living among you, among people who knew who I was and spoke to me, not the host. I think some of my responses might have been me." Her hands gripped a little tighter. "I have to have my own emotions now, somehow, because this host feels nothing but blind terror. I've blanked that out."

Startled, Abel looked up, straight in her eyes but he still managed to get out, "But you've been showing emotions, haven't you?" He dropped his gaze to their hands. Slim hands with long fingers, their skin dark against his, and he really didn't want to start thinking Ferryl's hands were beautiful. He'd end up wearing a blindfold or avoiding her entirely.

"At the dance I tried to enjoy it as she would and couldn't. There was nothing to use, so I tried to enjoy it as me. It isn't easy, but I think I had a good time." Her hands gripped tight, and her voice hardened. "I must learn! This host shouldn't be left with memories but no emotions. I have to learn how to like."

"You don't like anyone?" Abel felt a definite stab at that. He'd counted Ferryl as a friend, and thought she liked him, Rob and Kelis at least.

"Without any real comparison I'm not sure if I do, or just copy what I think I should feel. The hate and excitement and triumph in the fight with the fursomnium felt right, because I have fought all my life. I felt real pride in fixing the vase, even if I lied about how I learned. It's the same affinity glyph I used to gather gravel, but more controlled." Another of those silences fell, but this time Abel wasn't going to open his big mouth. Ferryl didn't even like any of them? Except Zephyr though she'd hadn't said like, just no regret. "But looking back, I find times when I didn't want to disappoint you, any of you, and wanted to help. Not just because of our agreement. I am certain I felt something at the end of the dance, something that was only me."

Lost in thought Abel almost missed the words, and took a second to understand. "After the fight?"

"When we followed you out to meet the dryads, I felt worried. Not for me, but for everyone, for all the trouble they would be in if it didn't work. I wanted to burn a tree to get an agreement for you." Her soft exhalation wasn't quite a sigh. "Then pride, in you and when we fixed everything, and then excitement as midnight came near. I'm sure I really enjoyed it, as me. Which is a real problem."

"How?" Abel looked up and this time he kept talking. Ferryl looked worried, and a little frightened. "Surely that's a good thing? That's what you wanted, isn't it?"

Ferryl actually glanced away, avoiding his eyes, a whole new experience for Abel. "But I couldn't stop, I kept dancing and laughing. Then you kissed me, and then Shawn did, and others, and everyone gathered round and laughed and cheered, and I felt as if I cared about you all. I wanted to be your friend."

"Then you are. It's not that hard." Abel almost spoiled the whole thing by laughing, because he'd only ever had two really close friends before Ferryl turned up, Kelis and Rob. Even now he couldn't really take in how many people smiled and said hello when they saw him. "If I can learn, so can you."

"Could you help me? This woman will need more memories than the dance." Ferryl turned her head to look at him but Abel glanced down, then wished he hadn't. "When I said I wanted to be your friend, I meant it. Not just as one of the group. I have to learn to let someone get closer." Ferryl laughed but it was quiet and brittle, nerves, not humour, which meant she'd found another emotion. Unless all this was her pretending, Abel realised.

"Like I said, half the lads at school will be happy to make friends." Maybe that was what Ferryl meant, she needed to practice her pretending. "You're doing a pretty good job now."

"I'm frightened and it isn't pretence, because even the memories I have of past hosts won't help this time. The world has changed too much since then. Before I went into the pit there were two sorts of girls, unless they were heiresses. By eighteen the girls had kissed one or two boys and were married, housewives and mothers, or too many boys and had become a fallen woman. Now I'm building a new life in a world where women can be anything." Her hands squeezed harder and she started to say something, then stopped.

"It's all right, I'm a good listener."

Ferryl hesitated, then instead of answering out loud her 'voice' sounded in Abel's head. "But now I can't get the words out. If these are emotions, they are scary. They swirl and rush, and maybe I've suddenly found out why you blush and move away when a girl gets too close. Maybe why you have careful rules about kissing. Because letting emotions run around uncontrolled is dangerous. When someone gets too close, and you want to get closer but think maybe you'll be pushed away?" Abel understood that all right. He knew how short and skinny he looked among lads the same age and how the likes of Claris and Arabelle, the girls in the Acro team, always treated him like a freak. "I'm a freak. I'm terrified of allowing myself to like someone in case they are frightened or disgusted."

"I've had some of that. None of us feel that way about you. We all know what you are and I'll bet every one of us considers you a friend." Abel floundered a bit because he couldn't understand how Ferryl couldn't know.

At least his answer pushed her back into speaking aloud. "But you pulled away when you realised you were kissing me." Ferryl didn't sound bitter, just resigned.

"Because you are possessed, not because of you. I like you, the you that's Ferryl." Finally plucking up his courage, Abel told her the one thing that might make a difference. "I enjoyed the last dance, and the kiss afterwards. I felt really guilty about it later, but not because of what you are. Just about the possession part."

Her little chuckle came as a real relief. "But I told you she isn't possessed, not really. This host can never give permission, or ever be allowed to remember her life before now. That dance and kiss was all me, a me who had stopped acting and pretending." Abel was looking at her now, and Ferryl had a smile but looked cautious. Abel couldn't keep up. He'd just told her he liked her as Ferryl, so what now? "This is ridiculous. I can scare a leech glyphless, and stand off a sorcerer." Ferryl's smile faltered and the worry came through much stronger. "I should have asked before I felt anything, but I didn't know I'd need to."

"Can you talk or think in Latin or Greek, or Danish, because English has stopped making sense. What do you want, Ferryl?" Abel wanted to hug her so she stopped worrying, but had no idea what Ferryl wanted. He shut his eyes, which might be an improvement over looking away.

"When I try to say, my throat locks up which makes no sense because I control this body. Everything has stopped making sense, now I've let some emotion in. How do I get closer to someone, to learn more? Can I trust them, let them inside my defences? Because now, after that first taste, I want to feel all those emotions again, as me." Even as only thoughts, her words seemed rushed, running together as Ferryl pushed on. "The more I talk about it, the more I'm sure it was me that really liked that dance, being a normal girl at a party. But not so that I could build someone a new memory. After that dance I want my own friend, Ferryl Shayde's friend, so I can learn more. Someone who'll take me on my first moonlit walk, share a milkshake or fairground ride, all the things I saw on your TV late at night. I've even found someone who seems to like me. He knows what I am and isn't frightened." Her hands lifted Abel's and when he opened his eyes she kissed one knuckle, very gently. "What should I do next?"

Abel knew just what he wanted to do, kiss her. He couldn't, Ferryl was too pretty. That stopped his head spinning. Too pretty was a really stupid reason. The truth was that girls, or getting close to them, terrified him because he expected them to suddenly start laughing at him. Except this girl felt that he might be disgusted or frightened. He really didn't think of Ferryl and her body as two people, not anymore. Maybe because she'd been a companion in three different bodies, so he knew her, not her disguise. So what was his excuse now? Abel screwed up his courage. "I don't know." Then very slowly, carefully, he pulled her hands forward and kissed her knuckles.

"That doesn't feel like don't know." Ferryl leant forward and kissed his knuckles again, so their faces were centimetres apart. "I've never done this as me, without using a memory to guide me."

"Neither have I, not really. Nor shared a milkshake or a rollercoaster." Not without magic or possession, Abel meant, but for once kept his trap shut instead of launching into a long explanation. Abel's head crept forward.

Ferryl barely breathed but Abel felt it on his lips. "We could make a list?"

"As long as you like."

They lowered their hands and her head came the last few centimetres, or maybe Abel's did. The kiss wasn't like with Kelis, a zing of magic, or the carefully measured ones with Jenny and Claris, or anything like those at the dance, but it felt very nice. The sort of nice he'd like to do again. With that in mind, Abel leant forward to put his arm round her, and Ferryl's arm came round him, and the second kiss definitely lived up to expectations.

"Oh. Oh! Abel?" Oddly enough, for once Abel didn't leap back and turn scarlet. He turned very calmly and smiled up at Kelis.

"That's me, and this is Ferryl. I think we've just sorted out the handholding communication problem." Since they'd both got an arm around each other, well past sorted out.

"You actually needed to practice? What happened to oh, no, I won't do that?" Kelis glared at Ferryl. "What did you do to him?"

"Ferryl did nothing. We had a talk and now I know her better. Ferryl, not the host, who will never wake up. I admitted I think she's pretty but I also like her, the real Ferryl. The real Ferryl likes me enough to hold my hand in public without any rules." In some part of his mind Abel noted he wasn't blushing for once. "Now would you like me to have this conversation with Emst, or Laurence, or the next sucker?"

Kelis looked shocked, then confused and a little lost before turning on her heel. "No. You're right. None of my business. Though I'd better warn Rob and Jenny." She strode off down the corridor. Abel stared at the open door, baffled. Kelis kept giving him grief about not kissing girls properly or teasing him about never having a real girlfriend, so why did she stomp off like that?

Ferryl sighed and leant on his shoulder, so Abel hugged her. "I hope Kelis isn't really mad at me. I really don't want to upset any of your friends. Do you think Jenny will be upset?" Her tone lightened. "Rob will complain and make me a better offer." After hugging tighter for a moment Ferryl sat up straight again. "No more acting. That will be strange." She stood, with a little smile that seemed much less sure than Ferryl Shayde's usually did, still holding onto Abel's hand. "We should go and tell Rob ourselves, because Kelis went straight upstairs."

Abel would have rather sat here quietly, but Rob would soon find out and he'd rather have reinforcements when Kelis came back. Instead, he and his thousand-year-old girlfriend went to face the music. Or not, because Rob claimed he'd known all along which was why he'd volunteered to ride with Emst to the New Year dance. When she came downstairs Jenny seemed to find it hilarious. She kept looking at the two of them sat together, then making jokes about older women and giggling. Even Kelis seemed better when she came back downstairs. She eventually made a few digs about watching out for the quiet ones, because a thousand years of experience hadn't saved Ferryl.

Abel walked back through the village hand in hand with his new girl, and kissed her goodbye at Kelis's gate without any heart-searching about if he should or shouldn't. They sat together that night for the Bonny's Tavern meeting, and Ferryl escorted him to the door at the end of it. Rob putting both hands over his eyes while they said goodnight more or less set the seal on the whole thing. Abel wasn't sure if his mum would just roll her eyes because she'd expected it or give him grief when she found out. Rob insisted anyone with half a brain and one eye would have seen the way Abel had been looking at the new Ferryl.

*   *   *

Maybe Abel had been looking at Ferryl too much, even at the dance, because the Taverners at school didn't seem surprised. Tobias, the student who'd talked of getting a tent, made his usual comments about clean living, country air, and yet another pretty girl. This time he definitely looked at Kelis when he said pretty and asked if any of them wanted a partner to play Bonny's Tavern on Skype. Within a couple of weeks, Fay Shayde, from Germany, settled into Stourton Comprehensive. According to Ferryl, these schooldays were definitely brand-new memories. She'd never attended any sort of school before meeting Abel.

Unlike the previous handholding just for communication, and awkward moments when the girlfriend charades meant hugging and kissing, Abel relaxed. Ferryl liked him, and she knew him better than anyone except his mum, Kelis and Rob. Better yet, with a sorcerer-length life ahead he'd got time to work through all those first milkshake and rollercoaster ride moments. From the comments Ferryl made about film experiences she wanted to try, Abel would definitely need more than a normal lifespan.

There were plenty of others either breaking up or chatting up, and the gossips soon turned to Claris and her new bloke. The rugby player who had been dressed as a frost giant certainly matched her usual boyfriends a lot better than Abel had. Claris began to act more like herself, laughing and flirting, though the nasty edge seemed to have gone. Rob started spending break times with Kathy, a girl in the same year who took sciences but had only just started playing Bonny's Tavern. When she mentioned that she'd been playing the game with Rob over Skype to understand the science involved, that finally diverted Kelis from tweaking Abel.

The rest of Abel's life settled down, giving him a chance to catch up on his schoolwork. After coming back from town without her earrings, his mum asked Abel to help her look on the internet to decide between three used cars. When she finally traded in her old car and arrived home in the newer one, Abel put hexes under the bonnet and the boot carpet. He even filled the Fiat Punto logo up with magic, just in case it was a real hex.

It wasn't just his mum's car being traded in, riding around in the BMW wouldn't be an option much longer. As soon as the divorce had been finalised it would be swapped for a minibus and a small second-hand car. Mrs Ventner couldn't drive, so the minibus would be her investment in the company, but she wanted Kelis to have a car. It would be a terrific incentive for Kelis to pass her test as soon as possible after her seventeenth birthday. According to Kelis it wouldn't take long, because she'd put the Highway Code on a wit.

Even creating wits wasn't real pressure, more like a necessity. The additional courses they were taking, especially the biology and the extra work on human biology, were probably too much without magical memory sticks. Abel, Kelis and Rob gritted their teeth and etched the biology information into a wit. The results were strange. None of them were sure how much they actually remembered from the lessons and how much from the wit. Abel and Rob stuck to using a shin bone to start with but Kelis wouldn't confirm where hers went. Jenny could put a locking glyph into compressed earth, but getting one into a branch without marring the surface still defeated her and school work interfered with magic practice.

The only real pressure came from trying to launch the game, Bonny's Tavern. Mr Forester, or Jenny with him watching over her, cut back the scale of the launch again and again but there still wasn't enough cash in the kitty to make a decent impact. At the very least there should be adverts in gaming magazines and online, on some of the forums. The only way out seemed to be another loan from Mr Forester, but Jenny warned he'd want more shares.

Even a loan wouldn't help with making the church into another refuge. The alterations were just too expensive to be practical, because of the rules and regulations about really old buildings. Even if the Tavern relied on Jenny's dad again, or his firm, and he did it for cost, they couldn't afford the amount of work needed. Kelis's mum offered furniture, including fitted wardrobes and the kitchen if necessary, because when she rented somewhere that sort of thing would be included. Even if it wasn't, everything from the big house wouldn't fit into a flat or two bedroom house.

Unfortunately the church needed a whole additional floor fitted with internal walls to create upstairs bedrooms, and serious plumbing and drainage work to accommodate bathrooms. Some of the windows would probably collapse once the boards were removed, while repairing the others would be specialist work and expensive. The wiring and plumbing would need a full inspection and might need replacing.

At the moment, every penny from the Stourton magic contracts went into Frederick's house. The place had been spruced up enough for renting as bedsits, but needed more work to cater for abused women who might have children or tenants with real medical problems. There'd be no skimping because with the charity link, the place would get close scrutiny once the game launched. Any of the Taverners with spare time provided labour, but too much of the work needed professionals.

The Taverners filling the protection hexes for the new contracts reminded Abel about the client who wanted to meet the sorceress, so he arranged a visit. Fay would be the sorceress with Abel as her assistant, allegedly so Ferryl would be along to help if necessary. Shawn sniggered at that part because he thought Ferryl lived in Abel's arm but all the Taverners called Fay, Ferryl. It had even caught on as a nickname at school with people who had no idea of the reason.

The day after a serious meeting between the parents and children about the state of Bonny's Tavern the game, Abel contacted Woods and Green. Despite the short notice, the magical solicitors fixed up an appointment for the same day as the hexing contract meeting. Ferryl thought Abel would get a lot of priority at the solicitors for at least one normal human lifetime, because of the coin.

*   *   *

Ferryl insisted on the Taverneers meeting in Castle House the evening after Abel made the appointments. Despite the weather, she insisted on Jenny coming over, which meant serious business. Abel tried to find out, but she wasn't telling him in advance. At least she didn't beat around the bush once they'd helped Jenny to get dry with reverse water glyphs and everyone had a seat and drink.

"Everyone here knows I have a charred glyph from the entrance, but the information is damaged. I have been carefully testing what is there, sometimes with Abel or more often Zephyr to help." Ferryl glanced down at their held hands and up at Abel. "Though not everything, because some of the glyphs might be dangerous if I get them wrong. I have experimented alone because I can heal this body, but now I can let you all know about one." She let go of Abel, stood up and moved into the middle of the room before making a small hand movement. "Cast glyphs at me please. Not strong ones or you may damage the room."

The four teenagers trusted her enough to agree, though they all threw very small wind glyphs that wouldn't harm her. Not that a big fire glyph would have mattered, because each glyph snuffed out before reaching the smiling sorceress. Kelis came to her feet, her hand outstretched, then stopped. "A shield! How complicated is the glyph?" She moved her head from side to side, trying to see. "It's invisible."

"I can see the flows. It looks like something else but there are differences." Zephyr flew out of Abel's arm to circle the room, connecting to everyone but Ferryl. "It is a globe, very close to the top of Ferryl's head and perhaps touching her feet. There is a resemblance to a veil but more complicated, and it will not let me connect spooky-phone."

Ferryl pointed to the shimmering form. "Zephyr will be telling you she sees a globe. Keep explaining, Zephyr."

Nobody else saw anything change, but Zephyr kept up a commentary. "The globe is changing, shrinking but not all over. Now it follows Ferryl's shape, but just a little bit away from her skin. The sorcerer! He had a shield like this!"

"What did Zephyr say?" Abel explained, bringing a smile to Ferryl's face. "I forgot she saw Pendragon's shield. The reason it is close to me, in my shape, is because that is the natural shape of a shield. It will normally include clothing and any small item carried by the caster." A faint tinge of blue outlined Ferryl. "I have coloured it now, deliberately. You all know you have a natural shield covering your skin, supported by your ward, which is why attacks from magic and creatures are blunted. This shield uses that natural protection, strengthening it and pushing it outwards." The blue glow moved out to create the globe Zephyr had first described.

"Why move it out? Isn't that harder work?" Kelis moved around Ferryl, tilting her head back and forth as she inspected the globe even closer.

"Does the globe use more magic, or more control?" Jenny rose to her feet to come closer, followed by Rob and Abel. She reached out, very tentatively, and touched the glow. "It tingles."

"The harder you push on the shield, the more it will hurt you. Heat or the shock of an impact can leak through a shield, which is the reason for the globe, so that the caster keeps clear." She chuckled and twirled to indicate the clear area around herself. "Though sorceresses don't keep a shield up in company because if two touch, the firework display can scorch walls and furniture. There is also a violent reaction if a shield touches items with magic in them, such as hexes. Two shields in firm contact drain magic from both sorceresses, very quickly, another good reason to avoid touching. Don't throw a glyph while doing that, because if it explodes on their shield it's still inside yours." Ferryl held out her hand to Abel and the shield disappeared. "Remember to banish it before holding hands."

"Even if the other person isn't warded?" Rob ignored comments from Kelis and Jenny about girls who might want to carry out scientific experiments.

"A shield won't hurt anyone who isn't magically aware because they have no natural barrier. A magically aware person, even if they can't actually control magic and have no ward, will be repelled. Unless they are included." When Abel took her hand Ferryl tugged him closer. "Ask Zephyr to come home, please." As soon as the Sprite disappeared into her tattoo, the blue glow outlined Ferryl and Abel, before opening into an elongated blob that included Abel. "Then the sorceress can let her guard down, because only someone trusted would be invited inside." She put her arms around Abel and kissed him.

"Oh yeuk, purrrlease. You could have made the colour stronger to keep that private." Kelis had a hand up to hide the sight.

"I'm more interested in how we test if we've got that part right. Do we have to kiss the other person to check if it holds when we're distracted?" Jenny looked at Rob, then Kelis, tapping her chin with a finger as if debating. "Hmm, that could be awkward."

"Safest to try with someone who can't see creatures, just in case." Rob grinned and pointed at Kelis. "Maybe Kelis had better stick to warded lads, or lasses, in case she binds the sucker." A quick flurry of teasing about who might carry out the test with who died down until they were all watching Ferryl again.

Kelis touched the shield very gently, as Jenny had. "Perhaps we'd better learn how hard it is to cast before sharing."

"Don't worry about sharing at all, not yet. I want you to drop all other practice and concentrate on learning to shield." Ferryl turned slowly to meet everyone's eyes, one at a time, obviously worried and trying to impress on them how serious this was. "I've been pushing, trying to get this right, because I want you all protected as fast as possible. My friends must be safe, now I am learning how friendship feels. Once you've perfected your shields, then it's up to Abel who else learns."

The others relaxed just a little because Ferryl always repeated the last part when telling them anything new. She would teach Abel as fast as he could learn, and he insisted she taught his closest friends. Ferryl still didn't seem to care about anyone outside the Taverneers except Zephyr.

"Even so, you usually let us sort of ease into a glyph for a day or two, to get used to it." Jenny looked at the rest for support and they all nodded agreement. "Why is this one so urgent?"

"Because on Saturday we will meet someone who definitely knows about magic. Not only will these protect you, they will send a message. I'm sure Pendragon will ask our client about the meeting." Ferryl's little smile had real wicked in it. "Only senior apprentices learn to shield, so we'll try to find a reason to demonstrate them to help with the scaring glyphless. There's also an outside chance whoever it is will hire a senior apprentice as a bodyguard when meeting a strange sorceress."

"So just how hard is it to learn the glyph, well enough to look as if we are competent?" For once even Kelis looked unsure, because a senior apprentice glyph sounded like very advanced magic.

"Not hard at all, so you will practice until you really are competent. Pretending would be dangerous if you were challenged. This glyph is similar to casting a veil and you all cast strong veils, very stable. Now you have to cast one, just inside your skin."

"Inside my skin? I still haven't perfected etching under the surface of wood, and I really don't fancy putting my skin through that sort of punishment!" Jenny really looked downhearted and the rest weren't pleased. The others could get down to their bones to create wits, but remembered the damage to the tree branches when they'd first practiced. Casting a new glyph inside their skin could be very painful.

Ferryl waited until the complaints stopped. "Not to do anything like staining or etching, just to get inside your natural shield. You can all do that, even you, Jenny, because you won't be trying to alter anything. The shield glyph incorporates the one for a veil but also combines with your natural defences. If you make the shield into a globe and then rotate it, that will also act as a veil."

"So anti-clockwise. Do we also have to spin a glyph clockwise to extend the shield, like we do with the veil?" Abel tried to see, but even from inside the shield there wasn't a clue. The blue faded away but left a very faint lemon-coloured hint. That suddenly disappeared, as Ferryl dropped the shield and launched into her explanation. The size and shape came down to intent, and the hint of lemon reminded the caster they had an active shield. Depending on the strength, the amount of magic available, the shield could repel physical attacks such as thrown rocks or arrows as well as magical ones. Her shield deflected musket balls, but Ferryl couldn't be sure about stopping modern bullets.

"Never mind bullets, it's a rain and wind shield." Rob smiled happily as they all looked at him, puzzled because they could manage that using wind glyphs. "I hate getting wet or cold because Melanie is walking with us and I can't divert the raindrops or wind. Now I can keep the shield close to my skin so it won't matter if my clothes are soaking wet."

Jenny perked up, holding out both hands and twisting one as if accelerating. "I'm all for that when I'm on my moped. Where there's no traffic to see me I'll put a shield right round it to stop the wind and any rain. It should act like an air bag as well, if I get in an accident." The four of them kept exchanging ideas on how to use the shield as Ferryl carefully drew the glyph. The shield consisted of a double veil glyph with the dashes forming the inner one offset to cover the gaps in the outer. Just as a veil for a person also hid solid items they touched or wore, so a shield tolerated any such items including the small patch of carpet they stood on. A shield cast while sitting in a chair included the chair. Standing up and breaking contact or trying to sit while shielded would burn the chair, though Ferryl felt sure she would find the solution on the damaged wit.

Ferryl insisted on two hours of concentrated practice, which included trips out into the garden to fill up with magic. Zephyr disconnected from Abel so she could learn to shield independently. The sprite would take a little longer because she'd never needed a veil to hide from most people, and didn't have enough magic to cast the stronger versions.

Eventually Jenny had to leave, but promised to work on her shield at home. She had kept the two belts of gold bars from the New Year party, so with her diamond she'd have plenty of juice for more practice. According to Jenny, using up more magic was an incentive in its own because filling both belts and the diamond still gave her a giggling fit. Once she'd recovered and ridden off home, the others left Castle House as well.

Ferryl hadn't been kidding. She insisted on practice at every opportunity, so by Saturday the humans could all cast a solid shield without any fluctuation. A last check by Zephyr confirmed everyone else's flows were steady, though hers wasn't that good yet. According to Ferryl, that was because Zephyr had never practiced her veil, and her outer limit wasn't as clearly defined as human skin. If shields were needed Zephyr would stay inside Abel's. Ferryl might think they were all safer, but her precautions left the rest feeling more nervous.

Mixed Results

The first visit on Saturday, to Frederick's house, combined business and pleasure. Frederick liked the idea of protecting Elmwood Park and his dryad friend. He became enthusiastic at the thought of offering a few dryads from the orchard new, young trees in the park so they could keep his friend company. Jenny and Kelis came up with that, giving a dryad three young trees to compensate for them being smaller, so that Frederick and the Taverners could use the magic in the orchard trees they vacated. Twelve Taverners walked to the park to set up the boundary, an echo of the first time the Tavern went there.

Dryad Elm, in its big Horse Chestnut tree, didn't seem keen on anyone claiming the park until Abel explained. The dryad would stay, but now it could ripen seeds to go into a couple of the other trees. The saplings weren't quite big enough to protect seedlings, not yet, but the protection around the park would deal with that. Explaining there might be other dryads coming, some extra company, really cheered up the old dryad. With ten other magic users to help, Abel and Fay soon set a dozen lead bars into the park walls to power a warning barrier around the whole area. That should claim the park and the trees until Ferryl could set up a feed from the trees to create a real deterrent to magic thieves.

She announced, through Abel and Zephyr, that she didn't want to put in the traps to zap any sorcerer poaching magic, not yet. It had been a while since she last cast those, so she'd prefer to inspect a working version first. Privately Ferryl admitted she didn't know how, not without the right wit. With luck, if Zephyr helped her to inspect one of Abel's new parks, she could work it out.

*   *   *

Shawn, one of the oldest Taverners, drove the BMW for the next visit because he filled the hexes for this customer. On the way, Abel warned Shawn to keep well clear of everyone else. He explained the shield, and that the best of the Taverners such as Shawn would learn as soon as Abel had got it perfected. At least Abel had an answer when Shawn complained about not having enough magic to practice yet another glyph. Providing he only took one extra lead bar's worth a week, Shawn could tap the young trees in Elmwood Park. If Dryad Sycamore told him that damaged the tree, Shawn had to cut back immediately or use several trees.

*   *   *

The security guard on the gate of the protected property called the house before letting them in. By the time the car reached the turning circle outside the front door, a man and woman stood there waiting. "That bloke is always here, but I don't recognise the woman." Shawn sounded worried.

Ferryl's mental voice didn't sound very happy. "The owner must be nervous about sorceresses, very nervous, because both of those people wear shields close to the skin. The man must be a permanent magical bodyguard. Pendragon or some sorceress might have loaned the woman, a senior apprentice, to help out. We must all be ready to shield very quickly." Abel waited a moment as Zephyr confirmed the shields, and the active hexes on the house. He knew about the hexes against creatures because Shawn topped up the magic levels every week, but there were also a couple of others not mentioned in the contract. "The extras are dormant, and have similarities to those in Woods' office so they could be there to protect against glyph users. We might be dealing with a sorceress, though not a strong one if Pendragon tolerates her living in Stourton."

When Zephyr passed the information to everyone else, Shawn released his seat belt and twisted to look at the back seat. "Will we be safe?"

"You four can handle those two, and I'll deal with the sorceress." Ferryl seemed really confident, so Abel did his best.

"No problem. Come on, introduce us." That part went smoothly enough, though neither greeter offered to shake hands. Magic users didn't anyway, Ferryl confirmed, in case the other person had an active shield. The usual liaison between Shawn and the owner preceded them into a large dining room, while the woman stayed in the hallway. He moved to the French windows looking over the rear gardens and stood with his arms crossed. When Zephyr sent out spooky-phones to remind everybody to keep an eye open, the man definitely saw them.

Large wooden double doors at the other end of the dining room opened, using magic according to Zephyr, to reveal a middle-aged man sat at a large polished desk in a luxurious office. "Welcome. I am known as Redwolf. I am here specifically to meet our new local protection. Which of you is the sorceress?"

Abel looked at Shawn who shrugged. "I've never met this bloke. I dealt with the man who met us at the door and he spoke of a woman."

"I am Ferryl Shayde, known locally as Fay Shayde." She walked towards Redwolf. "Is our contract with you or someone you protect?"

"The young sorceress from Germany? This is my private house, somewhere quiet where I can relax. I'd provide my own protection but Pendragon bought the monopoly in Stourton, though now it seems he has released some work to you. Please come through and take a seat." The sorcerer indicated a plush seat in front of his desk. "I would prefer it if your apprentices stayed in there. There are plenty of chairs." Redwolf nodded towards the offered chair. "Though not quite as good as this."

"Not as magical as that either." Abel asked Zephyr to let the others know, though not Ferryl because Abel felt sure she'd see the magic. Zephyr also primed Rob, so if those doors started to close he could put his rounders bat in the way. Abel had a bad feeling about this, because they'd been deliberately misled about the owner.

Ferryl walked through into the office before stopping to inspect the chair. "Perhaps not." She turned and a wind glyph snaked out to grab one of the dining chairs and bring it through. "This looks more comfortable."

The sorcerer, definitely sorcerer because when Ferryl cast her glyph Zephyr saw him raise a shield, sat down slowly. "That has answered my first question. You are a sorceress and one with better than normal magical sight. Someone has cast doubt on that."

"Pendragon? I've never met him. The trainees dealt with him the last time he caused trouble." Ferryl glanced back at the man who had shown them in, presumably Redwolf's apprentice. "Please explain to your apprentice, his shield will not protect him. Not only that, but it's not polite."

"Just a precaution with you bringing so many apprentices. Another rumour claims they are not tethered, so I worried about them being under control." The sorcerer pointed at Shawn. "That one is always polite, but one never knows. He only brings one other, yet they fill all my hexes.

An apprentice given that much magic should be tethered. One carrying a bound spirit definitely should be." Abel kept glancing around, uncertain where Redwolf might be going. This definitely wasn't a client checking the contractor knew their job.

"Sending more people would be a waste of time and effort." Ferryl finally sat, half-turned to keep an eye on the door into the office. "Perhaps I should introduce everyone?"

"No need. Since you give them so much magic, they should wait elsewhere. Just so I don't get nervous." Redwolf never moved, but the man at the French windows opened them and a woman came in. At the same time the woman who had greeted the party came into the dining room through the door, followed by another man.

"All have shields! Three are tethered to Redwolf."

"Tell Rob to be ready with the bat. Tell the others to put up shields when I call, and Shawn to crouch under the table in the middle. We'll cover him." Abel thought furiously, and something Redwolf had said made him smile. "If it kicks off, run at them and crash shields. Apprentices don't get much magic, he said." Abel gave it a few moments for his friends to get set, then called out "Shields!" He moved to stand opposite the newly arrived man. Beside him, Kelis put her hand up towards her throat, which looked like a nervous gesture, and moved towards the woman who'd just come in the door. Abel knew Kelis would be opening a button, for if she needed her big diamond.

"Are you sure about that, Abel?" Jenny didn't sound too confident.

Abel forced a laugh. "They haven't got half the magic you carry." He hoped Ferryl would order him to stand down if he'd got this wrong, but she sat back with an enigmatic smile.

"This could be a mistake, Redwolf. The trainees don't want to go. Perhaps you should have let me introduce them?" She glanced at Redwolf as he came to his feet. "Sit down."

Abel would never be sure if Ferryl put the contempt in her voice to deliberately provoke the sorcerer. If so, it worked. "Take them!" Redwolf gestured and the doors began to close.

Ferryl didn't move except to raise a negligent hand towards Abel.

"Deal with it. I'll slap Redpuppy down if he interferes."

That probably upset the sorcerer, it definitely shocked the man in front of Abel. He recovered, his eyes narrowing as he lunged forward to try and intercept Rob. Abel moved to block him, so Rob could get to the doors. After the Castle House fiasco, they'd cut the Tavern hex deeper on both sides of the bat, and melted lead into the grooves to hold more magic so he felt confident it would hold. The apprentice hit Abel, or rather his shield did, and Abel blinked and rubbed at his eyes as a firework display went off in front of him.

Through the showering sparks and flashes of coloured light coming off both shields, Abel could see the effect went right round the globe. The apprentice stopped, startled, then pushed again but Abel dug his heels in and both shields flattened where they met. He could feel pressure, and magic draining away, but with four belts he could handle that for ages. Lights reflected from the walls and the French windows and he glanced round.

Rob had placed his bat and now he locked shields with the other man, stopping him from getting to the doors. Jenny and the woman who'd come in through the French windows looked equally uncertain, so their shields were only clashing intermittently. Kelis had no doubts. She had a hand inside her blouse and was trying to herd her opponent into a corner. A brilliant idea, Abel realised.

"Drive them towards the walls, away from the doors and window and into a corner if possible. Once they run out of magic, they'll surrender." He certainly hoped so because his opponent redoubled his attempts to get to Rob's bat. A sharp crack and a whiff of smoke meant the doors had met the bat's hexes. Abel pushed back hard, confident he could stand the drain. He still hadn't seriously dented the first belt.

"What do we do once they surrender?" Abel turned enough to see Shawn. Instead of diving under the table, he'd crouched on top of it, a glyph boiling in each hand.

"If anyone drops their shield, Zephyr will confirm it. We'll herd them over to the far wall and you will guard them. First sign of a glyph, you fry them." Abel looked back at his opponent in time to see the shock on his face. "They'll keep their palms flat against the wall, Shawn, so you'll know."

"No problem." Shawn's laugh had just a touch of hysteria. "I ought to do something useful."

"Burn them?" Jenny wasn't saying no, but she sounded dubious.

"Their choice." Kelis meant every word. "After all, it's not our house." She laughed suddenly. "That's right, little girl, you are going over to that wall or getting a wonderful suntan. When your shield starts to fail you've got two choices." Since the woman had to be in her thirties, little girl probably made her more determined to win.

Abel's opponent started backing towards the door he'd come through but Abel crowded forward, because from the sounds of that Kelis would be free to help in a minute or two. The man reached the door, but Abel kept coming so there wasn't room to open it inwards. The part of the wall and the door touching the apprentice's shield began to smoke and blacken. "If you stay there, you'll roast long before the flames reach me." The apprentice, probably a strong one because he wasn't worried about the drain as yet, began to work his way along the wall towards the French window. More wallpaper smoked and charred as he moved.

"Mine's surrendered!" Jenny sounded triumphant, and definitely relieved. "Her shield stuttered so she's not very good at it. I've got loads of magic left?"

"Has she dropped the shield, Zephyr?"

"Yes, she is defenceless. The shield facing Rob weakened just for a moment, but he might have been distracted by the smoke. Patches of wallpaper and some of the chairs are smoking where a shield has touched them but none are on fire, not yet."

"Can you come out a little so they can see who is watching, please? Providing the shield won't hurt you." Abel remembered to say the next part out aloud, this business of talking in his head then in words was confusing. "Her shield is down, Shawn. Watch her please. Jenny, could you put out any fires, then block the French window so none of these get away?" The man facing Abel glanced desperately towards his exit, then at the shimmer by Abel's shoulder. "Had enough?"

"Perhaps I should ask you that. I have more magic and a better shield than the others, so I'm not even close to finished."

"Not yet but soon it'll be four against two, because Rob has his opponent on the run. Kelis has hers trapped in a corner, and when she gives in it'll be four to one. How much have you got?" Abel put his hand inside his shirt to draw more magic and saw the man's eyes narrow, wondering why. "Shawn brings extra magic in lead bars to fill the hexes." A terse nod acknowledged that. "He's not our strongest. Us four carry a lot more magic, in belts, and know more glyphs. Sort of like senior apprentices." The apprentice's eyes flicked towards the office where Ferryl sat. "Not Ferryl's apprentices, we don't work like that. Us four have our own tree to supply magic. It helps with training."

Zephyr reported that the woman who'd surrendered had her hands against the wall, with Shawn watching every move, and Jenny had moved to the window. Though Jenny must have been feeling much more confident now because she kept going. "I'm going to help Kelis, Abel, but I'll cover the window if anyone tries to get in or out."

"Mine's had enough, he's backing away. I reckon he'll be done in a minute or two." Rob sniggered as light flickered and flashed behind Abel. Zephyr reported the man's shield had started to fluctuate and wouldn't last much longer.

A man's voice called out from behind Abel. "Mannan, his shield hasn't faltered and he's still pushing hard. Mine's nearly done, and there's no point waiting until I run out and get burned."

"I understand. I'll tell our master I ordered you to stop, both of you. You're no good to him badly burned or dead." The man in front of Abel, Mannan, tried to move back towards the door again but Abel had pressed in off-centre so he couldn't get past.

"Come on Kelis, you're slipping." Rob herded his victim towards the wall, though Abel had to rely on Zephyr to let him know because his opponent wasn't done yet.

"Oh, this one is going down, believe me Rob." As Kelis spoke a brighter flash caught Abel's attention. He looked over to see that Jenny had pressed her shield in alongside Kelis's, doubling the assault on the apprentice trapped in the corner. Kelis laughed. "Hi Jenny. Just give her another nudge or two. Ooh, did I just feel the strain on her shield? Do it again." A voice murmured. "What's that, you want to be good? Drop the shield and lean against the wall then. I'll keep my shield up until you've assumed the position."

When he glanced over again Abel saw Jenny headed his way, her eyes on Abel's opponent. "Hello, my name is Jenny. Want to dance?" It had to be some sort of hysteria affecting them all. Jenny had a bright smile, momentarily obscured as she rammed her shield into Mannan's. "Budge up a bit, Abel, so I can get proper contact. This is like a cross between bumper cars and Guy Fawkes. Anyone got candy floss?"

Maybe it was Jenny's obvious confidence, or the thought of Kelis or Rob joining in that finally decided Mannan. Abel saw the fight go out of the apprentice, his shoulders slumping and a resigned expression crossing his face. "How do I stop without dying?" The man wasn't beaten, but now he thought he would be. If two shields or more were still pressing when he ran out of magic, Abel could only assume the result would be horrific.

"Kelis, guard the French windows please. Rob, cover the double doors to the office." Abel glanced towards Jenny and smiled. "If you back off that way, and I back off this way, he stays pinned." He turned back to the apprentice. "You drop your shield when I say and head for the wall. Once there, spread your legs and put your palms flat against the wall." Abel narrowed his eyes and tried to look threatening. "We'll pull our shields in tight but we'll keep them up. I'll know if you try anything and there'll be no second chance."

"I heard you confirm the other shields going down, so whatever you've bound can see them. Just for the record, we weren't to hurt you. My master was told you could be subdued and possibly recruited because you weren't properly trained or tethered." The man glanced at Jenny as her shield stopped sparking on his. "I don't want anyone feeling vindictive."

"None of us are hurt, so fair enough. I'm Abel." He almost stuck his hand out but remembered the shield. "Zephyr, please tell me when his shield goes down."

"I'm Mannan. Our master, Redwolf, likes Celtic names." The apprentice moved to the wall and with a wry smile assumed the position as instructed. "Please don't pat me down."

Abel had to smile at that. "Not if you behave. Will you help Jenny to

217

watch them please, Rob?"

"I'll do it, Abel. Rob's got to put a bandage on his bat." From the humour in Kelis's voice it wasn't too bad. Abel turned to see Rob scowling at his magic club.

"I've got another scorch mark to sand out, but not as bad as last time. Just for future reference, a seeming isn't fireproof." Rob held up his bat. "The tape caught fire." He'd put gaffer tape over the lead in case it came loose, then disguised it as wood.

But Abel wasn't looking at Rob, his eyes had gone past him to the doors and the office. The two doors hung open, both with a charred section at the bottom corner where they'd met the bat. One had half-opened then jammed or just run out of magic. The other had almost opened, but hung at a drunken angle because the bottom hinge had broken and the middle one was warped and stretched. Beyond them Ferryl still lounged in the chair, while Redwolf had stood up and backed off about three steps. "He has a full shield up, out in a globe." Abel nearly laughed aloud, because he'd have bet money on that. Redwolf looked like a man who'd stuck his fork into his spaghetti and come up with a rattlesnake.

Ferryl smiled, raised her hands and patted them together. "Well done." She turned back towards Redwolf and her voice hardened. "Sit down." The sorcerer looked at her, back to the dining room full of unfriendly faces, and back at her. "They aren't going to attack you, you fool. They came to discuss business. Now sit down, Redwolf." Her tone lightened, becoming thoughtful as he moved carefully towards his chair. "You do know that your namesake was female? The Red Wolf was a form taken by the Morrigan. If I had come to these shores a little earlier we might have met."

His eyes and face looked shocked now. "But you are newly orphaned, a child."

"No, just arrived in Stourton with a new identity. You are a child compared to me and Pendragon is an infant." Ferryl turned to Abel and beckoned. "You should have listened when I offered to introduce us. You asked to see the sorceress, so I came. If you had asked to meet the man in charge, you would be talking to the master of Castle House."

Now Redwolf seemed to think Abel was the rattlesnake. "You?" he croaked. "No, you were in the gardens but the house remains sealed."

Abel would bet on that information coming from Pendragon. "There's a terrific library in there, and a really nice aquarium. I don't think much of the wardrobe, but Jenny fancies a few of the frocks as fancy dress." Once again Abel had to stop himself sticking out his hand. "Is the shield still up?"

"Yes. His, not Ferryl's."

"Abel claimed the right to Celtchar's estate, by power and blood, while holding the token in Woods and Green's office. As you can see he survived." She frowned at Redwolf. "If we are being polite, you should drop the shield."

Abel would have to ask Ferryl how the sorcerer sat down without burning the chair. He dropped his eyes to her. "What happens now?"

"We talk business. Younger sorcerers do this, beat their chests and shout at each other to sort out some sort of pecking order. Now it's all over, Redwolf will talk sensibly." Ferryl frowned again, her hand moved and a glyph smacked into the plush chair Zephyr had warned Abel about. It spun away across the room, shedding scraps of burning fabric before toppling over. "You'd better get another chair, Abel. That one is ruined." She turned to Redwolf. "I said put the shield away. What did you expect, after offering a chair like that?"

"Ferryl did that on purpose. She hit the chair as soon as his shield went down so he put it back up again." Then she'd told Redwolf off about the shield. Ferryl kept telling Abel she'd forgotten most of her glyphs, so was she running a bluff? It was working, the sorcerer looked lost for words instead of objecting to having his furniture trashed.

Abel turned away, dropping his shield and calming down enough to send a wind glyph to bring a dining room chair. Some of the others were toppled over or scorched. "We all may as well drop the shields and sit down, the prisoners as well. They can use the floor and keep their palms flat on the boards." Abel smiled at Shawn. "You can stay on the table, or pick a chair. My bound spirit will warn you if they start anything." Shawn would think Abel was hiding who Ferryl really was.

Shawn sat with his legs over the edge of the table, an active glyph still in one palm. "I'll keep an eye on them from up here."

Abel turned back, catching the chair as it arrived and setting it next to Ferryl's. He sat down and took her hand so he could hear any hints. Zephyr connected to her, and everyone else. "Phew." Abel could hear the humour in Ferryl's mental voice. "I feel quite useless. That was a really good idea, clashing shields like that, because it stopped them throwing glyphs. Redwolf daren't interfere because he doesn't know how strong I am." Abel remembered, sorcerers didn't get involved in fights, not personally, in case they woke up bound to someone.

"That was a bluff?"

"Of course. Now it's worked, he'll be a good boy and negotiate. Charge him a penalty for the glyphs hidden in the chair I damaged, and the glyphs in the doors, because we have the contract to maintain things like that. Everyone cheats, but he's been caught." Ferryl squeezed his hand, smiled into Abel's eyes and chuckled. "So how much is the penalty clause, Abel?"

"For hexes he's been maintaining himself? I've no idea, but it'll be in the contract someplace." It was, and a substantial sum, but Redwolf paid for the chair, doors and the extra hexes outside. He also admitted that the woman Kelis had faced wasn't his apprentice. He'd been offered extra help just to make certain. Abel didn't even bother to push him; it had to be Pendragon. After a few minutes Kelis complained about the catering. Abel turned to find her lounging in a chair in a very similar pose to Ferryl's.

Redwolf took the hint, despite it coming from an apprentice. He very politely asked Abel to release an apprentice, to let the kitchen know. Abel chose the woman Jenny defeated, since she seemed the weakest, and she took their orders for tea, coffee and cola. When the refreshments arrived, Ferryl called the young woman over and passed her hand over everything on the tray. Redwolf looked offended, but she ignored him until the apprentice had re-joined the other captives. "Yes, I just insulted you. You insulted my employer, so perhaps you should consider it payback and not get any silly ideas?" The sharp jerk of the head showed that Ferryl's bluff still held. Abel really didn't fancy the consequences if Redwolf ever found out the truth.

Interestingly, after the basic business had been sorted out, Redwolf began to ask about how much of Pendragon's business had gone to this charity. Some of his interest was in finding out how they managed to pocket the money once it had been paid over. He seemed surprised it really was a charity and promptly lost interest in that part. Abel wouldn't have understood without Ferryl's hand to guide him, but the next questions were to find out if Pendragon had lost his precious monopoly. Abel confirmed the rest of the business in Stourton, such as creating or charging hexes for manufactured goods, remained Pendragon's.

"According to my sources, you have up to forty apprentices." Redwolf wouldn't call them trainees despite being corrected several times. "I'm not sure why the Council have allowed it, but with that number you could do with more business. I have friends who would be willing to make an arrangement to find them some."

"He means steal business from another sorcerer."

"I am not looking for a fight." Abel shrugged and told the truth. "I'm more interested in sorting out my legacy and finishing school."

"The school part is interesting. Too many older sorcerers have trouble with computers or driving, that sort of thing." The wry smile had to mean Redwolf wasn't very good at something modern. He glanced at Ferryl with a little question in his eyes.

"Which is why I am attending school here. Others sorceresses should do the same." Ferryl spoke seriously, but Redwolf laughed.

"Can you imagine that." Redwolf laughed again, then sobered and turned back towards Abel. "My apologies, we were discussing ways to find your apprentices more work." The sorcerer leant forward, intent. "No fighting involved. If say, twenty of your apprentices turned up and threw a few spectacular fire glyphs at a tree or a wall, that would have a devastating effect. With two or three sorcerers present, along with their tethered apprentices, some sorceresses might want to reconsider their position."

"Don't say a flat no. Let everyone think you might, if the deal is good enough." Ferryl's hand squeezed just a little, and Abel saw Redwolf look at it with a little frown. "Tell Redwolf you will have to think it over, because you don't want to make the wrong enemies right now. It'll keep them all wanting to stay friends."

Abel passed that on, and asked Redwolf to contact Woods and Green with any proposals so they could advise him. From the way Redwolf's face fell, Abel didn't expect any more offers. The conversation wound down until Abel and Ferryl stood up to leave. Redwolf looked at their hands again and Ferryl chuckled. "Tell me, how often do you find genuine youth with so much power? Totally irresistible. I came for a holiday, but I might stay for a hundred years or so." She laughed at the shocked look on the sorcerer's face and put an arm round Abel. "That should help slow them all up as well."

Abel smiled and hugged back. "I'm up for a hundred years or so of private tuition. Who'll be showing us out?" He looked back at the captured apprentices and remembered Mannan giving one of the others permission to surrender. "How about Mannan, so we can keep an eye on him?" All the way out of the house Abel kept expecting something to happen, but Mannan led them to the front door where the BMW still sat, untouched. Abel finally gave in to his good manners and after checking the apprentice still didn't have a shield, put his hand out. Mannan looked at it for long moments, then shook.

At least Abel didn't have to explain to the rest, because Zephyr had been keeping everyone informed. Now everyone hoped Ferryl's bluff and the bloodless victory over the apprentices had worked.

*   *   *

Shawn drove them to their next appointment, but didn't come inside. Shannon had been thoroughly disgusted at missing an entire afternoon, and warned the other Taverners about the way Woods and Green's waiting room made hours flick by in minutes. After checking Abel had his mobile number, Shawn went back to Frederick's to see how the orchard dryads had taken the offer of a new home.

Abel felt sure every visitor didn't get to see one of the partners, but once again he ended up in a room with Terese Green. Once again he unwrapped a small selection of expensive-looking items. "We've thought about what you told us last time. I'd like to sell two or possibly three items. One to give us about…" Abel stopped for a moment because it still seemed a ridiculous amount. "A hundred thousand pounds to invest in launching our game. I'd also like a smaller sum to be donated to the charity side, enough to renovate a church." Abel turned. "Jenny?"

She passed across a sheet of paper. "I got this from dad's computer. We might have to forget the windows, replace them with plain glass, and the same with some of those fancy carvings. That's if the heritage people allow it."

Terese Green took the page, scanned it and shook her head. "The church is eight hundred years old, so you won't be allowed to get away with anything. You can build the new interior because it's an independent wooden construct that doesn't impact the original structure, and could be removed at some time. Unfortunately you will have to repair or at least preserve and protect the windows and any old carvings and inscriptions." She started to smile. "But there are different ways to do so. How good are your Taverners, how precise is their control of heat, wind and colour?"

"It varies." Abel looked at the rest, but even Ferryl didn't understand.

"Renovation on churches is costly, because the church protection stops our magic working and the bishops are too busy elsewhere. If the church de-sanctifies this building, remove all their hexes, the windows will be easier." She glanced up at them. "A combination of heat, cooling, and control of colour can replicate any stained glass, matching the original shape and appearance as well as colouring. Glyphs can even warp the glass a little or put bubbles inside it to make it look older. The leading is, I was once told, much more complicated so you will still need an expert for that part. Someone non-magical will probably be cheaper because magic users never take the time to perfect those sorts of skills. Unless one of you already has experience?"

They all shook their heads as Jenny answered. "I asked but none of the others even has a relative who works with stained glass."

Terese's eyes dropped back down to the list. "The carvings and inscriptions, even the stone ones, can be built back up or recreated by someone competent with the necessary glyphs. New timber panels can be carved, stained and even aged using magic, so they are a perfect match. Any pillars or walls that are painted can be completely restored, then covered in a thin sheet of glass, and a shield to stop any further damage. Drains and wiring are non-magical work. Magical repairs will disguise where they've been installed." She had a wicked smile when she turned it loose. "Check where the drains come out before throwing air glyphs down them to clear any blockages." She handed the list to Abel. "You can hire senior apprentices for parts of the work if necessary. Some sorcerers might take on the work out of pure curiosity."

Abel handed the paper on to Jenny. "Can you revamp this, and come up with a new figure please? We'll start with fifty thousand but if it's a lot more we'll flog something else." Abel wanted the church set up as part of his personal mission to give his mum and Kelis's a bit of income. His mum could be hired for the office work, for starters. "Redwolf might know someone who does this sort of work."

Kelis plucked it from his hand. "I'll sort out what we can do magically, first, with Ferryl's help. That's if I can ever pry her off your arm. That youth and power is sticky stuff." Abel glanced, but the grin looked genuine.

"I can help Jenny with the launch of the game and pricing the rest, as long as I can count on my fingers." Rob did so, very slowly with a frown.

"You'll be busy on your computer, buster, changing graphics and producing some new promotional material. If we're getting the cash, I want to do this properly." Jenny rubbed her hands together. "I'm going to get a fabulous grade in my Business Studies A-level, if I can remember the dry legal bits."

"Which brings us back to these." Abel reached out to the vase he'd brought in last time, the really expensive one. "I also want something like this sold, but not in a hurry and not publicly. The money will be used wherever a Tavern player discovers magic. It will cover transport and accommodation for someone to help them get past leaf fluttering, and maybe some assistance in setting up a local branch if there's several people in one area."

"What is the eventual goal? Are you setting up an organisation to take over areas of the country? That could cause serious problems with an increasing number of sorcerers." Mz Green looked totally serious and a little worried. "As your solicitor, I advise against it."

"We won't take over anywhere that's claimed, just fill in the gaps. The idea is to do this on the cheap. Creepio told me that there's huge areas of the countryside without magical protection, and we know the poorer parts of Stourton have none." Abel warmed to his theme, though he'd never really thought it through before. As he talked he could suddenly see it, in his mind, a whole network of Taverns spreading across the country to fill in all those gaps. They'd be in remote or impoverished places, council estates and villages where few believed in the church and none knew about magic so there wasn't any money to be made. With no contracts or worshippers at stake, neither church nor sorcerers should object. Abel's new woodlands would provide the magic to allow new Tavern recruits to progress quickly, to where they could protect their own little village or maybe housing estate.

First the new Taverners would be taught enough to hunt down and drive out or destroy the likes of skurrits, globhoblins and ganshbaal. Once they'd cleared the worst, the new recruits would be shown how to place hexes to keep out smaller pests such as fae, hoplins, and thornies. Stronger Tavern members would visit to help them with any larger creatures such as varglin, beinsnork, grelf or blood leeches that preyed on humans. Coastal villages may have problems with amanatik, and Abel had no idea what nasty creatures might live in the waters off the coast. As each small group of Taverners became strong enough they could put up a magical barrier like the one around Brinsford. In towns they could achieve a similar effect by hexing lamp posts, fence posts and street signs. Those who lived on farms could plant stakes or power hexes with the magic in hedgerows to deter some of the magical grazing creatures. Crops would be healthier with fewer grazers sucking magic out of the plants, and herds could maybe have hexes painted on them to stop the likes of fae. Pictsies and piskies could be encouraged into stock yards and barns to protect the new-born animals.

Human babies, pets and old folk would be safe from the pests, and their cars and computers freed of gremlins. Once the local Tavern were more adept, they could let the helpful faeries, pictsies, brownies, and pixies back in, and the piskies to help keep the chickens, dogs and rabbits clear of pests. There'd be fewer illnesses when the helpless weren't targeted and drained of enough magic to weaken them. Pictsies and piskies would cut down on gnats and fleas, and if rats or mice were a problem Abel could arrange for the local Tavern to adopt a small goblin meld. Those would also eat discarded food and help with litter and, with a few batlins, would deal with any small creatures who came through a barrier inside cars. The Taverns could then extend their protection to the local non-church schools and colleges. Bit by bit they'd drive the nasties away from all the inhabited areas in the country.

When he finally stopped, Abel realised how hard Ferryl gripped his hand. He looked at her, and beyond, surprised by the stunned looks from his friends. Kelis recovered first. "Wow, Abel. You've never put it like that before. We just sort of bumbled through inventing the game, and fell into magic, and then managed to get a bit of finance. We protected Brinsford because it's where we live, and other Taverners are working on keeping their street or village safe, but that's a life's work you've just laid out."

"One human life, or two or three. Since you've told me I'll live that long, I've got that to spare and more. I'm in." Jenny giggled, shockingly loud. "Dad would have kittens. You never mentioned profit once."

"We'll have to make some money, someplace. We can't steal Abel blind to get it done." Rob's rueful smile accepted they were here with goodies from the house to do just that.

"So we make the Bonny's Tavern game profitable. You get the graphics and the rules and those descriptions as perfect as you can, and I'll sell it." Jenny hesitated, then leant over to hug Rob. "Sorry, it's just that sort of moment. I won't tell Kathy if you don't tell, um, anyone?"

"Deal." Rob looked at Kelis with a little half-smile.

"Not likely. Jenny got lucky but I'm not risking it. I could end up in a furry catsuit if I get too near to you. All that power and youth gunk means Abel's too dangerous for any woman under a thousand years old." She smirked at Abel and Ferryl but it faltered.

Ferryl hadn't said a word, still looking at Abel with a little half-smile. "Power is over-rated and youth passes. A mission though? I've never had a mission, or thought beyond finding the next host." Out loud she answered Kelis. "Yup, he's still covered in the stuff." She turned to Terese Green and continued in a brisker tone. "So we'd better get this carnival on the road. Can you do what Abel asked, Terese?"

Terese didn't quite shake herself, but she definitely needed a moment to get her professional persona back in place. "That is definitely ambitious, but technically feasible. I'll need to know how much of this money has to become public. Private sales between sorcerers will be taxed at one percent but can't be spent openly. Those sorts of sales in the public domain will attract at least twenty percent tax, but there is a middle ground. Funds from sales to sorcerers can become public if we create the right story, but only be taxed at seven percent. The tax is allegedly to cover adjusting public records." Terese checked the notes she'd been making. "You need a hundred and fifty thousand after taxes, a third to be donated to the charity. If it isn't incredibly urgent, I can arrange that with the seven percent tax option." Abel nodded. "Then a large sum of cash, three hundred thousand or so, from a private sale. That will be used here and there, quietly so it doesn't attract attention. You would only pay one percent on that part unless you are careless."

Abel nodded again, even if the figures still didn't seem real. He'd just arranged to get nearly half a million quid in cash, but couldn't spend a penny on his mum. "There's no hurry for the last part. We don't expect many more recruits unless the game actually sells." He tapped the vase again. "This will be more than enough, until we know how it's all going to work out."

"Charitable work will be a novelty for Woods and Green." Terese hesitated for a few moments. "You might want a different firm representing you for that part."

"I want Woods and Green involved in the business and the charity, even if it's just a little. Jenny's dad already has one solicitor working on both so you'll have to sort it out with them." Abel repeated what Creepio had said about any clients getting very good service in disputes. With a smirk Terese agreed, and promised to arrange minor roles in both the business and charity if he signed the necessary papers. If Abel and Mr Forester didn't know someone suitable, Woods and Green would find solicitors and accountants more at home with dealing with charities. After discussing which items would sell quickest, Abel asked her to keep the rest for him. On the way out he once again stopped and went back to hand her a note, and an extra vase he'd put in his school pack.

*   *   *

As he caught up with the others, Abel took out his phone to text Shawn. "Not yet, Abel." Kelis sounded very serious and Abel realised all the rest looked sombre. "We need a corner seat in a coffee shop, because it's too cold for us to be sat around outside."

Abel tried to find out why, but Ferryl's hand wasn't answering. Nobody would until they'd found a place with a table Kelis considered private enough. Even then everyone seemed intent on putting sugar or cream in their drinks. "So give. Either Ferryl or Kelis, because neither of you have any problem with bad news, not normally."

"My turn." Rob hesitated, then went for it without cracking a joke, which really worried Abel. "It isn't bad news. You can't keep giving us money."

"Why not? If it's my money." Abel didn't understand, he thought he'd explained it all. "I'm not really giving you it, because it'll all be invested. It's not even real to me, just some crazy accident in my DNA, and I'd never have inherited anything without you four."

"But I came in late, so I'm not entitled to the same share." Jenny looked dead serious, she wasn't giggling now. "Those vases and suchlike you've left with Terese might be worth a lot of money, but there aren't many and unless you get through the next door that's it. You've got a nice little windfall for one person, enough for a lifetime if you aren't too extravagant, but not when it's split five ways."

"You saved my life, bought me a new one, and now you are filling it with memories. What if you find a girl one day, a real one? Then you will wish you didn't have me as part of your business." Even Ferryl's mental voice sounded more serious than usual. "I came in even later, in some ways."

Abel opened his mouth to shout in sheer exasperation, but remembered where he was so he tried to think instead. The harder he thought, the more confused Abel felt. He knew it had to be this way, that he couldn't do anything else but share, but couldn't put the why into words. Not at first, though as he rejected every logical reason he came up with, Abel was left with something very clear and straightforward. He had real friends, people he felt comfortable with, and the thought of losing them terrified him. "I'm scared. If I get all rich and stuff, and you don't, we won't have anything in common and then I lose my only friends. You hear about it all the time on the internet and on the TV. The lottery winner says it won't change them, but a year later they're in mansion a thousand miles from everyone they know. That's not happening. You all have to share so we stay together."

A very heated but quiet fifteen minutes later the rest conceded, but reluctantly. Abel didn't care how reluctant they were. They'd get used to being equal partners over time and if the game made millions and it still bugged them he'd accept the money back again. If the game flopped, in three hundred years the money wouldn't matter. Ferryl kept arguing, through her hand, right up until Shawn arrived to pick them up. As the rest got into the car Abel held her back, then twirled her round and kissed her really hard. "That will help so you don't lose the memory."

"I'll definitely remember." Ferryl looked shocked, then curious. "What memory?"

Abel kept his voice low, so nobody in the car would hear him. "The memory of when you let someone do something to help just because they like you. Not because you are an ancient sorceress or spirit hunter, not because you can teach them magic or you scare them glyphless. Not even because of those eyes, or what your host looks like. Just because you are a friend." He got into the car and patted the seat. "Come on."

"There's not enough room for all of you. She should sit on your knee." Rob laughed but the rest groaned because he said that every time.

This time Ferryl shut the door, half-turned and hooked her legs over Abel's. She snuggled in. "There, more room. This is another one on the bucket list."

"Who told you about bucket lists?" Kelis looked suspiciously at Rob.

Rob smirked at her. "More importantly, what did they tell her goes on them."

Kelis mimed a finger in her throat. "Not back seat snogging? Yeuk."

"No snogging, I promise. On one condition." Ferryl waited with a little half-smile.

Eventually Kelis just had to ask. "What?"

"The same applies to you and Emst, or any other sucker." As Kelis spluttered and denied back seat anything with anyone, ever, Ferryl reached across to high-five Jenny.

*　*　*

Despite Abel's revelation, the discussion, and giving Terese the goods, none of it had an immediate result. For now, Bonny's Tavern was under-financed despite a small influx of cash. After Christmas, Abel, Kelis, Rob,

Jenny and Ferryl had become true investors, using the seven-thousand-five-hundred pounds from the additional pieces of jewellery 'found' at the same time as the Christmas presents. Not a fortune to some people, but now it wasn't only Mr Forester's ten thousand pounds financing the proposed launch. Jenny had revamped her plans for the launch, but not as much as she'd have to very soon. Not yet, she could hardly tell her dad there'd be another surprise windfall.

The others helped her prepare, in between discussions about Abel's mission. Abel wouldn't call it that, but the rest did when he wasn't about. The more they thought about it, the more the four of them thought Abel was right. The sorcerers and church had turned their backs on the poor or isolated communities, leaving them at the mercy of a myriad of small, continual magical attacks. Even if the Accord meant no magical wars or large magical predators such as ogres, thousands of people were being targeted day after day for tiny bits of their magic. That left them weaker, maybe easier prey to disease or just feeling unhappy, and in some cases it might kill them. Now, if Abel could let others have access to the magic in his trees, teenagers all around the country could make a difference. No monster slaying, but even a relative newcomer could squish globhoblins, thornies and fae if they had training and extra magic.

Though Abel's mission would have to wait for a little while, until the money came through, and even then it had to be spread carefully. Selling the goods and organising payments would take time, but despite knowing that, Abel dashed down to check the post every morning. He wasn't the only one impatient to get started, he had four texts first thing every morning asking if he'd had any news. Unfortunately Kelis did receive some news, much less pleasant than the good news the Taverneers were waiting for. Her mum received notification that Mr Ventner's case was coming to court. Kelis's dad's lawyers had run out of ways to put off the final reckoning.

The only person in Brinsford who had to give evidence, outside Kelis and her mum, was Abel because he'd called 999 the night Kelis's dad really lost it. He didn't enjoy the experience. Abel said his piece, then denied being Kelis's boyfriend at the time or lying about what he'd heard and seen to help her out. To be honest, he didn't think the defence were too worried about him. With a definite sinking feeling, Abel waited to find out how Kelis got on.

She surprised him, and probably the lawyers. Kelis wasn't shy and frightened these days, and much to Abel's relief she didn't lose her temper. Instead she clearly and calmly recounted a long list of instances where her dad had bruised her or slapped or thumped her mum. It had been worse than Abel and Rob ever realised, and started long before she arrived in Stourton. The defence got stuck in, but Kelis replied calmly and refused to be rattled. Afterwards she told the Taverners that when it got nasty she'd imagined filling the lawyer's pants with fire glyphs. Jess, Kelis's mum, looked nervous when it was her turn but she stuck to her guns, backed by the medical evidence and the police reports.

Abel couldn't skip school to attend court as the case dragged on, though it wouldn't be much longer, according to Kelis. After that the divorce proceedings would be tied up within weeks. She sounded a lot more worried about moving house than if her dad ended up convicted. According to Kelis, if the slimeball got off he'd better move a long way away and never walk down dark alleys. Ferryl offered to come along to watch her back and hold her cloak, or help bury the body.

While Kelis was still giving evidence, the meeting with Mz Green finally bore fruit, though the news didn't come through Abel's post-box. A fortnight after Abel signed the papers, Frederick called to tell him they'd just had an anonymous charitable donation of three thousand pounds. The bank insisted a stranger walked in and paid it into the right account. There wasn't a mistake, he'd had the account name and number dead right. Abel let Frederick wind down, smiling happily as the older man tried to figure out who would do a thing like that. Hopefully his blood pressure could survive the rest as it arrived.

Abel passed the news on, hoping it helped cheer Kelis up as the lawyers fought it out and tried to rip verbal strips off her mum. A couple of smaller donations kept the good news coming, but it wasn't enough to stop Kelis brooding. Abel, Rob, Ferryl and Jenny thought of one way to snap her out of it, for one night at least, a dance. Luckily, a very good excuse wasn't hard to find.

*   *   *

As Kelis's dad tried to weasel out of the consequences of his drinking and violence, February crept towards Valentine's Day. Kelis, wrapped up in the court case, never realised her friends were making plans to take her to her very first proper Valentine's Lurve Dance, in Stourton. The dance would also be a first for Abel, Rob, Jenny and Ferryl. Last year, Valentine's had been a damp squib for Abel, because he'd just broken the magic link with Kelis and didn't want a kiss, let alone a girlfriend. This year even Jenny's dad agreed she could go into Stourton, though he'd be providing her taxi both ways. To Abel's surprise, his mum offered to ferry the four from Brinsford there and back in the BMW. According to her it was because she'd never get to drive one again, but Abel wondered if it might be thanks for the earrings.

Ferryl broke the news four days before the dance, and it took Kelis's mind off the court case but for the wrong reasons. When the pair of them came into Castle House, Abel could hear Kelis arguing. "I can't. I won't. Not again. I didn't realise the first time, but now I know."

Abel stood up and moved to the library doorway so he could see them come in from the entrance. "Know what?"

To his surprise Kelis looked at him, opened her mouth to answer, then blushed bright red! Kelis hadn't blushed for ages, not since she'd first started going out with Laurence. Ferryl turned with a big smile. "Kelis doesn't want to wear that leather catsuit and the red cloak, even though she looked fantastic dressed like that. Tell her, Abel, it suited her."

From the look she gave him, that wasn't what Kelis wanted to hear. "It suited a tall, slim someone who wanted to stun at forty paces. Maybe Kelis doesn't want that?" He frowned a little, because that made no sense. "So why did you wear it, Kelis?"

"Because somebody," the glare at Ferryl told Abel who, "produced it at the last minute and told me it would be more practical for fighting. Then kept me in front of the vanity mirror helping to fix my hair and makeup until Laurence arrived. I never actually saw the full effect until I came home. I went to the wardrobe for a dressing gown before I got ready for bed, and got a good look in the mirror." Kelis turned her full glare on Ferryl. "Why did you do that? I looked like, like, like…."

"A new character, according to quite a lot of the lads. They're waiting for K'ress Bloodclaw to appear in the game. That's the most popular of the names we can use in a game for children." Jenny might have a laugh in her voice, but Kelis looked utterly horrified. "Emst seemed impressed to the point of speechless."

"What's the problem? You seemed happy enough stood in the doorway swirling that cloak. You did a lot more swirling once we got there, and chased all over the place after the fursomnium in just the leather. I'm surprised a couple of lads didn't cut off their legs by mistake when you came bounding past." Rob nodded towards Ferryl. "I reckon Ferryl was just as startling in her own way, and certainly had a bigger effect on Abel." He chuckled, coming through the door from the kitchen and offering Kelis a can of cola. "Though I'm well known for liking fur, not leather. Here, this is chilled and you need to cool down."

"You don't understand!" Kelis turned and now she looked even more horrified, if possible. "People were looking? When we were supposed to be fighting? Why didn't somebody say?"

"I can't believe you didn't notice the looks from the lads? At least four of the girls want to know where you got it, and how you squeezed into it, but couldn't really ask while fighting." Jenny kept trying to kill her giggles, and almost succeeding. "If you were so worried, why didn't you put the cloak back on afterwards?"

"Because Emst wanted to wear it, as a costume. Oh, flobberclomps." Looking shocked rather than horrified didn't stop Kelis's blush. "Then he wouldn't give me it back until we got home. He didn't do that on purpose, did he? So that…?"

"So you didn't cover up all that tight leather and those high boots? Probably. Haven't you noticed how many boys have asked what you're doing at Valentine's? They'll be disappointed if you go back to that K'liss Windcatcher outfit." Ferryl smiled happily, completely oblivious to the sheer horror on Kelis's face. "I'm looking forward to the dance. This version of Saint Valentine's Day is a new thing entirely and not even a little bit religious."

"I liked the Windcatcher outfit. It suited the Kelis I know much better than the leather, though which one she wears is up to Kelis." Inspiration suddenly struck Abel. "This isn't a Tavern dance so why go in a costume at all? How about one of the frocks from upstairs? Some of those Victorian ones must be all flouncy and romantic."

"Says a boy, a creature well known for having no idea what is or isn't romantic." Jenny stopped and frowned, then turned to Kelis. "Though since I'm wearing that blue dress again, and that definitely isn't a game costume, you might have a point. Come on Kelis, we'll go and look while Ferryl explains romantic to dumbo here." She pulled a grateful-looking Kelis towards the stairs.

"How do I do that?" Ferryl looked from Rob to Abel, completely baffled. "The whole idea is I'm supposed to be learning, and I thought the leather was a great success."

Rob held up both hands as he backed away, finally getting words through his laughter. "You're Abel's girl, not mine, and apparently one of us is dumbo, so luck with explaining anything." He shut the door into the sitting room, leaving Abel and Ferryl.

"Maybe we can go into the library? Then I can try to explain the difference between Kelis in leather and Kelis in her robes. Or in a Victorian frock." Abel rolled his eyes. "If I can. You must have some idea?"

"I lived for hundreds of years in places where people didn't wear any clothes at all, or a few beads and scraps, and nobody cared." Ferryl had lost her smile, starting to look worried. "Did I do the wrong thing? I knew Kelis wouldn't wear that leather if she saw what she looked like, but it really suits her. She definitely attracted the boys, which I thought was the idea." With a sigh she put her arms round Abel and rested her head on his shoulder. "This is a new sensation. Maybe another emotion. Am I feeling guilty?" Abel had no idea, and still wasn't sure after they'd sat in the library for half an hour discussing romantic. Ferryl seemed happy with whatever she'd come up with, and returned to inspecting the aquarium.

This time Abel joined her, bringing another chair over. "If you ever work out what it is in there, what will you do?"

"It's a wit, or something that acts very much like one. To have all those instructions and control all those glyphs it has to be inscribed the same way. I want whatever is on there, so somehow I have to get it out. If you'll let me." She hesitated, definitely uncertain. "In the past I would have bound a shade to carry out each individual task, copied the glyphs and taken the wit out. Those glyphs can't be anything I've seen before, because I never had anything to do with fish. I really want to see how they work."

Abel avoided the bit about binding anything, because he wasn't agreeing to that. "You can't resist them, can you? Glyphs I mean. I saw how you looked at the one in Creepio's hospital van." He chuckled as Zephyr flowed out of his tattoo to join them watching the fish. "So did Zephyr, but she couldn't memorise it all."

"I did." Ferryl smirked, forgetting about the aquarium for now. "I copied it straight onto a wit, or rather I put half onto each of two wits. Unfortunately I daren't test it because I am in a human, so if I made a mistake I'd kill myself." She put a hand on Abel's arm as she saw the alarm on his face. "Just the host, but I'm enjoying this one so it wouldn't be fair."

"So you'll just keep it tucked away. Why bother?" That sounded like a really tempting mistake waiting to happen, Pandora's Box style.

Ferryl sighed, her eyes looking over Abel's shoulder and her mind far away in the past. "I can't resist a new glyph. My life has depended on knowing the right one, time after time, and now I've lost most of them. I feel helpless, because I can remember being able to do much more but haven't any idea how. Worse, if anything happens to my friends, and especially you, I will always believe I could have stopped it if I'd had the right glyph." She turned back to the aquarium, her hand almost stroking the glass. "Having a wit in here, probably full of glyphs and almost in reach, is really frustrating. I can feed magic into the glyphs that will be scribed into the bottom of the aquarium to keep it working, then take the wit, but without shades to control them the glyphs will just keep working."

"Surely that's the idea." Abel tried to think why working glyphs were a problem.

"The salination one will keep adding salt, the feeding ones will keep producing food, the heat glyph will keep pushing out heat. Within hours everything in there will start to die. The shades are needed to moderate what the glyphs do." Ferryl suddenly stood up and turned away from the glass. "Talking about it is really annoying and frustrating. How about some dance practice?" Even as he practiced dancing, Abel tried to work out a way round Ferryl's problem with the aquarium before it became too much of an obsession. After stepping on Ferryl's toes twice, or the wind glyphs protecting them, he gave up on that and concentrated on his feet.

Eventually Kelis and Jenny came down carrying three dresses that might be wearable after some work. Abel wasn't sure if Ferryl offered to help as an olive branch, but Kelis took it as one. Kelis cheered up even more when the sorceress pointed out that she'd been in the minds of people who made their own clothes. Maybe her happier mood came from watching Abel's dancing practice, or the fiasco as they all joined in. Rob danced with all three girls, but as usual Abel and Kelis kept strictly apart. This time he didn't feel quite so bad about it, maybe because Kelis didn't make any comments about stupid sorcerers.

In a way Abel, and Rob when he mentioned it, thought the dress and leather fiasco had to have been a good thing. Kelis had been getting more and more pre-occupied with the court case and what would happen after the divorce. The bank would take away her home, and she didn't want to leave Brinsford. The impending dance might not have been enough, but with the new dress seemed to have temporarily driven all that into the background, exactly as they'd intended.

* * *

On the night before the dance Abel realised why Rob, Jenny, and Ferryl had been whispering, then obviously changing the subject or stopping as he came near. Kelis had been the same lately, but since they all kept smiling at him for no apparent reason he assumed it was to do with the finance for the game. Now Kelis, Rob, Jenny and Ferryl triumphantly produced a frock coat and waistcoat, resized for him, and a cloak with a new, electric blue lining. Abel had mentioned liking the getup but being too small for any of Celtchar's clothes. Before Abel could speak, Kelis told him that if Abel could give people whatever he liked, those same people could do the same so he should shut up and smile. Abel shut up and smiled, not difficult because he really did like the outfit.

Kelis, Rob and Jenny also wore Victorian clothing for the dance, though Kelis's dress had been altered to brighten it up. Rob found a top hat that fitted and snaffled a cane with a silver top, but Abel refused because he'd have all on controlling his feet while dancing. Ferryl's outfit, when she came out to join Kelis, wasn't Victorian. She'd gone for something slimmer, right down to her ankles but slit to her knees, made of riotously coloured silky cloth that looked just a bit oriental to Abel. According to her, nobody who'd actually had to wear the old styles every day would ever turn down modern fabrics.

On the way to town, Abel let the others answer his mum's questions about the clothes. They'd been rented, allegedly, compliments of Fay Shayde's allowance, her thank you for everyone welcoming her into their homes. Abel started to get tense about all the strangers but he soon found out he'd know more people than expected. Kathy stood outside waiting for Rob, and Kelis had a date. Tobias's comments about fresh air and fresh veg attracting pretty girls had been aimed at one in particular. Kelis must have finally realised, because as she got out of the car she accepted his arm. When Jenny arrived in her blue gown she'd also arranged for a partner, Laurence. He wore a jacket with gold braid across the front he swore had once been military, with a frilled shirt. Abel relaxed because compared to the others, he wouldn't look too conspicuous.

By the end of the evening Kelis seemed to have shed all her worries about where she'd live and Abel no longer cared what he looked like. No magic, no sorcerers, no leeches, no Creepio, no charity and no Tavern business; he wasn't even in a Tavern costume. Ferryl insisted on him trying every dance including the Conga, and nobody made fun of either his clothes or dancing. As far as Abel was concerned, the evening turned out to be an entirely different sort of magical.

*　*　*

The lack of magical problems didn't mean there were no other distractions. Plenty of things were happening in the non-magical part of their world, enough to keep all five of them occupied. A few days later, as they walked past on the way home from school, Kelis didn't notice the 'SOLD' sign on the village shop. Abel did, and the 'Flat for Rent' sign in an upstairs window, but he kept quiet. He'd rather someone else brought it up just in case Kelis was suspicious.

When he arrived home, Abel thought he knew why he had a text asking him contact Woods and Green. Instead, a bland voice asked him if he wanted to sell six trees. They had been dug up from one of his properties to facilitate the transport of magical entities, as agreed, and would have been replanted. Now, someone local was in the market for trees and the sale would help defray the expenses. Abel agreed. He'd never even thought about where the trees to shift the dryad seedlings would come from, or how big they had to be.

Jenny didn't come over that Saturday, unusual because she liked to top up her diamond at weekends. On Sunday the others found out why, once Jenny recovered from her giggling fit. She'd had to refill both her gold belts and her diamond, a huge fix of tree magic because they were all empty. Jenny had spent Saturday with her dad, and put a protective hex on almost every vehicle and machine in her dad's construction business, and all his workmen's huts and sheds. Mr. Forester had been really chuffed she'd spent the day with him while he checked on progress at all his contracts, and hadn't minded her wandering around while he dealt with his site workers.

That led to a bit of a discussion, because everything but the buildings should be Pendragon's business. Eventually the Taverneers decided that since Mr Forester didn't know about magic, it wasn't stealing business, and most of the equipment had been outside town when Jenny protected it. Since Jenny wasn't fit to ride her moped straight after such a big tree-magic fix, Kelis and Rob offered to help her perfect her combined shield and veil. Ferryl asked Abel to keep her company while she checked the barrier around Castle House gardens. She talked about this and that, but even Abel could see she had something on her mind.

After a long period of silence, Abel pulled on her hand to turn her towards him. "Come on, give. You don't usually have any trouble telling me what I've done wrong."

Ferryl looked startled, then embarrassed. "I don't tell you off very often." She put her arms round him and rested her head on his shoulder. "This is asking, and it might mean people starting to wonder about me, exactly who or what I am. It could make trouble for you if they do." She hugged a little tighter. "It's just a bit selfish as well."

Abel waited, but the silence stretched on until he'd had enough. "Am I supposed to guess?"

At least the little chuckle sounded happier than she had a few minutes ago. "No, silly. I want my name, all of it. Ferryl Shayde."

"You've got it. Woods and Green put your name on all those bits of paper they created to give your body an identity." Ferryl obviously didn't agree so Abel thought harder. "Ah, right, it's Fay Shayde on your passport but everyone calls you Ferryl unless…. Oh. Unless Zephyr is there. Then they call her Ferryl because they think she is the sorceress from the pit."

"I answer to Ferryl but my name is really Zephyr, a puff of wind. Or Ffod, the Flying Fist of Doom, if it's time to bop. I have to try and remember that I am Ferryl, but only sometimes."

Zephyr must have connected to Ferryl as well, because she chuckled again. "Exactly. You told everyone the sorceress in your arm is called Ferryl Shayde. Then when I needed a name for Jane Doe, and used Fay Shayde, you told them I had inspired the name for the game character. The smart ones must have already figured whoever lives in your arm adopted the name from the game and isn't really called Ferryl Shayde. Can you or Zephyr confess that's true, and ask them to call her a different name because now the real Ferryl Shayde is here?" Her grip suddenly tightened and she tensed. "Not Braeth Huntian, or one of my old names, or the church will look closer and might take Zephyr."

"Why not call Zephyr by her real name? We, the five Taverneers, call her Zephyr anyway so it'll be easy. Though we shouldn't tell everyone about Ffod, the real one, not the one in the game." Abel smiled quietly to himself. "A Ffod bop should come as a complete surprise if we need one."

"Would you mind, Abel? Zephyr?" Ferryl hugged a little, a smile starting at the corners of her mouth. "My memories say that kissing you about now would help you make up your mind, but I want you to decide without cheating." She snuggled in a little bit. "Though I've started enjoying the sensation and the emotion when we kiss, so maybe I'm just looking for an excuse."

"No need for cheating or persuasion. Ferryl Shayde really is your name and the ones most likely to be suspicious, the Taverneers, know the truth. This just stops Rob or Kelis looking at the wrong person when they say Ferryl, or saying Zephyr by mistake." Abel heaved a big sigh and hugged Ferryl a little tighter. "It'll be easier for me as well. The name Ferryl means someone very particular, regardless of which tattoo or body she lives in."

"That's definitely a cue for a thank you."

Abel barely felt Zephyr leave. She claimed that emotions were messy close up, so she preferred hunting. "Whew. I should agree to rename Zephyr more often."

"Not likely. She'll sulk if you alter either Zephyr or Ffod." Ferryl tugged on his hand. "Come on, let's tell the others."

The others were relieved rather than surprised. Rob, for one, had been expecting someone to notice he sometimes looked at the wrong person when asking Ferryl a question. Some of the lack of reaction had to be because they were distracted. Kelis had been telling Jenny her bit of news. The flat above the village shop was for rent and her mum would be phoning the estate agent in the morning! The excitement wasn't just about that. After Kelis described sitting on the floor in Frederick's house because there wasn't much in the way of furniture, her mum offered any she wasn't keeping. Now, if the flat was cheap enough and big enough for the two of them, they'd know how much furniture to keep.

"Three if possible?" Ferryl pointed at Abel. "I've still got to stay in Brinsford, near Abel."

"Ooh yes, all that power and wealth. It's still sticky then?" Jenny's eyes narrowed. "Now I think about it, going by his face when you arrived, it's definitely still working." Abel felt his face heat up, just a little as Jenny raised her hand to high-five Rob. "It's getting harder, but he's definitely blushing."

Though Rob didn't join in the teasing, because he'd realised one possible flaw. "I doubt there'll be room for Ferryl. Mr. and Mrs. Summers wouldn't need three bedrooms." He looked from Kelis to Ferryl. "I suppose you could share? Either that or Abel will be sleeping on his settee because I'm sure his mum won't let his girlfriend sleep in the same bedroom, even with the door ajar."

"Ferryl could use a storeroom as a bedroom and stay with Kelis. Stick a bed and a couple of wardrobes in there, and then she can help out with the rent." Abel tried for an innocent smile. "Or maybe Kelis would like a room-mate?"

"Not likely, or not if there's another way. No offence, but I'm sort of used to my mess, without adding someone else's." Kelis's eyes narrowed this time. "How come you know there's a storeroom in the shop? If it hadn't been up for sale before we'd opened Castle House, I'd wonder if someone's wealth had been sneaking about."

"Common sense. For all I know there's three storerooms, or the Summers kept the stock upstairs in their bedroom." Abel shrugged. "We don't even know if the shop is in with the rent. That would make a big bedroom." Abel knew the letting agent would alter the amount of rooms available to make room for Ferryl if the upstairs flat wasn't big enough, but daren't even hint it. Kelis still hadn't fully accepted she would get a fifth share of the investment money.

"It might also make the rent too high for me and mum, even with Ferryl helping." Kelis threw a wind glyph that snatched up twigs and twirled them around in the air. "Botheration! I just wish it was all over. Slimeball will be sentenced this week."

"They've found him guilty?" Jenny looked surprised because nobody had mentioned it, though it certainly explained Kelis's erratic mood.

"No, but he admitted being guilty to some things, and the jury are out on the rest. It'll be settled in days. Then his slimeball lawyer will make sure my slimeball dad doesn't give mum a single thing except the divorce." This air glyph exploded twigs, leaves and dirt up into a fountain.

"But you don't need anything from him, do you?" Abel opened his arms to encompass the others and the wood. "You've got magic and the Taverneers." The rest joined in to cheer Kelis up, eventually getting her into a competition to see who could construct the tallest totally unstable stack of leaves and twigs. They all used magic to cheat outrageously, except Ferryl who insisted on being the judge.

*   *   *

Kelis's mood swung back and forth during the next few days despite everything her friends could say or do. She threw herself into magic to try and distract herself, even practicing glyphs in her room at home. Sentencing on Thursday left her in a foul mood. Her dad got four years, but as she pointed out, that would only be two with parole and then the slimeball would be free. She worried about her mum being harassed, but Abel thought any sort of aggravation wouldn't last long.

Unfortunately, with the glyphs Kelis had learned and the amount of magic in her diamond, any showdown with her dad would end up with

Kelis in jail. Ferryl thought an early grave would be the best cure for Mr Ventner but agreed that might cause trouble for Kelis, so she came to Abel with a solution. If Mr Ventner ever turned up, Ferryl would put on a seeming of a big muscular man and use wind glyphs to slap him around. She'd tell him to clear off or he'd get a proper beating. Abel agreed because that had to be better than Kelis stood in a heap of splintered ribs and the police closing in.

On Friday morning Abel received something that would definitely take Kelis's mind off her dad. It did, she switched to berating Abel. Abel agreed he was stupid, an idiot, not fit to be let out without a keeper, and generally unsafe around sharp items. He still asked his mum to call a proper meeting of the management, with all three mums and Mr Forester attending. This time the five teenagers would be springing the surprise, sort of payback for being caught out over the church.

*　　*　　*

Saturday evening, as Jenny and her dad came into the old library in Kelis's house, Abel knew he daren't spin it out. Jenny looked ready to spill the beans, while Kelis might be about to explode. He knew Kelis intended making some objection, but she wouldn't be able to. He might have given her the money to offer to her mum to help with accommodation, but Mrs Ventner had been bursting with her own news. The shop itself wasn't for rent but the two-bedroomed flat was, as a three-bedroom maisonette with a storeroom at the bottom of the stairs converted to make an extra bedroom. The letting agent claimed the shop had too much storage and the new owner wanted to maximise the rental value. From her looks, if it hadn't been for the other news, Kelis might have been giving Abel the third degree.

"Right, what exactly is so urgent? Madame here is almost bursting with something, but won't tell me." Mr. Forester looked at the three puzzled mothers, but didn't get chance to push further.

"We've found a real investor for the game. Someone with real money, enough for a proper launch." Abel took out his envelope and extracted the papers and four cheques. "We have been scouring the internet and the boot sales. That jewellery got us really interested, but this time we tried to be smarter." Abel hoped his little laugh sounded natural. "We ended up with a heap of old plates, ornaments and vases that will help to decorate Stourton Tavern Refuge, but which are barely worth the pennies we paid." He glanced towards Rob, who took his cue.

"All except one. We were blindingly lucky because at first it went to Frederick's house as a failure. Someone there said the vase looked familiar, expensive sort of familiar, so we searched the internet again." Rob turned towards Ferryl. "We all paid an equal amount towards every single item, deliberately, but Fay refused to cash in. She has her own money, from her parents."

Ferryl smiled and took out a cheque, pushing it into the middle of the table. "I want to loan twenty thousand pounds to your company. Our company, if I am allowed to buy a stake." She pushed eleven one-pound coins across the table.

"We'd like extra shares as well, so we've all got eleven." Abel pushed one-pound coins across the table, as did Rob, Jenny and Kelis. "Which will give us fifty-five percent between us. That seems fair, because we'll have the most money invested." He pushed the cheques forward. "Four cheques, each for twenty thousand pounds, from a solicitor. Each cheque clearly states they are being paid to the company on behalf of one of us. Loans, the same as the one you put in, Mr Forester."

"Where did you get that?"

"What solicitor?"

"Why didn't you tell me?"

"Are you sure about this?"

None of the four teenagers got a chance to answer before the same questions came from a different parent to a different child, along with a wide selection of others. Despite being tempted, the four teenagers waited for the storm to die down a bit, just answering "please wait a minute" or something similar until their parents listened.

"Right. We're all waiting." The glare Rob's mum gave him didn't bode well.

This time Abel passed the papers across to Mr Forester. "You'll all get to see that, but I reckon Jenny's dad will be more likely to know how legal it is. We sold the vase, a private sale through a solicitor, to an undisclosed purchaser. The solicitor was asked to pay us the money, after sorting out any taxes, in these cheques. When the money goes into the company, we all want the earlier loans back, the ones from the jewellery we didn't give our mothers. That's fifteen hundred quid each. I want to buy a bike with mine so I can get to town." He looked straight at Kelis. "There's an alternative. If we ask, the solicitor will re-issue the cheques payable to whoever we ask."

"The reason we can get the cheques changed is so you can have my share mum, if you want. As a deposit for a house?" Kelis's wry smile took in the others, because they all had the same option. "All of us are willing to consider that, giving the money to our parents if they want it, but we'll never get this lucky again. We want to give Bonny's Tavern the best possible chance of success, and we also want to be in control once we are old enough." Her look at Jenny was another cue.

"Bonny's Tavern needs investment, and any investor will want some control. Every time we need a few more quid, we'll lose a share or two. Now, even if we have to borrow more money, the five of us will always be a majority." She smiled at her dad, her patent innocent one. "You taught me that there's a time to strike, to take the plunge, to put your money where your mouth is. So we have." No giggle this time, Jenny turned to Rob.

"This way the five of us can outvote anyone else, once we are eighteen. Even so, we won't do something stupid because it will take all five of us. Fay can't afford to throw her inheritance money away, but she's had advice and believes in us. We want her in because she's one of us, our age and outlook and actually put in a fifth of the price of the vase. Technically she's entitled even if she won't claim it." There wasn't any sign of the joker as Rob looked his mum in the eye. "The four of us have parents who will advise us, or even shout at us if necessary. I really can't see all five of us doing something utterly stupid, and anyway we can't until we are eighteen. Until then, the money will get the game off to a good start."

That did it. "Good start! That's a fortune."

Now Rob let his smile come. "Do you want the twenty thousand, mum? You can have it."

His mum leant back in her seat and stared. "Of course not. It's yours."

"You'd all change your cheques, give the money to your parents?" All four nodded, so Jenny's dad shifted his attention to Fay. "Leaving you the major investor." He started to smile. "Which Jenny knows I won't want, because regardless how these four feel you are an outsider, an unknown. I came today prepared to offer a small loan, just to get some sort of launch. I would have asked for a few shares, though I wasn't sure how many I'd get." His eyes went round the table, pausing on each teenager in turn. "That presentation covered all the main points, and the way you all took turns had to be planned so you've really worked it all out. There's a chance we could legally stop you, because of your age, but personally I'm quite proud of my daughter and wouldn't dream of it." For once, Jenny was the one blushing as her dad switched to the other three parents. "So, I recommend we take the money and do just what they've asked. Providing these papers really do cover the legalities."

"Which solicitor did you use?" Abel's mum reached for a cheque and read it. "Who are Woods and Green?"

"The same ones who are advertising through the game. The man who bought the vase wanted to use them so it didn't cost us a bean." Abel hesitated, then asked, "You could have a new car?"

"I haven't worn out the last one you gave me." Her happy smile came as a relief to Abel. "Keep your eyes open for any more vases or earrings, then you can afford your own instead of a moped." Around the table, parents and children worked through the same sort of thing, but none of the parents would take the money. If it had been enough to buy a house then Abel thought more than one of them would have been tempted to ask, but it wasn't even a substantial deposit. Even so, twenty thousand pounds was more than two of the families had ever had in a lump sum, while the money that provided Mrs Ventner's lifestyle had never been hers.

"When they wanted to advertise through Bonny's Tavern, I checked up on Woods and Green. They have a very good name for dealing with rich clients and confidential business so I'm sure the sale is legal. These cheques won't bounce, so if you ladies agree I'll pay them in tomorrow and get the shares issued." Jenny's dad smiled at her and scooped up the pound coins. "Meanwhile the least we can do is leave you and your friends to have a majority shareholder's meeting." He glanced at the three mothers. "If one of you ladies doesn't mind me bending your ear and drinking your tea until Jenny is finished?" Mr Forester stood up and put out his hand. "Welcome aboard, Mz Shayde. I will admit I wasn't too sure why you were so interested, but that sort of investment means you are serious."

Ferryl looked a bit uncomfortable but shook hands. From the talking as the parents left, they'd all be bending each other's ears and supping tea together for a while. As the door closed, Kelis opened her mouth but Abel held up a finger. "Zephyr, just check outside will you? I'm not certain anyone will put their ear to the door, but Kelis might be shouting loud enough so they don't have to. Tell my friends what you are doing, please."

Moments later spooky-phone connected to them all as Zephyr disappeared through the crack round the door. "Nobody with an ear to the door, but everyone is hesitating and looking at each other. Now they are starting to move away slowly." After a pause Zephyr finished with "They are down the corridor, going through the door into the lounge. Kelis can shout now. Should I wait out here?"

"No thank you, Zephyr. I doubt they'll sneak back." A shimmer reappeared around the door to hover by Abel.

"I was not going to shout!" Kelis subsided with a rueful smile. "Or not much. It still seems wrong but splitting the money into individual cheques means I'm stuffed. You gave me a clear chance to give mine to mum, but now she's said no I can't not put it into the company along with the rest of you. No more, right? I'll pay you back one day, but it could be a while." She turned towards Ferryl. "And regardless of all the fancy talk, we know where Ferryl's money came from as well."

"I offered to find my own money, but Abel wouldn't let me make magical gold ornaments." Ferryl put her arms round him. "So, I'll just have to say thank you and accept." Abel had already told Ferryl she'd earned every penny a hundred times over, just by saving them all from the sorceress with the bound shades.

"Later, purrrrlease. Preferably without embarrassing any spectators." Rob pointed at Jenny. "Jenny hasn't finished blushing yet so don't start her off again."

"Yeah, well, dad doesn't say stuff like that, not in public. Who wants a drink?" Everyone took the hint and changed the subject. Once they started talking about the launch, Jenny forgot all about blushing. She'd made plans based on about eighty grand, or thereabouts, but hadn't shown her dad. Now she could feed him the updated paperwork over a couple of weeks while Rob produced the extra graphics.

Becoming investors had passed off fairly simply, but none of them really understood how much work it would be.

Fishing for Snakes

The Taverners already knew what one part of the extra work would be. The character list for Bonny's Tavern needed one more update before the launch, and Kelis had the job of drawing the new creatures and players. After seeing Rob create a hole in the road to trap the leech-ridden priest, Shannon wanted an earth wizard in the game. Provisionally named Rock'n Rolla after Rob's preferences in music, he had to have armour made of magical granite. His mace would be a nod towards Rob's rounders bat. K'liss Windcatcher was mistress of wind and, according to Kelis, water, so the Taverners wanted a fire sorcerer to make up the set. Provisionally named Flamm, he had to be black-skinned with a cloak of flames. Kelis had already refused to create a sorceress dressed in black leather, some sort of necromancer, so several Taverners had tried drawing one. She eventually gave in, because K'ress Bloodclaw would definitely become a character so Kelis wanted the sorceress drawn properly.

Abel's new task wasn't connected to the game launch, it involved the magical Taverners. Now that he was seventeen Abel could buy a 125 cc motorbike, pass his CBT and visit the nearest of his parks and patches of woodland. Ferryl would also buy a motorbike though passing her CBT should be a doddle because she'd done it once as Jenny. Not only would seeing a couple of the locations give Abel a better idea of his inheritance, but Ferryl might work out if he could let anyone else have some sort of access. Hopefully she would also work out how to create proper protection for Elmwood Park, the sort that didn't also bar the non-magical. The town houses were another big mystery until Ferryl and Zephyr could visit a couple to find out why Abel, the owner, couldn't access rented property.

Group visits relied on Jenny passing her car test, then she could borrow the minibus. Rob didn't fancy a bike, so he would wait until he'd passed his driving test and then borrow a car if necessary. Kelis would definitely have a car, according to her mum, but she had to pay for lessons and pass her test without spending her fifteen hundred pounds. Since her mum didn't have a convenient no-claims bonus to help out, Kelis would need that to pay for insurance. Rob offered to help out, so if he learned to drive he could borrow the car now and then or take a turn with driving.

A more immediate chore awaited them all the following weekend. Jenny arranged for drivers and borrowed her dad's pickup truck so the Taverners could move the first of the donated furniture from Kelis's house to Stourton. That took the shine off Kelis's excitement over the proposed launch. As she pointed out, from now until they moved out her house would be slowly emptying, sort of bleeding furniture. Not all of it, because Kelis and her mum would keep their own beds and dressing tables, as well as some of the comfy chairs and kitchen equipment. It was all much better quality than the Summers left behind. Ferryl insisted on furnishing the empty storeroom with furniture already in the rented flat. Abel really wanted to tell her not to worry, he'd chuck the lot away if she wanted better stuff from Kelis's house, but daren't admit what he'd done to anyone.

At least Kelis's mum wouldn't be skint because she'd sold the brooch from Kelis, and all the jewellery her husband had given her including her wedding band. The money would last a long time because the flat would be cheaper to heat, the Council Tax would be a lot less and there weren't the huge gardens to maintain. The divorce proceedings were moving along quicker than expected, as if Mr Ventner just wanted this part over. Kelis kept saying she didn't care about moving, the house meant nothing, but Abel saw her face as he helped the others to remove the huge dining table. He began to wonder if he could cheer her up again, long-term.

*   *   *

Almost a week later Abel stood in the sitting room in Castle House, eyeing up the remaining ornaments. There hadn't been many so he had to use the money from them with care. Unfortunately, all the ones left in here were magical constructs. Perhaps he should sell them anyway, because some were downright ugly. Most buyers wouldn't know about the magic, so he'd get a decent price. "No, you don't. Enough is enough."

When Abel turned round, despite her light tone Kelis looked absolutely serious. "Don't what?"

"Sell that lot to buy mum's house so it can suddenly and miraculously appear at just the right price in a few years' time." Kelis suddenly burst into laughter. "I knew it! It's all over your face."

"It wouldn't be a crime."

"I know it wouldn't. It would be incredibly generous and sweet, and a complete waste. I don't ever want to live there again, and neither does mum." Despite Kelis looking and sounding completely serious, Abel didn't believe her.

"I've seen your face when we carry furniture out of there. You were really sad to see the dining table go." Abel flopped down on a settee. "I was looking straight at you."

"Not sad about the table, just the memories. I hate the house, and nearly everything that ever happened in it." Kelis started towards the settee, swerved and sat in an armchair. "But I remember that table when we had Christmas dinner, all of our families having a wonderful time together. I remember coming back to that house with your magical mark." Her hand strayed unconsciously towards her arm and stopped. "Chasing all those creatures out of my bedroom, and drawing the first Tavern shield." Her hands went up above her head and waved back and forth as she sang "I can do magic" very quietly. "That library was slimeball's den, but it's also where Ferryl flew the first time, and...." Kelis paused for a moment or two, looking wistful. "Where I kissed a boy, the first time. Lots of memories, but the house can burn for all I care." Her voice strengthened. "So, don't you do anything noble."

There wasn't much point in Abel denying it now, even if he didn't consider buying the house particularly noble. "I thought you might want to go back sometime?"

"Nope, never. Though if you're feeling generous, I have got one request." Kelis had a little smile now, just a hint of tease. "I'm pretty certain we'll prise that second door open sometime, and then there'll be more bedrooms. I reckon some will be even fancier, in which case I'd like the big one upstairs in case I need some me time. Mum can hardly object if I occasionally sleep ten houses away in my own, admittedly sumptuous room. There's even room to park my car out front, once I can drive it."

Abel laughed at her big smile because despite it being permanently parked up behind the shop, Kelis loved her little hatchback. "If we park the minibus here, you could sleep in that." Abel preferred the eight-seater minibus, the larger part of the BMW trade-in, because it would double up as a van. He'd suggested Mrs Ventner getting some cash and a cheaper vehicle for the Tavern, but all the adults agreed the two vehicles were better value.

"Not likely! A sorceress likes her comfort. I might even move in here permanently after I leave school, once we can work out how to explain you owning the place." Kelis lifted a quizzical eyebrow. "That's if the master of Castle House won't get embarrassed?"

"You can move in tomorrow if you like. Why would I get embarrassed?" Abel shrugged, then smiled at her. "I don't even blush much now."

"I know, but you might not want me in here with you and your new girl. Hah! Gotcha!"

She had, Abel could feel the heat in his cheeks. "We don't do anything that would be embarrassing. Why do you do that, keep switching on me? You tease me about not getting a girl without magic, then about getting one, and now, just because I like Ferryl you're trying to make it something more."

"I just like to keep you on your toes, make sure you know what you're doing." A magnificent smirk spread across Kelis's face. "It might be my behaviour that embarrasses you." She held up her hands in mock surrender as Abel glared. "All right, I'll quit. Just remember, no giving me or anyone else all your ill-gotten gains, right? So why are you in here instead of the library? You usually keep Ferryl company while Zephyr helps her stare at the aquarium for hours."

"I'm actually doing homework in there, but Ferryl definitely stares. Too much, in my opinion, although I'm hoping she'll stop before it becomes a real obsession. Ferryl knows I won't let her bind any shades to power glyphs to control that aquarium, so she can't get the wit out. Maybe a wit, but she'll never know. I feel guilty but I can't do it, let something die just to find out." Abel sighed, patting his arm and tattoo. "Ferryl might stop if she hasn't got Zephyr helping her, though I'm sure she already knows exactly what's needed."

"Five shades, six to be certain in case there are inactive glyphs we haven't detected."

"Six shades according to Zephyr." Once more Abel tried to think of a way round it.

"What a waste. You only need six to get to something important, while the sorcerer slaughtered things wholesale to make stuff like walking footstools. I wonder if they're bored now you've stopped them wandering...." Kelis stopped mid-speech, eyes wide as Abel lunged out of his seat with his arms open and a big smile starting.

"Brilliant!" The smile died before Abel reached her and he turned on his heel. "Er, thanks Kelis. Good idea." He headed out of the door without looking back, completely missing Kelis's half-lifted arms and stricken look.

*   *   *

Abel marched down the corridor berating himself. A hug wouldn't have mattered if it had been Jenny or even Una or Petra who'd come up with the idea. But it had been Kelis, and he'd nearly grabbed her and maybe reactivated that ruddy magical link. He had to be more careful because even if Kelis had got herself past the whole thing and had boyfriends, it only needed him to be stupid once to wreck her life. Abel stopped outside the library and calmed down. Maybe this idea wouldn't work so he'd sneak up on it.

Ferryl looked round as Abel came in. She'd knelt with her nose almost against the glass instead of sitting on the swivel chair as usual. "Hi Abel. I'm trying to see whatever it is, but it's just out of sight. If I could see it, and it isn't a wit, I'd stop beating my brain to death trying to get it." She stood up, still looking into the glass tank.

"So how would you get the whatever out if you could reach it? Do the shades actually inhabit the tree or dead dog, or are they attached to a bit of something else? Those bound shades that were in the garden, the dead trees, had two of your wits in them." Abel looked into the tank, deliberately not meeting Ferryl's eyes. He was hopeless at fooling her or anyone else, so she'd twig immediately. "Does everything with a bound shade have a wit inside or is it something else?"

"A bound shade without a vessel is usually kept in a tattoo on whoever binds and controls it, only released when it's needed. That ogre the churchman, John, brought to Castle House is a bound shade. A live creature that is controlled through a tattoo is a bound servant. I have a tiny spider one for the leech." Abel almost asked where it was but shut up for two reasons. Firstly, he didn't want to be sidetracked. The other reason was Abel had seen Ferryl in a miniskirt and crop top when she dropped the fur seeming. There'd been no sign of a spider tattoo so maybe it embarrassed her. Ferryl had continued, oblivious to his minor brainstorm. "If a shade is bound into a vessel, it has to be anchored to something solid containing magic and instructions. The anchor can be wood, stone, or bone, not necessarily a wit. Wits can hold very complicated instructions, because of how the bone is altered to hold knowledge. The wits in the trees still had all my information on them but the sorcerer had also inscribed his own instructions, tied to whatever he'd killed. I wiped those off again, healed them."

"So, if you take the solid thing out, does the shade come with it? Or can you move the shade to another instruction?" Abel kept his eyes firmly on a big striped angelfish.

"The shade has to stay bound to the original solid medium with the magic in it, or finish dying. Though if new instructions are inscribed, then the old ones erased, that would alter its purpose." Abel saw the reflection of Ferryl shrug. "A sorceress wouldn't bother because it would take time and care to avoid killing the shade. It's a lot easier to bind a new shade."

Abel braced himself and turned towards her, trying for expressionless. "But if the sorcerer didn't want to kill something new, and found a better use for a shade than controlling a walking footstool?" He saw her brow furrow, then clear, and Ferryl gave him a single penetrating glance. Abel couldn't keep his face completely straight, a smile tugged at the corner of his mouth.

"Really?"

"They're dead already. An aquarium might be more exciting for them. After all mmmph." Abel quit trying to talk and kissed back.

"That's for thinking about my problem long enough to find me an answer."

"Kelis came up with it. I told her the problem and she said the stools might like a change." Abel smiled and pointed. "She's in the sitting room, with five bored footstools."

A few moments later he tried to get his breath back while Ferryl gave him a wicked smile. "That's because I can't kiss Kelis to say thank you." She whirled and set off down the corridor. Abel watched her with a wry smile. Actually, Ferryl could kiss Kelis even if it might shock the hell out of her. Him kissing Kelis was the problem, though after those two from Ferryl it seemed a lot less problematic.

"Can I go to help? I will be able to see the flows. Then if you have to remove shades again I can tell you how."

"Go for it, Zephyr. Just knock before you go in." A shimmer shot off down the corridor and around the edge of the door without knocking or opening it. Since there'd been no yelp of alarm before she did, Ferryl must have restrained herself. Abel sat down in an armchair and relaxed. Ferryl would be busy working on the solution now rather than fretting, and he hoped transferring the shades would distract Kelis from her worries. Actually, wondering what might be on the wit, if it was one, might distract him. Though instead Abel curled up with the Highway Code, trying to memorise who had right of way and stopping distances. Perhaps Kelis had the right idea, inscribing them all on a wit would be quicker than learning them.

*   *   *

Abel wasn't learning the Highway Code during the next eight days. He barely had time to keep up with his schoolwork. Rob and Jenny joined in with the great wit rescue as well, because the first chore had to be extracting the shades from the stools. Dismantling the stools without disturbing the magic that preserved the shades turned out to be slow, careful work, just as Ferryl had warned. Twice Jenny lost track of time and stayed until her dad texted to ask if she was okay. He still didn't like her riding her moped in the dark. Because the house always had lighting, none of them had noticed the garden getting darker, though nobody could see the lights from outside. Despite being able to see through them from inside, from outside the windows still looked boarded up. Eventually Ferryl had six small, carved cubes of wood.

The distraction wasn't working properly for Rob because Melanie had reported the toadstools another four times, and swore she'd seen a troll twice. She'd seen all of them from her bedroom, though they'd been hidden from the downstairs rooms by the back fence. Unfortunately, Rob's bedroom faced the street, and by the time she'd brought him through there wasn't a sign. Ferryl still couldn't identify the toadstools, because they were very ghostly, misty, so Melanie only had a vague description.

Now she'd been allowed to play Bonny's Tavern again, Melanie used the sightings in an attempt to wangle an invite to play at Kelis's house.

The five Taverners still held some meetings in Kelis's house, in the original Bonny's Tavern, because they didn't want any parents knowing about the house. So far none of the parents seemed to realise they'd got inside, even making remarks about the amount of time the teenagers spent in a cold cave. Rob had ordered a cheap garden shed over the internet, to put up in the garden so they could allegedly meet there. Late in March, Rob turned up at Bonny's Tavern with his little sister. Melanie, now almost fifteen, clutched a battered toy fox and looked frightened. That warned the others there must be a real problem, because she should have been triumphant about getting into the original Bonny's Tavern.

Rob pointed to a seat. "Sit down please, Melanie." He turned to the others. "Melanie the trainee sorceress. She's fluttered a leaf half a dozen times, but daren't tell me. She didn't contact Ferryl Shayde because she recognised the email domain and knew it would come to me." He went to the little fridge, opening it and putting in a dozen cans he'd brought in a carrier bag. "Tell them why you didn't tell me the first time, Melanie."

"I wasn't sure, and didn't want Rob to laugh at me. Then Diane said she thought her leaf moved. She didn't say so on Skype, during the game, she texted me afterwards." Melanie hugged her toy harder. "She daren't tell Jenny, but we wondered if you all flutter leaves, if that's why it's in the game. I know you go into that spooky wood because I've followed you, but I've never worked up the nerve to go inside so I don't know what you do in there." All those present knew she never would, because the barrier would stop her.

"So why tell him now?" Kelis paused, looking a little bit guilty. "Sorry. Would you like a drink first?"

For some reason the answer shocked Melanie. Her eyes widened and she clutched her toy fox to her, her eyes darting from one to another of the older teenagers. Eventually, after a couple of tries, she managed to answer. "Yes please, because it's really true, isn't it? I was worried about imagining things because of the stuff over the fence.

Then Rob fluttered a leaf and said it was real, but he's always winding me up." Behind her Rob shrugged, totally unrepentant. The winding up

255

went both ways. "None of you are even surprised. Why didn't you warn me?"

"Rachel was watching for the first signs. Most people mention the funny feeling down their arms, and we tell them then." Kelis smiled happily, turning to Abel. "You told the others about Ferryl really being called Zephyr so everyone could call Fay Ferryl, which confused the hell out of them. Now's your chance to explain to someone who never got used to the other version."

"Zephyr, fly out nice and steady please." Abel pointed to the shimmer. "Melanie, meet our resident sorceress. She is called Zephyr." He held out a hand to Ferryl. "Both resident sorceresses because Fay is the real deal, the original Ferryl Shayde."

"Rob explained where the name came from." Melanie sounded distracted, her whole attention on Zephyr. "Are you invisible, er, Zephyr? Sorceress? I can see a smoky line out of Abel's shoulder and a fuzzy bit." She squinted, then ducked her head to look from a different angle. "Is that because I can't see properly yet? Rob said I'd start to see weird stuff, and gave me this." She dug inside her sweatshirt and held up a Tavern hex. Another dangled from a cord around the toy fox's neck.

"You will start to see creatures, the smaller ones described in the Bonny's Tavern booklet. You'll only see the harmless ones inside your house because it's protected, and most of them are kept out of Brinsford. School is protected as well, but your first bus trip to town will be an education." Abel deliberately looked up and to the side at Zephyr's shimmer to make it clear who he was talking about. "Zephyr isn't easy to see at any time, just a shimmer in the air. If you let her use spooky-phone she can explain it all to you a lot faster than we can, from inside your head." Abel glanced towards Rob because Melanie didn't look convinced. "Rob? I think you should be the demo."

"No problem. Spooky-phone please, Zephyr." The misty line shot out. "Maybe you could show Melanie where the phone line comes from. I reckon that will make her feel better, especially if Zephyr will put on a bit of a show?"

"Zephyr? Catwoman first, please, then have fun but don't show Ffod. Melanie knows all the game characters." Abel rolled up his sleeve.

"There, you finally get to see her. Zephyr lives inside the tattoo." On his arm a furry Catwoman stood up, wearing a polka dot summer dress, and turned to wave hello. Her tail waved as well, and a little bird landed on one ear. Zephyr had full control these days.

Melanie stared, wide-eyed. "Oh wow. She's the one in the game, sort of, in a dress, not shorts." The tattoo blurred then wore shorts before spooky-phones connected to everyone, and a connection waved in front of the new member. "That's, er, can you be anything? Or is that how you really look? No, you were a shimmery. Do I touch this thing?" Rob nodded and Melanie put out her hand, clutching the fox with the other. If it had been a real one she'd have probably strangled it. The connection met skin, Melanie looked startled, then she relaxed. "Hello, Zephyr. You sound, um, human?" Instead of her usual explosive enthusiasm, Melanie sounded cautious and very, very polite.

Half an hour later a cowgirl on a hare waved from Abel's tattoo as Rob took Melanie home. The stunning had worked off and, as expected, Melanie wanted to know everything now and work every possible glyph immediately. The teenager clutched a handful of Tavern hexes even though her home was protected, and instructions to stick with wind because it was fairly harmless. Not completely to wind, because she'd already wheedled the colour changing glyph out of them. That would slow her up a bit and probably make work for Rob, fixing her mistakes.

Jenny stood up, looking decidedly unhappy. "From what Melanie said about Diane, I'm going to get the same once I get home. Super. Do you mind if I insist Diane keeps her trap shut and just plays with leaves until I can get her here?" She looked after Melanie and heaved a big, resigned sigh. "That won't work, it'll take a bit more to fend her off. I'll give her the colour glyph as well because Melanie will probably tell her anyway. Trying to get that right should keep her occupied and maybe willing to slow up and listen."

Though the tone of voice and jaundiced look meant Jenny didn't expect it. "I really don't fancy the questions about me and Abel. She'll start on about love charms or some such rubbish. Sorry." Her look towards Abel and Ferryl might have held just a little suspicion. "Little sisters don't think any lad is good enough. She's already suggested you might have used drugs or hypnotism. Worse, she'll want a love potion to use on some oik from a boy band."

Ferryl started laughing as Abel's cheeks blushed pink. "I promise, I never used anything like that. Though if she really wants to capture a pretty boy we'd better be careful what witch charms Diane learns. I'll bet there's one on my missing wits that creates an attraction, because they've always been a good seller."

*   *   *

Two days later Mr. Forester gave in to a barrage of pleading and nagging from Diane and brought her to a real Bonny's Tavern meeting. The five Taverneers were pleased it wouldn't happen very often, because Melanie came as well. Either Melanie or Diane were full-on, but together and after discovering magic, the pair were irrepressible. Despite pleading, begging and a few very false tears, neither were allowed to go beyond wind and colour until they had full control. Promises to be good weren't very convincing because Rob had already changed several seedlings in the greenhouse back to green, and luckily Jenny had seen her cat's red tail before anyone else. Jenny cringed over the number of times Diane played the sorcerer's ex-girlfriend card, and how her younger sister should get preferential treatment. Melanie wielded the little sister argument like Rob's rounders bat, or possibly a real mace.

Despite pleas from both the younger sisters, neither were allowed in Castle House gardens. Abel wasn't sure if they actually believed the story about dangerous magic in there, or if Melanie had accepted she simply couldn't walk in. That left the five Taverneers free for the big wit hunt.

*   *   *

While the two almost-fifteen-year-olds were coming to terms with magic, the Taverneers pushed forward with extracting the shades from the animated stools. Ferryl now had six wooden cubes, each containing a bound shade, and two more stools were partly dismantled in case she needed more. The next chore was emptying the bookshelves beneath the aquarium so the woodwork could be dismantled. Ferryl couldn't see any other way of getting at the bottom of the aquarium where the wit or whatever had been hidden. "Later Kelis. You've got years to read them all." Abel smiled as Kelis reluctantly closed a book and put it onto a stack.

"Yes, I know, but while we were moving it I thought I recognised part of the glyph on the front." Kelis patted the book. "But now I've peeked inside it will have to wait until I learn whatever language it's written in." So far Ferryl had identified seven languages in the library including Latin and Greek, an old version.

"Right now I want to read the glyphs hidden in the shelving, or at least understand what they do." Ferryl laid on her back with her head actually inside the shelves, her hand almost touching the back panel. Zephyr floated, almost touching the back of another empty shelf. "I've got something here I'm not keen on touching. Am I right or is it just the catch, Zephyr?"

"I agree that it shouldn't be touched but can't see exactly what it does. There doesn't seem to be an attack element, so maybe that's a trigger to warn something? Not us, something in the house. Like an alarm bell?" Zephyr floated into the next shelf. "The catch is here, the glyph to open the back or maybe the complete section of shelving, but I can't see any hinges."

"With all this training you'll soon be able to pass as Nikk Smartish, the Warlock thief." Ferryl sounded distracted as she shuffled back out, her hand running along the bottom edge of the aquarium where it met the shelving. "The shelving and aquarium don't quite touch in some places. Can you get through the crack, Zephyr?"

The shimmer moved up to where Ferryl had her hand, and hesitated. Zephyr moved closer and closer, then a tendril of shimmer eased out and disappeared into the crack. "Ouch! There is something in there!" Zephyr shot back across the room, a hint of smoke trailing behind her. "That hurt. Something lives in there, or it's a shade that can cast a glyph."

"A glyph-casting shade is possible, but unwise." Ferryl hadn't moved far, and now she inspected the shelving again. "The glyph didn't damage the wood so it was meant for you, Zephyr, which needs carefully controlled intent. Shades aren't that precise. Maybe the alarm bell is for whatever cast the glyph?"

"If we drag the shelves out, or open them, and all of us are lined up?" Abel raised his hand. "Then blast it. It can't be very big, so five of us should be able to break its shield."

"Perhaps not. I doubt the sorcerer would put something really strong in his library with all these fragile books, but the house magic might supply a shield." Ferryl looked back at Abel with a little smile. "Which is why we shouldn't try blasting away. Too much magic would break the wit, and maybe the aquarium."

"Whatever is in there is strong enough to hurt Zephyr. Maybe we should take cover first, then pull the shelves out?" Jenny eyed up the timbers. "If the shelving actually opens when you activate that catch, Rob can stick his bat in the way to stop it closing." A quick discussion led to Rob standing up against the shelving one side of the aquarium, with Kelis the other side and Zephyr above. The others spread out, Ferryl and Jenny behind armchairs and Abel behind a settee. After second thoughts, the furniture was laid down so nothing could throw glyphs underneath it and hit someone's foot. The furniture wouldn't stop a glyph, but Ferryl didn't expect the defences to start a fire in the library. Everyone would stay hidden just in case she was wrong.

Abel asked Zephyr to touch the catch, then zoom up out of sight. He ducked down and waited, but nothing happened. Just as he was going to stick his head out Kelis called out. "It's moving, the whole section of shelving under the aquarium is sliding downwards. The top is now flush with the floor so the hole is big enough to get inside. I can't see in from this angle."

"Don't try! You're too close to dodge. Sorry." Abel knew what came next.

"Since I'm not a boy, my brain functions even when it's excited so I worked that bit out." Kelis sounded excited, too excited to keep teasing. "Something is moving in there. There's some sort of low lighting inside so I can see shadows. Two somethings, one each end."

Moments later Abel heard a clattering noise and a startled yell from Rob. "Cursing mippygrobs. Something smacked my bat across the room."

A brief silence fell as everyone tried to come up with the best way to see into the hole without becoming a target. Ferryl spoke up first. "That was wind, not fire, so whatever is under there knows two glyphs. It's controlled as well, because it hurt Zephyr but didn't damage the shelves. I'm going to peek and find out if these are just warning shots." Abel looked across without showing himself and saw Ferryl stick her head out and quickly pull it back. Two fire glyphs flew through the space where her head had been, tight enough so they didn't scorch the chair.

"Those looked a bit more than a warning." Abel didn't have chance to continue.

"Look behind you Abel. Ferryl and Jenny as well. Those glyphs died before they hit the shelves." Abel twisted round and just as Kelis said, there wasn't a mark on the fragile wooden shelves or books along the far wall.

Abel drew in a mental line, but at least one of those glyphs had to have hit well away from the window. "Watch again please, everyone this time. I'm going to pop my head up over the top of this settee but I'm going to put up a shield first in case a glyph blows right through the upholstery." Abel shuffled back from his cover, pushed out a shield and then rose up to show his head. He got a quick glimpse of two strange shapes, wide but waving about on a single leg or stalk, before ducking and moving sideways. Two glyphs flew over the settee, almost dead centre but once again clear of the upholstery.

"Weird, they shouldn't have done that because you are the master. Weirder still the glyphs just snuffed out for no reason, just before hitting the window and a bookshelf." Kelis sounded thoughtful rather than surprised. "The room must have put up shields."

Zephyr's connection shot out and then back again before anything could target them. "No flows, no shield. Glyphs just stopped."

"I took the chance to look at the two creatures, so I didn't see it. The glyphs dying means the guards under there aren't meant to harm the library." Ferryl chuckled quietly, then again at the surprised looks from the others. "I'd wondered why the sorcerer set up a firefight in his library, but the snakes under the aquarium are only here to stop others from getting to the controls."

"Snakes that throw glyphs? Are they like a magical spitting viper?" Having moved to the end of the settee, Abel saw Jenny almost peek out then think better of it.

"The guards are flying snakes." Ferryl sighed loudly, her exasperation clear in her voice as she continued. "Which doesn't help us much, because there's only one sort of winged snake that throws glyphs. Pterotos snakes are intelligent enough to fight smart, and will be supplied with endless magic by the house."

While Ferryl sulked, the rest tried to work out how to get past the guards. Rob still sounded grumpy, maybe about his bat, but wondered about shoving a chair or books across in front of the opening. Even if that would work, it wouldn't get Ferryl into the hole under the aquarium. After discarding a couple of other suggestions, Jenny suggested bagging the snakes. Wildlife programs usually showed snakes quietening down once they were caught. Ferryl perked up, she hadn't thought of that. Eventually they settled on using curtains to shield and wrap the snakes, then cushion covers to bag them up.

"Are the snakes magical, Ferryl? Will a bag hold them or will they just filter out through the cloth like Zephyr can?"

"Ophis Pterotos are real snakes with feathered wings, Rob. They used to be confined to Africa, where the local birds keep them under control. The snakes protected the source of frankincense, allegedly at the bidding of some godling, so they probably belonged to a sorcerer. These must have been brought in deliberately, and bound to the house. Bound servants, still alive because they are thinking rather than acting like a shade." Ferryl snatched a cushion. A fire glyph flew past but disappeared before striking another cushion.

"That settles the main question, the snakes won't hurt furnishings. I really hope the wit or whatever in there is worth all this trouble." Abel heard the door open as Kelis finished with "I'll get some curtains from the other rooms."

When Kelis came back with two floor-to-ceiling curtains from the sitting room, Zephyr slowly lowered one across half the opening. Neither snake damaged it, even when Ferryl gave them a very brief target. Only one threw a glyph, because the other would have hit the cloth. Kelis brought two more curtains, so there weren't any gaps, and soon wind glyphs held all four against the aquarium, hanging down to close off the entire opening.

After cautiously experimenting, the Taverneers gathered in front of them, where Kelis and Ferryl took the cushion covers. Ferryl could heal herself, while Kelis had the longest arms and could reach past the rest to bag her target. Abel counted down, and a short, frantic struggle later Ferryl and Kelis each held a bulging bag. Very still bags, which worried them all a little until Jenny remembered some of the snakes on the TV played dead once they'd been captured.

Kelis inspected a scorch on her sleeve, and one on Rob's jeans, while Jenny, Ferryl and Abel all had lightly scorched hands. The snakes had to banish their glyphs almost as they threw them to avoid damaging the bottom of the aquarium or the bookshelves each side, so they hadn't been very hot. As Ferryl healed hers, Jenny wagged a finger but with a big smile. "I'd be really annoyed about you doing that, but scorched clothes are actually a bigger problem. A curious parent one."

"Only until I get to school. I'll nip out at dinner break and get another pair of jeans." Rob smiled at Abel and shrugged. "I've still got most of my fifteen hundred quid so I can probably run to that." He turned towards Ferryl, already wriggling under the aquarium on her back.

Zephyr disappeared after her. "I do not burn. The glyphs hurt and I become a tiny bit smaller, but I am a much bigger puff of wind now." The tone of the voice down the spooky-phone changed suddenly. "Look, Ferryl! There is the wit. It looks like a wit. I'll get the bound shades!"

"Let me see first, Zephyr. I have to read whatever instructions the sorcerer scribed so I can copy them. If he has written the parameters as one set of rules, it might be easier to just scribe new ones for whatever each shade has to control." Ferryl's legs moved sideways as she twisted round and almost disappeared. The hole, with the shelves out of the way, gaped four metres wide by a metre high, stretching over three metres back into the wall. Her muffled voice sounded resigned. "I can't split these instructions up, not without rewriting each section anyway, so we'll start from scratch. Will you get my notes from the internet please Abel, the ones we made about the salinity and temperature, and the list of species and requirements?" Ferryl considered the internet a special kind of magic, a giant type of wit because of the sheer wealth of information it held. "Between them and what is on here, we can make sure there's nothing we missed."

"Can we scribe some of it for you, Ferryl?" Kelis went onto her hands and knees to peer inside, as did the rest. Even Jenny looked, though she probably wouldn't try to help with this job. She'd only just scribed her first wit, human biology of course, though she'd be starting on all the dry legal parts of Business Studies as soon as possible.

After inspecting the wit again, Ferryl spent two days creating six sets of instructions to split up the control of the aquarium. Abel and Jenny worried about the snakes being bagged up too long, so with Rob, Zephyr and Kelis they helped by scribing the basic instruction set exactly as Ferryl showed them. Ferryl further modified each one for the particular glyph and to give them their own parameters. The Taverneers made a little ceremony of wiping out the original instructions that told the shade to animate their stool. Zephyr and even Jenny could do that part, so they each took one and fixed all six simultaneously. Zephyr and Ferryl set into installing the bound shades before disturbing the wit, but only put in two the first night. Before they could finish the job something else cropped up.

*   *   *

Abel had already noticed that the younger players such as Melanie and Diane embraced the Tavern ideals with particular enthusiasm. Ten days before Easter break, he found out just how enthusiastic they were. Melanie caught up with Rob and his friends on their way to lunch. "Come quick. We've got a Tavern problem." She tugged on his arm, and the rest turned to follow. Abel had a sinking feeling as Melanie led them round towards the school rubbish bins, because it had to be more bullying. He'd thought most of that had been stopped. Now Abel hoped one of the Taverners hadn't got carried away and really injured someone. God's medics might not be interested in covering up that sort of problem.

At first sight the thick-set boy and the girl stood side by side against one of the bins didn't even seem to be restrained. A moment later Abel realised they were being held by strong wind glyphs. Using obvious magic, even on bullies or thieves, would lead to awkward questions so he opened his mouth to stop the glyph-casters.

"That lad is a Taverner. He's a magic user, a new one, I recognise him." Jenny sounded as shocked as Abel felt. They'd never had serious fighting between members.

"So is Natalie. They've been using magic to get money out of the kids in year nine. We haven't got many thirteen-year-old Taverners so nobody noticed at first." Rachel, Justin's fourteen-year-old younger sister, an advanced magic user and unofficial leader of the younger Taverners, scowled at the pair. "Well it stops right now."

"Where's the victim?" Abel wasn't sure what to do about this pair but any non-magic user who'd seen them pinned had to be mazzled, sharpish.

"Gone. We told her the Tavern would fix it and she promised to keep quiet if we did. To be honest, I doubt she realised anyone used magic. These two are still learning wind, but Carl uses it to enhance punches." Rachel pointed at the girl. "She's got better control so she trips anyone trying to get away. Carl is bigger than most his age so he doesn't really need magic, it just makes it easier. We turned up with older pupils and numbers, so the victim will think that's all we needed."

"Good. Keep an eye on the victim anyway, and if she says the wrong sort of things tell me. Ferryl or Zephyr will smudge her memories a bit, mazzle them." Abel saw the gleam in Rachel's eyes. "Not a chance. Even Kelis isn't good enough to learn that one. What have you told this pair?"

"If they want to be the bad guys, there's a price. We've taken their lead bars away for starters." Rachel pointed again, at four grim-looking youngsters. "Those four over there are thirteen and fourteen, in year nine the same as Natalie and Carl. I reckon they'll want to tar and feather them, or the magical equivalent." From Rachel's tone, and look, she might be wielding the tar brush. "We should take away their magic, all of it. They've disgraced the Tavern!"

"I think you might have disciples." Ferryl squeezed Abel's hand, gently. "Take care they don't start a crusade."

"Connect me to just Ferryl, please, Zephyr." Abel waited as the spooky-phones retracted from the others. "What do you mean? We aren't a religion."

"You could be, and now something about that Tavern sign is scratching away in my mind. I told you the way it worked felt familiar." Even mentally, Ferryl sounded very thoughtful.

"Never mind that, what about crusades?"

"Remember when you described your plans, your cause, in front of Terese Green. You saw our reaction, me, Kelis, Jenny and even Rob. I'm an ancient, jaundiced, embittered sorceress and I signed up on the spot. Not because of your scintillating wit and personal charisma, or because I owe you my life, it's the idea of it." Ferryl sighed, out loud. "All through the ages most sorceresses and religions have been interested in money and power, not in helping out the poor and powerless. Sometimes holy men and women were real saints, squandering their lives, wealth and magic to help others. Some had followers, but as soon as they died their work was corrupted by the leaders who took over. Yours might survive because if it works there'll be an army of dedicated young sorceresses and witches scattered around the country, none of them under anyone's control."

"That depends on who inherits. Nobody if I die without having a son. Can I change that? No, later. What are those like Rachel going to do?" Abel looked around at the silent faces watching him. "I'm getting advice from Ferryl and Zephyr, and it's quicker this way." Several heads nodded, though Kelis's look promised she'd want the full story later.

"I believe it is a combination. Many young people are idealistic. They wish they could make a difference, help others and change the world. Magic gives these youngsters a chance to do so, and every single Tavern member knows their discovery of magic is down to you. That makes you their leader. Kelis and Rob also lead, to a lesser extent, as does Jenny, but you are the one with the pet sorceress." She chuckled and her hand squeezed. "Two pet sorceresses. You could have kept magic to yourself, or charged everyone for lessons, or tethered them before they understood. Instead you've given it all away, and now you've given them a mission."

"But not a religion, and this goes beyond what I outlined. I didn't call it a mission." Abel pulled himself back to the immediate problem. "You still haven't told me what Rachel might do."

"Whatever her high priest or guru tells her, right now. If you want to stunt this pair, take their magic away permanently, she'll do it without a moment's hesitation. I'm trying to remember how, because it can be done." Ferryl paused, looking around at the gathered Taverners. "All the younger ones are angry. I doubt they'll kill but the keenest want to see that pair suffer, really suffer. They feel betrayed and some of the older ones are as bad. Right now they aren't thinking about consequences."

"No stunting. That's disgusting. I'd rather stop this guru thing as well."

"Difficult. Perhaps you should just guide them towards tolerance. As they grow older, most of these girls and boys will be less intense, though the charity sections in the rules of your game will tend to attract a certain type." Ferryl swept her eyes over the patiently waiting teenagers. "Look at them. Even Jenny and Kelis are waiting for your decision, though they might argue once you tell them. Some of the others will never argue, and if you don't guide them they'll make up their own rules and punishments. Then you'll have a crusade."

"That's all I need for now. We've got to talk properly, and not just you and me."

"I know, Kelis, Rob and Jenny."

Abel turned and forced a smile. "First off, no stunting, permanently taking their magic. Not if this pair behave." He'd never stunt them anyway, but the Taverners didn't want to hear that right now.

"There has to be a penalty!" Rachel spoke first but others were agreeing, even Kelis. "If the Tavern stands for good, then we have to punish members who pick on the helpless." Glyphs flared in Rachel's hands, proving Ferryl's assessment of her mood. "They can try picking on me any time they like."

"Calm down. There will be a punishment, though first I'd like to talk to the culprits. Let them go now. If they start to form glyphs, pick them up off the ground." From the number of hands that suddenly sprouted a wind glyph, Abel realised he'd have to be careful what he said. "Not too high or someone will see them. Just enough so it'll disturb their casting when they're dropped."

"Neat, I like it." Kelis sneered at the two apprehensive faces. "You are magical babies. A month ago you'd have been the ones being bullied so what started all this?"

"We should all act like proper sorcerers and sorceresses. The mudbloods should pay us for protection." The boy looked around in alarm as laughter rang out. At least half the Taverners had banished their glyphs to join in.

"Mudbloods? You idiot, magic is nothing like the books you've read, and nothing to do with your bloodline. The adepts told you, every single living thing is full of magic and anyone can learn to use it." Diane shook her head in disgust. "You really are stupid. It's a wonder you didn't blow your own hand off the first time."

"What?" The boy looked horrified, staring at his hand, but the girl wasn't impressed.

"Ignore her Carl, she's only just learned about it herself. We can do magic, and most other people can't. That means there must be something better about us, so we deserve to be in charge." Natalie tried to look confident, and almost brought it off. She certainly believed what she'd said. "We don't have to stick to their stupid rules."

"Zephyr, it's time for some scary. Is there enough dust to make a really visible shape?"

"I'll use water vapour as well. After all, they are beginners so they will not understand." Abel felt her flow out of his arm and wind gusted around him, picking up rubbish and dust.

"Now you've done it, you've annoyed Zephyr. You really think humans are the only ones who can control magic? Or do you think this creature is special and should be in charge, just because she's much stronger than you?" Abel glanced to the side, then stifled a smile. Zephyr had been creating solid-looking varglin and small deer with dust to keep herself occupied while Abel studied. Now he suspected she'd spent her nightly patrols and the hours when he slept getting more ambitious. Vapour billowed up, and up, until it almost reached above the boiler-house. The top blew sideways as the shape began to solidify. Massive limbs, a thick tail and long horns bent forward onto all fours as the burning green eyes of an almost-solid ogre glared at the suddenly-tiny humans. Abel felt the steady pull of magic down the tether, then a shield surrounded the three of them.

"Tell them to attack me." The humour in Zephyr's 'voice' didn't match her appearance.

The two youngsters, and most of the Taverners, were staring bug-eyed. "Okay you two. Hit it with your best shot." Abel had to give her credit, the girl tried. The boy's glyph didn't really have much intent, but neither even sparked Zephyr's shield. "Now tell it you are special, and should be in charge. Or explain why it's got the same special magic blood as you."

"What is that! I thought you said the big creatures in the game weren't real." Diane looked horrified. "That's an ogre!" Her identification and obvious shock added to the effect.

"Zephyr can be an ogre if she pleases, and if she hits you with those claws you'll bleed. Please be harmless-looking for the children, Zephyr." Abel nailed the girl with his glare. "Note that I asked. This is a powerful sorceress and she hasn't got a drop of blood, mud or any other liquid. Get it?" The short jerky nods as Zephyr evaporated and the wind died down meant Natalie, and several others, definitely got it. Quite a few looked relieved when a relatively harmless-looking shimmer hovered by Abel. He did his own double-take, because that looked like a very big shimmer.

"Some of me stays inside, most of the time. It is more comfortable and safer for me."

"Is there still enough room?"

"It doesn't work like that."

Abel wanted to know how it worked, but right now he still had to find a punishment. "Fly free, Zephyr, just around the Taverners to show you have no tether please."

"Back soon."

"As you can see, the tether isn't permanent so Zephyr can find you anywhere, at any time. You two have a choice. The first is to leave the Tavern. You will receive no more training or extra magic. You will be weak and alone if something powerful comes for you, something like Zephyr, but that's your choice." Abel paused, working on a punishment.

"But we'll mark you first, a magical one so any Tavern member, anywhere, knows you aren't welcome." Kelis shrugged at Abel's look, while beyond her most of the Taverners were nodding.

"What is the lesser punishment?" Ferryl fought back a laugh. "You don't know, do you? You won't physically hurt them or magically stunt them, so the worst you can do is give them a smaller dose of being alone. No extra magic and no training." Her voice suddenly became more thoughtful. "Better yet, a real shunning. Nobody even talks to them. That might work because there's whole tribes who managed using nothing else."

Abel hesitated, but Zephyr flowed back into her tattoo and connected so he could answer. "How do we stop them having magic, even temporarily? They'll keep absorbing it from the air."

"Drain them into a lead bar, then keep doing it. It'll be a boring chore." Ferryl glanced over his shoulder. "Though your disciples look keen enough."

With a sigh of relief Abel turned back to the pair. "If you don't leave, you serve a sentence. For the next three… months you will not be allowed to practice magic." Abel had been going to say weeks but the looks on the faces of the young Taverners wanted a real punishment, something that would sting. "Every morning, when you arrive at school, you will drain all your magic into a lead bar and give it to a Taverner. Each night before leaving you will drain what you've absorbed during the day into another bar. On your days off school, a Taverner will call round twice a day."

"No Tavern meetings, no playing the game." Rachel's curled lip promised she'd have a magnificent sneer when she grew up. "Not that anyone will want to play with you."

"Which I was about to say, thank you Rachel." She mouthed sorry and actually looked it. "Zephyr, or an experienced Taverner, will test you at any time without warning to make sure you haven't taken magic from somewhere else." From the looks, both the culprits were hoping it wasn't Zephyr. "You will not use your wind glyph until you are re-admitted into the Tavern." Abel drew a deep breath, mentally crossing his fingers. "Do you accept your punishment?"

"Yes. I'm sorry, I really am." Carl sounded it, but the girl still didn't seem repentant.

Though after a long pause, Natalie nodded. "I accept."

She'd barely spoken before Rachel held out a lead bar. "All your magic, now." Natalie hesitated, but Carl reached for the bar someone offered him. Rachel turned to Abel, her face hard. "We'll arrange the draining, Abel. The Taverners in year nine will watch them in school, and the rest of us will work out a rota." The younger Taverners including Melanie and Diane moved closer to Rachel, obviously eager to volunteer. Looking at their faces, Abel could see what Ferryl meant, the youngsters were totally committed to whatever they thought the Tavern represented. He'd have to sort that out as soon as possible.

He felt a bit better when he'd talked to his friends, on their way to a rushed lunch. All three had been chatting to the young Taverners while Abel consulted his two sorceresses. The group with Rachel were determined to succeed in their self-proclaimed mission, ridding the school of thieving, violence, intolerance and drugs. There were some non-magical teenagers just as keen, Tavern players who hadn't been invited because this situation involved obvious magic.

When Abel mentioned the crusade thing, his friends didn't think enough of the Tavern players were that dedicated. Most of them still played Bonny's Tavern as a game, and only one in four or five had found magic. The magical ones did tend towards youngsters who liked the charitable side, but there were plenty of non-magical blood and guts type players.

Even after the reassurances, Abel wanted a full meeting of the magical Tavern as soon as possible, to sort out some rules, but events caught up with him before he had a chance.

*   *   *

Abel, Kelis, Rob and Ferryl were baffled when Mr Sanders, the Graphic Art teacher, told them to report to the headmaster. Finding Jenny outside the headmaster's door settled one thing, it had to be about the Tavern. Zephyr quickly connected them but some muttering and head shaking confirmed nobody had any idea why they were here.

All five were even more puzzled and worried when the deputy head opened the door and invited them all inside. They'd never heard of something serious enough that it needed her as well as the headmaster. Despite the five chairs facing the headmaster's desk, it wasn't those that caught everyone's eye. The headmaster had a small stack of paper on his desk, and they all recognised the photocopied top page.

"Please sit down. From the way you looked at this, I can see I have the right people." He tapped the drawing of Bonny's Tavern. "The Parent-Teacher Association brought this to my attention."

"It's just a game. Sir." Abel wanted to curse, because his cheeks warmed. He concentrated on not blushing rather than what had to be a copy of the game rules.

"Don't worry, Abel, you aren't in trouble. If you are worried at any time, any of you can ask to defer this discussion until a parent is present. You are here because we, the school, have to understand your game better." Mrs Poole, the deputy head, sounded friendly, which alarmed Abel. Apart from a year as his English teacher, she'd never spoken to him. "As I understand it, this is a beta version, just a test. Despite that, over twenty percent of the pupils have played at least once and it seems to have had a distinct impact on the school."

Abel thought hard before he opened his mouth. "We can't help it if they skip homework. We've never encouraged anyone to do that."

"But a few probably have. Those are the same ones who already play computer games instead of completing homework so that isn't your fault. Your game might or might not be responsible for a strange phenomenon, but to be certain I must understand the whole scenario." The headmaster smiled at them all. "The subject has become urgent because the parents on the PTA have asked why other schools have a dance at Christmas, for instance, but we don't."

Now Abel's mouth definitely dropped open, and a surreptitious look showed the rest were in various stages of shocked and baffled. The deputy head smiled, probably at their expressions, but she quickly sobered again. "The answer is that we've never had any demand for one, especially with about a third of our pupils living out of town in villages or farms. Now it seems that if we allow fancy dress we will get most of your players, at least a hundred students, who will no doubt attract more. According to the parent representatives, your test players want somewhere to meet, but can't afford a venue that will hold you all?"

Since Mrs Poole looked straight at him, Abel answered. "We had the first meeting at Kelis's house, but there's more Taverners now. That's what we call the players. We've been waiting for summer, so it can be held outdoors."

"Enough of your players are complaining to their parents for them to ask if we can provide a venue. As a school we can't just let anyone use the facilities. We've both read this stack of paper, but want to ask a few questions. If the students are using the characters as some sort of role model, we want some guidelines." Her smile widened a little. "We'd like some clarification on exactly what we might be encouraging."

The headmaster turned over the top page, and started asking questions. Abel's mind whirled, wondering why the PTA had become involved, while answers from the others showed they weren't exactly calm and collected. Things went better once the creatures and characters had been explained, though both teachers seemed really interested in the background scenario. At one point Abel considered referring them to Creepio, because some of it was his idea. Jenny took over, reverting to the business plan and the link to charity. At least neither of the teachers seemed upset by any of the answers, eventually concentrating on whether the charity part really had been included in the game.

Eventually the two adults sat back and explained. The school had to be careful not to support a business venture, not unless Bonny's Tavern hired the school hall and organised the entire event. That would include financing and complying with security and Health and Safety regulations. Stourton Comprehensive, however, could have a school event that also advertised a local charity. According to the headmaster, since many of the pupils attending would be in Tavern costumes, the local media would pick it up. The school wanted to take advantage of that, encouraging the publicity to attract sponsors for the school itself. After agreeing that Easter would be a good time for the dance, the students went back to their lessons.

Before splitting up they agreed that discussing school business and Bonny's Tavern with teachers had to be one of the weirdest things ever. It wasn't until then they realised neither Mr Gordon nor Mrs Poole had explained what the strange phenomenon was, or why it might have anything to do with them. The jubilation in the following days washed away any concerns about the meeting. The school announced an Easter Fancy Dress Ball, with a Bonny's Tavern theme to support the Stourton Tavern Refuge.

The school would get their publicity, because Jenny's dad set into making sure he got Bonny's Tavern the maximum possible local coverage.

*   *   *

Despite the rest of the school being excited about a dance, the Taverneers were more interested in reclaiming the wit from the aquarium. Jenny even skipped Acro practice to help out, something she rarely did. Four interested teenagers passed the little bits of wood with the shades so Ferryl could install them, while Zephyr hovered next to her to watch for any variations in the magic flows. There had to be some alterations to the installation, because these shades would be more active than most. A skein of thin steel wire connected the shades and glyphs to the feed supplying house magic to the wit, then Ferryl turned it into gold. After some careful inspection, a hole in the back wall, protected by glyphs, had to be where the snakes came from.

There'd already been a long discussion about the snakes, because Abel wasn't keen on them being locked up in that hole. Unfortunately, he couldn't allow two wild snakes to fly around the neighbourhood casting glyphs at anything that offended them. Until Ferryl could come up with a way to alter their instructions, the snakes had to go back under the aquarium. Curtains were magically hung across the hole before air glyphs tipped the snakes out and quickly snatched away the bags and curtains that swaddled them. Opening the curtain enough to invite a wind glyph attack on Rob's bat proved they'd survived, so Ferryl activated the magical catch. The snakes were ready, but while she healed her burn, the empty shelves rose from the floor to seal the hole. Once the books were replaced, everything looked as before. Ferryl spent an hour watching the aquarium, but nothing altered. She went home with the wit, promising to put it in that night.

*   *   *

Despite her age, Ferryl Shayde still enjoyed teasing and grandstanding, or the young body had led to her rediscovering them. Nobody could get a hint out of her the following day. Jenny's dad commented about homework and Acro dancing, but Jenny insisted on coming to Brinsford to help Kelis move house. Ferryl made them wait until that chore had been dealt with.

Jenny's dad had already sent some of his workmen to move most of the remaining furniture and belongings from Kelis's house to the flat. Almost everything ended up in the right rooms, but needed unpacking and organising. Kelis's mum seemed impressed when the five of them reported they'd finished organising both girls' bedrooms, but she hadn't seen the glyphs or the puff of wind floating furniture, boxes and their contents about. She certainly had no idea the walls and doors now contained protective hexes, because they'd all been hidden under the surface. Leaving Mrs Ventner sorting out her own room, the teenagers headed for their last meeting in the old library, the original Bonny's Tavern.

"Firstly, it is one of my wits, and secondly it is intact." Ferryl waited for the excited questions to calm down. "The most important information that you can use immediately is better control of shields." A shield glowed around Ferryl, deliberately coloured, held to her body shape. Both Abel and Kelis started to warn her as Ferryl sat on one of the chairs, but it didn't burst into flame!

"That's what Redwolf did!" Abel moved his head side to side, but couldn't see if the shield went into the chair or not.

"The flows are right. It is a real shield."

The glow flowed out to include the chair. "There are two ways to sit on a seat and keep a shield up. The simplest involves adjusting the shield so part of it is just below your skin, exactly where you first cast it." Ferryl stood up, smiling, and one edge of the globe shrank until the glow disappeared from one arm, then came back. "Once inside my skin, you can't see it. An attack would inflict superficial damage, perhaps shallow cuts, and any heat or physical force would be felt, although the effect would be reduced."

Everyone had to try, but it wasn't as easy as it sounded. Casting a shield meant imagining the whole thing inside their skin, then pushing out to relocate and enhance the natural defences of their ward. Now everyone tried to imagine not doing so, but only on an arm. They were all keen to learn, because this would let them make phone calls without dropping the whole shield. A shield cut phone and radio signals, and Zephyr's tether, and according to Ferryl it would interrupt a sorcerer's tether but not break it. The alternative, pushing the shield out to deliberately incorporate a chair, for instance, might be much harder. There wasn't a natural magical boundary such as that around a person. Nobody would be practicing on real chairs in case they burst into flame, but Rob suggested using the plastic milk crates in the little cave.

Nobody would use the chairs and desk from Bonny's Tavern for anything, because tomorrow they would be stored until someone came up with a new location. So would a large number of Mr Ventner's tools, the ones neither Rob's nor Jenny's dad bought. Jenny's dad sent a couple of men to unbolt or unscrew the bigger tools, and move everything useful to the shop. The shelves and worktops had been dismantled and put in a skip, because the bank wanted the garage cleared.

The agents renting out the flat and shop had agreed to Mrs Ventner putting the tools and furniture in the shop, temporarily. Every time something like that came up Kelis shot Abel a suspicious glance, but he ignored her. The health food had all gone, taken by a large van, but all the racks were still in place. Abel still hadn't decided how to deal with the rest of the space, though the shop itself would make a terrific Bonny's Tavern. That would also blow his cover.

While they all played a last game of Bonny's Tavern, without cheating, just for old time's sake, Rob brought them up to date on the animated toadstools. Melanie could now see magical creatures, but still swore a few of them looked like toadstools. Unfortunately, those only appeared at night, outside the fence at the bottom of the garden, so nobody else had seen them. Ferryl racked her brains but nothing magical looked like a toadstool. Abel had helped Rob to set several fae-traps, but didn't catch anything unusual. Since the creatures never came past the fence, and the school dance was approaching fast, Abel almost forgot about them.

*   *   *

Two days before the school dance, Abel wished he'd thought more about the meeting with the head teachers than the dance itself. This time none of the other Taverneers were waiting outside the headmaster's study. When he was invited in and found Curtis the ex-bully stood in front of the headmaster's desk, Abel realised this could be real trouble.

"Good morning, Abel. I see you recognise this young man."

"Good morning, sir. Yes, his name is Curtis."

"You are either Abel or the sorcerer, according to him. I don't usually get involved in something like this, because it isn't strictly school business, but Curtis's parents asked me to intervene." The headmaster didn't seem very pleased, but Abel still couldn't work out how much trouble he was in.

"It seems he is one of those who play this game, Bonny's Tavern."

"Yes, sir."

"No, sir, because he has been banned. That is rather strange. How exactly does a child end up banned from playing a game that the whole school has access to?" Mr. Gordon leant forward. "More to the point, how can you possibly enforce it?"

"He only asked me to stop, sir."

"I wasn't talking to you, Curtis. Well, Abel?"

"I asked him to stop, sir."

"Now he refuses to play the game, even on his own at home, until you say he can. What will you do if I insist he plays Bonny's Tavern, right now, in my office?" From the look on Mr Gordon's face, that might have been meant to show Curtis that Abel couldn't do anything, but Curtis's eyes were fastened on Abel's arm and he looked horrified.

"No, sir! It's my fault, sir. If I'm good I'll be let back in." Curtis shut up and swallowed hard. "Sir."

"If you are good? As far as I'm aware, I deal with discipline at Stourton Comprehensive." Mr Gordon leant back. "This might be a good time to ask for a parent, young Conroy."

Not a chance. Abel really didn't want his mum wondering about the game. "No need, sir. The players have certain standards. If someone doesn't meet them, they aren't allowed to play for a while."

"For three months." A knock sounded on the door. "Come in." Mrs Poole, the deputy head, came in with a sheaf of papers in her hand. "So far we have confirmed that Curtis has broken some rule, and the banning is real. Did you get any sort of sense out of the other schools?" Abel's head whirled, what other schools?

"None of the junior schools are involved. The college and St. Agatha's have both noticed similar phenomena, though St. Agatha's isn't as bad to start with." Mrs Poole spread some of the papers out but Abel couldn't read them upside down. "There don't seem to be as many players in the other two locations, and the staff hadn't connected the game with the reduction until I asked."

The headmaster looked through whatever he'd been given, then fixed

Curtis with a look. "I'm going to make what is definitely not a wild guess. You were bullying or stealing." Despite an appealing glance from Curtis, Abel couldn't help. "There's no point in looking at Abel, he's got his own questions to answer. If it helps you to make up your mind, I don't think I'll have to talk to your parents about it. Well?"

"Yes, sir. I threatened some of the others and took money from them. I've stopped now." Curtis's glance went from Mr Gordon to Abel to Mrs Poole and then dropped to the floor.

Mrs Poole nodded, tapping one of the papers, then turned to Abel. "What happens if they don't stop?" As Abel opened his mouth to ask who they were, she narrowed her eyes. "Petty thieves and bullies, verbal and physical, and possibly racists and those dealing in drugs."

"I don't know because it's not me doing the whatever. Some of the game players want to carry the ideals into real life. I'm sorry if they've caused trouble." Both teachers were still looking at him, so Abel racked his brains for something more. "I'll talk to them at the next meeting."

"So you really are in charge." Mr Gordon put a finger on one of the papers. "Either the white wizard or the Wind Chaser?"

"It's a joke, the white wizard part. Wind Chaser is just a game character, not even a major one." Abel still couldn't get his head round it. What had been said, and did they think the Tavern were a gang of some sort? "We're not a gang, just people who play a game, sir, miss."

"Cult was the word that came to mind when this blew up, but it isn't. I'd like to work out exactly what this Tavern is, but first I have a request." From the tone of voice, Mr Gordon wasn't taking no as an answer. "Will you allow Curtis back into your Tavern so he can attend the Easter dance?"

"No, sir! It's my fault, sir. I don't want to go. I didn't ask. Sir." Curtis stood stiff as a board, going the same sort of colour Abel had managed too many times in the past.

The chuckle from Mr Gordon came as a big relief, to Abel at least. "No you didn't but your mother did. She came in to ask me why you were banned, and you aren't. You didn't tell her anything, but you've been complaining there hasn't been a place for everyone to gather and wear their costumes. Then when the dance was announced, you didn't want to go. The next time you argue over whose fault it is, keep your voice down." Mr Gordon turned to Abel. "I'm assuming Natalie Cutler was his accomplice?"

"Natalie, but I don't know her surname, sir."

"Maybe not, but I doubt she'll be here on Thursday evening. Since neither Natalie or her parents have approached me, that's not my concern. So, back to the question. Will you allow young Curtis to rejoin your little club? He seems to be sufficiently penitent." The tone and look meant Abel had some really difficult questions to answer if he said no, not least of them how he'd enforce it.

"Just for one night, please? I'll work in the refuge every weekend?" Curtis flinched from the scowl as Mr Gordon turned towards him, but Abel jumped in quick.

"I'm sure the other players will agree to that." Now he got the scowl.

Though Mr Gordon still had some scowl left for Curtis. "I'm sure they will. Curtis, I would appreciate it if you don't tell the rest of the students about this meeting, or I might have to take official notice of your past misdeeds. That means you don't tell Natalie, because I'd rather not find her parents on my doorstep tomorrow."

"Yes, sir. Thank you, sir."

"I'm not terribly impressed with the reason you ended up banned, and I really hope there'll be no repeats." Mr Gordon glanced at Abel. "The school have their own ways of dealing with such things, a little more robust than being banned from playing games. Off you go and remember, no gossiping." Curtis got out sharpish, but Abel felt sure he wasn't going to be so lucky. "If you won't be calling in your mother, perhaps you should sit down, young man. This could take some time."

It did, but Abel finally found out about the mystery phenomena. Schools tried to estimate the amount of unreported bullying, violence, racist behaviour, theft, problems with integrating, self-abuse, the list went on. Stourton Comprehensive had noticed a very strange trend. Even if the teachers couldn't catch all the culprits, they had a good idea who most of them were, and most of the suspected bullies in the school had stopped. Perhaps all of them Mrs Poole admitted, and pilfering had reduced to almost nothing. She had been putting together remarks from parents, pupils, and snatches of overheard conversations along with a regrouping of some social groups.

"Does your game disapprove of litter, Abel?" Mr Gordon's question came out of the blue, catching Abel still trying to think of the answers he expected to need pretty soon. After all, he could hardly admit Zephyr had been bored, so she'd hung around the lockers and some classrooms and solved the pilfering problem. For a moment he almost smiled, because he'd definitely stopped the goblins from littering in Brinsford.

"No, sir. Why?" Too late to bite his tongue.

"Because apart from your gang signs, that shield with a flower, the level of both graffiti and litter has dropped off. Any idea why?" At least both teachers looked curious, as if they had no idea.

Abel knew the reason for the lack of litter, but not the graffiti. "The sign is supposed to be magical protection, sir, not a gang sign. I'll ask the players to stop putting it on walls." They wouldn't need to draw it in view any more. As a side effect of reaching into earth to make it more rock-like, then putting a locking glyph in it, several Taverners could now place hexes beneath the surface. Others found it funny to practice air glyphs by blowing litter into bins. It had become a game, combining precision and careful timing so they weren't spotted. "I'll ask them to scrub the others off."

"Those on the computers, photocopiers and the overhead projector as well? There's a little shield on every single one in the school, except those in this office and the teachers' common room." Mr Gordon stopped and his eyes narrowed. "Correction, my printer seems to have acquired one. No doubt it'll be in permanent marker like all the rest."

"We swapped it out when it broke down." Mrs Poole shook her head at Abel. "You really have no idea, do you? I'll ask the players, you say. If you weren't a minor I'd make a small wager about the amount of graffiti disappearing once you've asked. I remember you from year nine English Language, Abel Conroy. Shy, blushed at the slightest opportunity, and almost melted into the woodwork if you were asked to stand up and speak. Now there are a significant number of children who consider you or one of your close friends a hero or role model of some sort." Her sudden, bright smile seemed totally genuine. "Actually you are a hero, for saving Jenny Forester."

"It's just a game, I swear. Kelis and Rob did as much designing as I did, and then Jenny joined in, and Fay." Hero? Abel really wanted to cast a veil and have a good look at those papers.

"The Parent-Teachers have asked others, very quietly, what they have overheard or been told. Several of our pupils are very proud of what they are doing, and not shy about telling their parents. Abel Conroy, Kelis Ventner, Robert Tyler and Jenny Forester are the people who set the rules. Somehow the new girl, Fay Shayde, is given the same sort of respect by a large number of them. Not just here either. Teachers at St. Agatha's and the college have asked who you are." Finally Mrs Poole held up one of the bits of paper, but not long enough for Abel to read it. "Once they looked into it, several of the more violent pupils seem to have quietened down, and there's been a small but significant downtick in pilfering."

As she paused, Mr Gordon leant forward. "So I have to ask a very strange question, Abel. What exactly are you trying to do with your game? The word mission has been bandied about so exactly what is it? You have players representing every race, colour and religion in the school, even some who are gay. Some of your players have definitely protected minorities from abuse. Who are the targets of your mission?"

"Nobody, no targets because there isn't a mission. Not as such, although as we explained, charity work is rewarded with increased health points. We are still testing the game, but it'll be for sale everywhere in a few months." Abel tried to explain that maybe some players were really getting into their roles and had begun to watch out for others, like some quests in the game. The headmaster seemed to think that quests to rescue goblins and dryads, different races, and players adopting characters with blue or green or brown skin might be significant.

Abel got the impression the teachers had already talked about most of this. He felt sure the pair knew exactly who was taking the game to heart, those like Rachel, but they seemed more interested in how it was done. All Abel could suggest was there were enough Taverners to stand off the smaller numbers causing trouble. At least the teachers let slip none of the pupils had complained, or seemed to be injured beyond bruising. Even Abel hadn't been sure about the last part, because Rachel and her cohorts were very intense at times.

When he finally got clear, Abel still didn't know what the headmaster wanted, or even if the teacher knew. He seemed pleased by the results, but worried about the methods. At least Mr Gordon would get a chance to watch the Tavern players at the dance, and could see they weren't some sort of street gang. Kelis, Rob, Jenny and Ferryl agreed, they'd ask Rachel to be very, very careful not to get caught. At least Petra had an answer to the graffiti question. Taverners who didn't like some of the comments written here and there were using colour glyphs or moisture and wind to make them disappear.

Apart from passing on the request about not writing Tavern hexes on walls, there wasn't much else Abel could do. None of the five Taverneers were happy about that part because they'd be the ones putting most of the hexes under the surface, which was slow, difficult work. One definite request had to be accepted, one way or another. The Tavern really had to forgive Curtis for one night, or any tolerance from the teachers would disappear.

Disorderly Conduct

The meeting with the headmaster finally led to the other meeting Abel had been after. Once they heard about it, the magical Taverners agreed that they had to sort out some rules as soon as possible. The more adept, senior regardless of their age, also wanted to discuss the problem of trainees who never learned to be full sorcerers. Others thought there should be a method of reporting things like the misuse of magic and a scale of punishments set in place. Generally speaking, they all wanted to get properly organised. With the launch of the game planned for the summer, both the charity and the players expected a lot of scrutiny and wanted to be ready for it.

Knowing they'd be expected to suggest some sort of structure for the magical Taverners kept distracting Abel and his close friends, more than the impending dance. They all had work to do on their costumes, especially with the dance being held at school, but that could be done at home. Most of their time together mixed shield practice with trying to write out some version of Abel's idea, his mission, as the others kept calling it. This time it had to be right, because once the first real charity case moved into Frederick's house, the big magical meetings there would have to stop.

The written version couldn't mention magic, just groups of players setting up a series of Bonny's Taverns across the country. At the meeting it wouldn't take much to explain the magical version, but Abel wasn't risking his mum seeing that written down. Equality, even if the written rules mentioned race and religion, also meant all levels of magic so that the weakest witch and the strongest sorcerer were all equal members. The charity would finance new refuges where there were enough Taverners interested in the idea. Although it wasn't written down, Abel's mystery cash would finance the hiring of premises for the magical Taverners. Any locals who fluttered a leaf would be able to train up in private, until they could protect the locals from magical creatures.

The whole thing still looked a shambles to all five of them when dance night came round. Since the meeting at Frederick's would be the following morning, Abel collected all the notes together and left them in his bedroom. He hoped the rest of the Taverners could make sense of them. Tonight he wore the same Wind Chaser outfit he had at New Year, with the same Angry Birds balloons because he daren't have Zephyr piloting one about at the school. When he came out of the door to meet Rob, on the way round to Kelis's to get a lift, Abel forgot all about creating rules and missions.

"Those can't be granite. What exactly are they?" From the waist down Rob looked at if his legs were two slabs of rock that widened to cover his feet.

"Bell-bottom jeans from a charity shop. I stuck papier-mâché to them, then hardened it and coloured the result." Rob waddled forward. "But now I've realised the tiny flaw, I can't bend my legs."

"Don't fall over or we'll need a fork truck to shift you." Abel eyed the jeans, and the stiff waddle Rob used instead of walking. "How are you going to sit in the minibus?"

"Good question. I'm hoping Ferryl has the answer. Maybe she can soften a strip around where my knees are." The pair of them walked, or in Rob's case waddled, to the old village shop. Zephyr inspected Rob's jeans but daren't alter anything in case the whole lot disintegrated.

Though Rob's costume wasn't the only surprise. "Do you like it?" Ferryl turned to show off what looked like a knee-length leather dress.

"What happened to your usual outfit?" Abel looked closer. "Those whiskers are drawn on."

Ferryl turned round again. "And I've used makeup for my eyes and fixed the tail outside my dress rather than poking out of a hole so the teachers can see the wiring. The dress is real leather, not a seeming. Is it long enough?"

"Ferryl's worried about the teachers. It's all that nagging you did about showing her fur when she was a tattoo." Kelis wore a neck to floor robe and a cloak, so hemlines didn't really come into it. "Though I'll bet Petra has a similar problem, what to wear instead of her shorts. What's the betting Una leaves her sword at home?"

"Never mind that, what about Rob's knees?" Abel explained, ignoring the laughter from Ferryl and Kelis. When Ferryl complained about students who didn't think things through, and worked on a solution, the rest wondered who else had toned down their fancy dress for the school. At least they'd be able to wear the proper costumes tomorrow, at the meeting. By the time Samantha, Rob's big sister, arrived to drive them, Rob's knees were flexible. Even so, he'd have had trouble if it wasn't for the extra leg space in the minibus.

He wasn't the only one taking up extra space, Melanie needed some for her Crone's hat. She spent the trip ridiculing Rob, and talking about the dance, which stopped the rest getting in more than the occasional word. They'd be able to talk tomorrow, because neither Melanie nor Diane, Jenny's sister, would be at the meeting in Stourton. Only the reasonably adept would be there, because they had more experience of the practical aspects of magic. Just as well, as both youngsters would have used being younger siblings to push their agendas, and both had embraced Rachel's mission.

*   *   *

"Good God, it's like one of those gaming conventions." Samantha stared at the children in costumes streaming in through the school gates. "Cosplay, that's it. I'm pleased I refused to babysit. A bit of string in the back of my shorts ain't gonna cut it tonight." She turned in the driver's seat to point at Melanie. "I told mum and dad you don't need a keeper, so don't mess up. Believe me, you'll be sorry if I have to watch over you another time."

"I'm all grown up now." Melanie stuck her nose in the air. "If I can come to school on the bus I can go to the school dance on my own." Her face broke into a big smile. "Ooh look, Diane's here, and Rachel! Bye."

Samantha turned to Rob. "Best of luck. I'll be back to collect you at 10:30, so don't get thrown out early. You owe me big time for this."

"Tripe. If you'd borrowed dad's car for a night out in town it would have cost you petrol." Rob carefully swivelled his hips. "Now leave me in peace so I can concentrate. It'll spoil my entrance if I fall out of the door." He paused, shocked by the cheering.

"Why are they…?" Samantha inspected the pupils waving at either Rob or one of the others. "Tomorrow we'll be having a talk, little brother, to decide how you buy my silence about your fan club. Especially about the girl wearing silver hot pants and netting, and the one with tight leather, fur and a club. They must be waving to you for a reason." Rob's vehement denials didn't slow her up at all, especially when several members of the local archery club turned up in wildly differing versions of Bullseye the Bowman, or Bow-woman. "How did Robin Hood sneak into the game?" She kept up comments about the costumes and Rob's reception as the rest climbed out, then set off for town.

"I'd rather they'd kept it quieter, toned it all down." Abel waved to some of the Taverners. "Mr Gordon is watching."

"And he'll see everyone wearing daft costumes, laughing and making jokes. No dark, mysterious cult or nasty gang stuff." Ferryl slipped her arm through his. "They'll have to relax the school rules about couples tonight. Some of these are from the college or St. Agatha's, or have left school." She waved to Lovingly Sculpted, wearing more leather and fur than skin tonight. "Quite a few have covered up, and not just because it's cold."

"Phew, I'm pleased she's gone before Kathy arrived." Rob shrugged at the curious looks, because his girlfriend wasn't a secret. "You haven't got a big sister, especially one looking for payback after the grief I gave her over some of her boyfriends." He looked around, then pointed. "Crikey, are those TV cameras?"

"I hope not. Smile everyone, because we're on someone's home movies. Let's get indoors out of sight." Though Abel's hopes were dashed. As their small group came to the double doors, Bonny the Barmaid came out, all frills and petticoats and cheap flashy jewellery. Jenny really, because she'd finally finished a proper Tavern costume. She put a finger to her lips as the deputy head and a smartly dressed stranger followed her.

"Abel, or should I call you Wind Chaser tonight? Could you and your friends spare a couple of minutes for the media?" Mrs Poole's happy smile swept across them. "We can use one of the empty classrooms. I'll be here in case the reporters need any clarification on how the school feels about your invention. Don't worry, the TV cameras will stay outside." To Abel's huge relief he soon realised Mrs Poole also meant to stop anyone giving her pupils a hard time. Even so, by the time the five of them had answered all the questions, some of the shine had gone off his evening. The practice when the teenagers had explained the game to their parents or teachers came in handy.

Abel would never be sure if Mrs Poole or Mr Gordon set the next part up, or if it really was coincidence. He could hear the music from the hall, but then it stopped and the headmaster could be heard welcoming everyone. As the deputy head opened the door to let them into the school hall, Mr Gordon paused. "Just a moment, we have some late arrivals." Everyone turned to look. "Just as well we waited. I'm told no Tavern would be complete without a Bonny the Barmaid. She seems to have brought Ferryl Shayde, Ka-liss if I've said that right, a Rock and Roll sorcerer, and I'm sure that's the Wind Chaser."

"Don't worry, no media cameras in here. School policy." Abel barely heard the deputy head because the Taverners, magical and otherwise, were laughing and cheering. "Though there'll be plenty of pupils with a phone so smile for your fans."

Not really, Abel realised with huge relief because for one awful moment he'd thought it might be that crusade thing Ferryl had been on about. Some really were cheering for Abel, but a good few Taverners were cheering the headmaster for naming the game characters, and others were shouting to his friends or just chanting "Tavern, Tavern." Even so, walking down the lane that opened for Mrs Poole left him bright red. The headmaster finished by hoping everyone had a good time, and the music started again.

"I hope you've remembered the dancing lessons." Ferryl's hand caught hold of Abel's so she could 'talk' silently. "I saw Curtis. He's dressed as Champ the Bouncer and cheering like a lunatic." A mental giggle tickled Abel's mind. "Rachel and a couple of others are watching him, but I don't think he's noticed. They've left it to the non-magical Taverners to actually talk to him."

Abel almost asked Zephyr to connect him, but some of the non-magical pupils might be the type who almost saw magic. "Zephyr? You'll have to stay in the tattoo in here. Would you like to fly free outside?"

"I can have a party with the dryads."

Abel laughed out loud, even as he felt Zephyr leave the tattoo. "Sorry, someone has gone to party with dryads." He looked down at Ferryl's feet. "If I've forgotten the steps, I'll just have to fake it and try to miss your toes." As they started dancing, Abel glanced round and relaxed, because he'd no idea who most of the other dancers were. Between the non-magical Tavern players, the non-players, and the total strangers who had come with some of the pupils, he was almost anonymous. He should do this more often, instead of being surrounded by magical Taverners or people like Creepio.

By the time Samantha turned up to collect them, Abel felt sure neither the headmaster nor deputy head harboured any real suspicions about Bonny's Tavern. At any other gathering like this there might have been the occasional glyph but the magical Taverners, nearly fifty of them, all knew better tonight. None of them even mentioned the meeting tomorrow. Una complained about not having her sword, but with a smile because Rob offered to give her his plastic one for the next dance. Even Zephyr felt happy and relaxed when she came back, and really had been to visit the dryads.

The good mood lasted all the way home, helped by Melanie being totally worn out and dozing off. Either that or none of them saw Ferryl hit her with a sleep glyph. For once the four of them could talk in front of Samantha without worrying about what they said, because nothing magical had happened. After bidding Ferryl goodnight, Abel walked back home with Rob and Melanie. He let himself in, sneaked upstairs and fell asleep without even thinking about tomorrow, or the big meeting.

* * *

Abel's good mood persisted the following morning, even while he stuffed the notes about the Tavern into his school bag. Rob wasn't quite as cheerful, because he'd had to deal with Melanie complaining because she couldn't come to Stourton. She thought the four of them were going to help out at Frederick's and wanted to meet up with Rachel. Shannon had borrowed her mum's little car so she could get to Brinsford and act as chauffeur, because she wanted to drive the minibus. Her parents were a little bit snobbish about her going to St. Agatha's, the church school, and hadn't wanted her to go to a dance at the Comprehensive. Now, once she'd picked up Jenny, Shannon wanted to know everything that happened.

That kept them all busy until they reached Frederick's house. "That's strange. There's usually a few people out the front, even if they have to be careful not to use magic." Abel looked up the path towards the house as

Shannon pulled up. "I'm surprised nobody is at the front door."

"Maybe they've already started. We aren't late, but if everyone else was already here?" Kelis shrugged as she carefully felt for the step with her foot. She couldn't see it properly because of her Glyphmistress robe.

Rob jumped out without any problem. He'd decided to wear ordinary jeans, stone-washed of course, until he could design something better than the last effort. "No goblins either, even as gargoyles. Though if there's a barbecue in the back garden they'll be round there scrounging."

"We'll know in a minute." Abel turned to Shannon. "If you park on the grass with the others, we'll wait for you before we go in." She nodded in reply and drove along the road to the driveway, where part of the lawn had become a temporary car park.

Meanwhile Kelis led the way through the gate as the front door opened. "I thought you were all asleep in there." She stopped and the rest crowded up behind her as the first person came out. "Natalie?" Effy and then Claris followed the shunned fourteen-year-old Taverner out of the door. One look at Claris's face told Abel there was a big problem, because she looked terrified. He soon realised why as Pendragon followed Claris outside, a hand on her shoulder.

"Welcome to Stourton Tavern, a subsidiary of Pendragon Enterprises." The sorcerer let go of Claris and moved to the side, away from the doorway. Natalie followed him, but Effy brought a baseball bat out from behind her back and raised her other palm to Claris.

"Follow your new master, or I'll burn you." Effy's entire manner and voice had altered. Gone was the quiet, nervous woman they all knew, replaced by someone who looked ready to do just that, burn someone. "Move it! You'll learn, once Pendragon puts your tether on." Her vicious smile disappeared, replaced by something much softer as she looked towards Pendragon. "Though you won't get a special one. That's just for me. Maybe he'll let me keep you as a maid, since you're useless at magic."

"Come on Effy, stop chattering. Your friends are confused." Pendragon ignored the happy smile that answered him, his whole attention on Abel, Ferryl, Kelis, Rob and Jenny. "Before any of you do anything unfortunate, I already have some of your friends on tethers." A scream sounded from inside the house. "That's the one called Justin, which will keep that little spitfire of a sister behaving herself. She'll take a tether eventually, if I hurt him enough. Would you like to hear five screams? More?"

"How? You can't force tethers past the ward." Abel turned to shout a warning to Shannon, but she'd stopped on the driveway and was climbing out of the minibus. She had her hands up, because a man wearing some sort of security uniform pointed a pistol at her.

"All voluntary. I gave Justin a choice. He could accept the tether or I'd force one on his sister and he could watch her die." Pendragon pointed towards Effy, without taking his eyes off the group of five horrified teenagers. "I threatened to do the same to Effy, so Shawn and Frederick let me put tethers on them as well. Threatening some of the others gave me more volunteers, including Una and Petra. Effy told me which weak ones to threaten and which to tether, the strongest ones most likely to cause trouble. That includes all the ones who can shield, apart from Rachel and you five."

As Abel wondered why Pendragon didn't know Shannon could shield, Ferryl took his hand. "He used a tether just before that scream, so that part is true."

"I saw the tether. Sorcerer bop?" Zephyr didn't sound keen. "He has a shield, held close to him."

Ferryl's hand squeezed. "He has a shield. I have one ready to snap around us both. Ask what he wants."

"What do you want?"

"An army. Your trainees to be exact, and you can't stop me. Your sorceress fooled Redwolf, but not me. I investigated, and none of the older sorceresses have disappeared from Germany recently so she really is young. Her father was a warlock, so she's not even properly trained." The sorcerer gave a big, expansive smile and turned a little to look at Ferryl. "Redwolf will be very annoyed. I might hand you over if he pays enough, once you are tethered."

"No!" Abel braced himself but Pendragon just laughed.

"In that case she dies. Though I want her dealt with before I try to tether you, because I'm wary about the one in your tattoo. Effy and Natalie tell me you bound a sorceress. Since she must be a bound shade, she won't have enough magic to fight me but she might be troublesome. If I see any sign of her, I'll kill one of your friends inside. A young lady." Pendragon gestured towards Claris. "I brought her out here to stop any heroics. You have a soft spot for pretty girls and I'm sure you don't want to watch her burned." His eyes tracked to Rob. "Your young lady is here, Kathy, and very confused because she hasn't seen magic before. I've got thirty of your friends in the lounge, all sat on their hands. If they move, my apprentices will burn one."

"I told you magic made us special. My new master will let me boss who I like, and he'll teach me the fire glyph." Natalie poked at Claris. "I'm not like this fool, afraid of magic. I told him everyone at school who can shield, and about your sorceress, so I get a reward. I asked for that Rachel on a tether so she can make me stronger and burn who I tell her to. Let's see how she likes that!"

"Calm down, dear, or I might have to teach you manners." Pendragon shook his head in mock despair. "Youngsters today. Enough of the chatter, time for decisions. I've had to rush this, borrow help from other sources, because you started teaching them all to shield. Though a shield is useless if you care too much about your friends. I want two of you young ladies to come over here and kneel. I'll tether both, which will keep the rest of you from shielding or fighting when we go inside."

"In your dreams!" Kelis raised her hand, a glyph swirling. She hesitated as a cacophony of screaming came from inside the house.

"Zephyr might break those tethers, if we keep Pendragon occupied." Ferryl paused for a reply, then realised Abel couldn't without letting Zephyr connect. "We worked on the ones to the bird, remember? Mazzlement broke the link to the watcher at the school, which helped us to work it out because all tethers are basically the same. We believe we have the key to Pendragon's version, if Zephyr has time to work?"

"Can you do that, Zephyr? You'll have to get out of my arm and into the house without being noticed." Abel raised his voice. "All right, we get the message. Stop it." The screams stopped.

"No, Abel, you can't agree. Once he gets a tether on us he can make us do what he likes." Kelis glared at Pendragon. "I'll die first."

"Going now." Abel daren't even glance towards his arm but he felt the link part.

"He can't tether us all, because some of us won't allow it. He's trying to find out who'll agree by threatening the weakest. He just told us that's how he tethered the others." Abel turned his full attention on Claris, trying to look and sound apologetic. "I'm sorry, Claris. Some of the monsters are human."

"You can't stop him?" Claris looked horrified as her eyes tracked to Effy. "Or her?"

"I gave you the bat for monsters. It was the best I could do and it works on some." Abel looked pointedly at Effy. She might have fooled them all to spy for Pendragon but he had a good idea of Effy's magic skills. Even if she'd managed a shield, it wouldn't be a good one.

Pendragon didn't seem to realise Abel was winding Claris up. "Effy is a special case. She doesn't need a tether, do you, my dear?"

The silly smile spread over Effy's face again. "No, master. I have a special link."

"The sort that can't be seen. There's no communication but she's totally loyal, which makes her a perfect spy." Ferryl's little sigh probably wasn't heard by anyone else. "It's what I thought you'd done to Kelis."

"Very special, and you've been a good girl. If you want that one as a maid, you can have her." Pendragon's voice sharpened and he glared at Kelis. "I'm waiting. Two women, now!" A scream echoed inside the house to punctuate the last word.

But Ferryl, not Kelis, answered him! "On two conditions. You don't give me to Redwolf, or try to give me a link like Effy's." Before Abel could react, she continued but in his head. "When he's distracted, hit him with everything. Rob has his hands behind his back and is building a glyph. Jenny has her shield up so she's going to resist. You heard Kelis's opinion. We need to distract him, keep him here while Zephyr works." Ferryl let go of Abel's hand and took a step forward. "You'll find me more useful as a willing apprentice. I might be young, but I'm ambitious and I'll bet I'm stronger than any of your other apprentices." She straightened and her voice strengthened. "I'll tell you how to get into Castle House?"

"No, Ferryl, don't do that!" Abel let a glyph start up in his hand, but

Ferryl laughed.

"My real name is Fay, as you know, and you really aren't strong enough to stop me without using your bound slave." She turned back to Pendragon. "Well, master? I like power and wealth, and Abel hasn't got either now. His last lesson in sorceress politics."

"Agreed. If you really are that strong, I wouldn't let anyone else have you anyway. Come on then. If you accept the tether without a struggle, you can control a couple of the weaker ones in there. There's too many for me to manage on my own." The sorcerer smiled triumphantly as Ferryl walked towards him. "I'll just make sure we aren't interrupted." The door opened and two more security men came out and stood on the front step, pistols in their hands. Abel assumed Pendragon used a link to one of his apprentices to send them but without either Ferryl or Zephyr he already felt half blind. He'd relied on their ability to see magic, and spooky-phone, too much.

"You can't let her." Rob muttered very quietly but Pendragon's eyes flicked to him so he'd heard.

"I can't stop her, Rob." Abel put all the bitterness he could into his voice. "When it's your turn, Claris, let them tether you. Don't resist. It's all right, it won't be that bad, no worse than the leech." Abel felt mean when he saw the horror rising in Claris's eyes but he needed a diversion, any sort of diversion. He also saw both Kelis and Jenny stiffen. They both knew what Claris thought about the blood leech, so hopefully they'd be ready for trouble. "You don't have to do this, Ferryl. We could take him."

"Don't be a fool, Abel. He's a proper sorcerer, not like those two." Ferryl gestured towards Effy and Natalie. "I doubt they could manage a shield between them, and Natalie never got past learning wind. I could take both of them with that baseball bat." She knelt in front of Pendragon. "Ready, master."

"No foolishness, no suddenly casting a glyph or shield. I am only reducing the shield on my palm, so if you try anything it will bounce. Then I will force the tether until you submit or die." Pendragon reached out towards Ferryl's shoulder but watched Abel, a glyph swirling in his free hand. Abel activated his shield, slowly extending it. He hoped it would slow up whatever Pendragon threw.

The double flash and ear-splitting crack caught him totally by surprise! Ferryl lurched to her feet, spinning away then going to her knees again, one arm in flames up past her elbow. Her skin, he realised, as the fur seeming disappeared and he saw charred fingers. Pendragon yelled in pain and surprise, staggering backwards with his shoulder blackened and torn open deep enough to show the bone. The glyph in his hand stuttered as he lost concentration so Abel threw one of his own, fire. It couldn't break through, but Pendragon had his shield close to his body so the heat scorched his hand and he lost the glyph entirely. He staggered as Kelis's windhammer smashed into his burned shoulder.

With a cry of mixed fear and rage, Claris did what Abel and then Ferryl had been trying to suggest, she snatched the baseball bat off a distracted Effy and swung. Abel had recognised that bat, Claris's own special one inscribed with a magic-filled lead glyph. Effy, already turning towards Ferryl with a glyph forming, turned back towards Claris and raised her hand to cast. Too late, the redhead connected. If Effy hadn't had a ward forming a natural shield she'd have been out cold.

Even with her protection Effy went down to one knee and lost her glyph, shaking her head as the flash ruined her vision. "Look out, Claris." Jenny threw a quick wind glyph that staggered Natalie. Claris turned, snarled and swung again. Natalie abandoned her glyph and raised her arm to stop the bat, spinning away as her natural shield failed to absorb the physical impact.

Claris went after her, bat raised. "Burn me, you little shit?" The bat came down again. "Put a tether on Rachel?" Smack. "Come on then!" Smack. "Burn me!" Smack. Natalie reeled back until the house wall stopped her, but Claris didn't let up. She'd lost it again, and she'd got a target. Behind her Effy recovered and formed a glyph, but a Windhammer from Jenny threw her forward onto her face. She rolled, throwing fire back, her eyes wide in shock as Jenny's shield took it without any sign of strain. Effy rolled again, frantically, but Jenny's Windhammer followed and smashed her flat again.

Meanwhile Abel and Kelis threw everything they had at Pendragon. He'd been rattled but now his shield pushed out into a globe, absorbing the attacks while his shoulder began to heal. Abel wondered why Rob wasn't doing anything, but a series of explosions off to the side distracted him. A glance showed smoke and flame outlining Shannon's shield as she pressed forward between two parked cars. Ahead of her the security guard kept firing as he backed away, but so far her shield held. A scream snagged Abel's attention, but he dragged it back to forming another glyph to throw at Pendragon.

That meant Abel missed Rob's contribution. The two security men in the doorway opened fire on Ferryl when she attacked Pendragon, though her shield stopped the bullets. They must have understood because both of them switched to aiming at Claris. As they hesitated, worried about hitting Effy or Natalie, both were yanked forward by reverse wind glyphs. One fell to his knees, hanging on to his gun, but the other screamed and let his go. He twisted, crying out again as he reached for his broken ankle. As he fell his foot had remained upright, held by a concrete clamp growing out of the step.

The first guard, on his hands and knees, looked up and raised his gun. Rob's Windhammer knocked it aside and out of his hand, but he twisted to lunge after the weapon. He didn't move far because the paving stone under his other hand had flowed up and around it, then set to lock him in place. The first guard lay clutching his ankle, but another loop of paving slab came up and around his forearm to make sure he stayed there. Rob could control his earth glyphs much better than the last time he'd needed them.

Abel could hear voices yelling inside the house, mixed with the shooting and the shouting outside, but so far nobody had started screaming. He threw another frantic glyph, trying to force Pendragon into keeping his shield up. The attacks weren't working, the sorcerer had healed and Abel could see a vicious smile forming. Now that the sorcerer's shield had spread out into a globe, the heat from the glyphs wasn't reaching him. Ferryl recovered enough to throw a crystalline web at Pendragon's shield, where the glittering strands clung and ground away with a high-pitched screeching noise. Sparks flew and Pendragon turned towards her, startled, his smile dying as he cast a slow, swirling cloud in reply. It flowed over Ferryl's shield, then slipped and dripped to the floor which seemed to surprise the sorcerer.

"I should get in there and deal with the apprentices guarding the Taverners. Can you hold him, Abel?" As Ferryl asked, behind her Effy rolled over again and started to sit up.

Jenny brought both hands down, fisted together. This Windhammer came from above, flattening Effy as she let out a short, startled yelp. She lay still afterwards, spread-eagled on the grass while Jenny threw a fire glyph at Pendragon. "I'm on it now, Abel." A bush produced a long sharp branch which shrivelled and burned as it hit the sorcerer's shield.

"Me too." Rob's voice came as a relief, as did the chunk of hardened earth that shattered on Pendragon's shield. "Go for it, Ferryl."

"Just keep him off my back for a minute or two." Ferryl turned to the house, now showing no sign of the burning except scorch marks on her leather top. As she moved past them she tapped the two security men, Rob's victims. "Sleep." Despite any wards, sparks flew as her glyph punched through their personal magic and both slumped. The door opened and an apprentice started coming out, hands lifting to cast. Ferryl's red web wrapped around him too fast, clamping his arms back down to his sides. He staggered back, his shield sparking and scorching him as the mesh tightened and forced it into his skin.

Pendragon must have felt secure in his shield because he ignored Jenny, Abel, Rob and Kelis, looking straight at Ferryl's back as he formed a big glyph with both hands. Abel heard Rob grunt with effort just as Pendragon cast the glyph, and it never reached its target. A wall of earth surged up in a curve that blocked the sorcerer from both Ferryl and the other four. Smoking chunks flew outwards as the glyph, a murky red with light blue flashes inside, hit the earth and disintegrated before it had chance to activate properly. Ferryl disappeared inside the house, the last Abel saw of her was a silver web spreading out ahead of her hand. The scream that followed wasn't from the same direction as the captives.

The shooting around the cars had stopped, but Abel daren't look because two spots of red appeared on the earth wall between him and Pendragon. "Aim there in three seconds. Give it all you've got. I'll need a moment to recover." The strain from lifting all that earth showed in Rob's voice. Jenny glanced at Abel, pointing to the left glyph as her other hand dragged moisture into an ice spear. Abel built as hot a fire glyph as he could. Kelis kept moving her hands and seemed to be muttering to herself. The earth wall started to crack as the sorcerer hit it with something but just as Rob promised, on the count of three, two neat holes appeared.

Jenny hurled her ice at the startled face beyond, and as it shattered on the shield Abel's fire followed it. He hoped heat and cold, close together, would cause more stress. "Stickybangs!" Kelis screamed the nonsense with real feeling, venom really, and a cloud of small black somethings flew from her palms. They hit the shield before extending little legs that stuck and held them fast. Pendragon's shield began to spark and glow around each one.

The rest of the earth wall crumbled, revealing Pendragon, so Abel hit the edge of the sorcerer's shield, hoping the strength had been concentrated at the front. His fire swept around the curve, but had no real effect except to startle Claris. Natalie lay crumpled while Claris leant against the house wall with the bat dangling from one hand, still panting. The wash of heat, though not dangerous, brought her head around and her eyes fastened on Pendragon's back. Her lips peeled back in sheer hatred and she ran towards the sorcerer, both hands swinging the baseball bat up and round.

Abel opened his mouth to warn her but too late, because the black things stuck to the shield exploded in a rapid series of crackling sounds. Claris would have never heard him over that so Abel threw another fire glyph where the series of explosions had left a bright red network of cracks. The cracks faded, though they'd brightened slightly as Abel's glyph hit. "Do it again, Kelis."

"Can't. No time." Kelis reverted to ice shards alternating with fire, maybe with the same idea as Abel, that she might stress the shield. Meanwhile, Claris connected. Pendragon turned at the loud bang, but didn't cast the glyph. The baseball bat shattered and Claris staggered back then spun and fell, hugging her hands to her sides in pain. She came to her knees, looked up and started to crawl away from the fight as fast as possible. Pendragon cast again, at Kelis, and this swirling cloud of sticky stuff clung better than it had to Ferryl.

"Use slippy-glyph!" Abel cast the simple protection onto his own shield with one hand. With the other he threw a small fire glyph at the gunk, angled to glance off Kelis's shield, and it burned off a wide swathe. Several more small fire glyphs flew from Jenny, clearing more and the rest dropped away. Pendragon had been building something else, which he cast at Abel. A series of long gleaming shapes streamed out, spinning and looping around each other. Abel braced himself, pouring magic into his shield. The first ones struck and spun, trying to drill in and he felt magic draining, but the rest of the storm were swept away by a stream of fire.

Jenny grinned, turning back towards Pendragon. "I thought you could do with a hand." She hurled a fire glyph at the sorcerer. "I didn't think slippy-glyph would stop those."

"Good thinking Jenny. You help deflect attacks while we clobber him. I'll cover you if he switches targets." Abel knew Jenny didn't have the same skill as the others, so hopefully that would work out better. Though despite them all hurling glyphs as hard and fast as possible, none of them had scored on Pendragon. Worse, Abel had already gone through a whole belt of magic and the sorcerer showed no sign of weakening.

*　*　*

As Ferryl offered to surrender, Zephyr crept down Abel's leg under his jeans, a long thin tendril of self. She eased out of the back, where Pendragon wouldn't see that Abel had pulled in his shield, and slithered out of the garden into the road. Behind her, glyphs began to fly, but Pendragon was concentrating on Ferryl. When the last of Zephyr drifted over the edge of the kerb to lie hidden from sight she would have heaved a sigh of relief, if she'd ever been able to sigh. The rest of her, already several metres along the gutter, had something more important to do. Zephyr didn't like fighting without her tether, in case she lost who she was, but Abel trusted her.

A wisp of almost-nothing drifted back across the path to a manhole cover, then bled through the crack around the lid. The rest of Zephyr followed, too slow but she couldn't thicken up in case someone spotted her. The stink in the sewers made no difference to the wind spirit, a plus to not being able to sigh. Zephyr thickened once all of her arrived in the sewer pipes, flowing quickly along them and up to one of the bedroom en-suites. A cautious peek showed no sign of anyone lurking, so she poured out into the room.

Zephyr flowed down the stairs, sticking to shadows, until she located the prisoners. Thin again now, her shimmer bled through the cracks around a light fitting and into the space between the ceiling and the upstairs floor. It didn't take long to spread out across the right room until she could drift enough of her down around another light fitting to see her targets. Furniture had been scattered, pushed to the side so all the Taverners could be crowded together on the floor.

Most of them sat on their hands, glaring at four apprentices with live glyphs swirling in their hands. A small group in the centre sat, listless, with their hands in their laps. Those had to be the ones on tethers, obeying the last instruction. She poised, but none were dying so she checked on ways to get to them. A wiring duct led down to the skirting, and from there Zephyr trickled between floorboards and across until she was beneath her target. She listened. The Taverners were quiet but the guards were talking about the sounds of fighting outside.

"I'm worried." A woman, the one Kelis defeated at Redwolf's, paced back and forth. "You didn't see those four. No finesse but they are strong and willing to go all the way. That sorceress is no pushover and she won't let them surrender."

"Don't lose your nerve, Ginny, just because you were captured once. You've got more magic this time, and we have Pendragon with us. If there's a problem we've got another four apprentices inside the house, and the others outside ready to pitch in." The man laughed and strode forward towards the seated Taverners. "The master checked and that sorceress ran a bluff, a good one, but it won't work now. I'm going to look these over, because there are too many for our master to control. We'll all get a few, on our own tethers, which will make us as powerful as some sorcerers."

"You might, but my master only hired me out. If there are any extra apprentices, he'll get them." This man seemed disgruntled and definitely uneasy. Gunfire thundered out the front, shouts and a cry of pain. A scream followed, quickly cut off. "One of us should check, to see what's happening."

"No need, Pendragon is stronger than your master. He'll deal with Ferryl Shayde and the bound shade, and four real apprentices will sort out those beginners if they won't take a tether. There's plenty of shooters as backup if necessary." The four descended to bickering about whose master was strongest.

*   *   *

Zephyr could hear gunfire outside, she daren't wait any longer. She sent a tendril up through the floorboards, tight against Eric's back, and felt for the tether. It took her a little while because it wasn't in use, but then she found the invisible glyph anchor on the top of his shoulder. A slightly thicker part of her coiled around it, very gently under his shirt, and inspected the flows. It looked right, close enough to what she'd worked out with Ferryl for her to unravel it. Portions of the mazzlement glyph would loosen it, letting her get into the flows. More tendrils drifted up behind other Taverners until one wrapped around the anchor for every tether.

Zephyr paused. If she just broke them, the guards might notice. Many Taverners might die before they had time to fight back. Unfortunately, if she warned them, that might trigger the tether so Pendragon could hear. She inspected the anchor again, while also trying to follow what must be happening outside. A long scream towards the front of the house startled Zephyr, and Pendragon's apprentices!

Ginny, the woman apprentice, spoke first. "That was inside the house. Celeborn, go and see what's happened."

"It could have been a glyph from outside and if not, Denny is waiting for anyone coming through the door. Pendragon told us to stay here and you know what he'll do if we disobey." A startled yell from the back garden stopped them arguing.

"It's going wrong. I knew it!" The woman shut up, then murmured, "I hope he didn't hear that."

"I'll go. Pendragon isn't my master so I'm allowed to think for myself." As the speaker opened the door, glass smashed somewhere and the smell of smoke wafted in. "Someone's inside and fighting!" The apprentice set off at a run while the other three stared anxiously at the door as it closed behind him, so Zephyr took her chance.

Just like talking to many at once, she thought. The same thing down each spooky-string. Each tendril twisted tighter and began to unravel the swirls and flows of magic, dismantling the glyph. An endless time passed as she worked, totally engrossed, until she felt a loosening. Zephyr paused on the ones that had started to break, waiting until the others gave way. Some tethers seemed to be stronger than others. If she'd had a mouth, Zephyr would have smiled because Una had definitely resisted hers, leaving it a little looser than others.

More shouting, then screaming, then a crash in the corridor was all the distraction she needed. The tethers dissolved and Zephyr connected spooky-phone to each victim. "Don't move! Stay very, very still and say nothing. I have broken the tethers, but the apprentices will hurt many Taverners if they realise." Zephyr paused, but nobody did more than twitch slightly. She'd been thinking while waiting, and they had one chance. "I will tell everyone to hold hands when Una shouts, 'Go.' That way Shawn can put a shield around everyone, and give them chance to get set. I will try to provide a diversion. Back soon."

The door rattled for a moment but nobody came in. Instead, a voice in the back garden called out in obvious alarm and someone ran past the window. Ginny took a couple of steps that way, trying to see what had disturbed the apprentices outside. "We should run, get out of here. There's too much noise for a public place, the church will notice. Then if Pendragon kills a priest we'll all be dead or on church tethers!" Another window broke somewhere and the door rattled again as a dull thump echoed down the hallway outside.

"You fool, he'll kill us if we run. Unless he's dead. Curses, I can smell smoke. For once I wish he'd contact us. Apprentices or not, they're making him keep a full shield up and stopping the master from using the tethers. Maybe he does need help." The man paced up and down then pointed at the seated Taverners. "You! Sit still."

Zephyr froze her spooky-phones, all connecting out of sight though a few little sections might be visible if the apprentice looked hard. She detected magic over to one side and sent a tendril to investigate, then wished she could smile or maybe snarl. Pendragon had made the Taverners throw their lead bars to the side of the room, but hadn't drained the magic from them. "Everyone knows. I will distract the apprentices. Pick a time, Una."

"Go!" Una didn't hesitate, she shouted straight away and caught hold of the two nearest hands. For a moment chaos reigned as Taverners pulled hands from under them and fumbled to get a grip. All three of Pendragon's apprentices were frozen in shock for vital moments as the tethered victims burst into action, then they raised their hands. Before anyone could cast, the air in one corner of the room howled and began to boil, something growing up and out. Glyphs flew, one from each apprentice, but the cloud of vapour had a shield!

"Kill the kids with tethers, the strong ones." The oldest apprentice, Celeborn, realised the real danger. He was in a room with thirty magic users and had just lost control over them. Too late, the volley of glyphs crackled and died against Shawn's shield, a shield that spread over everyone sat on the floor. Though casting such a big shield had weakened it, and the apprentice-strength glyphs caused showers of sparks and cracks spread in several places. "Deal with whatever is inside that seeming, Ginny, we'll stop the kids." More glyphs grew in the man's hands.

"Drop the shield. Everyone hit mouthy first!" Una had no intention of sitting under a shield while Zephyr fought her battles. "Kathy, lie flat!" The shield dropped and a storm of hastily formed glyphs shattered against the apprentice's shield. It didn't break but it sparked and glowed, a spider-web of cracks blotting out his view of his glyphs so he lost control. Eric cried out as half his hair burst into flame, a very near miss, while a Windhammer bowled several Taverners over. Another wind glyph knocked more of them down as the other man loosed his glyph. Petra and Rachel bounded forward, snatching up lead bars then crashing their shields into him, locking him in place.

As his shield recovered and cleared, Celeborn saw all the hands raised towards him and frantically tried to finish his own glyphs. "Help me!" He was too late, because the Taverners had concentrated properly this time and over thirty glyphs were poised.

The third apprentice, Ginny, daren't take her attention off her own problem. She threw glyphs with both hands, but the vapour boiled higher and two burning green eyes appeared. As the form strengthened and became clearer, she lost concentration and her next glyphs barely sparked on the thing's shield. "Someone's brought a bound ogre and it's shielded!" She took an involuntary step backwards, towards the door.

Celeborn glanced over, hesitated over what he should use his glyphs on, and lost the chance. He might have survived if he'd concentrated on his shield, but maybe not because the Taverners threw everything they'd got without any real thought for the consequences. His shield blew out in a maelstrom of fire and ice, stoked by powerful Windhammers. The slower glyphs from the weaker casters were mainly wind, but there was nothing left to stop them. A brief storm picked him up and tossed

Celeborn across the room into the wall. He didn't get up. He'd barely hit the ground before three more Taverners were heading over to add their shields to Rachel's and Petra's.

Meanwhile Ginny backed towards the door, concentrating on her shield in case those lunatics targeted her next. She threw occasional glyphs at the ogre as it lumbered across the room, scattering furniture, but it didn't slow up. Zephyr had to concentrate hard, using up her precious magic to keep the shield solid. She could only maintain it in front of her while casting wind as if her paws were knocking things aside. Zephyr shaped wind to make a bellowing noise, then used the etching glyph to tear scratches in the floorboards under her claws while the woman's eyes grew wider. The sprite hoped she only had to look solid for a little longer, and that the woman didn't rally and throw stronger glyphs. Wind couldn't carry much magic so Zephyr was relying on the small heap of lead bars she'd connected to, and they were running low. But she would keep going as long as possible because the Tavern needed her, as the fearsome Ffod, not a puff of wind. Abel told her not to die so if her shield fell she would run, but until then…

"Use wind to knock that bitch away from the door, then we'll pin her with shields and drain her. Get your lead bars back first." Shawn ran to a corner of the room and picked up two lead bars. Other Taverners scattered towards the edges of the room, where they'd thrown their extra magic. "Come on everyone. Top up." Once again Zephyr thought being able to sigh would have been handy, because to her great relief a series of Windhammers staggered the woman even through her shield and she stopped attacking. Zephyr sent out a tendril to a nearby lead bar and felt magic flood through her. Her ogre reared up, hunched over to avoid the ceiling, and lumbered forward.

"Call it off! Call it off!" Behind Pendragon's apprentice, the door flew open and two men with guns ran in. Seconds later they finished bouncing off furniture and walls, lying groaning while Taverners kicked the weapons away.

"Drop your shield." Rachel's face, twisted with anger, should have been frightening enough without the glyphs in each hand. She pushed her shield harder again her victim, the last apprentice still fighting. A third and fourth shield joined hers and Petra's, and a dozen glyphs smashed against the startled man's protection. He flinched as a glowing sword hit his shield, the point punching through before it fell to the floor. "And pray your master doesn't hurt my brother again." She looked angry enough to throw the glyphs, but that would be foolish. As they hit the other shield, the backlash would be inside Rachel's, the magical equivalent of shooting herself in the foot.

"Pendragon can't touch me, Rachel. Zephyr, bust the tether." A pale-faced Justin kept clear of his sister, or of her glyphs and shield, but he had a couple of his own glyphs ready to help her. His announcement seemed to worry the trapped apprentice as much as the attacks.

*   *   *

The back garden of Frederick's house wasn't involved in any fighting, not yet. The apprentices Pendragon had left there as guards heard Ferryl assault Pendragon and the fight start, but had no idea what was actually happening. Zephyr had only just flowed under the floor beneath the captives when an apprentice standing near the orchard yelled in alarm, pointing at an area of dug-over ground. "I'm telling you again, I saw something. Something came over the wall and now it's over there."

"No it didn't, you saw a bird. You've been twitchy ever since the master told us who we'd be fighting." His companion, an older woman, looked and sounded disgusted. "I blame Ginny. She's been ranting on about the danger, trying to justify getting slapped down by schoolkids and a newbie sorceress." The woman turned as feet pounded and another apprentice ran round the corner, a glyph already formed. "Not you as well? Relax, it's just this fool shouting at shadows. We've got most of them nicely boxed up or tethered and the master will deal with the rest."

Gunfire rang out around the front of the house. "He's taking his time, and that doesn't sound like it's easy." The newcomer paused. "Forget I said that? Please?"

"Don't worry, we all speak out of turn when the tether is down." The woman eyed up the orchard. "These trees are past their best, but there's a lot of them once we throw the dryads out. Maybe we will be allowed a little more magic. Pendragon gave us these gold armbands for this job, but those kids carried lead bars all the time."

"My mistress wouldn't allow that." The original apprentice, the one worried about the patch of bare ground, inspected the old fruit trees. "Maybe I can get visiting rights to the orchard if my mistress and your master are splitting the proceeds." Leaves fluttered and some branches creaked softly. "Once the dryads are gone."

"I hope your mistress got the shares signed off in blood. Pendragon will wriggle." The woman nodded towards the house. "He wants to tether as many of them as possible to make a bid for the Council. I doubt he'll let any strong ones go and he'll split most of the weaker ones among us."

"What's happening in the house? I thought they were all under control but a window blew out at the front." The latest arrival glanced back towards the corner of the house as smoke drifted into sight. "I'm supposed to be round there." He dithered, torn between obeying his last instructions and being isolated. Pendragon had assured them he'd soon deal with the sorceress and the other four, but the battle out front showed no sign of easing off. "To be honest I'd rather stay here. Safety in numbers and all that. We all thought Ginny was exaggerating, but we tethered eight who were advanced enough to shield. They all claimed the ones who hadn't arrived were stronger, and Pendragon is being pushed hard enough to need a full shield."

"Yeah, he might have taken on more than he expected. Your master told my mistress Abel has a tethered spirit, but Effy swears it's a bound sorceress, a strong one." The original apprentice, the twitchy one, pointed at a window. "Now don't say I'm imagining that. What is it? It's huge. Has Pendragon bound anything that size?"

"Not likely. If it takes a big hit, healing something that large will drain a serious amount of magic. I thought only the church bound things that size?" The woman beckoned and all three moved a little towards the window, then got a good look at the shape. "Someone definitely miscalculated if one of those kids managed to let loose a bound ogre. Maybe we'd better get in there to help."

"Forget it. I'm sure my mistress's contract never mentioned fighting ogres!" Twitchy glanced at the other two. "I'll watch your backs." A deep bellow sounded from the house, and from deeper inside came the sound of screaming.

"Not likely. If there's an ogre loose in there, I'd better tell the master."

The third man glanced back at the corner, towards the sound of more breaking glass and another puff of smoke. "The tether being down gives me an excuse to be away from my post." He headed for the gate in the garden wall, hurrying as a bright flash in the front garden lit up the side of the house. A loud crash followed and a huge ball of smoke billowed up into sight from behind the wall.

Moments later the woman stiffened, then turned towards the fighting in the front garden. "My master called, he needs help." She glanced back at the loaned apprentice. "If I wasn't on a tether I'd run away about now. That's a big hint in case you missed it." She hurried towards the garden gate. Behind her the remaining apprentice, the nervous one, backed towards the trees before freezing in shock. He'd been right about something coming into the garden, though it had been a someone.

"I'd rather you didn't go out there." The calm voice shouldn't be in here but...

The woman apprentice turned to find a slim figure dressed in black, standing in the middle of the dug-over garden. One glance at the over-large cross told her all she needed and her hands came up. "Your stupid game costume won't protect you from me." Though a niggling thought wondered how a trainee had hidden from magical sight. Any niggling concerns turned to serious alarm as her glyphs fizzled out without even sparking the man's shield. A cloud of small white angular shapes flew back towards her.

"It isn't a costume, you fool." The white shapes became a swarm of crosses surrounding her, ones with vicious points at the bottom. Even as she opened her mouth to surrender, they all turned their points inwards. A millisecond later her shield collapsed as the glowing white missiles pierced it, and then her body. Creepio strode forward, towards the garden gate, hoping he'd be in time. He wasn't allowed to interfere unless attacked, so he'd tried to startle her. The response had been a surprise. Perhaps he should get a cloak and a wide hat to encourage more of the ungodly to make the same mistake. As long as the bishops didn't find out. The archbishop's face set as he neared the gate, still swinging closed behind the other apprentice. He might be too late to save young Abel, but now he could finally deal with Pendragon. That sorcerer had to have known about Father Curtis being seeded.

*   *   *

Behind Creepio an apprentice backed slowly through the orchard, careful to make no noise. Once out of the garden he'd activate his tether and report to his mistress, but right now the black-dressed figure might detect any magic usage. He might look like Vicar Creepio Mysterio from that daft game, but the attack looked like pure church and had blown straight through a senior apprentice's shield. A slight creak stopped the apprentice in his tracks and he quickly began to build glyphs and a shield. He'd come into an orchard full of dryads, just after discussing throwing them out of their trees.

A rustle warned him, but not soon enough and he staggered as the branch shattered on his shield. More branches swung or stabbed, while roots reached up for him. He had a shield and fire, but now the magic of six old trees closed in from every side. When the charred stumps of roots and branches drew back, they'd made sure the apprentice would never report anything to anyone.

Branches creaked and leaves rustled. "That was a risk. Sorcerers are nervous when dryads kill one of them."

"We only helped the Lord of this house. The wind whispers of a dryad helping sorcerers near Dead Wood."

"Against blood-bags. Though the new master of Sorcerer's Keep offered us safety if we defended this garden. Many whispers speak of his generosity to those who help him, and his word is true."

"The Lord here befriended a dryad, in the place of dead trees. His master offered us younger trees, protected ones." Not-wind rustled branches. "It was worth a risk to kill an apprentice."

"Yes, but only because he is alone. We should spread the whispers, about the Dead Wood and the contracts with dryads. About a sorcerer who treats magical creatures as allies, not prey."

"About apprentices without tethers, and how fast they grow. We have heard them talk of spreading out, so others should be ready to meet them." This time the not-wind sighed. "Perhaps a whisper will reach the Wild Wood, and we will have guidance." Silence spread through the orchard. It had been too long since the wind brought word of the Wild Wood.

* * *

As the dryads closed in on their prey, inside the house the Taverners closed in on the remaining male apprentice. His shield collapsed and he screamed briefly as four shields lurched inwards before they could be stopped. The woman, Ginny, turned to run but thuds and shouts outside the door, then more screams, stopped her. More glyphs smashed against her shield, the ogre raised huge claws and she made her decision. These Taverners had let her live once, when she surrendered. "I surrender. My shield is going down." After a moment, light wind glyphs buffeted her as someone checked. More important to her, the ogre put those claws back on the floor.

Zephyr could feel magic raging outside the door, in the corridor, some of it feeling like Ferryl's. She dropped her shield, kept enough magic in the ogre so it stayed solid, and reached out a tendril for one of the lead bars. With the magic boost she slid the tendril down and eased it between the bricks below the floor, into the corridor. She peeked through a crack in the floor, while keeping the ogre's eyes on the sorceress.

Ferryl Shayde fought two apprentices, two strong ones. Her webs and strikes were stopping them from casting many glyphs, because they were busy bolstering shields, but Zephyr worried. Ferryl's leather skirt and top were scored and burned, and one boot had split open, so perhaps she was weakening. One of the apprentices concentrated his shield to his front so he could strengthen it, blocking the corridor to avoid a glyph looping around him. Zephyr's ogre smiled, because the tendril in the corridor couldn't.

The tendril eased out onto the floor, thickening, while Zephyr drained the lead bar. She had enough magic for one good strike. After a brief assessment she decided on fire for the shock effect and carefully built the glyph, making it small but very hot just like Abel did. Ferryl cast one of her red nets at the apprentice's shield where it clung on, causing a few cracks to appear, though the spitting, glowing strands couldn't break through. Zephyr's tendril reared up and struck like a scorpion's tail, releasing the glyph inches from the back of the man's bare neck before recoiling. He screamed and one hand went to his neck, he started to turn, and too late he realised. A moment's inattention, a wavering in his shield and the net broke through, wrapping itself around him with a sizzling noise. As he staggered back Zephyr smacked his heel with a small wind glyph and he fell.

She had no magic to spare for another glyph, but when Zephyr looked she didn't need it. As soon as the net broke through, Ferryl Shayde turned all of her attention to her other opponent. A silver net, still attached to Ferryl's outstretched hand, clawed and ground away at the woman's shield, but despite the fine silver lines mixed with the sparks and golden flashes, it wasn't getting through. Now Ferryl's other hand thrust downwards and a Windhammer smashed a hole clean through the floor, the joists and the ceiling of the cellar below, right underneath the shield. Zephyr felt sure the woman would drop out of sight, allowing Ferryl to finish the man covered by the net. She didn't have time to watch, she needed everything to keep the ogre solid so she pulled her tendril back.

Outside in the corridor the woman apprentice lunged for the side of the hole, frantically trying to avoid the drop. A mistake because her concentration on her shield wavered. A silver spike grew out of Ferryl's free hand and she punched, right in the middle of the area still being weakened by the silver net. With a crack the shield parted, the silver spike carrying on through and into the apprentice's face. Silver fire wreathed her head, her shield disappeared and she dropped through the hole without another sound. Ferryl turned towards the apprentice still struggling in the red net, building a second one as she strode forward. She banished the glyph as she saw the charring on his neck and the blood welling slowly around the cooling mesh. That came as a relief, because she was running low on magic and there were too many apprentices. Already Ferryl worried she had taken too long, leaving Abel out there facing a full sorcerer.

A stab of something that must be an emotion hit Ferryl, making her wonder if she'd done the right thing. Maybe it was guilt, because she'd never meant to leave Abel unprotected, not for this long. There'd been gunfire, too much, and an explosion unlike any magic she knew, either of which might have breached Abel's shield. Ferryl hesitated, torn, almost turning back to help Abel, but she'd offered to free the Taverners. Abel would be relying on her to help his friends. A moment's thought and a seeming covered the damage to Ferryl's clothing. Looking unharmed might help her to cow those holding the Taverners, though from the sounds, the trainees were already fighting back. Zephyr certainly was. Ferryl raised a foot and kicked.

* * *

Inside the lounge the door crashed open again, hanging half off its hinges, and Ferryl stood there with glyphs boiling in each hand. She glanced at the crumpled figures and the one cowering in front of the ogre, and all the glyphs aimed at her. "Are there any more apprentices?"

Petra pointed. "In the garden, but there was shouting and a scream out there."

"Yeuk. The dryads got someone. There's nobody alive in the back garden." The three Taverners looking out of the rear window turned away.

"In that case Abel might need our help. I had to leave him." Ferryl did a double-take when she spotted the claw marks in the boards. "Nice ogre, Zephyr." She turned away, heading back through the door. "Hurry."

Eric glared at the remaining apprentice. "Any Taverner who is hurt, get bandaged or whatever and watch her. If the ogre stays as well, you'll know if she shields." He nodded with a satisfied smile. "From that look, she'll be good." True enough, Ginny's eyes were locked on the huge, threatening shape taking up much too much space inside a house. "Wait for us, Ferryl." He started running because Ferryl had already disappeared.

"Sit against the wall, Mz whoever." As most of the Taverners surged out through the door, following Eric, a pale-faced Justin sat down. "I'm a bit wobbly so I'll stay to dish out orders if your friends wake up." He tossed an empty lead bar towards the captured apprentice. "Drain your magic into that and throw it back, then I'll give you another until it's all gone." Ginny looked from the ogre to the half-dozen angry, injured Taverners and picked up the bar.

A relieved Zephyr settled down. She had enough magic to keep the ogre for a while, now she wasn't moving or shielding. Though she would have rather gone with the others, to help Abel. Zephyr really wanted to go and look, to make sure he was safe, but the Tavern needed her here. Would she know if Abel had fallen, now they had no link? Zephyr sent a tendril out under the floorboards to come up and check on the burned man. Despite his injuries he still lived, a powerful apprentice who had hurt Abel's friends and didn't surrender. Her tendril thickened over his mouth and nose, long enough to make sure he would never hurt them again. Another tendril checked the other fallen apprentice, but he was already dead.

She wished again that she could go to find Abel and curl up in her tattoo, be Zephyr again, but she had to be Ffod the mighty just a little longer. What would she do if her creator was dead, if her home, her refuge was gone? Who would remind her she was Zephyr, not a nameless puff of wind? Zephyr's ogre leant forward, glaring at one of the security guards as he roused. He was not strong enough to threaten the Tavern, so he could live.

*　*　*

Outside, at the front of Frederick's house, four teenagers and a sorcerer were engaged in a savage battle, glyphs flaring and sparking, tearing at shields and sometimes flesh. Abel started worrying, because his gold belts were running low while Pendragon seemed to be getting more confident. Again and again Pendragon's attacks broke through, long enough for a moment of heat or pain, though as yet nobody's shield had collapsed. That gave Abel some comfort; Kelis's, Rob's and Jenny's gold belts and diamonds still had enough magic.

Inside the house, screams, shouts and the occasional crash of something breaking meant Ferryl had a fight on her hands. Smoke and then flame blew out a window, followed by a blackened figure that landed in a crumpled heap. After a moment, whoever it was staggered to their feet and dived back inside, still trailing smoke. The second time the figure flew out, Abel recognised the red net wrapped all around it. The still figure didn't stir this time, even after the glow faded.

"Look out!" Rob's shout wasn't strictly necessary because with so many glyphs hitting it, Pendragon's shield stayed permanently visible. They could all see the rear shrink back towards him so he could use the tethers to his apprentices and victims. Kelis looped a glyph around the shield but the sorcerer swatted it with a contemptuous sneer. Even as the four of them redoubled their efforts, the sneer turned to alarm. Pendragon staggered sideways, blood pouring from his arm before the shield snapped back all around him. Claris marched into Abel's view, one of the security men's pistols in a two-handed grip, firing again and again. Sparks flew from Pendragon's shield, and as bullet after bullet hit it in almost the same place, red cracks showed.

"Hit those cracks!" Abel wasn't sure if the bullets were seriously weakening the shield, or if Pendragon's distraction as he healed his wounds had allowed it to falter. Either way, more little cracks appeared as more shots hit home. Abel smashed an ice spear into the same spot, though finding enough moisture for them was getting harder.

Claris tossed the gun aside and plucked another from the front of her jeans. "How d'ya like that? I've got plenty more!" She started shooting again.

But as Claris came past, Effy climbed to her feet and tottered towards her, fingers clawed. "Leave him alone! He's mine!" Claris turned, the gun steadied, and for a moment everyone thought she'd shoot Effy. Instead Claris yelled in alarm and threw herself backwards, the gun flying off to the side.

Abel had heard the engine roaring, but not really paid attention until Effy turned, opened her mouth and eyes wide, and was plucked off her feet by the minibus. Abel got an impression of white hair with charred patches still streaming smoke, staring eyes, and white-knuckled hands on the wheel as Shannon rammed Pendragon's shield! Flames and smoke exploded in all directions, and when they cleared, the sorcerer had definitely been distracted. The vehicle might not have actually broken through and hit him but his shield was down, he'd been thrown off his feet, and his clothes were on fire.

"Get him!" Kelis moved forward, firing glyphs with both hands but Pendragon only took a few hits before he shielded again. Although only to the front this time, and not because he wanted to use his tethers! "He's weakened, shield to shield!" Kelis ran forward, still throwing glyphs, until her shield hit Pendragon's with a flare of sparks. "Drain him!" Abel ran forward even though he had a horrible feeling Pendragon still had enough diamonds in his bones to drain all of them. The whoop from Jenny and the shout from Rob as they ran in sounded more confident.

Shannon half-fell out of the crumpled, smouldering minibus with a crazed smile on her face. "Magic airbags! Did I hit him?"

"Not hard enough." As Abel pointed, Shannon turned and began to run in the same direction. Abel's shield flared as it made contact, as did

Shannon's, forcing Pendragon to re-establish his full shield. Abel kept his smallish to make room for the others, but now he hoped the heat wouldn't build up too much. Through the sparks and washes of flame, Abel saw the sorcerer's face as he jerked his head back and forth, trying to work out what had happened.

Pendragon must have figured it out because his face calmed and he concentrated, his shield steadying. "Let's see how you like to hear friends die." The sorcerer took two quick steps back and as he broke contact the shield behind him shrank to nothing. He smiled, then looked startled. "How…?" They'd never know the rest, because a tubby green shape with thin arms and legs sprang out from behind a bush and wrapped its arms around the sorcerer's head. Everyone saw the shield snap back out around the sorcerer and goblin, because the goblin thrust an arm up into it and ignited. A ball of flame enveloped Pendragon's head, then filled the inside of the shield. As the globe faltered the five of them pressed back into contact, but it didn't break even when the flames died back to reveal a burning man. Within seconds the fire had gone, snuffed out by magical mist that left the remaining clothes smouldering. Through the smoke Abel saw huge blisters on the sorcerer's hands, face, and any skin showing through his ragged and charred clothes. For a moment Pendragon thrashed around frantically, then his eyes healed and his shield strengthened. He coughed out a cloud of smoke and took a breath. "Hard luck, help coming."

Abel's heart sank because Pendragon had to mean his apprentices, though he felt a flush of pride because that meant the Taverneers had forced a full sorcerer to call for help. Not bad for amateurs, but it hadn't been enough. As Abel rallied, pushing magic from his last belt into his shield, he heard cheering inside the house. At least Pendragon's apprentices had been forced to free the Taverners. "I've come back to discuss that tether." A cold, clear voice cut through the bedlam, and Abel, for one, stopped yelling. He peered through the glare and a relieved smile split his face, because his own reinforcements had arrived. A mini-skirted figure stood outside the front door, apparently unmarked, with a familiar glowing red ball growing between her hands. Behind her, Taverners poured out into the garden, most of them already forming glyphs with one target in mind.

Pendragon didn't answer. After one startled glance he stopped trying to heal or throw glyphs, relying on his shield as he turned away and started to run. A hail of glyphs followed, hitting him but the shield soaked them up even if Pendragon briefly looked like a mobile firework. Rob even threw his rounders bat, but this time it failed him. With a loud crack the small length of enchanted wood shattered into splinters. As the mob ran forward, already building or casting another volley, the door in the garden wall crashed open. A stranger ran through, hands raised and glyphs forming, then screeched to a halt. He had time for one startled yelp before an avalanche of fire, ice and wind threw him back against the wall. Perhaps he had a shield, but if so it didn't hold long enough.

Almost everyone paused and the shouting died down as it sank in. They'd just killed a man, because the torn, smoking body was well past any medical help. Abel realised someone hadn't come with the crowd and sudden dread filled him. "Where's Zephyr?"

"Playing with her captive apprentice." Eric found that funny, despite the red, burnt skin where half his hair should be. "She earned it. Some of the others have been hit with glyphs but mainly wind and they're all breathing." He looked past Abel and began to build another glyph.

"Look out, Pendragon's getting away." Kelis, for one, still had all her attention, and her stream of glyphs, firmly fixed on the sorcerer, and her words jerked everyone's attention back to Pendragon. The sorcerer had reached what looked like a parked van, but the seeming fell away as Pendragon opened the door and dived inside his Bentley. A belated storm of glyphs struck, but none even scratched the paintwork.

"Save your magic. He has a block of gold in there, filled with magic to feed the vehicle shield." Hands went up as a new voice butted in, glyphs swirled into life, but luckily nobody cast one. Abel, for one, didn't think Creepio would have appreciated it. "Hello, Kelis. It seems you've done the job without me, again. God's SAS will be redundant at this rate."

"Can't you stop him?" Kelis pointed towards Pendragon's car, already accelerating off down the road.

"Not personally." The nasty little smile Creepio turned towards the vehicle didn't seem too worried. "Oops. That's what happens if you speed in a built-up area." Abel didn't think the living battering ram that hit Pendragon's car cared about the speed limit. The three metre high, six-legged, fifteen-metre crocodile-duck with a beaver's tail and a big solid-looking swelling on the end of its beak charged out from between two buildings. Its beak smashed the Bentley sideways across the road until the wheels hit the kerb and the car tipped over onto its side. As it did the faint shimmer of a veil sprang up around the vehicle and creature.

The huge scaled creature rammed the car again, rolling it onto its back, then raised its beak and began to beat on the exposed underside with the thickened end. It ignored the flaring shield and the smoke and flames surrounding its head, hammering away until with a crackling noise, a shower of sparks and a nasty crunch, the protection failed. The next few blows crushed the bottom of the vehicle. Despite the charring on its head the creature continued battering at the crushed Bentley, even after the wreckage burst into flame. A priest ran out into the road and knelt nearby, followed by two others who began passing him crosses. The monster slowed its attack, then began to turn into a thick, dark billowing cloud. The Taverners stood, open-mouthed, as the smoke slowly funnelled in through the priest's clothes and disappeared.

"What on earth was that?" Even Ferryl sounded stunned.

"The tool for the job, if the job is an armoured and magically protected vehicle. When we heard that he'd hired in apprentices for an attack on someone, I thought we might run into Pendragon's car. I had the priest with the creature transferred to Stourton after we found Father Curtis, conveniently close if Pendragon broke the Accord." Creepio's smile and his tone lightened. "The creature is probably a mistake, created when someone attempted a war beast. We call it the platycroc, a platypus-crocodile. It feels no pain and will keep battering the target until one or the other fails."

"What about Pendragon?" Abel thought he knew the answer. Unless he could teleport, the sorcerer must still be inside the mangled heap of burning metal. One of the priests in the road cast a glyph and the flames died down. He peered into the wreck before turning to Creepio, sketching a cross.

"I think he's resigned." Creepio turned to inspect the garden, stooping to peer under the crumpled, smouldering minibus. "Is that one of your people, Abel?"

Shannon spun round and bent to look, then doubled over, went to her knees and brought up her breakfast. Abel answered, though he felt a bit queasy. "Effy, Pendragon's spy. She got between the minibus and Pendragon's shield. She was trying to defend him from Claris."

"How many of Pendragon's people survived?" Creepio hooked a thumb over his shoulder, back towards the garden. "Dryads aren't known for mercy, and the other apprentice in there thought I was one of your Tavern players." Several Taverners winced, which could be about dryad mercy or Creepio's reaction.

Voices murmured, trying to come up with an answer, but meanwhile Shannon had made it to her feet. She tottered towards Creepio and dropped to her knees again. "I killed her, Father."

"Deliberately?" Suddenly all the banter had gone, and an archbishop looked down at Shannon.

"I didn't see her. I had smoke in my eyes so I aimed at the glare of Pendragon's shield." Shannon started sobbing, barely getting the last words out.

"A valiant attempt to help your friends against a powerful enemy, self-defence against an unprovoked attack. You are blameless, Shannon. I will contact your priest if you wish but there is no sin." The archbishop's hand rested on Shannon's head, his thumb brushed her forehead and Abel saw the glimmer of blue-white church magic, just briefly. "Your conscience is clear. May the Lord bless you and go with you, Shannon." Either the words or the magic had their effect, because Shannon's shoulders straightened and her head came up a little. As she stood up several Taverners gathered, reassuring her, while others created a mist to wet down the minibus.

Abel had other worries, because one particular fighter still hadn't appeared. "Where is Zephyr? If she's all right, why didn't she come out with the rest of you?"

The laughter and smiles reassured him, even before Petra answered. "She's playing with her new toy, and watching over the wounded and prisoners." Though Petra and several others sobered as she continued. "She broke our tethers, then forced the apprentices to attack her until we could get organised. I owe her my brain at least."

Petra, her catsuit torn in a couple of places but otherwise unhurt, looked down at the two security men slumped on the steps. "What happens to these and any other survivors, the people Pendragon brought? Especially the apprentices. Is there a magic court or something, because I'm pretty sure the local plod aren't equipped to handle them?" One after the other, everyone including Shannon looked at the recumbent Natalie and the security guards, and then Abel, realisation slowly dawning.

High and Low Justice

Though before he worried too much about Pendragon's people, Abel wanted more information about Zephyr, and the Taverners who'd been hit. After reassuring him about Zephyr, Eric thought the wind glyphs had caused a definitely broken leg and possibly broken fingers and an arm that needed a hospital. The only fire glyph had been aimed at him, and almost missed when the Taverners' counter-attack landed. Other Taverners had painful bruising, scratches and a few were scorched, but Pendragon's apprentices had only launched one real attack. Several Taverners smiled when Eric said they'd had a bigger problem.

Meanwhile the concern about what to do with captured magic users had hardened to anger and resolve. "The captives have to pay, one way or another, especially the traitor." Kelis's glare at Natalie promised a lot more than shunning. She wasn't the only one, if looks really could have killed, then Natalie would already be dead several times over. "They tried to kill us."

"But they didn't, and compared to them we got off fairly light. Pendragon barely touched us." Abel glanced down, then looked around properly for the first time. "All right, he didn't quite kill us." He'd felt heat and pain several times, but lost in the fight he'd paid little attention since none of them had put him out of action. Now Abel could see that sometime in the fight half of one leg of his jeans had been shredded, the front of his leather jacket looked as if a tiger had mauled it, and scorch marks or tears ruined any otherwise decent bits of clothing. He became aware of aches and pains, and cuts, and grazes, and burns, and realised his exposed skin stung and looked too pink.

Kelis's robe sported a score of large burn holes, dozens of small ones and flapped open in several places to show patches of scorched or bloody skin. She looked down, suddenly embarrassed, and pulled her tattered cloak around to cover up as much as possible. Jenny couldn't cover up, half her frilly skirt had been almost completely blasted or burned away, while the rest of her clothing bore a selection of slashes, holes and scorch marks. She favoured one leg, the one weeping blood from innumerable pinprick holes between her knee and her shoe. The game version of

Creepio offered his cloak and Jenny gratefully pulled it around her over the rags. Rob hadn't escaped unscathed, his exposed skin covered in cuts or bruises and one hand badly blistered. He had holes burned or torn in his jeans, jacket and shirt, he'd lost a shoe someplace and one arm was bare and covered in tiny parallel cuts.

Shannon's hair and clothes had stopped smouldering, but she had bald patches, blisters on one cheek and her arms, and her thin plywood 'armour' was charred. The rest of the Taverners were relatively undamaged, though most had collected a few scorches, scratches, or bruises and looked generally knocked about. "How come you aren't hurt, Ferryl?" She dropped the seeming so Abel could see her clothes. Although she'd healed herself, the scored and scorched leather of Ferryl's skirt and top, and her split and burned boot, showed the sorceress had taken hits as well.

Creepio's thoughtful gaze lifted from the security men to settle on Abel. "I will take the prisoners if you wish, or you can deal with them. As the master of Castle House, and having defeated the other dominant local sorcerer, it is your choice. Under the Accord you administer High and Low Justice over anyone in your area of magical influence—demesne, in the original wording."

"Let him take them." Kelis's anger had evaporated, and now she sounded tired and distracted. She kept staring at her hands and then towards the wreck of Pendragon's car. "You'll just slap them over the wrist and that little bitch for one will cause more trouble."

"Stunt her this time. Or stick her on a tether so we can teach her some manners." Rachel pushed forward to glare down at Natalie. "By the time she's recovered from the beating Claris gave her, she'll have got the message and won't need another." Claris looked shell-shocked, hugging herself and staring at the battered figure.

Abel turned to Creepio for better suggestions, but the vicar just shrugged. "Not the worst possible fate. Most sorcerers would find amusing ways to kill anyone useless like those security guards. They'd concoct something long, lingering and agonising for someone who betrayed them, especially someone not well enough trained to make a useful bound servant." The vicar curled his lip when Natalie's still figure twitched at that. She wasn't unconscious, just faking. "I will take any prisoners you give me to the monks or nuns where their wounds will be tended. Once healed the prisoners will earn their keep by working in the gardens or wherever else we find them useful. They will have the chance to repent, but it will be genuine repentance because they will not be able to lie. Their tether will be held with a light hand, only a tether, not a full binding, but none of them will be allowed to cause any more harm, ever."

"We could do that, keep her tethered." Rachel still stood over Natalie, and for a moment Abel thought she'd kick the apparently unconscious girl. "She laughed when Justin accepted one to save me, and when Pendragon hurt him to keep me under control. Said she wanted me as her slave. How does the binding thing work? We could fix her so we'd know she wasn't up to anything, maybe give her some of what Justin got."

A look around the number of heads that were nodding worried Abel. Right now too many Taverners wanted payback and they didn't care how. "I don't want to do something that'll come back to haunt me later. But that's just me, so how do we decide?"

"Cre… The archbishop said it was up to you, Abel." Eric kept putting a hand towards his scorched head, then pulling it away before he touched it. "Right now I want to fry the bloke who tried to burn my head off, but I might not want that memory in the middle of the night."

"Not just me. The Tavern should decide." Abel looked around but few of them seemed interested.

"Kelis, Rob, Ferryl, Jenny and Zephyr can help you. The rest of us do what you say anyway." Una's usually cheerful face looked drawn. "The six of you could probably flatten us all if it came to it. I owe my brain to Zephyr for freeing me, and probably my life, so I'll trust her judgement." More answers came, slowly at first but then in a flood. Nobody else wanted to be judge and jury. Even Rachel declined when it came to deciding for all the prisoners, though she still wanted to bind or tether Natalie.

Abel turned to Kelis as Rob and Jenny moved up each side of her. He caught hold of Ferryl's hand. "Well?"

"High and Low means life or death, Abel." Rob looked sick at the thought. "I can't just kill someone in cold blood, execute them." Kelis and Jenny shook their heads to agree with him though Ferryl pointed out, through her hand, that it was the sensible solution. "The game rules don't

320

cover this."

"You wrote the original rules, even if this isn't a game anymore. Or if it is, it's a very different, very dangerous game." Una swished her sword, the bottom third of the blade blackened by something. "You did a good job with the first set so I'll stick by whatever you come up with. Better than that," she said, lifting her sword, "I'll help you make them stick if necessary."

"In that case, we'll hand the prisoners over to the archbishop. Too many of us would be looking to make them suffer but he's got nothing personal against them." Several voices objected, but they gradually died away as others pointed out the alternatives. "I'll check with Zephyr." Who Abel knew would do what he asked.

"There's a security man back there who'll need an ambulance. He might be in a bad way because I hit him really hard with a Windhammer, but I left him clear of the fires." A red-eyed Shannon sniffed, pointing to where two of the parked cars still smouldered. "Sorry about the damage. My shield wouldn't fit between the cars but I needed it to stop the bullets." Loud exclamations were followed by comments about trying to get the insurance to fix that sort of damage. Abel didn't hesitate, he told them the Tavern would cover it.

"If you want to hand over the prisoners, you'd better ask Zephyr if she'll give hers up." Ferryl's smile had a lot of wicked in it. "Come on. You can let the wounded know it's all over."

"I've just done it." Shawn limped out of the door, holding his head. "I've still got a lousy headache from trying to fight that tether."

"Just give me a moment, please." Abel turned towards the vicar. After a brief discussion, Creepio made a call on his mobile for the God Squad to collect the bodies and prisoners. They were lurking nearby, ready to clean up if God's SAS had found an excuse to join the fight. Creepio explained that part; the church couldn't interfere in sorcerer fights unless one broke the Accord or attacked a churchman. For once Creepio didn't seem to mind parting with information.

Abel now had the number of an anonymous doctor for magical wounds. He'd already called and a team was on the way. They would cost him, but the private practice in question used magical healing alongside the usual methods and wouldn't go near an official hospital. Abel even recognised the address, because the Taverners maintained the glyphs on the outside of the building. He'd been worried when they'd asked for his credit rating but Creepio took the phone, identified himself and suggested they sent the bill to Woods and Green. There were some advantages to being Celtchar's heir.

When the first Land Rovers and ambulances disguised as vans drew up and men spilled out, Abel invited Creepio inside to see who else needed locking up. Una had already been around to the back garden and reported two bodies, one among the trees. The one Ferryl had thrown through the window hadn't survived either. Following her through the house Abel passed several torn and crumpled figures. Taverners were watching over several security men who might live, providing they got to a hospital, but the three who must have been apprentices were stone dead. A cautious glance down the hole in the hallway floor revealed a still figure with a charred head, crumpled on the cellar floor. Further up the hallway lay another apprentice, blood still oozing around the web embedded in his flesh. Despite two more possibly dead apprentices in the lounge, one badly burnt, Abel had to smile when he came in. Two battered security men sat against the wall, with a woman between them. Abel recognised the woman, the apprentice from Redwolf's house, but the smile wasn't for her.

"Spare me. Please? I was on a tether. I didn't want to attack you again." Despite talking to Abel, the woman's eyes, and those of the two men, were riveted on Zephyr. The sprite hadn't been able to reach full size but a fairly large, very realistic ogre crouched among the furniture. Its bright green, burning eyes followed any movement her prisoners made. The other jailers, several injured Taverners, didn't even have live glyphs ready.

Abel didn't answer, waiting for spooky-phone to shoot out of the ogre and connect. "Handshake please. Do you like my ogre? It was a big surprise for her. I am pleased you are here because I have used up almost all my magic."

"That's a very realistic copy. Perhaps it's a good job you didn't see the platycroc." Abel felt some of Zephyr flow back into her tattoo, and shook hands. "Fill up, I've still got some magic left." Not much, but Abel knew there were four vacant trees outside to supply some more. The dryads had moved to Elmwood Park. "Did you block the tethers or break them?" While more Taverners and Creepio came in, Zephyr told Abel what had happened, though she didn't mention killing the burned man. She knew Abel would have spared him but Zephyr had promised to protect her creator, and she would do what was needed.

Creepio eyed up the ogre. "That's not full size. You should feed it more often." His brow wrinkled when he looked from Zephyr to the score marks in the floorboards, then to Abel and back to Zephyr. "Though it's much too solid for a wind spirit and it's not bound, is it? You had no tether outside."

"Zephyr comes and goes as she wishes, and takes whatever form is appropriate." Abel ignored Creepio's sudden interest, turning to explain the alternatives to the three captives. The woman, Guinevere or Ginny, seemed relieved that Pendragon had died but was terrified at the thought of going with Creepio. The two security men, on the other hand, seemed relieved they could go with the vicar. For the first time, the Taverners met God's SAS. Two men in military uniform, but wearing prominent crosses, arrived to take the security men away.

"Do you want to come home, Zephyr?"

"Yes please." The ogre began to fuzz, then turned into a boiling cloud that slowly shrank to nothing. Abel fought back a smile because Zephyr left the bright green eyes hanging in mid-air right to the end. He felt her relief as the sprite flowed into her tattoo. "I missed this." From her tone of voice, Abel half expected the sprite to purr.

"Where did your dust go?"

"Back under the floorboards where it came from. There was plenty."

The sorceress looked relieved as the last wisp disappeared, but not for long. "What about her?" Kelis glowered at Ginny, who flinched. She obviously remembered the last time they met.

"If she won't accept a tether, I can't take her." Creepio shrugged, apparently unconcerned. "So kill her or stunt her."

"No! I'll accept a tether, but not from the church. Never from the church." Despite being a captive, Ginny's look at Creepio promised carnage, or at least a feeble attempt at it if he tried.

"Your problem, Abel." Creepio turned to leave. "You'll need some serious redecorating before the place opens as a refuge." Abel had to agree. Scorch marks and gouges had wrecked a good bit of the new décor and damaged the furniture.

"It looks like a bomb went off." Shannon looked down at herself. "While I look as if I've been in a car wreck. Oh dear, I have. Though most of it was the heat." Her bright smile didn't fool anyone, because she kept bursting into tears. "When my shield hit the cars, they glowed, and that's hot." Most of her exposed skin looked almost cherry red. "I should have put sun block on this morning." Her voice faltered on the final word and Petra put an arm round her.

Creepio turned back from the doorway. "I am telling you this in front of your friends, Shannon, so they know I am not trying to influence you behind their backs. If you find that what happened today preys on your mind, the church will welcome you." He came back and took both of Shannon's hands. "Ask Abel to call me and a priest from your branch of the church, one who understands magic, will meet you. Just to talk, or to arrange a safe place if you wish to renounce magic, or to enrol you as one of our own. The Church Militant, God's SAS, would welcome a warrior like you."

Shannon looked around at her friends, settling on Abel. He smiled and shrugged. "Your choice, Shannon, it always was. Remember what we said right at the start, that maybe good is in the person, not the label? You can become a white sorceress or a bishopess, or abandon magic, but there'll always be a place for you at a game of Bonny's Tavern."

She smiled her thanks, turning to Creepio. "I think I can fight for good without joining your Church Militant. A sort of apprentice Saint Georgeous?"

"If the cause is just, the heart and soul don't care what armour they wear." The vicar smiled and sketched a small bow. "And now I must take my leave." Once outside, Creepio became sharper, more like his usual self. "I am assuming you don't want another sorcerer moving into Stourton?" He nodded very gently at the horrified headshakes from Abel and his friends. "Then you'd better get down to Woods and Green and stake your claim. Since you wiped Pendragon out, nobody local will want to object."

"We didn't kill him, you did."

"The platycroc finished him off, but all the hard work had been done. You defeated his apprentices and ran him off, left him alone and vulnerable. If he'd got away, the vultures and hyenas would have gathered. Pendragon would have been dead by tomorrow. I'd rather deal with a clean takeover by you and yours than all the others squabbling over scraps. To be honest I expected to have to fight him and wasn't looking forward to it, but once again your happy band exceeded expectations." An expansive gesture took in the street and, presumably, all of Stourton. "This town and all Pendragon's business is now yours by right of conquest, providing you get the paperwork organised. That does not include any area protected by the magic from a church cross."

"Is conquest legal?" Una looked a bit brighter. "Robin D'Ritche would want some plunder."

"Start with that." Creepio waved a hand towards the wreck of the Bentley. "Put a veil around it when we remove ours, then take the gold before the rest is carted off for scrap. My people put up diversion signs to stop any traffic and cast sleep glyphs over all the other houses as soon as the fighting started." He looked up and down the peaceful street. "The local residents will find this morning passed quicker than expected, but if you tidy up the garden nobody will think twice about it. The Bentley will show up as stolen so the police will believe a car thief crashed it, and will concentrate on finding the driver."

"That's it? What about Natalie, won't her parents come looking for her?" Abel gestured to take it all in. "All the damage and injuries get swept under the magic carpet? People died here, some of them security men who had no real protection against glyphs."

"Men who fired on unarmed children, Shannon, for one. Though she didn't kill that one, for which he should thank God because I would have. Natalie's parents will be told she died in a hit and run, a long way from here. They will attend a closed casket funeral, and skilled magic users will blunt their grief and blur their memories. That has to be better than their daughter disappearing without trace, or finding out she helped to enslave and torture other students. As an apprentice she would have left home anyway, despite her age." Creepio's face and tone hardened. "As for Pendragon's apprentices, they knew the score. When a magic user trains to be a sorcerer, they accept that they will be involved in disputes and one day a stronger sorcerer may kill them."

"We didn't accept anything. We started playing a game, then tried to clean up a village and a school because nobody else would." Kelis looked at the scorched patch where the Taverners had killed an apprentice, then down at her hand. The other still held her cloak over her torn robe. "Now we're all murderers."

"You heard what I told Shannon, Kelis. Self-defence. Everyone is entitled to defend themselves, or would you rather have accepted a tether?" Creepio nodded gently at her vehement denials. "So you fought back but with restraint, with what used to be called honour, an outmoded concept and a refreshing change." The vicar's hand swept across the garden where the security men and Natalie had laid. "Most magic users would have killed those men and the girl without a thought. Those earth glyphs could have driven concrete spikes through the men, much easier than restraining them. None of your people killed in cold blood and until one of you does, I will keep cheering your Tavern on from the sidelines. Very quietly because you are on your own now, a part of the magical hierarchy, a player of a different sort. Under the Accord the church must stay neutral in magical squabbles." With a sad smile Creepio took in the surprised expressions.

"So what happens now? You just walk away and leave us to try and sort this mess out? We've no idea how to fix the evening news, or police reports." Rob looked around at the other Taverners, who were all shaking their heads and looking more and more worried. "How can we keep the Accords, keep everything secret, if we've no idea how it's done? We don't even have a copy of the Accord."

"There'll be a copy in Castle House, and in Pendragon's headquarters, but I'll send you another. I know how you'll feel about the answer to the cover-ups, but this is the harsh reality of life. The church will still deal with those things, if you wish, but we will expect payment. We have a widely established web of agents throughout the law enforcement and medical services." For once Creepio looked embarrassed. "Considering what you have already done for the church, without asking for payment, I will not send an invoice for today. But this is the last time. It really isn't a game anymore, or at the least it's a very different game with very real penalties." With that he turned and strode off down the road. A small anonymous van stopped, Creepio climbed in, and moments later had gone.

"As usual, I still have a million questions." Kelis didn't sound even slightly amused this time.

*　　*　　*

It came as a shock to the Taverners, but the whole fight including the talk with Creepio had taken less than half an hour. Clearing up would take longer, and they'd better get started. A priest came over to introduce himself, and let the teenagers know they had one hour to regrow grass and generally make the front of the house look reasonable. After that the street full of possible witnesses would be awake again, unless Abel wanted to pay extra. At least the four vacant trees in the orchard had plenty of magic for fixing the external damage. Better still, when a shaken and subdued Frederick asked them, the dryads in the orchard were willing to trade magic for honey or boiled sweets. They seemed much more approachable today, though several Taverners suggested the good mood came from killing a sorcerer.

The anonymous medics also arrived in what looked like vans, but unlike the church medics many of them were women. The paramedics dealt with the walking wounded, while anyone who needed hospital treatment left in the disguised ambulances. According to the first assessments, all the injured would be able to go home today. The medics administered ointments and dressings, assuring Abel that both had been magically enhanced. The lighter burns and smaller wounds would be gone by tonight or possibly tomorrow morning. Phone calls to parents arranged for some of the lightly wounded to stay overnight, allegedly to help with decorating the refuge. That would give them a better chance of healing before parents saw them. Unfortunately Shannon and several others had injuries and hair loss that wouldn't heal quickly enough and couldn't be disguised.

"It's no good, I still look like a car wreck." Even as she said it, Shannon's face brightened a little. Her mood still swung from sentence to sentence. "Actually, that would cover it. We've got two damaged cars, both partly burned, one scorched and battered minibus and a large, heavy, completely wrecked car that has been on fire."

"I don't mind slandering the memory of Pendragon, though I'm glad I didn't actually see his body." Jenny grimaced, because whatever the God Squad removed from the wreck couldn't have looked good. "Creepio reckoned the police would blame a car thief. We could tell our parents a drunk in a Bentley ploughed into our Tavern vehicles, then ran away?"

"The rest of the brave Taverners rushed out and pulled their injured friends free, which is why they have sundry bruises and scorch marks." Jenny's words brought relieved smiles to a good few faces, and a rush to move the damaged cars into the road before the priests woke the neighbours up. Within an hour two different garages had come to take away the minibus and one of the cars, while the other scorched vehicle had been fit to drive to a third garage for repair. Frederick placed the orders using Stourton Tavern Refuge letterheads, but Abel would pay in cash so nothing showed in the books.

Abel called the private doctor, explaining they would use a car crash as a reason for the injuries. A voice on the other end asked what reason she should give parents for the private medical care. Abel floundered until she suggested the Bentley's insurance might pay for private medical treatment? Abel agreed, wondering how often this happened.

By then a possibly genuine policeman turned up at Frederick's house, though he didn't come inside. He certainly knew all about magic and keeping it secret, studiously ignoring the rapidly re-growing grass and new leaves appearing on the scorched bushes. He took their statements in his car, accepting the story about the wrecked vehicles without asking for more than the bare facts. The policeman stayed while concerned parents collected offspring, assuring them the police were looking for the culprit. Two hired medics stayed to meet the parents of the obviously injured and smoothed away any concerns, probably magically, considering how well it worked. A phone call promised the worst injured would be delivered home by ambulance. The docs were definitely worth the money, however much it turned out to be. Abel mentally allocated another of his vases or something similar to pay for it all.

There'd be plenty of money if anyone could sell gold. Abel, and several others when he mentioned it, had expected the magic store in Pendragon's car to be magically altered lead or iron. They'd checked anyway, carefully avoiding the inside where Pendragon had died. Despite the chunks of car crushed into the solid block under the boot, Zephyr and Ferryl both declared it was real gold. The Taverners soon had proof because melting it, under cover of a veil, turned out to be the only way to get the precious metal out of the tangled steel. Ferryl suggested that Pendragon used real gold so damage wouldn't leave him with a pile of dust.

*   *   *

Getting the medics, calling Woods and Green, sorting out the garden, taking the gold, organising car repairs and trying to tidy up the house itself kept everyone going until lunchtime. As the initial excitement faded, one after another of the Taverners ran out of steam. Rob was the exception because he spent most of the time sat with Kathy, showing her little magic tricks and trying to explain how magic worked. Eventually Petra pulled Abel away from a scorched stretch of plaster, telling him he had to sit down or fall down. Since he'd been staring at it while thinking of something entirely different, she had a point. Frederick helped Petra round up anyone else still working, and the Tavern meeting finally started.

Una cheered them all up a bit by passing round takeaway menus. "While you all decide on what to eat, we'd better organise shopping expeditions. You five, six with Shannon, need new outfits. Your costumes are ruined, but you can blame that on the crash as long as your parents never see the actual damage. There's several others who need clothing replaced, especially jeans or tops that aren't costumes. We'll need a mile of bandage as well. Then anyone who can cast a seeming on cloth can disguise their minor wounds if they don't want parents to notice." Una turned to Abel. "But first we'd better decide who'll be going. The rest will be having that meeting you wanted."

"We need rules more than anything else right now." Rachel sat holding her brother's hand, looking subdued. "I wanted to kill them all, especially Natalie, until Creepio said his piece. Even then I considered it, for Natalie at least. We need a set of penalties for anyone who breaks the rules, or betrays us, so nobody goes over the top." Her wan smile accepted that maybe she needed them more than most. "It isn't a game, so the rules have to work in the real world even if that's inconvenient."

"Excuse me, but did someone swap out my pestiferous sister for this serious young woman. Bring back Rachel!" A pale and still shaky Justin nudged her, bringing a little smile. "That's better. You weren't the only one, Rachel. I can promise you, if Pendragon or Natalie had been in here when the tether broke I wouldn't have cared if they were tied up. I'd have burned them both."

"I lost it again." Claris looked down at her bandaged hands as her frost giant hugged her. Splinters from the bat had driven into her palms when it shattered on Pendragon's shield. "I've got to stop doing that, losing it when I feel threatened. You know, leech sort of threatened. That's what set me off with the fursomnium, those things reaching out to get in my head. When I realised what tethering meant I nearly killed Natalie without any magic at all, and I meant to kill Pendragon when I shot him." After a long pause she continued, very quietly. "I can't be sure I wouldn't have shot Effy."

"How did you learn to do that?" Jenny frowned, obviously trying to remember. "You looked like those pictures on the TV, a proper police stance, not like a gangster or cowboy movie."

"Dad goes to a gun club. I asked him to teach me but without telling mum." Claris's faint smile looked a little guilty. "He's a soft touch really, since the divorce, and worse since I supposedly got into drugs. Dad sort of blames himself for that. Though he wouldn't get me a gun. Probably a good thing."

"We all felt like that, mad as hell and lashing out. That bloke, the apprentice in here, had to have been hit by at least thirty glyphs." Shawn looked a little embarrassed. "We shouldn't use fire glyphs inside, or against people, but I did both. We pushed on the other one's shield until it collapsed and fried him."

"But like Creepio said, not in cold blood." Una had her sword across her lap, cleaning the scorch mark from the blade. "I threw this at his shield, but I couldn't just stick someone who isn't attacking me. Even if I threatened to if that woman didn't behave." She looked upwards towards the bedroom where a shimmer on the ceiling, one with bright green eyes, guarded Ginny. The rest of Zephyr still curled up in her tattoo, content to listen and watch. Bit by bit everyone began to talk, while Petra made her list and several of them helped her phone for the food. The talk carried on, in fits and starts, right through the meal. A strange sort of discussion full of bursts of laughter and occasional tears, but most people got the morning out of their system, for now at least.

"Time for all those notes, Abel." Kelis looked round in alarm. "They didn't get burned in the minibus, did they? We took ages over them."

"No, I dropped my bag when Pendragon came out, and it laid on the footpath through the whole thing." Abel opened it up. "Even our phones survived, which will save some trouble at home, though explaining our clothes will be bad enough."

"Except my phone." Rob pointed to a blackened lump on the floor next to him. "My next costume won't have pockets, then it can stay safely hidden in a backpack like the rest. Though I haven't really got any pockets now." Several Taverners smiled as he pulled at his rags to demonstrate.

"My cue." Shannon stood up, zipping up her borrowed hoody. "You know how I feel. If I think I can go with whatever you come up with, I'm in. If it tends too much towards the dark side, I'm out. My preference is towards the Saint Georgeous end of the spectrum but not too saintly." She raised a hand to touch a couple of bald patches. "I want to let my hair down now and then, once it grows again. If I can borrow the taxi fare I'll deal with the shopping."

"I'll go with whatever you agree, as long as this place remains a refuge." Frederick smiled up at Shannon. "Since Abel is going to be generous and buy the clothes from the loot, I'll raid the petty cash for taxi fares." Three others announced they would go with whatever the rest came up with, and filed out.

*   *   *

An awkward silence followed, until Kelis raised her glass of cola in a mock salute to Abel. "To the master of Castle House. I suppose we'd better explain that bit first."

The ice giant nodded slowly. "Since that means you administer High and Low Justice in Stourton. I'm definitely nervous because I remember what that means, from my history lessons, and I'm fairly sure it was abolished long ago." Several faces, Abel's among them, looked shocked as they remembered what Rob said. "I'm really curious how that works because I'm sure the police think it's their job."

"I don't know exactly what it means in the Accord, but I've got an appointment with Woods and Green at 4:30 so I'll ask them. For anyone who doesn't know, the Woods and Green in the game is a real magical solicitor and they pay for the advert." At least that brought a few chuckles. "For now we do exactly what we intended, set out rules for Taverners. Some will only be advisory for non-magical players, for if they want to earn extra health bonuses in the game. After today, I think we can all agree that anyone wanting to stay in the Tavern once they have magic has to obey another set. They'll be the same as the game rules, loosely speaking, but not voluntary."

"Call them Taverners, while the non-magical are Tavern players, a nice innocuous name for when we are in public. If there'll be rules, that means setting penalties because some will realise just how much power this magic gives them." Justin hesitated, then pushed on. "Natalie was like that, but Effy was worse. She deliberately joined us, spied on us and betrayed us."

"Effy had a special tether, one that made her a different sort of slave, but she must have accepted it voluntarily. She lived a complete lie to get our confidence and tell Pendragon all about us, well beyond blind obedience. Though how guilty she was doesn't matter now. We have to decide on a penalty for the survivor, Zephyr's prisoner." Everyone's eyes glanced briefly upwards to the room holding Ginny before Jenny carried on. "She imprisoned and then injured Taverners, and being on a tether isn't an excuse. She accepted that voluntarily, to get training and become another Pendragon in time."

"Let me ask Woods and Green. There has to be a recognised way of dealing with her." Abel had a sinking feeling that tethering, binding, killing or stunting more or less covered it. Ferryl's hand crept into his and confirmed it. "First we set our rules, then we all swear to them, and then I'll go and see about the rest."

"When we agree to the rules, that means we agree with the mission. Um, sorry, the aims of the Tavern." Rachel looked embarrassed, but determined. "I've got to try and explain that to some of the younger ones, the less adept who weren't invited today. That it's just a set of ideals, so we haven't got to get too carried away." For once she didn't seem to mind a hug from her big brother.

"Though we can still stop abuse and pilfering at school, that sort of thing. We just have to accept the whole town can't be cleaned up." Kelis passed around some of the notes. "These don't really cover it, because we didn't know we'd suddenly become the Stourton super-cops. I reckon that means we manage the magical side, stop nasties from bothering people in the areas where we have enough magical Tavern members. Regardless of this High and Low Justice thing, law and order has to be down to the cops, more or less. If one of us wants to stop something non-magical, it has to be approved, no vigilantes."

"Unless someone tries to mug me." Grim smiles and nods greeted Petra's amendment. The Taverners gathered into small groups so they could share the printed sheets, and started working out just what other amendments they'd need.

*   *   *

Oddly enough, setting out the basic rules wasn't that difficult because they'd already been working that way. Help people in trouble and deter the bad guys, but quietly, without attracting public attention and preferably without seriously injuring anyone. Petra summed it up. As each new member joined, they'd found the rest acted in a certain way. As the first unexpected recruit, she'd accepted what Abel, Kelis and Rob, and Abel's tattoo of course, told her was the right way to use magic. The first group of betas were all geeks, not the most aggressive kids in the school, and they'd set a tone.

A good few had suffered verbal abuse from Seraph, or something stronger from Henry and the like, so they had a natural aversion to that sort of thing. Abel had set the bar when it came to payback, because once Seraph and Henry were dealt with he'd left them alone. He'd even given Henry some Tavern hexes so he could sleep creature-free. When the charity bit went into the game rules, the magical members were already trying to clean up their neighbourhood and the school. Doing so as the Tavern had attracted the rescued victims, minorities and misfits, to start playing the game. Any of those who had discovered magic became willing recruits when Rachel announced her mission. According to some of those present just being accepted by the other players, then the Taverners, had made a huge difference to their lives.

Gradually the sixteen of them decided on what was practical, back up to twenty-four by the end as the shoppers and some of the injured came back. The result wasn't a firm set of rules, but the Taverners came up with a rough framework they could all agree with. Abel insisted he wanted a full meeting to decide on the final version, all sixty-one local Taverners, including the very latest leaf-flutterer. The eleven other magically aware players, those living elsewhere who had learned about the Tavern through relatives, could be consulted by phone.

In the meantime Kelis took a deep breath and phoned her mum, explaining that the minibus had been hit but the other driver's insurance was taking care of it. She'd be home later, in a hire vehicle provided by the other bloke's insurance firm. That would be another bill for Pendragon's gold to hopefully pay for. Abel, Rob and Jenny phoned home at the same time, assuring their parents it was just cuts and bruises and they'd been treated. Jenny had the most trouble, her dad insisting on collecting her immediately until she played the "don't embarrass me in front of my friends" card.

By four-twenty only fifteen Taverners remained, three of them residents. Eric promised to stop overnight, to help Shawn guard Ginny until Abel decided her fate. She'd be drained into lead bars again this evening so she'd only have whatever magic she absorbed, leaving her almost helpless. The two thick gold armbands she wore were also emptied. Pendragon had locked those into place, magically, and so far nobody had figured out how to remove them. The ones on the bodies had been melted off before Creepio took them away, extra loot to pay for medics and clothes.

Despite the precautions, Frederick looked more cheerful when two others arranged to stay overnight to take shifts on guard. Pendragon had tethered him even though he couldn't shield, then hurt Frederick until Una agreed to a tether.

Una, Petra, Justin, Warren and Rachel wanted to come to Woods and Green with Abel, though they agreed to wait in the entrance lobby. Justin still looked pale after Pendragon's torture, but a magic-spiked drink from the medics and an invisible glyph drawn on his head had helped and he wanted to keep an eye on his little sister. All five of them were worried there might be more apprentices or someone like Redwolf lurking to attack Abel. From what Creepio had said, taking Abel out would give another sorcerer control of Stourton. Abel wasn't too worried because he'd got Kelis, Jenny, Rob, Ferryl and Zephyr, and with the orchard dryads willing to trade for honey, everyone's gold belts and diamonds had been filled up.

Claiming the Gryphon

Abel felt conspicuous trooping into Woods and Green with nine others. The entrance lobby had enough seats, but the receptionist definitely looked wary. He relaxed when Terese Green came in and smiled at Abel, though her smile wavered as she took in the rest. "Are they all coming with us?"

"Coming? Where?" That sinking feeling started. Abel looked around at the rest. "They're worried about another attack."

"That's unlikely, but we can bring them if I organise extra transport. It would be best if you travel with me." A little smile crossed her face as several people tensed. "With Kelis, Rob, Jenny and Fay, I assume? The rest will be right behind us."

Abel worried all over again when two cabs pulled up outside and Terese led him towards one. He wanted to know what was going on, but he couldn't talk in front of the driver. At least they were hackney cabs so all five could get in the back, with Terese taking one of the seats facing backwards so she could talk to Abel face to face. She gave the driver an address, then tapped a small glyph on the partition between him and the passengers. "We are now in a bubble, as it were. The driver can't hear a word we say. The company in question have no idea magic exists, but know we want our destinations and clients to remain discreet. It is a lucrative contract."

"Where are we going?" Kelis sat back and gestured towards Abel. "Sorry."

Terese answered her anyway. "To take over Pendragon Enterprises, of course. I thought that's what you intended?" Abel nodded. Creepio had told him he had to take over to stop any others, although the name came as a surprise. "To do that we must go to one of his business addresses, and you must claim it."

"Take over? Will that mean a fight?" Rob looked alarmed, understandably so. All five of them were wearing jeans, blouses or shirts and jumpers or jackets because their costumes had been ruined. All of them looked battered, and had more bandages, plasters, ointments, lumps and bumps under their clothes. Despite wearing leather, even Ferryl had needed new clothing.

"Perhaps, though it won't be much. If some junior apprentice hasn't realised Pendragon's tether has failed, he or she may try to defend the place. If another sorceress is trying to take over, I will serve notice on her." A smug smile appeared, briefly. "That usually settles the issue. Redwolf has been notified and asked if he will be making a claim, as he is the only other sorcerer with a residence in Stourton. I explained the extent of Pendragon's failure, and he has declined."

"Where will we be going?" Jenny glanced at her watch, remembered it was now scrap, and leant over to look at Ferryl's. That had only survived because Ferryl dropped it before going towards Pendragon, because she'd known her arm would be catching fire. "I can't be too late or Dad will start up again. We were supposed to be back by six."

"That is cutting it fine. This first visit will only take minutes, but the second location is thirty miles away. We can have you home by seven, or I'll leave you here after the first visit. My apologies, parents aren't usually a consideration." Mutterings filled the cab, and Abel quickly texted Petra in the other cab to tell the rest. Nobody wanted to be left out so despite it taking some frantic phoning, everyone arranged to be home a little later. By that time the cabs had pulled up outside an empty, boarded-up shop, allegedly for rent. Glowing glyphs on the boarding spelling out Pendragon Enterprises for the magically sighted.

*　*　*

Terese marched up to the door set back into the shop front, and placed her hand on it. A veil shimmered as it opened, preventing the non-magical from seeing inside. "Follow me. You must each place your hand on the door to open it, to tell the staff who is coming in."

Abel went first, until Ferryl pushed in front. "Guard and trainer, remember. You don't wander into strange magical premises first." She placed her hand as Terese had and the door swung open.

"There are magic flows, but just reading her hand. It may gauge the strength of whoever enters." Zephyr sounded amused. "It will not read Ferryl Shayde, only her host."

"Will it recognise you?"

"Perhaps, but just as a bound spirit. It will not be able to assess my strength while I am in my tattoo." Zephyr definitely sounded happy. "So if you need an ogre?"

"Naughty. We are hoping to avoid a fight."

"Ffod is ready." Abel placed his hand on the door and went inside, still wondering if that meant Zephyr wanted a fight or was just being reassuring. The inside resembled the foyer of Woods and Green, though not quite as large or luxurious. The receptionist looked worried as the rest of the Taverners trooped in, but before he could speak Terese flourished papers at him. By the time she'd finished he looked completely baffled and even more worried.

A door at the rear opened and a young woman paused before coming in, her eyes widening. "I'm afraid the proprietor isn't here at the moment. Would you like to make an appointment?"

Terese flourished the papers again and nodded towards Abel. "This gentleman is the new owner. Please take us to the gryphon." The woman hesitated so Terese pointed towards the rear of the shop. "Please check. The gryphon's claws may be red. Do you understand?" As the woman and the receptionist exchanged baffled looks, Terese Green abandoned her officious manner. "I'm sorry. Who is usually in charge here?"

"Mr Celeborn is usually in charge, but Mr Paragon took over for the day. Three hours ago he told me I was in charge and left. The manager doesn't usually leave during opening hours." The woman rallied, straightening up and sounding more formal. "I only answer the phone and deal with some typing and data entry, so I can't help with contracts or a new owner. I didn't even know the business was up for sale."

"But you've seen the gryphon, possibly called a griffin. A creature that is part-eagle, part lion?"

The woman nodded, glancing at the receptionist for confirmation but he just shrugged. "It's on the manager's desk."

"This gentleman"—Terese indicated Abel—"wishes to see it." She laid a hand gently on the woman's arm. "Will that be allowed?"

From the blank look that settled over the woman's face and the monotone "Yes," Abel thought she'd probably agree to anything right now. He decided against shaking hands with Terese, ever.

Ferryl took his hand, briefly. "I can see it in your face, but don't worry. It is suggestion, not control. If the secretary was vehement about stopping us going in there, she could still say no." Ferryl looked and sounded puzzled when she spoke aloud. "I thought gryphons were extinct."

"This way please." Abel shrugged and started to follow Terese, but Kelis, Jenny and Ferryl got in front of him with the rest following behind. When the secretary showed them into a large, luxurious office Abel felt a little let down. The brass gryphon on the desk only stood about thirty centimetres high. Maybe not just brass, the eagle's talons on the front legs were crimson. Terese looked at the woman and hesitated, but Ferryl reached out to tap her.

"Sleep." She caught the woman as she slumped. "I presume we need privacy."

"It helps, because she obviously doesn't know the first thing about the real business here. She's not even magically aware." Terese waved Abel forward and pointed at the gryphon. "Claim it, by blood and power."

"Don't sorcerers ever sign a document, or stamp a wax seal? That sounds the same as the inheriting thing." Abel eyed up the statuette, wondering if it was looking back.

"You are inheriting. Celtchar died and you inherited by blood. You defeated Pendragon and he died, so you inherit his wealth and business by power." Terese pointed. "Use the point on the end of the beak."

"What for?" Abel rolled his eyes. "Blood again?" Nobody answered so he put his finger up to the hook on the eagle's beak. It must have been very sharp because he barely touched it before it stung and a drop of crimson spilled out. A second later it had gone, absorbed into the beak. "By blood and power, I claim it." The red disappeared from all the talons bar one. "Is that it?"

"No, there is another claimant. A minor one, but whoever it is will be waiting for us." She tapped the gryphon's talons. "Whoever made the claim is not related, and was not in the vicinity when Pendragon died. The sorcerer or sorceress has claimed from another place of business, and is not officially allied if they only have one-eighth of a claim. That might even be an ambitious apprentice." She turned towards the door. "We will put the claim to Pendragon's gryphon."

"Zephyr, please ask Ferryl what is going on?" The spooky-phone connected.

Ferryl touched the woman on the floor, then cast a tiny glyph as she began to stir. Her hand caught hold of Abel's. "I've mazzled her a little. I've no idea what happens next. This taking over of a business is all new to me. I think it might be recent, to cater for the modern world. Normally if a sorcerer killed another he just marched into the castle or whatever and sat in the biggest chair."

"What about the gryphon toes?"

"I've no idea. From what Terese said there might be a real one, linked to the gold statuette." Ferryl didn't sound too sure about that. "They should be extinct."

Abel almost rolled his eyes, of course the statuette was gold. He had to stop assuming things were brass, around sorcerers at least. On the way out Terese suggested the receptionist shut up for the day, and told him a representative of the new owner would arrive tomorrow.

*   *   *

Once in the cab, Abel asked what representative Terese meant. She explained that a junior apprentice should run each branch of the business, though if Pendragon only had a few then he might give senior apprentices the job and income. She started to speak again, then paused. "Ah, of course. You have no apprentices so who will run your business? Their presence might be needed at any time, so schoolchildren aren't suitable."

"Eric and Shawn for starters, providing there's a decent wage involved. Maybe Frederick?" Jenny smirked at the realisation dawning on three other faces. "We wondered how to support a few Taverners so they were always available. Eric has a minimum wage job stacking shelves at the supermarket. Shawn works at fitting lawn mowers together and rides a beat-up scooter so anything above minimum wage has to be an improvement."

"Whoever takes care of the branch must be loyal because they'll know enough to sell out, join another sorceress and help her steal business." Terese looked from one to the other. "Loyal personally, through a tether at least because Pendragon Enterprises is now Abel Bernard Conroy's personal property. He just claimed it." She passed across a signet ring, one with a blank face. "Put that in your pocket and produce it when I tell you. A priest dropped it off earlier."

"So Ferryl could have done the same, claimed the business?" Abel cursed silently, because that would have meant she was financially independent and even if he was killed, the Tavern would have some income.

"Not with the same certainty. As the master of Castle House you would have had a quarter claim based on power alone even if Pendragon left an heir. Mz Shayde might have a quarter claim if you declined and gave her that ring, because she helped to defeat Pendragon, but she has no power base to fall back on. If that ring isn't what I think it is, her chances would be even less. We can't be sure until we get to Sheffield." Terese's little smile had some mischief in it. "As we represent both of you, I hope there'll be no dispute?"

"None. Abel claims everything and I will help him keep it." Ferryl's tone closed the subject.

"Can the Tavern claim it, Pendragon's business? Not Bonny's Tavern the game, but the magical Tavern." Abel turned to Jenny, hoping to get this away from personal loyalties and tethers. "You do all that business stuff, so how would it work?"

Jenny had barely started explaining before Terese pointed out magical businesses didn't work that way. No shares, no shareholders or dividends, and no vice-presidents. Everything, every tree, contract, house and car belong to the sorcerer, personally, linked together by his gryphon. Not a real one, a talisman of some kind linked to the smaller gold gryphons at each major location. Once Abel satisfied Pendragon's gryphon that he had the strongest claim, he would take possession of everything.

"You mean more woods and houses and stuff?" Rob looked over at Kelis with a little smirk. "You should have stuck with Abel, he could have given you a house." Abel opened his mouth to offer one but Terese beat him to it.

"There may be very few of either because Pendragon wasn't a strong sorcerer. He paid for his monopoly in Stourton, which means he bribed other sorcerers rather than challenged them. Pendragon may have only had one house and a few small clumps of trees, though I'm sure he claimed the public park in Stourton. Until we have settled Abel's claim, we can't even find out who dealt with his legal affairs." That wicked little smile came and went. "Someone cheap, no doubt."

Unfortunately Terese couldn't answer most questions, but one thing could be organised. A phone call to Eric confirmed he would be happy to take up a job which included increased wages. His first job was to look for the cars that brought Pendragon's apprentices to the fight, because according to Terese they now belonged to Abel. The batlins spread out and reported vehicles parked nearby on waste ground, under a veil. When Eric checked there were three BMWs, a Volvo and a Mercedes, all with the keys in the ignition but guarded by wards.

Abel asked Eric to bribe the batlins or goblins to stand guard. If the gryphon accepted him, Abel would own the cars and Eric would get one as his company car. A very happy Eric promised nobody would get near.

*   *   *

The head offices of Pendragon Enterprises were in a well-maintained, elaborately carved stone building in a leafy lane bordering a park. Both Ferryl and Zephyr told Abel the park had been claimed by someone, they could see the boundary magic. That didn't mean Pendragon had access. According to Terese there were four trees for every single person living in Sheffield, which made it popular among the magical community. Many of the most powerful sorcerers, including the master of Castle House, owned a house in Sheffield and claimed one of the numerous public parks. Abel buried the impulse to go and look, concentrating on the building they'd come to visit. One glance at the carving confirmed that Pendragon had taken his name seriously, dragons crawled or perched all over the front.

A group of four adults stood by the entrance, closely inspecting everyone in sight and especially the two cabs that had just stopped. Terese held out a hand to stop Ferryl opening her door. "That is either the other claimant, or someone hoping to ambush the claimant and take over. Word must have spread quickly. Stay in here while I investigate. There'll be no magical attack because these vehicles, their drivers and their owners are non-magical so an attack would be public and break the Accord. That's why we use them." She opened the door of the cab and got out.

Kelis's "Sneaky" followed the lawyer out of the cab. Meanwhile Rob called Warren in the other cab, explaining they should stay inside for now and why. Terese spoke to one of the waiting women, who looked a little alarmed at first but then laughed. After exchanging a few words Terese beckoned so Abel got out, although Ferryl insisted on being first. She seemed very protective today.

"Can I fly?"

"Not yet, Zephyr. We might need a surprise." As Abel walked forward he heard the doors on the other cab open.

The woman looked startled then caught herself, smiling nervously and looking from Ferryl to Abel. She kept glancing past Abel to the five from the other taxi, while her apprentices spread out a little. "She has shielded, and so have her apprentices. All three are on tethers."

Abel glanced back, realising the woman would be wondering about the game costumes the other five still wore. "Shields, everyone." Eight of the Taverners spaced themselves out while Ferryl caught hold of his hand and a lemon tinge told Abel he was protected.

The woman narrowed her eyes. "This is just a test, and invisible to the non-magical. It will not harm the unshielded." She cast a small glyph upwards where it burst into fine sparks that drifted down. As they touched the shields, including her own, each one glowed a bright electric blue but quickly faded. "Eight shielded apprentices?" She looked towards the offices with a big happy smile. "I'd love to see Boudicca's face when you walk in, especially the way some of you are dressed. She's here to claim Pendragon's little enterprise, because according to her you'll have nothing left to stop her." Her smile faded a little as she inspected Abel's group. "Though you've upset my plan. I intended offering you an alliance in return for a couple of morsels."

"Tell her it's still possible. You need allies, someone out in the sorceress community." Ferryl noticed the sorceress glancing down at their held hands and smiled brightly. "I am Ferryl Shayde, sorceress and personal bodyguard to Abel, master of Castle House and Pendragon Enterprises."

"Sorceress Verenestra, which is allegedly the name of a fairy. I doubt my master knew for certain. I am intrigued by a sorceress being a bodyguard, sorcerers usually use apprentices." The slim, black-haired woman bowed slightly to both Abel and Ferryl. "Greetings, Abel. That is an ancient name. Was your master called Adam?" She had a lovely smile, which Abel wasn't trusting an inch.

"I've never had a master or mistress, and neither have my companions. Abel is the name my parents chose, which I'm told is unusual." Abel tried out one of those little bows. "Since I'm new to all this, and I'm still sorting out Celtchar's holdings, there may be a morsel or two for anyone helping me." He really wanted to talk to Terese about keeping this sorceress here, but daren't risk letting Zephyr connect.

Though the lawyer must be psychic. "If you allow Verenestra to accompany us inside, she could witness your claim." She turned towards the doors, missing the huge smile from the sorceress. "I will go in ahead of you, so there are no unfortunate misunderstandings."

As Terese Green went inside, both Kelis and Rob spoke up. "We'll go in first, Abel."

"At least two of us should go in as well, just in case. We don't know how many are in there." Warren eyed up the door. "I don't really trust sorcerers. Sorry Veren, but we've had a bad day." He must have caught the look on the sorceress's face. "Sorry but I can't remember your full name. It all seems a bit silly to us. I'm Warren." The rest called out their names.

"After all those very ordinary names, I suppose I can live with Veren if only for the novelty." Her eyes drifted over them, noting the signs of combat. "How many did you lose?"

"None, or two, depending on how you count. We found two traitors. One is dead and one is on a church tether, along with half a dozen security men." Rachel's scowl meant she wasn't totally reconciled to Natalie's fate, not yet. "Pendragon got some of us tethered before Abel turned up, but Zephyr disconnected them before anyone had been badly hurt. Once they were loose, we helped Ferryl clean up the rest of the apprentices and then Pendragon." She saw the look on Ferryl's face and shut up.

"Who is Zephyr, and how did he or she break a tether?" Veren looked them over, definitely interested. "Were any of you among those tethered by Pendragon?" Petra, Warren, Justin and Una all nodded. "May I check one of you, please? My apprentices will drop their shields while I do?"

"Why?" Warren backed up a step, as did Justin.

"If a tether breaks when a sorcerer dies, rather than being deliberately removed, it leaves a remnant. The weakness makes it easier for someone else to attach another tether. There are sorcerers who specialise in removing the trace, though they charge huge fees. The sort of fees most newly-freed sorceresses can't afford." Veren hesitated for long moments. "If your Zephyr disconnected someone's tether while the sorcerer still lived that sounds as if it might have been done properly, in which case I'll be asking what your rates are."

"Your sorcerer died?" Inside Abel's head a smug voice assured him Zephyr had done the job properly. She didn't break the tether, she unravelled it.

"Mine and Boudicca's, the same man." A glance at the office showed a bit of venom. "I could offer some help just for that, to have the weakness removed?"

"If Zephyr can do that, Abel, I'll volunteer to be inspected. If Veren manages to tether me, get Zephyr to break it again and we'll know how to deal with her." Una turned to Veren with a wry smile and a hand on her sword. Abel almost asked her to put it back in the cab, but Terese didn't seem worried. "No offence, but I'm not really very trusting either."

"You'll have to be, just enough for me to touch the place it was attached. Where was it?" Una touched her shoulder, then stood very still as Veren approached. The sorceress paused, looking over Una's Robin D'Ritche outfit. "That's an old style of dress but you carry it off very well. Most apprentices who can shield are too old to get away with those boots." She reached out to rest her fingers on the same spot for a few seconds, then stepped back with a smile. "Nothing, not a sign. Can we deal?"

"Yes, after this is sorted out." Abel hesitated, then gestured. "Go in front of me, with an apprentice, so you get the full benefit of Boudicca's expression. Your other two apprentices come in last." Veren nodded and waited until Rob, Kelis, Justin and Rachel had gone through the door before following. Jenny pushed in to follow her, while Warren, Una and Petra closed in behind Abel. He felt like one of those VIPs with all the bodyguards, especially when the lemon tint around him tightened to let him and Ferryl through the doors together without losing the shield.

Inside he didn't need an introduction. Veren's smug smile and the murderous look from the woman facing her identified Boudicca. "Why are you in here? You refused to deal with Pendragon so you have no claim." She turned to Abel. "I'm told you have a seven-eighths claim, but you still have to make it stick. Pendragon Enterprises owes me for one apprentice, lost in combat while under loan. I want a quarter share or a senior apprentice and cash." Her face fell as more and more people followed Abel, then she recovered. "Is this all you have left, children?"

Abel hesitated, but Terese seemed more interested in showing paperwork to the woman at the desk. Ferryl said sorceresses did the threat thing before talking, though Veren hadn't. Abel tried to hit a balance, not too aggressive but no pushover. "These are all I thought I'd need. The rest are back in Stourton, sweeping up after Pendragon and your apprentice."

"There can't be many left if these are the best. Did you raid a fancy dress party because all your real apprentices died?" Boudicca pointed at Rachel. "How old is Red Riding Hood? She can't have been aware for long." One glance at Rachel's face and Abel got in before the fiery fourteen-year-old started a fight over her sorceress costume.

"Please be a little more polite. Depending on who your apprentice was, Rachel might be the one who burned him by locking shields." Abel was quite proud of that because it told the sorceress Rachel had a strong shield without claiming any particular level of skill. From the assessing look, it worked. "Pendragon attacked in the middle of our fancy dress party, but some of us had to change afterwards."

"Don't go by their ages, because all of them have shields. They let me check, outside." Veren's smug smile had grown to a wide grin. "You should ask who his bodyguard is." The sorceress pointed at Ferryl Shayde.

"Ferryl Shayde, sorceress and bodyguard to the master of Castle House, prime claimant to Pendragon Enterprises." Ferryl looked the sorceress up and down in a way that implied a sneer without altering her expression. "A real sorceress, not an apprentice who had a careless master and found herself free. I have never been tethered." Abel smiled to himself. Ferryl really seemed to have a knack for put-downs.

"Excuse me, are you the sorceress Boudicca, claiming a portion of Pendragon Enterprises on the grounds that you are owed for a lost apprentice?" All eyes turned to Terese Green.

"Yes. I want…"

Terese cut Boudicca off without even raising her voice. "Do you wish to pursue your claim by duel or will you accept the decision of the gryphon?"

"What? Duel?"

"An option laid down in magical law, though the method is rarely used. There is a duelling chamber in Sheffield. Each contestant brings whoever is currently accompanying them, or arranges a later date and brings reinforcements. There is the option of personal combat against the master's bodyguard, Ferryl Shayde?" Terese's smile could have cut steel. "To help you decide, I am willing to swear under oath that my client will bring forty apprentices who can wield wind adequately, thirty-two of whom are proficient with fire. Or you can fight now, at odds of almost three to one."

"Four to one." Veren might be smiling, but her voice snarled. Behind Boudicca her three apprentices looked decidedly nervous.

"I've never heard of this duelling chamber, and nobody is allowed to have that many apprentices. I'll settle now for a quarter, or the trees or the big house, or a senior apprentice and financial compensation. After all, nobody can be sure how the gryphon will decide." Boudicca looked rattled, but still seemed to think Abel would settle.

"True. Gryphons can be fickle, but possibly not this time." Terese Green turned to Abel. "If you would show the ring please?" He took it out and the blank face now showed an ornate medieval dragon's face with a large P on its forehead. "There wasn't much left of Pendragon, so this might have been just a ring and the talisman might have been lost." The barest flicker of Terese's smile drove it home better than a triumphant fist pump and a lap of honour. "The gryphon is unlikely to choose anyone but the bearer."

Boudicca's shoulders admitted defeat, or not quite. "What about my car? It doesn't belong to the apprentice."

"What was it?" Una wore a tiny smile and she'd put her hand on her sword hilt again.

"A Volvo. Did it survive?" Boudicca seemed to perk up a bit. Abel began to realise that he'd got the wrong impression of sorcerer wealth. Pendragon wasn't anything like as rich as Celtchar had been, and this woman had even less if she wanted to haggle over a car.

Before he could tell her to take the Volvo, Una answered. "Sorry, finders keepers. I claimed it as my part of the loot." She smiled happily and gestured at the others. "Most of these can't drive, so it was a no-brainer."

"Taken in battle is a legal claim, sorceress. Do you wish to contest it? If so, there is the question of your liability for damage to the house known as the Stourton Tavern." Now Terese Green looked downright predatory, poised to pounce. "Your apprentice contributed to the damage."

Boudicca looked from Abel to Ferryl to Terese to Una's smiling face, and didn't answer directly. "Come on, we're done here." Though as she passed Veren she added, "For now." Her apprentices didn't meet anyone's eyes, they seemed pleased to get out in one piece.

Abel watched the door close behind the last one and turned to Una. "Loot?"

"Robin D'Ritche, at your service." Una produced a big flamboyant bow, then sniggered. "Not the same without the hat but it wouldn't fit in the car. Hey, I just won a Volvo! If you let me keep it I can run people about without borrowing mum's car." Her face fell and she sighed, her shoulders slumping. "No I can't, because the insurance for a Volvo will be crippling. Tarnation and gadzooks. Robin Hood never had this trouble."

Abel laughed at her because just for a moment Una's usual good humour had surfaced, a relief after today. "You might not want it if the gryphon hands over the Merc or we have to blow the door off to get inside. What happens now, Terese?"

"You take that ring to the gryphon. Boudicca has just renounced her one-eighth claim so it should be a formality." As Terese answered, the woman behind the counter came out and opened a side door, obviously waiting for them to go through.

That came as a relief, though Abel wanted to clear one thing up because it bugged him. "Veren, how upset will Boudicca be about one car?"

"Very. We each kept our own cars of course, and we each took what we could before other sorcerers came to pillage our master's estate. Boudicca claimed the other cars, but she only has three left now. One of the other apprentices helped her take over our master's house once it had been stripped, but then she double-crossed him." Veren's smile seemed to be chiselled on, she'd loved every minute. "I only kept my own car but I reached the house before any sorcerers. There was only time to remove the easily portable treasures, but I filled my car. Boudicca has never forgiven me for what I got away with." The sorceress bowed slightly and swept an arm towards the waiting receptionist. "After you. I've never seen this done."

"Clean takeovers are the exception, but once the blood stops flowing it still comes down to the gryphon. Please follow me, Abel." He followed Terese, the receptionist and Veren, and Kelis because she insisted on going first. At the first chance, Rob got in front as well, they were all really protective today. The receptionist led them to an ornate door, carved with a huge representation of the crest on the ring. Terese stood to the side. "You must go in first, though I can follow and advise. Others can come in as well, to witness the claim." She opened the door and Abel went through.

"That's not a gryphon." Abel wasn't sure what it was except a very, very lifelike head. One without a body so it must be dead, or maybe just a block of wood covered in scales.

"No, that is a young dragon's head. There are several of all types and ages preserved here and there, though I haven't seen one used like this before." While Terese spoke everyone else filed in. "This room and gryphon must have originally belonged to a much more powerful sorcerer, presumably split between apprentices. Pendragon only seized a portion of the original estate, because this room is designed for witnessing a very substantial claim." The room held seating for about twenty, plush seating raised towards the rear so everyone would get a view. "Everyone please take a seat." Terese pointed to the huge head. "Approach it and claim it, Abel. Hold out the ring on your palm so the gryphon can see it."

Abel walked down the little strip of carpet with the ring on his palm, wondering how a dead dragon could see. The same as anyone else, a silly voice in his head pointed out when, about three steps away, the head opened eyes the size of a saucer, a sky blue saucer. "By blood and power, I claim it." Abel stopped right there, because it opened its jaws. Not far, just enough to show the tips of a lovely set of very sharp teeth. Moments later the tip of a pale purple tongue with violet and scarlet veins jutted out.

Abel stared at it. What did the thing want? Someone, probably Terese, cleared their throat and coughed, a stage cough. Right, blood and power, it needed blood and those teeth were fairly obvious. Abel reached out his hand, very slowly, to touch the tip of his index finger to a fang. "Good dragon." He really hoped nobody heard, but the thing scared him half to death. Blood welled and Abel let the drops fall on the tongue but it stayed put. Before he could think it through Abel dropped the ring in the blood.

"Welcome, master." A deep, mellow voice echoed in Abel's head a bit like Zephyr's did sometimes. The blood disappeared and left the ring pristine clean. Abel hesitated, then picked it up and slipped it on his pinkie finger. It felt a bit loose, then the metal band warmed a little and fitted perfectly. The dragon's tongue pulled back and it closed its mouth, though its eyes stayed open and fixed on Abel.

"Thank you, dragon." Abel raised his voice. "Is that it?"

"In the past there might have been a flowery speech or two but yes, that is it. Your receptionist will show you where to find out details of your inheritance." Abel turned and walked back towards the rest as Terese continued. "If you allow me access, I will give you an assessment. There will be the usual age problem regarding legal ownership, but magical law will allow you access to everything immediately." She paused while Abel was suddenly buried in congratulations and hugs.

"Shucks. My chance to get a house and I can't make nice." Kelis gave him a quick hug then cut Abel off as he opened his mouth. "A joke. Don't you dare give me a house so I have to move away from Brinsford."

"It might be really nice, with hot and cold running footstools and your own library?" Rob's running commentary on what there might be followed Abel to a small office.

As instructed Abel put his hand on a dragon carved into the front of a filing cabinet. After a couple of clunks it opened. "There you are, Terese. Knock yourself out. Though we've got to get home so don't get carried away." Terese didn't get carried away, just asked which files held the contracts and details of the properties. Abel drank coffee, provided by a secretary, who also fixed up drinks for everyone else. The magically aware man had a dragon's head hex on a chain around his neck but didn't know how to cast a glyph and didn't have a ward. Both the secretary and receptionist looked happier when Abel, prompted by Terese, confirmed he'd want them both to stay on. He was an employer! After promising to send someone to take charge sometime tomorrow, Abel followed Terese back to the cabs. Veren left him a phone number, asking Abel to call to discuss getting rid of the remnants of her tether.

*   *   *

On the way back to Stourton, Abel found out he now had two houses that he could access right away, and a flat above each of the two offices. Instead of a park, he had the rights to the tree magic in two whole housing estates of leafy streets. Two houses in one city seemed odd, but Terese guessed that one was for the apprentices. The three BMWs belonged to Pendragon, which probably meant the Mercedes belonged to another sorcerer's loaned apprentice. Abel let it wash over him, because he still had the same stupid problem. Whatever he'd won, inherited or whatever, he still couldn't buy his mum a really nice present or give her a BMW.

Kelis jerked him back to reality. "You were going to ask about the prisoner." Ferryl, Rob and Jenny were suddenly intent and Terese's eyes sharpened.

"What? Sorry, missed that." As Abel floundered, Kelis repeated herself.

Terese didn't flounder at all. "A live apprentice? Pendragon's?"

"Yes, Guinevere or Ginny. She wouldn't accept a tether from Creepio so now I've got to work out what to do with her." Abel sighed heavily, not looking at the rest because at least two of them wanted Ginny tethered or possibly bound.

"The usual alternatives are to kill or tether them. Some sorcerers bind strong captives for better control, or kill and bind sorcerers to get absolute obedience." Terese pursed her lips, thinking. "Woods explained your stance on binding, and you have captured her instead of killing her out of hand. That leaves tethering."

"Or setting her free if she pinkie-promises to be good. He's daft

351

enough." Kelis glowered at Abel. "This is the second time we've been attacked and captured her and I'm getting fed up with it."

"So you tether her!" Abel took a deep breath. "Sorry I snapped at you but what else is there?" He turned to Terese, knowing it was a long shot. "How about a contract, make her sign a non-aggression clause or something?"

"Even if she doesn't take another master to get his protection, this Ginny will have the same weakness as Verenestra. The first sorcerer to get the chance will tether her and then she isn't responsible for her actions. That or, being alone but skilled enough to shield, she will be killed as a possible rival or threat." Terese looked really puzzled, turning to the other four. "Tethering isn't close control, not if the sorcerer doesn't use it for more than communication. The tethered can't attack their master or mistress, and can be badly hurt if they try or their controller wishes it, but otherwise it is harmless."

"Seriously? Having someone in your head, moving you about like a meat puppet, is harmless? You didn't hear Justin and the others screaming." Jenny snorted. "You should see how Claris reacts to the idea, though her last one was a leech."

"Ginny wouldn't be a meat puppet, just obey instructions, though the threat of sanctions will ensure she doesn't disobey. Unless she has direct commands, your captive will have free will, and you can only know what she is thinking by deliberately activating the link. Would you want all the thoughts in eight or nine minds permanently cluttering up your head? An absolute command can immobilise her, for instance, but tell her to defend you or go on an errand and she will do so in her own way. When either of you shield, she will be completely free, except for long-term commands. If you release her, other sorcerers will consider it a sign of weakness, so tether her at least. That is my advice, as your solicitor of course." The solicitor turned back to the papers she'd brought from Pendragon's. "A senior apprentice would help you protect the weaker apprentices, especially any family members?" Terese started leafing through the documents while Abel grappled with the options.

"Whoa, hang on. I mean, wait a moment please, Terese. Protect family members? Are my sisters and parents in danger?" Rob had clenched his fist, his face pale and his other hand groping for the missing bat. "Will someone go after them?"

"Not unless they are magically active. A codicil added to the Accords by the Magical Council forbids attacks on a sorcerer's non-magical family members. The same applies to unwarded employees if they carry their employer's hex, which is why those two in Pendragon's office wear the dragon head necklaces. That actually makes them safer than most people, who can be targeted as long as there is no public display of magic." After a moment's thought Terese turned back to Abel. "There will be a copy of the Accord in your library, or I can supply one in modern English? It is relatively simple, one page of modern type which I suggest you memorise."

"Creepio is sending one but I'd rather have the modern English version. I'm going to put it on a wit." Kelis paused, then answered the inquisitive look from Terese. "Inscribe it on my bones?"

"You really do have a mismatched skill-set because I doubt any of Pendragon's apprentices could do that. We don't have a name for inscribed memory, because it is impossible to tell which is remembered by the brain and which is coming from the bone. I have complete legal libraries in my bones, but can't actually tell which part is genuine learning." The sorceress-solicitor had continued leafing through files even as she spoke. Now she explained that before the fight, Pendragon had four experienced and four newly-promoted senior apprentices, and two rank beginners barely capable of filling a hex. The missing Mr Paragon was one of the latter. Pendragon must have promoted and recruited on the basis of winning the fight, because the business didn't warrant more than four seniors and four hex fillers.

Abel called to offer Shawn the manager's job in Sheffield with a flat, car and a better salary than his current job. Once Shawn had checked out exactly what it entailed, and knew there were capable staff to help him, he gleefully accepted.

*   *   *

It came as a relief when Terese dropped them all off near the Stourton Refuge, next to the vehicles: three BMW cars, a Volvo estate and a Mercedes minibus. Una repeated her claim for the Volvo even though she knew it wouldn't work. A big almost-new estate like this one would cost a fortune to insure, especially for a teenager. Terese stayed while

Abel opened the three BMWs, just to check the gryphon's ring worked. "You have drivers, so I suggest you remove those three immediately. I will arrange a magical locksmith for the others."

"Not yet." Ferryl looked decidedly smug. "Zephyr will have a look at them first. She might be able to unravel the magic if they really are simple."

"Of course, and you can…" Terese caught herself before telling everyone Ferryl wasn't human. "I'll wait for a phone call." She turned to Abel, gesturing for him to walk with her towards her taxi. "Since nobody in our office observes Easter, we will have a proper report ready before start of business Tuesday. You may want to arrange for more of the work to be carried out at weekends when your assistants aren't at school."

"Great, and thank you. To be honest I won't remember most of what you've just told us, so being able to sit down in peace and quiet and read it will be a big help. It still isn't real, somehow." Abel looked back at his friends, playing with the BMW's electric windows, seat adjustments and music system. "I don't want to sound ungrateful, but I'm still stuck with a big problem. How do I help my mum, legally and without her finding out about the inheritance and magic? The others, Kelis, Rob and Jenny, have the same problem. I'm open to suggestions."

"I will bear it in mind, and ask a couple of our younger staff members to look at the problem. They have a more modern outlook. Once you have seen our report you can decide if you'll use gold, your income from rented properties, or Pendragon Enterprises to pay the medical and vehicle repair bills. Now I had better get back to my desk before Woods realises I'm not really necessary." From her smile that had to be some sort of joke. Terese turned away, then back, and the smile had gone. "Tether that woman or kill her, as soon as possible. She is an uncontrolled trainee sorceress of unknown power right inside your defences." With that, Terese Green boarded her taxi and left.

Abel turned back to watch the others play. "May I look at the hexes on the other two vehicles please, Abel."

"Yes, sorry Zephyr. You've been cooped up a lot since this morning."

"I needed some time in my tattoo. I feel more me now. Ferryl warned me to keep together so I don't split up and become many mindless wind spirits, but this morning I stretched very thin. I also split my thoughts to do many things at once, then worried about not getting me back together properly, and about you not being here if I did." As the sprite flew off towards the vehicle, Abel reflected that Zephyr seemed to be able to feel emotions. Maybe Ferryl just hadn't tried before?

He soon had other things to think about, because Eric came round to see if the cars were open. With a huge grin he accepted a set of keys and drove his prize back to Frederick's house. He would send Shawn to collect another BMW. That set Abel wondering about paying wages. Did he have access to Pendragon's bank account or did sorcerers keep a pile of sovereigns in a vault?

"We've been talking." From the set faces, it hadn't been about the BMW. "Jenny and I are both worried about our little sisters, so we want Diane and Melanie to tether Ginny." Rob looked as determined as he sounded, Jenny looked grim, while both Kelis and Ferryl were nodding agreement. "Then she can hear if they call for help, and be a bodyguard."

"If Zephyr tethers her as well she can let you know if there's a problem." Kelis glanced back to the shimmer hovering near the Volvo. "She can monitor the kids as well, make sure they don't play games with their new servant."

Abel thought fast because Rob and Jenny wouldn't take no for an answer. He couldn't actually stop them tethering Ginny if someone told them how, so they were being polite about it. It took a fairly heated discussion, but eventually Jenny and Rob accepted that as long as Ginny protected Melanie and Diane, she didn't have to take orders from them. Zephyr could give the tethered apprentice orders, and peek into her head now and then, though Zephyr insisted on not very often. "If Ferryl Shayde helps to craft the tether I will do it. I can adjust the tethers so Diane and Melanie cannot issue direct orders, but there will be a strong imperative to protect them and you."

Abel only had one reservation. "I've got two bodyguards already, possibly more going by today, so Ginny will protect anyone less adept."

Despite it being more or less what they'd wanted, Jenny and Rob kept asking questions as Una drove them round to Frederick's house in the last BMW. Una joined in, agreeing that Zephyr putting a tether on

Ginny would satisfy everyone. They'd all seen the ogre, and how much it frightened the captured woman.

Though oddly enough it wasn't being tethered to Zephyr that worried Ginny the most. "Tethered to two kids? Some sort of grown-up doll they can order about? Not a chance. Kids are cruel." Her eyes were on the shimmer hovering by Abel's shoulder. "I don't know exactly what that ogre is, but she let me surrender. Kids will have me doing all sorts of stupid or dangerous things and my healing charm is only good for superficial damage. You may as well kill me now."

"Healing charm?"

"But Diane and Melanie won't…" Abel tailed off as Kelis's exclamation registered. "What charm?"

Ginny looked really exasperated and scowled. "I'd hoped to use it to trade, get a better deal. Pendragon gave his senior apprentices two witch charms, one for healing and one to numb injuries. They aren't very strong but until I earn the glyph for healing myself it will help me survive. Do I still get to do that, earn more glyphs?"

"Yes, eventually, if you behave." Kelis waited for the apprentice's face to drop before finishing. "Eventually to Mr Softy here is nothing like as long as you'd wait under Pendragon, so your punishment is actually a win. We work on the basis that if you are adept at one glyph, you're ready for the next. At the very least you'll learn as fast as Melanie and Diane, and those are two very determined young ladies." Kelis's little smile looked downright mischievous. "Though you're lucky Abel's already got a girlfriend. He likes older women."

Abel saw the sudden alarm and remembered Effy's link to Pendragon. "That's Kelis's idea of a joke. My current girlfriend is plenty old enough for me, thanks." He smiled, hopefully reassuringly, and carried on before Kelis made a joke about Ferryl's age. "You really will learn glyphs when Melanie and Diane do, because you'll supervise their practice as much as possible. That means you stopping them or telling Zephyr if they get too ambitious. You couldn't do that on a normal tether, not if they ordered you not to." Abel did his best to explain exactly what he meant.

Eventually he ran down and Ginny looked around at the small group. "So I'm to be a part-time magical babysitter and bodyguard to a pair of fourteen-year-olds, tethered but only so they can shout for help or I can warn or protect them. I'm to be your chauffeur, and help out any other Taverner in trouble. The only one who'll give me orders down a tether is a being called Zephyr, who doesn't actually like being in my head so she won't be reading my thoughts very often. I get a car if I play taxi now and then, a home and some sort of wage, and extra magic to practice glyphs every time I fill up a few hexes." She burst into almost hysterical laughter as the eight heads now watching her all nodded. "That's a punishment? Oh Gods below I wish Denethor or Celeborn, or any of the other apprentices, could hear this. I left school at barely sixteen because I was already tethered and didn't need an education to learn magic." She broke into laughter again, a good part of it relief because she'd been sat for hours wondering if Abel would decide killing her was simpler. "I've spent the last twenty years as Pendragon's apprentice, living in a house with the others, taking shit from the seniors like Galadriel and Celeborn and filling hexes until I'd barely got the magic left to practice."

"I thought you were one of the senior apprentices?" Shawn wasn't the only one looking baffled. "Didn't you get a car and a big salary and all that?"

"Oh yes, but only so I could look good for the master. I've got a wardrobe full of expensive clothes, nice jewellery and shoes to die for. I had my hair and nails fixed in the best places, drove a swanky motor, and got to let my hair down in the nightclubs if the master hadn't got a job for me. That was after my promotion. Before that I had good clothes and jewellery and a decent salary but not much spare time. I spent my days going where the tether told me, when the tether said, filling hexes and being very careful what I said in case the tether was open." She waved her hands around, taking in all those watching her. "When you killed Elrond, all the glyph-fillers had to show the master how well they controlled air and fire. I won, so I got the promotion. Pendragon gave me Elrond's room, his car, two charms and taught me the water and shield glyphs. He promised me a healing glyph in ten years if I worked hard. I concentrated on the shield, so I've barely managed a bit of mist. Half of you were throwing ice, which is advanced water, heat and wind combined, and you're still at school! I want to hate you but I'm too damn jealous."

That sounded like a really complicated way to say yes, but Abel wanted to be sure. "So you don't mind the three tethers?"

Ginny undid a couple of buttons on her blouse, bared the top of her shoulder and smiled happily. "Bring it on." Her face fell just a little. "What about my clothes and stuff? Can I have some of it back? How many will be sharing out my wardrobe?"

"Our oldest female is nineteen so they probably won't want your clothes even if they fit. If you behave you'll eventually get your jewellery back." Because despite Una's attitude to loot, taking personal possessions seemed like stealing to Abel. He kept talking while Zephyr, coached by Ferryl through a ball of mist around her fist, extended a thicker version of spooky-phone.

"I will remove the rest of Pendragon's tether. Ferryl thinks anyone tethering the two escaped apprentices might learn how to break it, so we don't want it included. While working out how to break tethers we created a way to stop anyone else trying. I will add something that will bite back if interfered with." While Zephyr worked, Abel talked about where Ginny would live, in Frederick's house for now, and her wages. Ginny told him she'd earned thirty thousand a year, though she accepted she'd get less now. The thirty-six-year-old kept breaking into giggles or laughter when discussing her conditions. If she wasn't a magic user, Abel would have suspected drugs or booze. "She is telling the truth. The tether is in so I know. Ask her if she would prefer to be asleep while we put in her imperatives. I would like to come back home first? To be just me."

"Come home Zephyr, and take a break." During the break Abel took the two charms to Kelis, to stop her pestering for them. When he came back Abel asked if Ginny wanted to be asleep when Zephyr put in her imperatives, the ones that made her protect the kids and not harm them or Abel.

"I barely felt the tether going in. Maybe it was the imperatives, the instructions not to kill Pendragon, that hurt? Just in case, I'd rather sleep through that." Ginny looked down at her shoulder, obviously relieved. "Will the other two be as gentle?"

"We will instruct them. They will only do what we tell them, so there should be no pain." Ferryl leant forward and tapped her. "Sleep." As Ginny slumped, Ferryl looked uncertain. "I'll need a little time with

Zephyr to work this out, because neither of us have crafted an instruction like this down a tether. Judging the strength of the imperative isn't easy. Too much emphasis on protection and she won't let Diane or Melanie use a knife to cut food."

Knowing how little Ferryl cared about most people, Abel worried about exactly what the imperative might say. "Don't make her kill herself like some sort of kamikaze, Zephyr."

"A dead guard would be no good to Diane or Melanie." Though Zephyr would strengthen the order just a little. This one had attacked the Tavern, so now she would die if that was the only way to keep Melanie and Diane alive. Zephyr worried that Ferryl might tell Abel about the alteration, but she kept quiet so maybe Ferryl Shayde felt the same. Neither of them were sure how sorcerers did this but Zephyr agreed to dip in and out of Ginny's mind, with Ferryl coaching her. The tether allowed her to bypass every natural or magical defence the apprentice had. Eventually the imperatives were set, down below conscious thought, and the two tethers were ready. All they needed was for Diane and Melanie to connect their magic to the right spot on Ginny, briefly, to seal the connection. Meanwhile all the Taverners had copied the two charms, simple glyphs, and those with wounds used them. Both worked with just a trickle of magic. The soothing one worked immediately, but the healing charm must be slower.

By the time Zephyr and Ferryl were satisfied, Frederick called upstairs to say the hired minibus had arrived. After confirming it was insured for any driver, Frederick accepted it, so Abel, Jenny, Kelis, Ferryl and Rob could finally go home. Zephyr confirmed that with more time she could unpick the protection on the other two vehicles, so Eric promised the Taverners would keep them safe. They left Ginny answering questions about life as an apprentice, and the sort of places she went for Pendragon. The trip back seemed fairly quiet, with nobody speaking much except Una. She still kept hoping she could work out how to insure the Volvo.

Jenny's parting shot told Abel why she'd been quiet. "I've been mulling it over and we should stop worrying about business, both lots. The employees or Taverners can keep Pendragon Enterprises going, the income will help fix Stourton Tavern Refuge, and Terese reckons nobody else dare bother us for a while. The rest of the Taverners have a sort of system, to help newcomers get through the first few weeks, so they don't need us for that. The better ones teach basic glyphs, make hexes and help to rid houses of thornies, slimies, gremlins and hoplins, that sort of thing. We'll be having a meeting in a couple of days to finalise the rules, but then nobody really needs us except for extra magic. I'm going to forget the businesses and concentrate on school until after the exams." She giggled briefly. "Unless you go to visit all those trees in Sheffield?"

* * *

Abel wasn't looking forward to his mum's reaction, while Jenny really did think her dad might lock her up for a month or two. At least a combination of magical medics, new jeans and long sleeves had reduced or covered the worst of the cuts and burns. The accident and fire story would explain his reddened skin. One of the Taverners had even trimmed Abel's, Rob's and Kelis's hair a little to hide most of the charring. Luckily Kelis had plenty of hair to rearrange, while Rob's and Abel's hair rarely looked tidy. Jenny's hair had escaped, probably because Pendragon had concentrated on the stronger casters or maybe just luck. Her leg certainly hadn't escaped, but hopefully her jeans would hide all the little holes until they healed.

When Una parked up and headed for her mum's car, Abel fully intended heading for home. Instead, Ferryl pulled him inside the rear of the shop, waiting as Kelis went upstairs. Before he could ask, she wrapped both arms around him and held really tight, tight enough for him to feel her trembling. "What's the matter?"

"I nearly lost you. My first friend and I nearly lost you. I promised to protect you but I knew you wanted the others rescued. I thought you could hold out while I did that." Ferryl sounded close to tears, but didn't look up so he couldn't be sure.

Abel wriggled his trapped arm free and put it round her, stroking her back. "But you did. You clobbered the other apprentices and came back to chase off Pendragon." Abel chuckled at a memory. "Or to discuss the tether, I think you said."

"You were lucky, I was lucky. I thought there'd be three or four apprentices, at least two of them in the lounge with the Taverners. When I punched him, I hoped Pendragon's shield would drop and we could finish him there and then." Abel heard a little catch in Ferryl's voice, almost a sob. "It didn't work, it hurt too much for me to cast another glyph straight away. Pendragon called for help on the tether so then I had to stop the others coming out to join the fight."

"Punched his shield? Is that why your arm burst into flame?" Abel pulled one arm from around him to inspect her hand. "Not a mark."

Her hand promptly went back around him and hugged tight, but at least Ferryl's voice firmed up while she explained. "I told you, a close-held shield lets physical shock and heat reach the skin. I couldn't heal fast enough to follow up immediately. Once I got inside there were gunmen and more and more apprentices." Abel felt a long juddering sigh. "The last two were almost too much, because most of the apprentices were wearing gold armbands full of magic. Their shields were holding and most of my diamonds were empty, but then Zephyr popped up out of the floor and hit one from behind. I must make more diamonds for my bones."

"So you had enough. It still worked, and how else could we have done it?" Abel kept up the holding and stroking, because Ferryl's arms hadn't eased off.

"Zephyr should have stayed, and I should have stayed so we could stop Pendragon first. But that would have taken too long." This sigh was followed by a shaky laugh and her hands stroked Abel's back before tightening again. "Who would have expected Claris to start shooting and Shannon to use the minibus? Without them you would have been dead. Dead! When I promised. I might never have found another friend." Again Abel thought Ferryl sounded close to tears.

"Calm down. It all worked out and we might have made it anyway." Though Abel had to accept, privately, it was unlikely. Despite four of them throwing glyphs, they'd never even looked like getting through the sorcerer's shield. They'd have all run out of magic and Pendragon would have tried to force a tether. "You taught us well, especially how to shield. Though I give that goblin a lot of credit, it did more damage than any of us. I thought goblins never fought sorcerers?"

The little laugh sounded as if Ferryl was recovering. Her grip slackened, altering a little as she cuddled in rather than trying to crush Abel's ribs. "Another arrogant sorcerer mistake. The other goblins told me Pendragon made jokes about throwing a party, an old-style one with green fireworks. Otherwise I don't think even an Old would have risked attacking."

"That was an Old?" Abel hadn't had time to get a really good look.

"Yes. Not ready for the flame, not yet, but near enough to be willing to go early and old enough to be sneaky. According to the rest it squished down and disguised itself as a paving slab so Pendragon didn't realise a goblin had stayed in the front garden. It meant to warn you, but didn't have time. Dryads, goblins, and the church, you had some very strange help today." Ferryl finally let go, but only so she could push Abel towards her room. "Come and sit with me, please. Hold me for a while?"

"Not in your room, you know the rules."

"No mum so no rules, but we'll leave the door ajar if you want." Ferryl's arms tightened again. "I nearly lost a friend today. Maybe many friends, I realised." She pushed again and Abel went in. By the time Abel left and made his way home he was absolutely certain Ferryl had discovered emotions, and friends. Unfortunately, now she had friends, the ancient sorceress seemed terrified of losing them. He'd had to persuade her to let him walk home alone, and it was a stone certainty Ferryl hadn't introduced herself as his bodyguard on a whim. Though if he had to have a guardian, at least she was a very pretty one.

Abel barely opened the front door before he heard his mum's voice. "Rob went past here half an hour ago, and he's got plasters on his face. Where have you been and how bad was that accident? You said it wasn't much, but you didn't send any pictures of the minibus."

"Hi mum. My girlfriend was upset, so I stayed to calm her down." Abel closed the front door, hid his smile and headed towards mum and his roasting. He'd get the seventh degree, then a good telling off, then she'd tweak him about calming girlfriends. After today a good telling off would be a relief and absolutely, wonderfully normal. So would the rest of the school year because Jenny was right, there'd be plenty of time for magic after the exams.

Ferryl Shayde IV

Storm and Steel

is being written even as you read.

Abel's World

Brinsford - A small village in rural England, eight miles from Stourton

Consists of:

Main Street - With pub and small shop

Brinn Lane - Off village green, leads to a small bridge then up valley to local farms

Riverside Close - A dozen council houses

Castle Road - Road from village to main road half a mile away

Residents:

Abel Bernard Conroy - 16 - Lives with Mum, Dad died - accident at sea

Christine Conroy - Chris - 42 - Abel's widowed Mum, has part-time job

John Tyler - Rob's Dad

Terri Tyler - Rob's Mum

Rob Tyler - 16 - Abel's best friend

Melanie Tyler - 14 - Rob's sister

Samantha Tyler - 19 - Rob's sister

Jessica Ventner - Kelis's Mum, skint after recent divorce from abusive husband

Kelis Ventner - 16 - Abel's best (only) female friend

Stan - Local pensioner and reputedly poacher - has a shotgun and an old Jack Russell called Bugsy

Mr. Copples - Local farmer

Henry Copples - 17 - Local bully

Tyson Copples - 19 - Henry's brother - bully with crossbreed dog Cooch (Cuchelain)

Mrs. Turner - Local busybody

Stourton - Town eight miles from Brinsford

Briarley - Village six miles from Brinsford, seven from Stourton - home to Petra - active church

Kielby - Village seven miles from Brinsford, nine from Stourton - home of Jenny and Diane

Stourton Comprehensive - Local secondary school

School year groups: 11 = GCSE year, 13 = A-Level year

Mr. Gordon - Headmaster

Mrs. Poole - Deputy Head

Mr. Sanders - Graphic Art master

Mr. Beresford - Sports master

Mrs. Svengy - Biology teacher

Jenny Georgina Forester - 17 - Acro dancer for school team year 12

Diane Forester - 15 - Jenny's sister - year 10

Claris Ellsworth - 18 - Bubbly redhead Acro dancer, dates rugby players - retaking year 13

Petra - 17 - Game beta with cat-sorceress costume lives nearby in Briarley - year 13

Warren - 16 - Game beta in town - year 12

Una - 17 - Game beta in town with Robin D'Ritche costume incl. sword - year 13

Sarah Russel - 17 - Game beta in town - year 12

Justin - 16 - Game beta in town - year 12

Rachel - 14 - Justin's sister - year 10

Fay Shayde - 16 - New pupil - year 12

Kathy 16 - New player - not aware of magic - year 12

Tobias - 17 - Pupil who keeps teasing Abel about the benefits of country living - year 13

Carl - 13 - Pupil year 9 - new magic user

Natalie - 14 - Pupil year 9 - new magic user

Others:

Jake Forester - Jenny's dad, a local builder and businessman.

Stephanie Forester - Jenny's mum

Laurence Horatio Sperrick - 18 - Kelis's ex-boyfriend - minor nobility but not wealthy

Eric - 21 - Warren's big brother

Shannon - 17 - Game beta - St. Agatha's church school - carries a cross - year 13

Shawn - 19 - Friend of a friend of a beta

Mark - 19 - Neighbour of Petra's, game beta & devout catholic.

Frederick - 53 - Adult who sees magical creatures - befriended a dryad - lives near Elmwood Park in Stourton

Effy - 27 - Sees creatures, thought they were ghosts - Shawn brought her to the Tavern

Amanda - 17 - Found seeded in leech lair

Cecilia - 17 - Found seeded in leech lair

Vicar Creepio Mysterio - Kelis's name for a peripatetic archbishop interested in Castle House

Pendragon - Local sorcerer who has a monopoly on magical contracts in Stourton.

Elrond - 41 - A senior apprentice to Pendragon - hosted blood leech, killed defending Firstseed

Father Curtis - Priest hosting a leech (Thirteenseed)

Celtchar - Name used by the sorcerer owning Castle House

Redwolf - Sorcerer who has a house in Stourton

Mannan - Redwolf's senior apprentice

Terese Green - Powerful sorceress - junior (and only other) partner in Woods and Green solicitors

Celeborn, Denethor, and Galadriel - Pendragon's senior apprentices

Gawain and Paragon - Pendragon's newest apprentices

Guinevere - Ginny - 36 - Apprentice to Pendragon, recently promoted to senior

Verenestra aka Veren - A new sorceress (ex-apprentice whose sorcerer has been killed)

Boudicca - A new sorceress (ex-apprentice whose sorcerer has been killed) in Sheffield

Seraph Angelique Bellamy-Courts - 18 - Wealthy young woman who manipulated the rich, influential, athletic and good-looking until stopped by Ferryl Shayde - now left school

Kieran - 16 - First Taverner outside local area - in Hope Valley in the Pennines - year 12

Emst - 19 - Laurence's German cousin

*   *   *

Magical Entities:

Ferryl Shayde - Faded but powerful sorceress, species unknown, a shimmer in the air unless possessing a living creature

Zephyr - Created living magical creature - a wind spirit created, enhanced, strengthened and taught to have both awareness and a sense of right and wrong - lives in Abel's tattoo to replace Ferryl Shayde

Fourthseed - Senior blood leech possessing an apparently young woman

Dryad Chestnut - Strong, ancient dryad living in Horse Chestnut tree on village green in Brinsford

Dryad Sycamore - A mere two hundred years old, rescued when its tree blew over in a storm - now a stone glyph allows it to be the only dryad in Dead Wood, the magically protected woodland behind Castle House gardens

Dryad Elm - Lonely old dryad, the only one living in Elmwood Park - lives in a Horse Chestnut, the only adult tree left in the park, because all the Elms were killed by Dutch Elm Disease - has befriended a human, most unusual

Churchyard dryad - Lives in a very old Yew tree that predates the church in Brinsford

Dryad Woods - Very old dryad in a large bonsai - senior partner in a solicitors firm, Woods and Green

Magical Council - A group of powerful sorcerers and sorceresses who enforce the Accord and attempt to regulate the sorcery community

Ferryl's World

Magic - A power that permeates the air, but cannot be utilised in its raw form. All living creatures absorb magic but plants are unable to dissipate it. Trees are the greatest natural reservoirs of magic, if old enough. Animals from insects to elephants will dissipate any surplus in an uncontrolled fashion, unless they are sentient and learn to utilise glyphs and store more.

Glyphs - Patterns drawn or etched on solid objects or in air or water, used to control magic and give it specific purpose. The strength of a scribed glyph depends on the magic put into it, and the medium it is drawn on. Glyphs inscribed in metal are the strongest, scribed in air the weakest. Effect of a glyph depends on amount of magic, skill, and intent behind it. The four basic glyphs are air, fire, water and earth. Combined with each other and shaped by intent, they create glyphs of increasing complexity, until almost anything can be accomplished. Conversely, a slight mistake can be catastrophic or fatal.

Veil - A concealment glyph that can be anchored to an object or a person. The amount of concealment depends on the intent and magic poured into it.

Spun slowly anti-clockwise, a veil obscures living beings from non-magical sight, though the magically aware can still see through it and will detect the veil itself as a shimmer in the air. Spun faster, it conceals plants, faster still, dead plants such as wood. The same speed will conceal an object such as a car if the glyph is drawn directly onto it. Spun at very high speed, the glyph uses impractically huge amounts of magic but can conceal anything, including even its own shimmer, from magic users. Beings made of almost pure magic can still detect the intense magical activity, but not the veil or what is concealed.

Another identical glyph spun clockwise at the same time extends the size of the concealment globe, faster making it larger.

Shield - A glyph that increases the natural protection covering the skin of all warded magic users. Heat or physical trauma can be felt through the shield while it is next to the skin, though the effect is reduced. The amount of magic used strengthens the shield, and it can by pushed out to cover others and nearby objects. Two shields touching causes both to drain magic from their users, with a spectacular light and heat display.

As a side effect, a shield cuts all tethers, spooky-phones, telephone or radio communications. Bindings will hold and shades can be controlled through a shield, but the protection must be dropped to allow them in or out.

A part of the shield away from a threat can be collapsed in beneath the skin, to allow communication down tethers or to free a phone.

* * *

Gods - Possibly originally sorcerers who have learned how to draw magic from worshippers using a symbol or mark. Their power grows with the number of prayers, but old gods act quickly to crush young ones. Gods fade away as worshippers decrease but are eternal as long as one worshipper still lives. Legend claims that the glyphs were stolen from the first God.

Sorcerer or Sorceress - Advanced glyph wielder who has learned how to prolong his or her life with magic. Even after learning the secret, it takes many years to understand their body well enough to heal any injury or illness. They are usually wealthy, live in a well-guarded home and keep a wide area clear of any large or particularly dangerous entities.

Apprentice - Magically aware teenager (the usual age for awakening) who accepts a tether from a sorcerer in return for training in magic. Apprentices are used to fill protection glyphs for their mistress's customers, using most of their naturally absorbed magic each day. The amount of magic they are allowed to keep for practicing, and the speed they learn new glyphs, varies from sorcerer to sorceress. Some apprentices may serve fifty or sixty years before being given the healing glyph, for instance, while others are never taught it.

Once established, the tether allows the sorcerer to read their apprentice's current thoughts (but not memories), drain magic from them, and control their actions. With concentration the sorceress can treat an apprentice as a puppet, but this is hard work so most are left to carry out their orders without direct control. The tether includes imperatives that prevent any attempt to harm or betray the sorcerer, and can inflict excruciating pain.

Witch or Warlock - Minor magic practitioner unable to progress beyond wind and fire to complicated sorcerous glyphs. Sells charms and hexes, and removes or creates minor curses. They have a long but normal lifespan, usually training a replacement who will also support them in old age. The profession is dying out in the countryside and smaller towns due to the current disbelief in magic and magical creatures. There are few paying customers to provide a living so youngsters prefer to take up other jobs.

Bound Servant - A being branded with a mark allowing a glyph wielder to control it completely. Will ignore pain or injury, hard to kill because partly protected by brand.

Tethered Servant - A person or creature controlled with a less complicated version of the apprentice tether. They are not taught, nor rewarded, and are never released.

Creatures Visible to the Non-Magical

Dryad - Creature that lives in trees, utilising the accumulated tree-magic to protect its home tree and prolong both their lives. Gnarled, bad-tempered, rude creatures, they can manipulate magic to create a veil to hide or to change their appearance. Will sometimes give answers to questions in return for honey.

Stout woody torso, no neck, eyes large, round and are different shades depending on tree. Chestnuts are chestnut brown, of course. Torso matches bark of tree. Legs are short, stout, no knees and end in roots that often embed in ground to help dryad stand. Arms are thin branches with long twigs as fingers, no foliage.

Can work simple glyphs using tree magic, protect tree against magic, slow rot and disease, and control tree enough to drop branches on attackers, strangle small creatures with roots or hit them with branches. Full control of the roots and branches takes many, many years of practice.

Asexual, though they can produce very realistic facsimile human features to lure humans close enough to steal a little magic. Dryads occasionally ripen young, but not often because there are few unclaimed trees. The young are given a basic knowledge of the world, the glyphs dryads can work, and how to control a tree. Blend into a young tree as seedlings and grow together, very vulnerable until the young tree matures and accumulates surplus magic.

Blood leech - Old blood magic remnant that survives by possessing a human and feeding on fresh blood and the magic therein. Spread when a single leech infects healthy humans with seeds, which grow to create a nest of leeches. The originating leech, known as the Firstseed, dominates and is protected by the others. Leeches are connected both by sensing each other's presence and an affinity for the lair, the home of the Firstseed.

Adult leeches prefer pale skinned hosts to shed excess heat. Wear dark glasses because their eyes show red around the pupils. Most find a willing victim, usually demanding a fixed period of possession (forty years) for the curing of an otherwise fatal illness. Once vacated, the discarded host should be left young and healthy but with no memory of the intervening years. If the leech has kept the bargain they will then live out their lives normally.

Not all leeches keep the bargain, some leaving the host barely alive and often infected with a seed. These also leave the host with full memories of forty years spent hunting humans and draining blood. The host may survive but memories may drive them insane. If a seeded host finds enough fresh blood, another blood leech is created. Even if the host finds a priest or sorcerer fast enough, the seed will try to poison them as it dies.

Goblins - Visible to the non-magical because they eat large amounts of non-magical food. Goblins eat almost anything humans or animals do but prefer junk food (or fruit cake) to raw meat. Raid rubbish bins, cat and dog dishes and bird tables but also eat magical creatures and small animals and birds.

Hunted almost to extinction for two main reasons. Firstly, gastric juices and wind are very flammable, making them a severe fire hazard. Goblins sleeping near open fires could explode and set fire to the house if they passed wind. Sorcerers still believe a goblin with indigestion started the Great Fire of London. Considered vermin. Some sorcerers used captive goblins as entertainment at feasts. Guests would shoot burning arrows at tethered goblins, or heat them slowly until they exploded.

Periodic attempts to wipe them out failed because they breed fast. Goblins reach plague proportions as their melds (clan, family) keep expanding. Even goblins have no way to limit their numbers, except suicide. Periodic hunts scoured the countryside, but one survivor is enough to regrow the meld. Although goblins helped to keep rats in check, the fire hazard outweighed their benefits. A goblin infestation sweeping down from the north of England and wiping out the flea carriers might be why the Black Death petered out in the Midlands.

Goblins are dark emerald green, potbellied munchkins, vaguely humanoid. Two short skinny legs with fat feet and five fat flat grasping claws—can be used for perching. Two long skinny arms end in small palms with four long knobbly clawed fingers and a very fat, short thumb. Wide mouth, lots of tiny teeth, looong thin tongue and huge appetite. Round, dark green eyes, no apparent ears or nose.

Goblins live in melds (like a clan). Old goblins are called Olds. Skin crumbles as they get older until internal gases and juices mix with their magic, erupting in a small explosion. Olds may look for the flame (suicide) if there is a food shortage. When an Old looks close to exploding, keeps away from other goblins to avoid killing them.

Batlins - Smallest goblin, body the size of a thrush. Like other goblins except for large bat-like wings. Live in caves, barns and attics, very much like bats and usually fly at night to avoid notice.

Ratlins - Size of a large rat, not as rotund as other goblins, live in burrows and often steal flower bulbs or gnaw roots on living bushes and unprotected trees.

Stonelins - About metre tall. Disguise themselves with a seeming, looking like gargoyles or grotesque garden statues and ornaments.

Hobgoblins - Bigger, tougher and scarier and were used by some sorcerers as guards. Lived in wild places and deep caves, but are now allegedly extinct.

Troll: Several types, all allegedly destroyed by the church or sorcerers.

Cave Trolls still exist, hiding deep in the earth. An adult looks like a crusty slug with a pointed head and is the size of an articulated truck. Little magic outside of an affinity for compressing and strengthening earth and rock around tunnels. Trolls accrete rock and earth as they grow, bonding it into their skins as armour. Most glyphs bounce off an adult or only damage the crust. New-formed trolls are about a metre tall, looking like a fat half-worm on end but twisted like a swirl of cream or soft ice-cream (or a dog poop).

Swamp Trolls, Water (Bridge) Trolls and Ice Trolls are probably extinct, as they were more visible and killed on sight.

Varglin - The lesser descendants of what were called vargs, the children of the Norse wolf-god Fenris. Almost a large wolf but sickly green mossy fur with longer fangs and claws and a ruff of orange porcupine quills. Usually inhabit thick woodlands and prey on lesser magical beings or weak animals.

Amanatik - A spined, eight-legged turtle with a metre-long shell. The hunting hounds of the South American creator goddess Amana, who rode a turtle and had a mermaid's tail. Amanatik have huge heads sporting four long spiral tusks. Allegedly came from South America on Spanish treasure ships. Prefer seashores, where they wait for their goddess to return.

Fraggon - Long, frilled, many-legged dragon with a frog-like head, looks like a stone guardian. When it moves, the creature is living stone, both more agile and more intelligent than a guardian. Possibly a creature, possibly an advanced magical creation.

*   *   *

The following are invisible, unless the human is awakened to magic. Those with enhanced magical sight can see the glow of magic inside each one, the life-spark.

Free Spirit - Semi-sentient fragment of a force of nature that has absorbed a fraction of the life from a dying entity. A ripple in the water, a flame or a puff of wind can become alive though not really thinking, and will persist if it finds enough life magic to feed on. The amoeba of the magical world, hunted by a myriad of tiny creatures. Wind sprites are almost invisible, even with magical sight.

Feral Spirit - A free spirit that survives long enough to understand hunger, and seek out the stray magic leaking from non-magical beings. Any who survive long enough, the rarest of feral spirits, learn to deliberately take magic from fish eggs, tiny insects and free spirits. Feral spirits that survive for centuries learn how to drain the magic from larger animals and magical creatures. Although still very simple creatures, the strongest can kill animals the size of humans. Even those vanishingly rare examples are still ephemeral in nature, a cloud of magic with few defences, so any magic user or large predatory magical creature can drain them.

The final form, so rare it doesn't have a name, is when a feral spirit becomes truly sentient. If it learns to possess flesh creatures it becomes harder to find and much harder to kill, and may learn enough magic to be truly dangerous. The church in particular will use all their resources to hunt down any such creature once they learn of it.

Beinsnork - Old Norse for Bonesnake - metre-long yellow snake with tiny pincered legs, covered in short, sharp triangular blades of bone. Allegedly the creations of the world-snake, if it bleeds on the bones in a graveyard.

Satan-Steed - A white lizard two metres long with red horns, and jaws like a coachman beetle, usually found in bogs or where old bogs dried up. They are allegedly inhabited by the spirits of those buried alive in ancient rites. Six of these allegedly pull the Devil's coach, or in some mythologies they are the mounts of the Four Horsemen.

Ganshbaal - Glittering black nightmare scorpion rats - the survivors of the rats that bore the Indian elephant-god Ganesh in his final battle before fading from the world. During that battle, rage and magic transformed them into vicious poisonous combatants.

Wealth Toad - Sometimes called a luck toad. A fist-sized furred three-legged toadish thing with three straight, sharp horns. Not usually belligerent. Will sometimes use a simple seeming to live in homes as a small statuette where it absorbs stray magic from residents. Name originally comes from an affinity to gold.

Ruttlyte - Like a ratlin but grey and veined with virulent blue and purple. Originally a failed attempt at killing and binding ratlins. Secretive, and like ratlins, they prefer flight to fight.

Catspaw - Hand-sized beetle with cat's paws and claws and a single sharp spine down its back. Often used by ancient sorcerers as a bound servant, sacrificed to obtain information or simply for amusement.

Skurrit - Pack hunter. Long thin low-slung metre-long body with a variable number of short legs and clawed feet, all covered with long, matted dirty brown fur. Has a light brown bald tail and a nearly bald head each about 40 cm long. Tiny red eyes in a small skull with a long thin pointed snout, containing several rows of sharp teeth. One alone will probably run from a cat, two or more might hunt it.

Globhoblin - Warty, globular creature up to the size of a football with a variable number of legs ending in clawed feet. Will eat the magic from bacteria, maggots and flies on discarded food but prefers to prey on the helpless, like kittens, hamsters, caged birds, chicks and baby animals, as well as small, slow wildlife and magical creatures. Will also prey on drunks or the ill, using a stinger to draw magic directly. Easily killed by weak glyphs or banished by hexes.

Fursomnium - Dream stealer or eater. Spreads webs through bedroom walls to feed on the emotional magic given off by dreamers. Can sometimes follow a dream back to the sleeper, inducing nightmares to increase the emotions and therefore the magic. A dream shield, often known as a dreamcatcher, can thwart it using glyphs powered by the magic in the gems. If a fursomnium eats well, for instance if someone nearby goes insane, it can sleep for many tens of years. The ambience and rumours of ghosts in old asylums is often due to the presence of a huge, well-fed fursomnium.

Gremlin - Tiny creature whose skin and carapace look somewhat like a toothless old man in overalls. Live inside any type of machinery or electrical equipment, often cause malfunctions. Angry or frustrated humans touch the object, and the gremlin can feed from the leaking magic.

Thornie - Prickly creature the size of a mouse, vaguely humanoid, prefers magic from fruit but will graze from most human food. Infests canteens and rubbish dumps to drain magic from bacteria, flies and maggots.

Hoplin - Little predatory creatures looking like a miniature armadillo hopping like a kangaroo, with a mildly venomous bite. Hunt in pairs that can drain the magic (and life) from small magical creatures such as thornies, rats, mice, caged birds or a kitten. Useful for dealing with infestations of rats and mice, but will also eat your pictsies, pixies and brownies.

Faerie - Rough-skinned flying creatures in shades and patterns of brown, with long, thin horny wings and a variety of limbs. Absorb magic from grass, leaves, flowers or fruit. Eat a little to help remain solid, which leaves tiny blemishes. Too many can drain the magic, leaving the plant sickly or dying. Can kill grass or leaves, or rot fruit. The brightly coloured faerie that preferred blossoms, those giving rise to legends of fairies, were too visible and were hunted to extinction.

Fae - Faerie-like but leaner, predatory and larger. Some hunt faeries or small insects and are harmless to humans. Others take small amounts of magic from humans and animals, using stingers that can leave itchy marks and be dangerous in numbers. The natural magical food supply for larger versions is sucked like mosquitoes from grazers, animal or magical.

Pictsies - Extravagantly jawed tiny predators that often live with humans and their pets where they hunt faerie, fae, lice, flies, insects and spiders.

Pixies - Live with humans. Absorb the magic leaking from the residents of 'their' house or left on clothes, removing dandruff and loose hair to store a surplus.

Piskies - Live in gardens, stock pens, or in the wild, preying on the pests infesting animals. Are useful for dealing with ticks or fae. May cause unexplained accidents if trapped in a house.

Brownies - Good ones are fanatically tidy. Live with humans if possible and tidy up dust, cobwebs, dirt on clothes or pet hair for the traces of magic clinging to them. Will leave if humans are either too tidy so there is no food, or too scruffy. If trapped in a house where they can't find a small private place, will actually create a mess.

Grelf - Magical eel, fresh-water carrion eater covered in small spines. They are hatched in the bloated carcase of a drowned animal, gorging on the rotten meat, the carrion eaters from bacteria upwards and each other to gain strength and become solid enough to survive. Are rare now that waterways are being cleaned up.

Grazers - Non-flying creatures ranging up to the size of a bison, which feed on the magic in grass, weeds, shrubs and crops. Usually found in farmland, where an infestation may kill or stunt crops.

Slimies - These have a variety of names, none complimentary because they look like dull greenish slugs with brown scaly patches. Very slow, so tend to settle on stains or other food sources unlikely to move. Absorb the stain as well as the bacteria, were useful when stains were difficult to remove, less so with the advent of washing powder and bleach.

A profusion of small creatures exist, grazing or hunting the magic in anything from bacteria, moss and grass through fleas up to rabbits or small dogs. Those targeting spoiled food are actually after the microscopic amounts of magic in either fungi or germs, with any insects a bonus. Creatures also hunt each other. Cats and dogs can see them but not clearly, just enough to avoid them or fight back. Some are beneficial, but if aware, humans prefer to stop most from fluttering, crawling, hopping or slithering into their homes.

Allegedly Extinct Creatures

Kalkatrie - Once used as a tracker by the Greek gods. Short flat pointed beak with teeth, large eyes, ruff of tiny feathers, two small chicken-like legs with clawed feet, stubby wings and a long, scaled tail with a sting that causes sleep. Usually slither but can fly or run short distances. Live in tunnels. The cockatrice legends are probably based on glimpses of kalkatrie.

Skoffin - Icelandic creature. Breathes fire and turns prey to stone, or charcoal if hunting for food. Probably the source of both the Gorgon myth and sightings of basilisk. There are some accounts that claim a skoffin can turn a victim to living stone. Natural enemies of ogres.

Dragon - Many types, now all hunted and killed. Magically preserved trophies are still displayed by some people.

Aryadne's Hound - Man/spider hybrid created by Goddess Aryadne to serve her. Live in caves, eat carrion, four spider legs at the rear and four spider-like arms on humanoid torso, well over two metres tall. Allegedly died out when Aryadne faded.

The Last Paladin - Mythical figure, the first recorded sightings are three thousand years old. Originally on foot, then a mounted figure, latterly the horse and rider wear battered crusader armour. The Wanderer, now known as The Last Paladin, roams the earth looking for redemption and may appear if your cause is hopeless but just.

Ogre - Six metres tall by three wide with a tail and tall forked horns making them look even bigger. Four thick limbs with vicious talons, and burning green eyes. Descriptions can vary since few survive an encounter. Ogres only exist as bound shades, used as attack beasts as they fixate on any perceived threat. Their square scales can be mistaken for giant's armour.

Gryphon - Sometimes called a Griffin. Half eagle, half lion, traditionally entrusted with the treasures of kings and sorcerers. Actual creature is extinct, but the object magically bonding a sorcerer to his holdings is traditionally referred to as their gryphon. A small facsimile protects all significant locations.

Created Entities

Stone Guardian - Very hard to kill without magic. Usually a statue, the construct is charged with magic and set to guard. Once triggered, the magic will animate the stone regardless of any weathering or damage. The animating glyph is carved in the centre of the stone block, a very skilled magical task, and impossible to reach without destroying the vessel.

Bound Shade - A creature with its life-spark captured at the moment of dying and used to keep a semblance of life. Kept alive by burying it in a glyph deep inside the corpse or another dead animal or plant, or imprisoning the life-spark within a tattoo on the shade's master or mistress. The shade will obey direct orders from the tattoo wearer if sent on mission, or will follow imprinted instructions if left with a task. Some are carried as personal guards, but damage to a bound shade will drain magic from the tattoo wearer. Most, especially the larger ones, are left as guards and will usually appear lifeless. A few are novelties such as animated footstools, created to amuse a sorcerer or guests. While torpid, a bound shade needs only a little sustenance, though once roused its magic must be replenished and those left on guard may feed on the living to absorb their magic.

Platycroc - A creature close to a gigantic cross between platypus and crocodile. Fifteen metres from the tip of the three-metre beak to the end of the flat stubby tail, three metres high and a little wider, it has six clawed, webbed feet on short, thick legs. The creature is protected by thick scales that deflect anything but strong magical attack. At the end of the beak is a large, solid lump used for ramming or beating on an opponent.

Once launched it will continue battering at an opponent, immune to pain and ignoring damage, until one or the other is destroyed. The platycroc, supposedly a failed attempt at a war beast, is now a bound shade held in a priest's tattoo and used by the Church Militant.

Stickybangs - A very small short-lived magical construct created by an amateur sorceress, usually cast in numbers. The many-legged creatures cling to whatever they hit. Designed for combating shields because stickybangs suck magic from the target until saturated, then explode.

Pungh Hmmshtfun - (Very old type of Hebrew)

spiritus qui furabatur (Latin)

Koška Smerti (Russian)

Braeth Huntian (Olde Englishe)

Ferryl Shayde - name currently used by a faded sorceress

Bonny's Tavern
A proposed board game with D&D roots

The world of Bonny's Tavern is semi-medieval, where cruel tyrants, monsters, grasping nobles, and corrupt churchmen abound. An ancient pact between magic, church and nobility has failed, leaving most of the population, those lacking magic or armies, defenceless. The sorcerers, nobles, church and a variety of magical monsters fight to maintain their power bases, often crushing the populace between them. The best a peasant or small business can hope for is to scrape together enough to pay their tithes and taxes and be ignored. The game quests include clearing monster infestations, finding lost treasures and mythical weapons, freeing heroes or maidens, hunting fugitives, fighting small wars or rebellions, robbing corrupt bishops and barons or helping the local populace when famine or war wreck their lives.

All game quests start at Bonny's Tavern, which acts as a neutral meeting place for creatures and humans who would normally attack each other on sight. Bonny's half-sister is a mercenary, Robin D'Ritche, which frightens off any low-level ruffians who might risk fighting Champ, the ex-pugilist bouncer. The smith, Fe Hamma, insists on carrying out business there because he likes the ale. Anyone upsetting him won't be able to buy his enhanced armour or weapons, and might fall foul of his enchanted mace. Cackle the Crone wants a place to sell her charms and hexes, but if you interfere be prepared for waking up with a septic ear. Bullseye the Bowman has to buy new enchanted shafts somewhere. Nikk the Warlock Thief needs a place to sell his plunder, or will steal yours if you annoy him.

Stronger potential raiders, magical or otherwise, understand the message and the magic in the Tavern sign. A variety of humans and creatures, all dangerous in their own right, find having a safe house convenient. Even the nobles and church stay clear because potential enemies as varied as a Paladin, a Barbarian hero, a wild hunter and several sorceresses including a feline with her bodyguard, have agreed to enforce the truce. They enjoy a peaceful pint of ale or a good meal and a bed without fleas.

Characters:

Players can choose another name and sex when adopting a character. The standard types are not all human, and advanced players may choose different racial characteristics for their chosen character to enhance their skills.

Not all characters can be adopted by players. Bonny the Barmaid or Champ will supervise the game, much as a DM (Dungeon Master) guides a game of "Dungeons and Dragons." There are a wide variety of monsters, entities, and ephemeral beings, as well as magical traps and dangerous terrain, but the following characters will usually be found at Bonny's Tavern itself, the start of the game.

Some such as Ffod or Fe Hamma can be recruited, or persuaded to help. They will react according to their characteristics. Others such as Creepio may join you voluntarily, or obstruct a quest.

Bonny the Barmaid - Part-owner, half-sister to Robyn. Her Tavern has magical protection gifted by a mysterious customer, possibly another part-owner.

Robyn D'Ritche - Female mercenary, scruffy inebriate, Bonny's half-sister and part-owner of the Tavern. Buys or steals magical protection. She supports and protects Bonny's Tavern, her base, where she recruits for fighting contracts or sells loot.

Champ - Tavern bouncer and ex-pugilist.

Saint Georgeous (pronounced Jorjeous as in George) - Paladin, severe, androgynous, beautiful. Heavily armoured with innate magical defences. Weapons inscribed with mysterious and powerful magical symbols. Rides a white unicorn which can run down the fleetest foe despite wearing heavy armour.

Roughly Hewn - Barbarian adventurer with bluish-tinted skin, perhaps has some ice giant blood, who uses clubs or heavy swords which may be enchanted. Brute force fighter, all muscle and rage. His body is naturally immune to minor spells and can tolerate serious injury in the heat of battle. He (or she) buys medallions inscribed with spell symbols to provide protection and help him heal.

Ferryl Shayde - Half-cat sorceress. Powerful and skilled user of spells, knows many intricate symbols well enough to throw them from memory. Her origin is shrouded in mystery, but her mere name can terrify lesser creatures.

Shayde Warrior - Fighter-mage trained in both magic and weapons, a difficult skillset to master. Ferryl's bodyguard and apprentice.

K'liss Windcatcher - Tall, slim sorceress wearing a pale blue robe unlike the usual sorceress garb of black and red. She is an absolute mistress of all air symbols, and an adept at mixing them with other spells to enhance the effect.

Rokk'n Rolla - Earth sorcerer. Can shape rock to form shields and armour, or command the earth itself to bury an enemy. Very difficult skill to master, using large amounts of magic, but earth-wrought constructs are very resistant to both physical attacks and magic symbols. Wields a dwarven mace inscribed with powerful magic.

K'ress Bloodclaw - Sorceress dressed entirely in tight, magically-enhanced black leather under a crimson cloak. Reputedly uses forbidden blood magic to raise and command the undead. Malicious rumours claim she is related to K'liss, possibly a twin.

Spenz F'Lorinze - Foppish Rake, smitten by Bonny but often unfaithful. Disgraced, disowned fourth son of a noble. Has an allowance on condition he never comes home. Tries to join quests to show how tough he is, to impress the ladies. Dons a broad-brimmed hat with big feather, frilled shirt, striped tights, high boots and a rapier. He really can use the rapier, one of the few lessons he paid attention to. That and his wealth are both good reasons to include him in a quest, a man with gold can open doors where magic and brawn fail. Buys magical protection, and might have persuaded Fe Hamma to enhance his rapier.

Wind Chaser - Sprite trapper. Small, skinny, and may have dwarf or some other non-human blood, but is sensitive about it. Looks innocuous but catches and tames sprites as guards or hunters which takes considerable magical skill and knowledge. Will sell them, transferring control of their magical tether, but is always guarded by his personal, very powerful Wind Sprite. Loner, but invaluable as a scout or magical fighter if he/she can be recruited. Has been linked romantically with Verdant Bounty, K'liss, K'ress, and in the wildest rumours, Ferryl Shayde.

Ffod the Hunter - Magical creature, never fully seen but sometimes taking the form of an ethereal leopard, wolf, eagle or, allegedly, an ogre, though few believe the last. Never fully aligned, but might join a group if they can catch its attention. Superb night guard, being almost invisible without needing magic. Uses magic but can kill or snare an unwary victim without. Unexplained deaths, those which don't leave a mark, are often ascribed to Ffod. (Only a select few know the origin of Ffod's name, though there are many legends of a hunter on the wind.)

Nikk Smartish - Far Eastern warlock who fled to the West, changed his name and turned to crime. Uses skill, a personalised toolset, and magic to circumvent magical and mundane defences, either to steal or for hire. Has mostly defensive hexes, but carries enchanted knives, poison darts, throwing stars and a miniature crossbow with charmed bolts. Good ally on quests needing guile, but make sure your own valuables are safely locked away.

Creepio Mysterio - Church investigator and possible assassin. Sneaky, dangerous, magically powerful. Do not cheat or threaten him, your body may never be found. Take care if Creepio offers to join your band. He can call on terrifying allies, but they may consider your safety irrelevant. Creepio might betray you for what he sees as a higher cause.

Cackle the Crone - Very old, experienced witch using bound shades to animate a pack of small dead creatures such as rats, crows and foxes. Allegedly preys on children but more likely to pick on rich merchants. May join quests, but watch out for pilfering of magical artefacts. She knows many small but obscure spells to improve love life, remove warts, or cause a septic ear. She sells charms, and curses for warding houses, to local villagers or fighters such as Roughly Hewn and Bullseye.

Bullseye - Race unknown, slim with seamed and lined dark brown skin and phenomenal strength. Despite his rounded ears, rumours persist that he must be at least part-elven. Superb non-magical bowman, using arrows etched with symbols that can pierce most armour and even defeat some magical shields. Like a medieval longbowman, he is armed and armoured, a fierce, but agile melee fighter who prefers enchanted mail armour to heavy plate protection.

Fe Hamma (element joke - Fe = iron) - Allegedly troll/Dwarf hybrid, weaponsmith, muscular, gnarled hunchback, skilled in making weapons embedded with spells and gems to store magic and enhance their power.

Woods and Green - Magical solicitors with a small shack next to Bonny's Tavern. Quest contracts between players will include penalties for not fulfilling the quest, or lying about skill levels or abilities (these are not automatically revealed to other players). Players can earn or lose reliability points by their actions during a quest. Stealing the loot will make it harder to get another contract, but proof of charitable work on Low Earth (aka the real world, where we live) will increase health points.

Choose your character wisely, and let the game begin!

Review

If you enjoyed this book, please share a short review with us on Amazon, Goodreads or the platform of your choice. Help other readers discover new authors.

Vance reads each and every comment you post and loves to hear from his readers.

Want more? Check out all of Vance Huxley's titles - from dystopian to military science fiction, there's something for everyone.

VANCE HUXLEY

Vance Huxley lives out in the countryside in Lincolnshire, England. He has spent a busy life working in many different fields – including the building and rail industries, as a workshop manager, trouble-shooter for an engineering firm, accountancy, cafe proprietor, and graphic artist. He also spent time in other jobs, and is proud of never being dismissed, and only once made redundant.

Eventually he found his Noeline, but unfortunately she died much too young. To help with the aftermath, Vance tried writing though without any real structure. As an editor and beta readers explained the difference between words and books, he tried again.

Now he tries to type as often as possible in spite of the assistance of his cats, since his legs no longer work well enough to allow anything more strenuous. An avid reader of sci-fi, fantasy and adventure novels, his writing tends towards those genres.